MW01087868

| | |
|---|---|
| **Title:** | How to Survive a Horror Story |
| **Author:** | Mallory Arnold |
| **Agent:** | Courtney Paganelli |
| | Levine Greenberg Rostan Literary Agency |
| **Publication date:** | July 8, 2025 |
| **Category:** | Fiction |
| **Format:** | Trade Paperback Original Deluxe / Standard / Library Hardcover |
| **ISBN:** | 978-1-4642-2740-0 / 978-1-4642-5118-4 / 978-1-4642-5253-2 |
| **Price:** | $17.99 U.S. / $17.99 U.S. / $32.99 U.S. |
| **Pages:** | 368 pages |

This book represents the final manuscript being distributed for prepublication review. Typographical and layout errors are not intended to be present in the final book at release. **It is not intended for sale and should not be purchased from any site or vendor.** If this book did reach you through a vendor or through a purchase, please notify the publisher.

Please send all reviews or mentions of this book to the Sourcebooks marketing department: **marketing@sourcebooks.com**

For sales inquiries, please contact: **sales@sourcebooks.com**

For librarian and educator resources, visit: **sourcebooks.com/library**

# Praise for
# *How To Survive a Horror Story*

Blurb

tag

HOW TO
SURVIVE
A
HORROR
STORY

# HOW TO SURVIVE A HORROR STORY

## MALLORY ARNOLD

*Poisoned Pen*
PRESS

Published by Poisoned Pen Press, an imprint of Sourcebooks
P.O. Box 4410, Naperville, Illinois 60567-4410
(630) 961-3900
sourcebooks.com

Cataloging-in-Publication Data is on file with the Library of Congress.

Printed and bound in [Country of Origin—confirm when printer is selected].
XX 10 9 8 7 6 5 4 3 2 1

*To my family for their endless support
of my pursuit of storytelling.*

*And to my husband—I love you.*

Crystal Flowers

Winnie Roach

Chester Plumage

Scott Clay

Melanie Brown

Petey Marsh

Buck Grimm

FROM THE OFFICE OF

*the Mortimer Queen*

To whom it may concern,

    I write this letter with a heavy heart, as I must inform you that the great Mortimer Queen has passed away.

    Upon detailing Mr. Queen's assets and will, I am bound to share that you have been bequeathed an item of great personal value. As dictated in his last testament, **you are hereby invited** to the Mortimer Queen Manor to stay the weekend, accept your willed item, and celebrate Mr. Queen's lasting legacy as one of the greatest horror authors this world will ever know.

    I will expect you in a week's time.

*Sincerely,*
*Gia Q. Falcone, groundskeeper*

# Melanie Brown

THE GRAVEL ROAD leading up to Mortimer Queen Manor curves and bends like an uneven spine. Melanie Brown's Toyota quivers about on the vertebrae as gravel spits out from underneath its tires. The road is strangled by a thick forest, with trees bearing down on it, giants bending over to inspect something squashed on their shoe.

The car radio conked out an hour ago, and no matter how hard Melanie bangs on it, the comforting mumblings of lazy-afternoon NPR won't come back. She tugs on her uneven bangs, a product of rusty scissors and a terrible mistake made in front of her bedroom mirror last night. It had been a poor attempt to cover the fresh scar marring her forehead, which is now even more prominently framed by fraying strands of hair.

Her cell phone buzzes in the cupholder, and she answers it on the second ring. If it's her sister, Petra, Melanie is eager to talk. If it's her mother, making her wait for a third ring is liable to start an argument.

"Are you there yet?" Someone snaps in a taut voice from the other end before she can utter a greeting.

Melanie sets the phone on the dashboard, hitting Speaker so she can use both hands to keep the car from veering off course.

"Yes, Moth—yes, Cynthia. I'm just pulling up to the address now."

Only a few months ago, their mother decided they were old enough to refer to her by her real name. "It's about time I got back to who I really am," she told them. "I was your mother for so long, I feel neglected as a person."

Neither Melanie nor Petra pointed out that, regardless of how they referred to her, she was still very much their mom. There was no undoing that.

"Hmph." Cynthia sniffs.

Melanie waits, listening to the sharp whistling coming through her mother's nose. "Did you need something or—"

"How long are you staying again?"

"Just the weekend."

Another "hmph," followed by an aggressive slurp of coffee. "You're missing my bridge tournament."

"I know. I'm sorry."

"What am I going to tell my friends? That my daughter trekked across the country to sleep in a creepy old man's house?"

Melanie grips the steering wheel tighter, her knuckles whitening. "It's not like he's going to be there, Mother. He's dead."

"Oh, I'm sorry—sleeping in a *dead* man's house. Even better. What will people say?"

A crow flies dangerously low in front of the car, forcing Melanie to jerk the wheel and almost skid off the road. The phone slides off the dashboard and into her lap. She picks it up and is about to put it back when she realizes the call has dropped anyway.

She exhales a shaky breath. There's an ache in her neck that comes only from a conversation with Cynthia. The whiplash of her message was clear through the phone: *I do not approve*. It's why Melanie had waited until last night, while they were out to dinner, to tell her about the letter she'd received about a week ago. Cynthia nearly choked on her charred brussels sprouts at the news that Melanie was not only named in a will but in a *wealthy* man's will and would be leaving the next morning to hear what she was bequeathed. One would think a mother would be excited about this, but Cynthia preferred when her daughters were slightly down on their luck, just enough that they still needed her. Melanie loosens her grip on the wheel. *Who says I'm not still down on my luck?* she can't help but think.

After ten minutes of winding along, she gets spit out into an open valley where the Mortimer Queen Manor basks under the gray October sky. That's what it had been called in the letter—*a manor*. An outdated title that suggests an icky kind of wealth: a *manor owner* has money that is old and tinged with years of poisonous family history. At least that's what comes to mind when she hears the word.

Melanie pulls up to tall iron gates protecting the property, and with a melodramatic groan, the doors swing open. She drives the car slowly, inching her way forward so she can stare through the windshield up at where she'll be staying for the weekend.

"Oh...my..." she breathes, forgetting that she's driving for a moment and allowing the car to roll along independently.

The manor is an extremely tall house, though it's terribly skinny in width and slightly leaning like a stack of badly organized books, not at all what she pictured when she first received her letter. Did Mortimer really live here when he was alive? In *this* century? It looks uninhabitable, the sort of place she'd give a wide berth just in case there was an old caretaker with a shotgun perched at a window.

She pulls the car around to the side of the house, then thinks better of it and reverses for several feet so that it's parked a safe distance away. If the foundation is as flimsy as it looks, a bad storm would blow the whole thing over, and on her nonexistent writer salary, she can't afford for her Toyota to be crushed in toppling-manor-related incidents.

As she steps out onto the gravel and meets her destination face-to-face, Melanie can't help but tense, her muscles bunching like rusted mattress springs under the weight of the manor's eye. Even though the letter she received not even a week ago is clearly an invitation, nothing about this house is. If anything, it demands to be left alone, and Melanie suddenly longs to turn tail and head back down that winding road.

The exterior drips with Gothic foreboding: stone gargoyles and cherubs missing limbs, the fascia sharp, like canine teeth. Centered above the wraparound porch, there's an abundance of windows with two large circle panes that resemble beady eyes, crowned by a widow's peak with more cawing ravens perched atop, assessing. This house, it's… grotesquely human, the window shutters slanting like eyelids, the porch roof curving like a smile. Everything about the place makes Melanie wary, like she's about to step foot into an oversize Venus flytrap, the deadly plant peering down as she stands before it, feeling as small and insignificant as a bug.

She's not sure which is making her stomach ache more: the house or the prospect of walking inside and encountering strangers she'll have to talk to. Either way, she feels like vomiting up the banana muffin she managed to choke down on the way here.

After reaching into her pocket, Melanie withdraws the letter. It's sustained a series of wrinkles, creases, and a tear in the corner, but that's only because she's felt the need to read it a hundred times to confirm its contents.

*Why me?*

It's a good idea, she decides, to have it in hand just in case someone needs proof she's really been invited. Otherwise, who would believe her? Melanie pulls her suitcase out of the trunk. She's just realizing she forgot to pack a toothbrush when footsteps approach from a car now parked at her rear.

"Hey there," says a tall man as he bounds toward her, his springy, eager energy and open-mouthed smile giving off the semblance of a golden retriever. "Do you need help with that?"

Admittedly, he's a very *handsome* golden retriever, with sandy-blond hair and a long camel peacoat, a thin red scarf winding through the collar. Melanie wordlessly shakes her head.

"You sure? It looks bigger than you." The man grins, his smile devilishly crooked.

Melanie stares up at him through her bangs—for longer than is socially acceptable, she realizes, as the grin wavers and his expression turns confused, then concerned. Her hand tingles, as if Cynthia is standing there and whacking a hairbrush across her knuckles. Whack. *Sit up straight!* Whack. *Speak louder!* Whack. *Enunciate!*

"I'll manage," Melanie finally says. "Thank you."

She flexes her fingers, reminding herself that no one will be here today to correct her social inadequacies. Not even Cynthia—former Miss Teen Rhode Island. Melanie's sister, Petra, would have a fit if she knew Melanie was still feeling the press of their mother's admonishments. *You've got to grow a backbone!* Petra often tells her. *Mother—or Cynthia or whatever she wants us to call her—can go stuff it for all I care.*

Easy enough for Petra to say, having been born with silky chestnut hair and an intoxicating personality. It's always the most beautiful people who go around telling everyone else that life doesn't have to be so hard.

"I'm Scott," the man says, extending a hand for Melanie to shake. "Scott Clay."

She tries not to grimace as he squeezes much too enthusiastically. He then stares at her expectantly until she realizes she's supposed to give her name in return.

Whack. *Don't be so off-putting!* Whack. *Introduce yourself!*

"Oh!" She stumbles over her words. "Melanie Brown."

A cold breeze flutters through Melanie's hair, and her bangs fly up like retracting window shades.

"Whoa!" Scott frowns. "What happened?" He gestures to her forehead, where she can only assume he's seen the scar.

"Oh." Her face flushes, and she quickly smashes her bangs down. "Just a result of one too many drinks."

Scott snorts. "Been there. Done that."

Melanie hoists her oversize bag up by its handle, and she and Scott begin walking to the front of the house.

"Did you know Mortimer well?" Scott asks, gingerly brushing his yellow eyebrows so that they're nice and neat.

"No," Melanie admits, deciding it's better not to lie. "Not really."

Even though it's the truth, the response feels restless on her tongue. She didn't know him, but she did *meet* him. Once.

Problem is, she's been having trouble remembering that day.

"We were colleagues. You know, because of the industry," Scott says, seemingly disinterested in Melanie's answer. "I was floored when I heard he died, and then floored again when I got the letter telling me I was in his will. Mortimer respected my books, I think. Never came out and said it, but the old guy was a man of few words, wasn't he?"

Melanie doesn't say anything, but Scott continues anyway.

"Have you heard of them? The Dark Skies series? Quite a few have hit the *New York Times* bestseller list…" He seemingly accepts Melanie's silence as an answer. "No? You must not be a reader."

"I read," Melanie says. *And write*, she wants to say but doesn't dare. What if he asks what she's published? It would be mortifying to answer, *Nothing*.

"Well. Anyway, that's what I'm thinking," Scott says. "Maybe Mortimer was a fan, you know?"

"Maybe," Melanie says flatly. As friendly and…*bouncy* as he is, Scott makes her feel uneasy. Particularly extra-peppy people are always over-compensating for something.

"I think he must've been," he says, sounding resolute.

She nods in reply, only half listening. Her heartbeat thunders with every step that takes her closer to the manor. She should find solace in the fact that she's not the only one surprised by their invitation this weekend. But to her, it raises a new shiny red flag.

Once they're feet from the manor's wraparound front porch, both Melanie and Scott stop. She tilts her head up, taking in the peeling paint, outdated trim, and snarls of ivy crawling up the sides. Mortimer Queen was not shy about how much wealth he accumulated over the course of his career—he actually griped on countless podcasts (*Authorfiles*, *Armchair Expert*, *Read and Weep*...) that he had *too much* money and no idea what to do with it. Melanie tries to swallow her judgmental thoughts while her eyes scale the molding porch, but it's hard not to question if Mortimer was putting up a front this whole time. Surely someone with money would make proper repairs to their house.

Neither she nor Scott moves for a moment, and she wonders if he feels as reluctant to go in as she does.

"Well?" He takes a big breath. "Shall we?"

*No, no, we shall not*, she wants to say. But even though Scott is a bit bigheaded and too boisterous for Melanie's comfort, she's glad she has someone to enter the manor with.

She steps across the threshold into the entry hall and immediately snaps her neck back, unable to look away from the ceiling. It's dizzyingly tall, decorated with ostentatious painted scenes—characters Melanie recognizes from Mr. Queen's novels. There's a half naked man dragging himself from a broken grave (*The Rise of Bartholomew*); two women dressed in black robes, holding melting candles, the wax dripping all over their hands (*Veiled to Death*); a mountain of skulls with ruddy-cheek

children playing among them (*Playmates of the Shadows*); and more
Melanie doesn't know. All are cast in light and shadow from the sparkling
chandelier dripping from the center.

That's when she notices the ticking.

Melanie draws her chin down to see the maroon walls crammed
with clocks. And not just everyday time markers. No. These are strange-
looking ornate cuckoo clocks, some with swinging pendulums in glass
cases and others with carved animals or faces within their bodies. In every
shape and size. The worst part about them was the sound.

*Tick, tock. Tick, tock. Tick, tock.*

Every clock is in tandem, their hands synchronous, producing a
terribly loud chorus of ticking, worsened by the grand acoustic ceilings.
It sets Melanie on edge, as if there's an immediate countdown to something terrible. She notices that the biggest clock in the room is the only
one inactive. The towering dark brown grandfather clock stands on its
own; the gold pendulum in the glass case hangs limply. It must be a lot
of upkeep to make sure all these time pieces stay in good condition, so
it's no wonder at least one of them is broken.

The hall is so very strange that Melanie notices the people in it last,
which is incredible, considering both her rampant social anxiety and how
vibrantly they are buzzing about the space. As Scott leaves her side and
thrusts himself toward the five fellow guests smiling at one another and
exchanging polite chatter, Melanie can't help but think they look like
chess pieces arranged against the black-and-white-tiled floor, the ticking
meter timing their every move.

It's easier for her to catalog them that way, really. Scott Clay—who
is now pawing at everyone in greeting, his shoulders back, his grin
wide—is clearly the king piece. Which makes the young woman to his
right—somewhere around twenty-five, with milky skin and platinum
hair in a tight bun at the nape of her neck—the queen. She's wearing
a tailored black pantsuit with a deep neckline showcasing her sallow

sternum, her outfit could be construed as sultry, but because of how the woman's eyes flash dangerously as she surveys the hall, seems fearless to Melanie.

A few feet away, an older woman hasn't reached Melanie's same conclusion, glaring disapprovingly at the girl's bare flesh. This, Melanie decides, is the bishop, in a floor-length dress with flowy sleeves that spill over her hands, like the garb of a disapproving religious figure. Her hair is chopped at the chin and dyed an unnatural maroon red, clashing boldly against her purple eyeshadow and coral lipstick.

Then there's the knight, a bear of a man who towers over everyone. He seems to be bursting out of his tucked-in plaid dress shirt and faded jeans. His unruly beard is amber, making him look like a Texan Santa Claus. He seems like he could weigh four times as much as the rail-thin man next to him, who is glued to his cell phone. The light from the screen reflects off his shiny face, his equally greasy hair combed back with far too much gel. Melanie assigns this man as the rook, mostly because looking at him makes her so uncomfortable, she would like to move him as many spaces away from her as possible. His facial features are too small for his face, beady like a scavenger, and his eyes keep darting restlessly around the place.

Melanie turns away from him, her nerves rising again when, yes, there he is. The pawn appears. A squat balding man with thick round glasses looks about as nervous as Melanie. He dabs at his forehead with a handkerchief, his lips moving slightly like he's mumbling, inaudible above the clocks.

*There*, Melanie thinks, satisfied. *Everyone's accounted for.* This eases her social anxiety a bit, and she plans on standing safely on the outskirts of the room until someone forces her to do otherwise.

This, unfortunately, happens too soon.

The queen approaches, her tiny kitten heels clacking against the tile floor. Up close, Melanie sees that her eyes are slightly bugged and lined with charcoal, making her look like some kind of dark fairy in a fantasy book. She half expects a pair of spindly wings to unfurl from the queen's shoulder blades.

"Should we leave our bags here?" the woman asks.

This is such an odd thing to ask that Melanie has to do a few mental backflips before responding.

"Uh, I…I'm not sure."

"I just wondered if you all would be taking them to our rooms or if we should do that ourselves," she continues, turning to point to a winding staircase at the far end of the room. "I don't entirely trust myself hauling my bag upstairs wearing *these* shoes."

She gestures to her heels and laughs sheepishly. "It seems inappropriate now, but I wore them because… Well, I guess I just wanted to look nice." She swallows visibly. "For him, you know?" Her eyes suddenly look watery. "That's silly, isn't it? I'm sorry."

This is a worst-case scenario for Melanie. Talking to a stranger is bad enough, but addressing their emotional turmoil while trying to relay that she's, in fact, *not* the manor's baggage girl, is painful.

The woman taps at her eyes, slightly smudging the liner. "Anyway. Bags?"

Melanie can't tell if Scott walking up to join them is a saving grace or simply adding to the nightmare. His smile so big, there should be a long pink tongue hanging out of it as he pants excitedly. "I'm sorry to interrupt, but are you Crystal Flowers?"

Of *course* her name is Crystal, like her parents already knew she'd be sparkling and gorgeous when she grew up. Someone like her couldn't possibly be named something like Sarah or Helen or Mary.

"Yes," Crystal replies easily, her eyes turning toward Scott. "And you are?"

If Scott had a tail, it would fall and get tucked between his legs. "I'm… Well, I'm…"

"Kidding." Crystal smiles. But it's a cool smile—not too big. "I know who you are, Scott Clay. Doesn't everyone?"

This makes Scott boom with relieved laughter. "You had me going for a second," he says. "I can't believe you're here." He turns to Melanie. "Can you? I mean, of all people…Crystal Flowers."

"Yes, well…" Crystal curls a piece of hair behind her ear, which Melanie sees is studded with diamonds. "I was good friends with Mortimer."

"I see you've met Melanie," Scott adds, nodding her way.

"Yes," Crystal says. "I was just asking how the bags will be handled."

Scott frowns, looking between the two of them. "She's not… Er, Crystal, this is Melanie Brown. She was also invited to the will reading."

The clocks fill the awkward pause. *Tick, tock. Tick, tock. Tick, tock.* Ugh. Melanie wishes the floor would swallow her.

"Oh my gosh!" Crystal's hand flies to her mouth. "I'm so sorry! I had no idea… I guess I thought…you just looked like someone who… Not that you… Uh…"

"It's nice to meet you," Melanie says, fumbling with the words. "And don't worry about it. If it's any solace, I don't know what to do with my bag either."

Crystal laughs gratefully, and Melanie knows she's said the right thing. "Thank you for being gracious, but I'm still embarrassed. And if you've seen any of my work, you know that's a rare feeling for me."

Scott chuckles like she's just said a dirty joke but stops when he sees Melanie's eyebrows furrow. "Don't tell me you don't know who she is?" he asks. "Now I feel much better about myself." He addresses Crystal. "Melanie didn't know who I was either. I was more than a little surprised, to say the least, but now I can only assume she might not be a big reader."

"I read," she repeats for the second time. Annoyance twinges the back of her throat.

"Maybe she's just not a fan of our genres," Crystal says, coming to her aid.

"Wh-what genre is that?" Melanie feels utterly incompetent.

"Horror. Well, I write erotic horror. Scott keeps it pretty PG, from what I've read," Crystal says. "I'm a little...dirtier."

Melanie's face grows hot, and she suddenly wants to look anywhere but at Crystal.

Scott's expression is practically giddy before he leans in and speaks quietly out of the side of his mouth. "So, Crystal, have you recognized a few of our fellow peers in the mix here today?"

She swings her head, her hair flying as if in slow motion over her shoulder. "Yes, I think everyone here is an author of some acclaim."

"A *horror* author, at that. How interesting."

At the same time, both Crystal and Scott's eyes fall back onto Melanie with a mix of sympathy and bemusement. She's the odd one out, it seems. In the game of chess, she's the lone red checker that was accidentally tossed into the box.

"So, what *do* you do, Melanie?" Crystal asks in a placating tone.

Melanie feels her mouth open, but nothing comes out. Thankfully, she is rescued by the harsh clanging of an iron door, abruptly bringing the conversation around the room to a halt.

At the top of the spiral staircase, a woman emerges. She is slightly gray-skinned with straight black hair, her smile unwavering as she descends the stairs. As she nears, Melanie clocks a large black mole above her lip, the image of a smashed beetle flashing unpleasantly through Melanie's mind.

"My name is Gia Falcone, and I'm the manager of Mortimer Queen's estate," the woman says, spinning slowly on her heel to make eye contact with the guests. "And I'm *so* happy you're all here. Please make your way into the parlor room for a short cocktail hour and introductions before dinner. You may leave your luggage here, and we'll have the manor staff take it to your rooms."

Gia has a sort of transatlantic accent, the kind used in old-timey black-and-white movies in the 1930s. Her dress, Melanie notes, looks equally vintage, like she's just been plucked from another era and landed here.

"We'll be doing introductions?" tasks the bishop—the older woman with the blunt red bob. "To one another, you mean?"

Gia opens her mouth to speak.

*Brring! Brring!* A familiar peal sounds—the chime Instagram makes when you have a new like. A few people glance at the rook with eye rolls, and the greasy man looks up from his phone, gives a contrite smile, and shoves it in his pocket.

"Yes," Gia says, trying to ignore the interruption. "It was very important to Mr. Queen that you all get to know one another before we begin."

"Begin the reading of the will, right?" Scott clarifies, and Melanie thinks he might pounce on all fours and wag his butt in eagerness.

Gia's black eyes slowly fall on his. After a long beat, she finally says, "That's correct."

"Would you mind telling us…?" interjects the burly man, the Knight, his Southern drawl prominent. "I mean, I haven't heard or seen anything in the media and… Well, would it be rude for us to ask how Mr. Queen died?"

Melanie watches closely as Gia considers the question. She assumed Mr. Queen died of old age—he *was* old, wasn't he? He certainly looked it. Her lack of certainty makes her stomach plummet, vulnerability leaving a chill up her spine. God, what *is* she doing here?

"Mr. Queen was ill," Gia says sadly. "It was incredibly sad but expected. He was prepared to die."

Melanie hears Crystal whimper. *Of course she's upset,* Melanie thinks. *They must've been close.* And then there's her, a stranger among the mourning.

A sharp creaking breaks the melancholy atmosphere, and a young South Asian man steps through the front door. He's wearing a bright pink suit jacket with matching pants and white saddle shoes.

"Hello? Oh gosh, that was loud, wasn't it?" he says, wincing apologetically. "I'm looking for Winnie Roach? Winnie, doll? Are you here?"

"Over here, dear!" The bishop—now dubbed Winnie—lifts her hand and flaps it.

The man hurries over before dropping a peck on her left and right cheek. Winnie's face is flushed, from excitement or embarrassment, Melanie isn't sure.

The man looks around, his mouth turned down. "Yikes, Win. This place... It's interesting, no?"

Gia clears her throat loudly, her face suddenly hard, her smile gone. "Who is this?"

"This is Felix," Winnie links her arm with his and lovingly rests her head on his shoulder.

"No last name," Felix adds, flashing a cheeky smile. "Like Cher or Madonna. It's a thing I'm trying out." He has a diamond stud on his canine tooth, and it's glinting like a broken piece of the chandelier.

"You did not receive an invitation," Gia says icily. "You cannot be here."

"Come now!" Winnie scoffs. "He's my friend! I invited him here this weekend as my plus one—I need him for emotional support!"

Felix nods, pouting.

"This isn't a spa weekend," mutters the greasy rook, back on his phone.

"You have not been invited into Mortimer Queen Manor." Gia is angrier this time. Melanie thinks her voice has a surprisingly strong tremor for such a small woman and hopes Winnie will make her guest *go* so it doesn't get even louder.

Felix doesn't look so confident anymore, the diamond smile disappearing. He pats Winnie's arm, and as he tries to ease out of her grasp, he says, "Look, doll, maybe I should just go..."

"No! Stay! This is unacceptable." Winnie tilts her chin up. "You never expressly said we couldn't bring someone along. You asked us to come all the way out here for this—what's the harm of housing one more person?"

The entry hall is quiet. Melanie holds her breath.

Then, unexpectedly, Gia breaks back into a smile. "Of course, how very inconsiderate of me," she says. "Felix, you're more than welcome to stay in the manor for as long as you can."

"Oh!" Felix perks up. "Rad! My bags are in the car. I can go get them—"

*Brring! Brring!* The rook's phone chirps again.

"We'll have someone do that for you," Gia says, procuring a satin sack. "Now, before you head into cocktail hour, please turn in your cell phones. For legal reasons, no electronic devices will be allowed on your person during the will reading. You may collect them later."

Most everyone appears slightly vexed by this, their footsteps especially heavy as they walk over and drop their phones into the sack. Melanie tosses hers in, knowing the only text she'll miss will be from Petra, probably asking something like, *How much blood can you donate in a day?* or *Do you think any online perv will buy my toenails? There's a site for it.* Her sister, who dropped out of college when Cynthia stopped paying the tuition, is always looking for ways to make a buck. She's saving for a 'round-the-world trip, desperate to get as far away from their mother as possible.

The rook opens his mouth like he's going to argue, but then he deposits his phone. It makes a few more muffled *brring, brring* sounds as he walks away, and Melanie watches his hand reflexively twitch toward it.

"Wonderful!" Gia says. "Now please make your way to the parlor room. I have some things to prepare before the will reading, so I can't stay for cocktail hour, but I'm sure you'll all have a nice time getting to know one another."

There's a shuffle as the guests follow Gia, but Melanie hangs back. She expects an army of staff to come take their bags, but no one appears. The hall remains empty, save the persistent chattering of clocks.

*Tick, tock. Tick, tock. Tick, tock.*

Melanie wavers by the spiral stairs, her hand brushing against the cold metal railing. Suddenly, a strange sensation beckons her, like something is waiting at the top of the stairs for her, just out of sight. She feels compelled to climb. *Up, up,* it says. *Don't you want to see…?* She licks her lips and sets one foot on the bottom stair. The moment she does, a low hum seems to sound from the walls, drowning out the clocks, growing louder and louder…

"Melanie," Someone says into her ear, and she jumps away from the stairs. Silence falls immediately. Even the clocks momentarily pause before picking up their ticking again.

Gia has materialized next to her, the smile still plastered onto her face. Her skin is thin and pale, like mist hovering over a bog. "I'm so glad you could make it," she tells her. "Mr. Queen would be pleased that you came."

"Oh!" Melanie says, her heart still beating hard against her rib cage. "Th-thank you. I was hoping to talk to you in…in private. I was wondering if you could tell me… I don't mean to be rude or ungrateful, but I'm not sure why…why…"

Gia tilts her head. "Why what, dear?"

"Why I'm in Mr. Queen's will."

This gets a boisterous laugh in return. "Very funny, dear."

"I…I didn't know him," Melanie whispers conspiratorially, like she's sharing a secret. "And, like I said, I don't mean to come across as rude, but I would hate to be included by mistake."

Gia leans forward and raises a brow. "You didn't know him?"

"Well, I did meet him once. But it was just that one time." Melanie cocks her head. "I wondered if maybe he meant for someone else to get the letter. Someone more…"

"Someone more famous?" Gia finishes for her.

"Someone more well acquainted," Melanie says firmly.

"Mr. Queen didn't make mistakes," Gia says. "You're very much meant to be here, Melanie. You'll see. For now, please join the rest of the group."

Gia is wrong. Melanie is not meant to be here. Yet she still chose to get into her car and drive out here, to answer the call and enter the manor. Something told her to come. Something deep inside.

Melanie nods, and Gia smiles even wider.

"Go on," she says pleasantly. "I'll be in soon."

The sound of friendly clinking glasses and popping champagne corks from the parlor indicates that happy hour is now in full swing. Melanie takes a few steps, her stomach walloping.

"Actually, Gia, I don't think I can do this," she says, moving to collect her bag. It's only then she realizes that hers is gone, along with everyone else's belongings. Her clothes, toiletries, wallet—her *car keys*—have disappeared, killing the chances of her slipping out the front door. Melanie spins to face Gia again, but like the bags, she, too, has vanished into thin air.

# Scott Clay

A FINGER OF *gin, a slice of cucumber, two fresh basil leaves, an ounce or so of simple syrup, and a freshly cut lime rubbed around the glass rim.* This is Scott's signature cocktail, one he's dutifully preparing at the bar while the others meander about, chatting casually about the weather, deadlines, and funny *can you believe my publisher said this?* stories, as if this is just another industry mixer.

But Scott can't stop shaking. He's making a good go of it, flashing smiles at everyone and offering firm handshakes to those who introduce themselves, but his guise can't hold up without a stiff drink. He finishes his cocktail and brings the glass to his lips, swallowing half of it in one gulp.

Something is *off* with this place. For one thing, Mortimer had a strange preference in decor. Every room they've been in so far is cluttered with *clocks*. They're not even nice new ones either, more like the kind you'd see in a decaying grandparent's home. Aside from that, the parlor room is nice enough, he supposes, with warm rustic stone countertops and floor-to-ceiling deep-brown cabinets. The serve-yourself bar he's just been rummaging through consists of a colorful array of wines, a few bottles of gin, and a thick jar of whiskey with a red wax seal. Neatly tucked next to the alcohol is a tray of sodas, a jar of orange and lemon slices, a bowl of cherries, a bundle of herbs, and a small tin of ice.

But, *Christ*, the place reeks of mothballs and death. Or is that just Scott's imagination? Mortimer was a millionaire—he always showed up to book conventions in Tesla limos. Tesla. *Limos.* Couldn't he have afforded a maid or professional decorator? And there are these eerie patches of warm air. The entire manor is cold, but then suddenly Scott feels like he's enveloped by hot breath. He shudders, swallows the second portion of his drink, then jostles the glass so that the ice cubes clink together.

"Well, Scott Clay!" exclaims Winnie Roach, a fiftysomething woman who acts and dresses like a distressed Hollywood starlet from the silent-film days. "If I knew you were coming, I would have gotten more dolled up."

The unwelcome guest, Felix, is glued to her hip. Scott gives him a little nod of greeting.

"You always look great, Winnie," he says good-naturedly and allows her to kiss him on each cheek. "It's good to see you."

"What has it been, almost five months?" Winnie simpers, a glass of wine in hand. "You never call."

"My schedule is packed," Scott says with a tight smile. "I'm pretty busy, you know."

"Babe, look at him," Felix says, swishing his hand in the air. "The man is a tall drink of water—he's probably so busy fielding women, he barely has time to ring his mother, let alone *you*."

Scott and Winnie share the same publisher, who, much to his dismay, try to parade their two bestselling horror authors around to as many events as possible. Over the years he has had to endure countless book signings, conventions, and tours with Winnie's irritating cackling and flirtatious come-ons.

"But I'm never too busy for *him*," she says, grabbing Scott's hands. "What happened here?"

Scott flinches as she brushes a thumb against his bruised knuckles. Last week the colors were blue and purple, but today they're a sickly shade of yellow. He should've worn his gloves to avoid all the questions.

"Ooooo." Felix tsk-tsks. "That looks bad."

*So does that rock drilled into your tooth.*

"I shut my hand in a car door by accident." Scott looks over her head, willing her to go away.

"Hmmm," Winnie says, looking at him skeptically. "Is that right?"

"Yep," he says, keeping his brows relaxed so his expression appears unbothered. "So I didn't know you knew Mortimer Queen well."

Winnie sniffs. "Well, maybe if we spoke more often, you would've."

The last event Scott did with Winnie was last year's ThrillerFest in New York City. They were on four panels together and were ushered around, practically hand in hand, all weekend. Fans ate up Winnie's dramatic flair alongside Scott's chagrined squirming. He suffered through three days of incessant chatter, blatant bragging, and far too much touching. After that, he refused to do anything with Winnie. No book signings, no promotional tours—not even a lunch date.

"Right." Scott clears his throat. "I'm going to top off my drink."

"Don't go getting sloppy, dear," she says in a taunting tone. "We should represent *our* publisher with class, right?" Then she adds a wink that makes him want to gag.

As he stands near the bar, not needing to top off the one sip he's taken, a large form sidles next to him, exploring the whiskey options. Scott immediately recognizes him from the back cover of one of his favorite slasher novels from college: *Blood Bath*. So this must be the talented Buck Grim, author of a book so terrifying, it once stopped Scott, as a pimply nineteen-year-old, from leaving his dorm to chase college girls and drink crappy beer for a week.

Scott realizes too late that he's been shredding the basil leaves with his fingers. Quite honestly, he's used to being the most successful (and often the most handsome) person in the room, and anything to the contrary is uncomfortable. He doesn't *mean* to be arrogant, but it's sort of second nature at this point, thanks to a formula of only-child syndrome, daddy issues, good genetics, and a haltingly bad temper.

When he published his bestselling horror novels, the Dark Skies, he knows his ego got a whole lot bigger. His fans are not only interested in his work but in *him*. Magazines feature his photo on their covers, he's pulled onto talk shows to discuss his dating life and fitness routine, and Hollywood agents are at his heels about starting an acting career.

Yet, here in the Queen Manor, Scott finds himself surrounded by people who not only don't care about his fame, but are even more successful than him. He tells himself this is good practice of humility.

Now, standing next to a goliath of a man—both in stature and success—Scott feels very, very, very small.

"Can you pass that?" Buck points to a top-shelf whiskey, his Southern-accented voice low and masculine.

"Sure," Scott says, handing him the wax-sealed bottle. He realizes he's speaking lower than usual, perhaps instinctively trying to match Buck's baritone. "Good selection here. Mortimer knows how to host, even from the grave."

As soon as he says it, he's worried it might sound a little off-color, but Buck gives a hearty laugh. "Yer right. Hell, I might stick a bottle in my jacket," he says. "I'm Buck. Buck Grimm."

"Good to meet you," he says, deciding not to relay that he already knows who he is.

"And you're Scott Clay."

"That I am."

The two men shake hands, Scott's carefully moisturized palm snagging against Buck's rough one. Though the gin had not yet calmed his nerves, Scott leans against the bar in a nonchalant pose before his palm slips a bit against the cold marble. He straightens, embarrassed.

"So, where are you from, Buck?"

Buck sticks a thumb through his belt loop and bobs his head, a tiny smirk underneath his unruly beard. There's no rigidity in his demeanor, no puffing of the chest like there usually is when another man sizes Scott up. "Oatmeal, Texas."

Scott blinks. "You're kidding. That's really what it's called?" he asks.

"Sure is." Buck grins in a way that makes Scott think he enjoys the effect this fun fact has. "Population of around two thousand. Everyone pretty much knows everyone."

"Wow. Sounds peaceful. Too peaceful, probably. I can't go to bed without the New York City sounds of car horns and sirens."

"I had my fair share of that when I lived in Los Angeles," Buck says. "Crazy place, though, I'll tell ya."

"And how did you know Mortimer?" Scott wishes idly that Buck would ask *him* something, anything to showcase that he, too, belongs here.

Buck's smile vanishes, and he stares into his drink. "I was his publishing assistant," he says. "A long time ago."

"Wow. I take it you two were close?"

"No," Buck says curtly.

Scott coughs into his hand uncomfortably, and Buck angles away, single-handedly ending the conversation. This allows Scott to finish his drink, but it also leaves him alone to panic.

He lifts his head and looks around the room, his paranoia growing. With every *tick, tock* those awful clocks make, Scott thinks someone is going to burst from the walls, point a finger at him, and shout, *AHA!*

*Got you!* And he'd deserve it. He is ignorant for being drawn out here by curiosity. He lost sleep this past week, tossing and turning over what rare personal artifact Mortimer could have left him in his will.

But *still*. He feels like a burglar waltzing into the very house he just robbed, expecting tea and cucumber sandwiches. *Surely Mortimer wouldn't have left you in his will if he knew what you'd done*, Scott tells himself as he swallows another mouthful of watery gin. *So stop freaking the hell out!* Sure, he and Mortimer weren't exactly close, but had they not been friendly with each other? Attending each other's release parties? Sitting at the same table during charity functions? Perhaps he'd been fonder of Scott than he realized.

Forcing a smile, he straightens and makes a beeline for Crystal, who is gazing out a window into the manor's sloping grassy grounds. She's different from what she looks like online. It's not like she would wear lingerie or a tight dress to a will reading, but in all the photos he's seen online, her hair drapes over her shoulders in bouncy waves. Today it's restrained into a knot. Her face, while still dewy and beautiful, is modestly done.

He quickly wets his lips, thinking he might offer her a shoulder to lean on, which could turn into exchanging numbers. Only, when he gets up close to her and sees the genuine pain in her eyes, he can't bring himself to switch on the charm.

"Are you going to be okay?" he asks, lowering the register of his voice, as to not embarrass her in front of everyone else.

Crystal lifts her watery eyes to his, her features strange but striking. "I just can't believe he's gone," she says, her voice wobbling.

Scott inhales. "In the end, it's not the years in your life that count, but the life in your years," he says as stoically as he can muster. He's pleased with how the words sound coming out of his mouth and reaches for his phone to jot it down into his Notes app before remembering it's with Gia. Damn. If he can remember it later, that quote could become a great chapter opener.

"That's beautiful," Crystal says. "Spoken like a true writer."

"Thanks." He suddenly recalls where he got the phrase from—it was something Abraham Lincoln said. Never mind. No harm in Crystal thinking he's profound. Or, rather, more profound than she already thinks he is.

She sighs and looks back out the window. Rain has begun to splatter against the pane, a low rumble of thunder echoing in the distance. The wind picks up, bending trees back like asparagus stems.

"I guess I was lucky to know him while I did," Crystal says. "Right? We all were."

"Yeah." Scott shuffles his weight from one foot to the other.

"He was always…larger-than-life. Like a sort of legendary character I didn't think would ever actually… Well, you know. Sometimes, I swear, he seemed inhuman. That's how brilliant he was."

Scott tries not to prickle at all the praise, but it's hard not to. *Brilliant?* Sure, Mortimer was somewhat of an icon, his celebrity spilling from niche horror fans to everyday people. But some of that, Scott has to believe, was luck. Brilliance? That's a bit much.

As if sensing his reluctance to agree, Crystal wipes her tears away. "I'm sorry—maybe I'm being too much. I know people like to exaggerate the dead once they're gone, and I don't want to be like that… He certainly wasn't perfect, that's for sure."

"No, no," Scott finds himself saying, if only to stay in Crystal's good graces. "I agree completely. Yeah, Mortimer was… I always thought he was a great guy."

Suddenly, from outside, a pebble rockets through the air and whips into the window, leaving behind a long splintering crack. Both Scott and Crystal leap back.

"Shit!" he exclaims, his heart in his throat.

Hot breath tickles the back of Scott's neck, and he jumps again, nearly colliding with Chester Plumage, who stands with his hands slightly raised. His eyes dart back and forth as quickly as his tongue, which pops out to lick at the dry crusts in the corner of his lips.

Even though they've never formally met, Scott requires no introduction to Chester, nor would he *want* one. Chester is a polarizing figure, with some claiming he has a great "artistic mind." Scott's opinion is cemented, however: the guy is a creep.

"What happened?" Chester urges, his eyes sharp.

"Nothing. Something just got tossed into the glass, that's all," Scott barks, stepping away from Chester's greasy face.

"Are yeh okay?" Buck comes around to inspect the crack. That's when Scott realizes the hum of conversation around the room has paused, the rest of the guests staring their way.

"We're fine," Scott says irritably. "We were just standing here talking about Mortimer, and I said that I thought he was a great guy and—"

Unprovoked, the splinter in the window spreads with a loud *crack*, reaching each corner of the pane. The group gasps, the rest of the guests—Winnie, Felix, Melanie, and a short balding man Scott doesn't recognize—pulling closer.

"Wh-wh-wh-what was that?" the unknown man says, speaking with a pronounced stutter. "D-d-did something b-break?"

"That was mighty odd," Buck says, staring at the crack. "It broke all on its own."

"Doll, did you bring me to a haunted house?" Felix demands, facing Winnie. "Because I am not down for that. You know I believe in the power of ghosts like Jennifer Aniston believes in the magic of moisturizer."

"It's *fine!*" Scott insists forcefully, feeling like everyone is watching him too closely, like this is his doing. "It's *nothing!* The wind is…The wind is bad. And so are these windows. I bet they haven't been replaced in…in…"

*Count to ten,* he can hear his therapist say. *If you're still angry by the time you hit ten, then count to twenty.* His blood feels hot at the attention, burning through his veins. The pent-up steam funnels through his muscles, down to his very fingernails. He coils up.

"Scott, are you okay?" Winnie asks, resting a hand on his forearm. "You seem stressed, dear. We were just asking what happened. What's wrong?"

"NOTHING IS WRONG!" Scott shouts, louder than necessary.

The window suddenly shatters, the glass disintegrating into tiny shards that fall at their feet, the wind howling through the empty frame masking any scream.

As the others stare at the destruction, Scott suddenly feels sick.

"I...I have to use the restroom," he mutters, crossing the room to duck out into the entry hall, then navigating down a side corridor on his left. He moves down the hallway, away from the group, and as he gains some distance, Scott feels his anger dim. But still, he's an anxious mess.

As he paces, replaying the incident, Scott suddenly realizes he's alone in the hallway, finally in silence away from the ticking clocks. He glances around and finds a line of nondescript doors dotting each side of the hall. Not ready to return to the parlor just yet, he moves to the one closest to him, rubbing a thumb across its worn copper knob, the square corners dulled from use. Slowly, Scott tugs.

He almost shouts, but the words are lost in the back of his throat. A woman hangs there in a long purple trench coat, the black buttons done up to the collar.

No—not a woman. Not even a person. It's just a *coat*. Feeling stupid, Scott brushes his hand on the pilled fabric. It's the kind of thing his mother wore when she was alive, a little worn but obviously well loved. He pushes it aside to see that the closet is almost three rows deep, practically a cavern of fur-lined jackets, puffy ski coats, floor-length trenches. He shuts the door and moves to the next. More hanging coats.

He can tell these don't belong to Mortimer. They're all too human, too normal to fit in with the manor's collection of things. Plus, Mortimer was known for his itchy-looking sweaters and expensive coats, like every clothing item he wore was made from the bristly backs of warthogs.

"What are you doing here?" Someone snaps.

He jumps a little, surprised to see Gia suddenly standing next to him with pursed lips.

"Jesus! I didn't hear you coming. Sorry, I was looking for…the bathroom," he says. After a beat he asks, "What's with all the coats?"

Gia narrows her eyes into slits, as if offended by Scott's inquiry. "Mr. Queen always had company," she says. "Many guests visited the manor."

"And they forgot their coats?" Scott asks in confusion.

"Would you like me to show you the restroom?" Gia says, ignoring this question.

As she guides him back down the hall to a different door, Scott wonders if he should tell her about the window. But if he does, then she'll assume *he* was the one who broke it, so he decides not to say anything. Gia gestures to the bathroom and then waits, her hands clasped in front of her in a way that makes him believe she intends on staying right there until he's finished.

He shuts the door in her face and unzips his pants.

The bathroom is incredibly dark, made of black walls and single light fixture dangling over the sink. Scott can hardly see in front of him and has to fumble for the toilet handle to flush. When he goes to turn on the sink, he immediately yanks his hands out of the scalding water. No matter which way he twists the faucet knobs, it only gets hotter.

"What the heck?" he mumbles as steam quickly rises and fogs up the mirror.

Scott gives up, turning off the water and gripping the sink with unsteady hands. There's a slow burn in his chest, and he's holding back tremors, side effects of going off his medicine. He didn't tell Dr. Murphy he was skipping pills, didn't want to hear the same lecture about anger management and self-regulation. Dr. Murphy would ask why Scott didn't want to take the meds anymore, and he would have to admit he *likes* feeling angry. He *likes* the rush. It's powerful and intoxicating.

It makes him a better writer, more potent. Nowadays, his motivation to write is more about his own fame, but when he first started, what got him to put pen to paper was the low-bubbling fire lit from within. His anger made for great stories.

Scott goes to wipe the mirror clean, but he notices a smeared handprint forming in the steam.

He stares at the mirror for a beat, wondering if he's seeing things. Wondering if he pressed his own hand to the glass and already forgot. The door rattles, and he hears an annoyed Gia on the other side.

"Scott? I implore you to finish up in there," she says.

Scott turns back, and the foggy fingers have disappeared; he questions whether they were there at all. When he opens the bathroom door, Gia watches him suspiciously.

"What were you doing in there?" she asks.

Scott blinks, taken aback. "I was using the restroom," he says, confused.

Gia takes his arm and starts escorting him back to the parlor. He has an uncanny feeling that she doesn't trust he won't wander off again and wonders what *she's* so paranoid about. He watches her carefully as she reaches out and drags one finger along the wall, like she's skimming the surface of a pond or dipping into the top of a neatly frosted cake.

"Uh, the manor is… It's beautiful," Scott says, forcing conversation even with his anxiety turned back on high. "Such unique design choices."

"I'm glad you think so," Gia says happily, her finger still pressed to the wall. "The manor is quite magnificent, but not a lot of people understand it. The guests who have come through here have often asked me why I gave up so much of my life to take care of these halls. They don't understand the sacrifice."

"I do," Scott says quickly, seizing the opportunity to gain her approval back. "The architecture is a feat of ingenuity. It's not even a house—it's *art*."

Gia pulls herself away from the manor and smiles at Scott, tilting her head slightly. She inches even closer until Scott thinks she might kiss him. Instead, she whispers in his ear, "I like you, Scott. I hope you make it."

# Buck Grimm

I T'S BEEN FOUR years since Buck had a drink, a fact that moves across his brain like a neon news ticker as he pours himself another helping of bourbon. He flexes his fingers around the glass, only just remembering how it feels to firmly grip alcohol. It's not the same as holding water nor coffee nor soda—not nearly the same.

He's normally not a weak man. In fact, his sobriety has been—dare he say—easy. Buck drank himself stupid when he was ambitionless and lost in his late twenties, but once he discovered writing, he never felt the need to numb himself like he used to. Why would he want to when everything in his life was finally exciting?

But today Buck feels more than just weak. He's uneasy. The minute he stepped into the house, he felt watched. Maybe that's because he's surrounded by his peers, the handful of famous horror authors he competes with on a daily basis, eyeing one another like birds of prey. Since Mortimer is gone, the pen-and-ink-lined throne is now empty, and any one of them could ascend to take it.

But the competitive tension isn't the only thing producing goose bumps on the back of his neck. Buck also vividly remembers how it felt to have Mortimer Queen's eyes boring into him from his office seat day after day, and this feels similar. Like Mortimer is watching from behind the manor's walls.

He shudders and takes another sip of bourbon.

Never did he imagine Mortimer would own a house like this. Buck only really knew him within the confines of the publishing company, Deacon's Group, but during his time there, Buck gathered that Mortimer was not a fan of *things*. He used paper mugs for his coffee, owned a single pen he'd buy replacement ink for when it dried out, and used email for everything—absolutely no paper. His desk was sparse, except for a solid gold box with precious stones across the lid, an antique too rare to be out of a museum and far too grand for a humble office. Buck assumed it served as a reminder that even though his space was bare, Mortimer Queen had *wealth*. He could do whatever he pleased, even use a rare artifact to store his office supplies.

It's crazy to Buck that a man who hated clutter so much would own a home packed to the brim with antiques, figurines, and hundreds upon hundreds of clocks, all of which seemed to be ticking even louder now that Scott's incident with the broken window has left the parlor eerily devoid of conversation.

Buck suspects Scott only ducked away out of embarrassment following his tiny temper tantrum over the shattered glass. So the seemingly spontaneous breaking window was odd—big deal. Aren't horror writers supposed to have backbones? After Scott stormed out, Buck simply warned the others to give the shards a wide berth before moving to fix himself another drink.

Scanning the room, he can tell people are trying to decide whether they should appear excited to be here or deeply mournful. He eyes Crystal, who's on the latter end of the spectrum, and the others near her seem to be following her lead. A few of them are speaking in quiet tones; even the louder-than-most Felix, has lowered his voice to a respectful decibel. But for the most part, everyone hovers in place, waiting for direction to move to the next room they should haunt.

Everyone, except one sweaty, squat man with pants hiked far too high. Buck watches him closely, this man eyeing the dusty decor and antiques with hunger. He recognizes him vaguely, but only remembers his name when Crystal hisses, "Petey, watch out for the glass!" as he gets too close to the mess under the window.

That's right, Petey Marsh, whose author headshots, Buck now realizes, are *intensely* edited to make his balding head appear full and weak jaw chiseled. Petey wrote *Shrieking and Shrinks*, a well-known horror classic that's so highly acclaimed, college professors include it in their fiction curriculum and lit snobs constantly cite its merits. Some have called him a genius, but the industry has a different name for Petey: a one-book-wonder.

Buck has never been good with names, a trait that can be accredited to his upbringing in Oatmeal, Texas. Back there, people didn't often address each other by God-given names, but by casual handles and terms of endearment. When Buck and his grandma—referred to as *Nan* by all—would walk down to the corner market on Saturdays to pick up brown-speckled eggs, the man behind the counter would say, *You want them wrapped up darlin'? Right away, ma'am. What about you, bucko? You want a caramel apple? Seventy-five cents apiece, but I'll tell you what, sonny: you can have it for fifty if you promise your Nan here that you'll brush all that sugar out of your teeth real good.*

It doesn't seem appropriate to refer to anyone here as *sugar* or *pal*, so Buck takes a napkin off the bar and withdraws a pen from his front shirt pocket before writing the guests down.

*Scott Clay.*
*Petey Marsh.*

*Chester Plumage.*

Just as he's finishing the *e* in *Plumage,* Chester approaches, much to Buck's disappointment. They've never officially met, but the wiry towhead has a terrible reputation in the industry, inspiring his fans to do dangerous feats, like playing on railroad tracks or swimming in alligator swamps, all in the name of "conquering fear."

"Inspiration strike you?" Chester asks, leaning in too close. His breath smells like slightly sour milk.

"I'm just…" Buck tries to hide the napkin, but he's already been caught. "Tryin' to wrap my head 'round everyone's names."

Chester gives a mossy grin. "Please. Half these people aren't worth remembering. But I'll help anyway." He points to his own name. "Looks like you already know who I am. I'm assuming my reputation precedes me, and not in a good way. Otherwise, you would've introduced yourself—you did to everyone else straightaway in the entry hall. Real Southern thing to do, eh? Ingrained in your big bones?"

Buck offers a noncommittal shrug. Slippery, calculating men like Chester make him jumpy, like cattle when there's a mouse in their stall.

Without asking, Chester takes the pen and finishes the list.

*Scott Clay.*

*Petey Marsh.*

*Chester Plumage.*

*Winnie Roach.*

*Crystal Flowers.*

"And whoever that nobody is over there," Chester finishes, jamming his thumb in the direction of the pale girl with bangs attempting to blend into the decor.

"She told me. Hang on." Buck thinks hard. "Started with an 'm,' I think."

Whenever he shakes women's hands—especially those smaller in stature—he always worries he's going to break them. But he'd been pleasantly surprised to feel her grip was firm. She doesn't exactly look confident standing in the parlor with her arms wrapped around herself, but Buck senses there's some fight in her. After a moment, he takes the pen and writes:

*Melanie Brown.*

"What do you think *he's* doing?" Chester asks suddenly, his eyes narrowed in on Petey across the room.

Buck looks up and scratches his beard. "I guess gettin' the lay of the land." He shrugs. "He's kinda an odd guy, ain't he?"

"He's certainly jumpy," Chester sneers. "Like an overweight rat."

Buck says nothing. If he were the ruthless type, he'd say Chester is more the rodent in the room, while Petey resembles a beetle prowling on its hind legs.

A clap of thunder splits through the air, and the lights flicker. The sound is even louder now that the window is gone, and rain blows in, wetting the floor.

"So," Chester continues, much to Buck's dismay, "I take it you're not too familiar with anyone here?"

"Uh." Buck's eyes fall on the woman with silky white hair and a thin, albeit athletic, frame. Crystal Flowers. "No, not really."

Nan used to always catch him in fibs, like when he said it wasn't him who dug their hands into her gooey butter cake or that he'd gotten a black eye from falling by the creek, *not* from being punched at school. *You're fixin' to lie like a rug in church*, she'd tell him, her eyes going bug-eyed, she was so mad.

But this is a lie he's fine with telling. Buck has been trying to keep as far away from Crystal as possible ever since he saw her standing in the foyer. He moves when she does, like a bee circling a flower. She doesn't know who Buck is, but he certainly knows her. *Too* well, in fact.

And not for the reasons she'd expect.

"God, I wouldn't be surprised if this place was knocked over by the next strong gust of wind," Chester says, looking up at the ceiling. "You'd think Mortimer Queen would own something a little more… substantial."

"I was a little shocked myself," Buck says, tearing his eyes away from Crystal. "It doesn't seem very…Mortimer. But what do I know? I guess it's nice 'nuff. Pretty big place."

Chester gives a closed-mouth smile like he might disagree.

Another round of thunder sounds, rattling the house. This time, the lights flicker, darkening for an extended beat before the room is illuminated again. Buck hears a murmur of trepidation, the loudest being from Winnie, who is standing with Felix by the southernmost wall, the only bit not covered by clocks. Instead, it features a large oil painting of a woman in a white blouse with thin straps, exposing soft shoulders, a cream-colored shawl fallen across her arms. The subject is not looking at the artist, her head tilted slightly to the right, and her hair is drawn up into an effortless knot. Though the date isn't anywhere on the canvas, Buck guesses by the style and outfit that it's an older painting, maybe early seventies.

"…can't even afford to have solid *electricity* out here," Winnie's muttering. "Ridiculous."

"Ser-i-ous-ly," Felix agrees, breaking the word into exaggerated chunks. He leans a hand on the wall. "I just can't believe—"

Then, just like that, Buck watches as the wall behind the painting gives way, spinning on an axis, and Felix falls through to the other side. It stops rotating as the group rushes forward, Buck following suit when he steps forward to press against the space. *Sealed? What in the hills?* he thinks, putting his shoulder into the wall with force.

"FELIX!" Winnie shrieks, pressing into Buck's side. "FELIX! Can you hear me?"

"I'm fine, babe!" he says, his voice muffled through the plaster. "Woo! That was crazy."

"A trapdoor!" Chester remarks, a glint in his eye. "Maybe this place is cooler than I thought."

Winnie pushes her palms against the wall again, throwing her weight against it, before giving up.

Buck brushes his fingertips along the wallpaper, trying to find the crease or hinge. There's nothing there.

"Maybe 'ss stuck," he guesses.

"Maybe?" Chester repeats. "I'd say definitely."

"Wh-wh-what's back there?" Petey asks. His pants, once hitched too high, are now drooping at the sides, dragging past his belly. "What do you s-s-see?"

"Well, it's certainly not clean, I'll tell you that," Felix says. "But there's a long tunnel sort of lit with torches? OMG, are these real? Winnie, this is so castle-core in here. You should see."

"I'm incredibly jealous, dear," Winnie says, rolling her eyes. "But do you see a way out?"

"Nowhere but down this tunnel!"

"What kind of house has secret passageways?" Crystal asks, frowning. She's staring at the wall with more malice than the others, a tiny vein in her forehead pulsing.

A small voice pipes up, and Buck has to tilt his head down to see the girl with the choppy bangs, Melanie, now at his side.

"*The Hounds of the Baskervilles, The Secret Garden, Jane Eyre, Dracula…*" she lists.

"Huh?" Crystal crinkles her nose, annoyed. "I can't hear you."

Buck watches as Melanie startles, caught by their attention. Her face turns as pink as rhubarb.

"I…I was just saying all the books I could think of that have houses like this," she says. "With trapdoors and secret passageways and…"

Buck has to laugh a little, beaming at Melanie. He doesn't know a thing about her—in fact, he's sure she's the only nonfamous (at least by publishing standards) person here—but still, there has to be a reason Mortimer invited her. Perhaps this is it. She entertained him with her oddities. Or maybe they're related. He wouldn't doubt it.

Crystal scowls, and Buck jumps in before she can respond.

"We should probably wait until Gia gets back," he advises, after Melanie tentatively returns his smile. "Don't know where that tunnel leads. He could end up lost back there."

"Oh, please." He hears Felix blow a raspberry. "My sense of direction is just like my sense of style—*sharp*. I'm going to go explore."

Winnie, seemingly placated, laughs.

"Okay, dear!" she says in singsong. "I'll see you later then!"

"If I'm not back by dinner, send some hunky firemen in after me!" Felix calls jovially, his voice getting farther and farther away.

Buck's nerves prickle. First rule when you get lost in the wild is to stay put, and Buck is wondering if the manor is wilder than he first suspected. "You really shoulda told him to stay put. A house like this? Gotta have a lot of twists and turns back there."

"And I still want to know why we can't open it again. The door just completely sealed." Crystal frowns. "I don't even see a hinge."

Winnie flaps her hands. "Please. There's no need to be so ser-i-ous."

That word again. Buck wants to groan.

"Who even is that?" Chester asks, gesturing to the portrait that marks the trap wall. He sounds bored again, Felix's stunt only a fleeting moment of excitement for him.

"Liotta Queen," Crystal answers quickly, a slight edge in her voice.

Buck raises his brows and locks eyes with Melanie, who appears to have noted Crystal's tone, too. *Was that...resentment?*

"Is it really?" Winnie walks close to the frame, her nose almost brushing it. "I hardly recognized her. This must have been done *years* ago, of course."

Crystal offers an ambiguous grunt.

Not a moment later, Gia walks into the room with Scott behind her, looking far paler than he had when he left. The others quickly give them the play-by-play of what happened to Felix, Chester embellishing a few details, describing how high-pitched Felix's shriek was and how scared Winnie was.

"Oh, I was calm, cool, and collected," Winnie tells Gia. "Do you know who I am? It takes more than a secret passageway to scare me."

Gia is unperturbed by the whole retelling.

"Of *course* there's no need to be concerned," she says. "I'm sure none of you are surprised Mr. Queen has all sorts of tricks up his sleeve. Part of the fun, no? And all the passageways are very safe, I assure you. That particular one your friend went through should spit him right back out in no time."

For the first time since he arrived, Buck sees a bit of Mortimer in the manor. On the surface, this house is ancient, off-putting, shrouded with a dark authority that demands respect. But on the inside, real deep down, there are twists, tricks, and traps waiting to take you somewhere you never agreed to go.

"Now." Gia claps twice. "Has everyone become familiar with one another?"

Buck pinches the napkin in his pants pocket as her question is met with silence.

"Oh, come now." Gia clucks. "I suppose we can proceed with introductions formally, if that's what it takes. One by one, if you please."

"Th-th-hen we can m-m-ove on to the w-w-will reading?" Petey asks, rubbing his fingers together.

"Then we have *dinner*," Gia replies coolly, eyeing him with a pinch of disdain. "Who would like to start?"

Shocking no one, Winnie steps forward with a flourish of her hands and sleeves. She reminds Buck of the weather vane on top of his farmhouse.

"My name is Winnie Roach—yes, that's right. *The* Winnie Roach."

She pronounces her name *Roashay*. "I'm a bestselling author, a hand model, and an active guest on several daytime talk shows."

Buck knew there was a good reason he didn't own a TV.

"How did you know Mortimer?" Crystal asks, almost suspiciously in Buck's opinion.

"We were neighbors in LA," Winnie says simply, her answer short compared to her extended bio.

He remembers hearing Mortimer complain about Winnie—loudly—through the walls of his office. She was never referred to by name, just *that nosy bitch*. Something about Winnie really set Mortimer on edge, something Buck knew firsthand after being tasked with combing through neighborhood ordinances to find some loophole to get Winnie evicted years before.

Buck wonders what she'll be receiving in the will—probably a dead tarantula.

Chester steps forward next, giving a sarcastic bow to the group before speaking. "Chester Plumage," he says. "Author of the I Dare You to Scream series."

Scott snorts, and Buck gives him a sideways glance. Chester is less of an author and more of a cult leader. His books center around a group of teens who want to conquer their fears by doing the most dangerous, most horrifying acts possible. While the writing is a bit redundant and formulaic, Buck thinks he might be able to stomach it if not for all the controversy surrounding the series.

"How's that lawsuit going?" Scott asks, scowling.

Chester smirks but offers nothing more than that.

"Lawsuit?" Winnie arches a brow. "What lawsuit?"

Before Chester can answer, Scott does for him.

"I should have clarified—lawsuits, *plural*. Chester has inspired so many young people to do stupid shit that he's got parents across the world suing him for personal injury and endangerment."

"No comment," Chester says, nonplussed.

"Scott, since you're so vocal, why don't you go next?" Gia asks.

He snaps his neck around, his expression somehow both wary and offended. "Everyone already knows who I am, I'm sure."

This time it's Buck's turn to snort. The others join in, chuckling under their breaths. Scott gives a chagrined wince and clears his throat.

"My name is Scott Clay," he says quickly, his face reddening. "Author of the Dark Skies series and American Horror Award winner. I'm a New Yorker, always have been. And… What else…? I have a beta fish? And… Well, shit. I just realized I forgot to feed him, so he's probably dead by now."

"Were you and Mortimer close?" Winnie asks, sounding suspicious and a little hurt. "I've never heard you talk about him."

Scott's face turns stony. His eyes dart toward the broken window, then toward Crystal. He takes a deep breath. "I've actually never met him," he admits. "Always wanted to. Seemed like an amazing man."

At this, Crystal furrows her thin eyebrows, staring back at Scott. He won't meet her eye. Buck watches as she blinks rapidly before making her introduction.

"I'm Crystal. I write horror erotica." She pauses, swallowing loudly. "I…I was good friends with Mortimer. Very good friends."

Buck prays she doesn't start crying again. He wonders if she knows what happened between him and Mortimer. She couldn't possibly, otherwise her tears wouldn't be from mourning but from rage.

"Excellent." Gia urges them along. "Melanie? Why don't you go."

"Me?" Melanie gulps and fusses with her hair. "Um, okay. But I'm not a writer… A real one, I mean. I like doing it, but I have never been published, so…"

"You still got a name?" Buck encourages her with a smile.

"Yes." She relaxes her shoulders and drops her hands. "It's Melanie." She looks around at the others sheepishly. "I don't know what else to say. Can I be done?"

In an attempt to rescue her from her own discomfort, Buck volunteers to go next.

"The name is Buck Grimm," he says gruffly, avoiding eye contact with the others. "I'm an author."

"*Poetic!*" Chester kisses the air.

"I don't like to get personal," Buck grunts. "Petey? Yer last."

"P-Petey Marsh!" Petey blurts too loudly. "Author of *S-S-Shrieking and S-Shrinks*. I—I like w-w-alks on the b-b-each and the s-smell of f-fresh laundry."

Everyone laughs, Buck included, as the man dabs at his wet forehead with a handkerchief in surprise. Grateful that the formalities are over, Buck stretches his arms in front of him. He hasn't eaten since lunch, a greasy fast-food chain at the airport when he landed, and the promise of dinner was calling to him.

"Last item to attend to before we eat," Gia says as Buck's stomach growls indignantly.

She takes three long steps toward Petey and stops inches away from his face. His eyes grow wide, and he leans back, his mouth slightly agape. Gia unfurls her empty palm.

"You are to give me back the items you stole from this room," she says darkly. "Don't you know by now, Petey, that it is rude to take what is not yours?"

Then, as if in full agreement, the cuckoo clocks on the walls bleat on the hour.

*GONG.*

*GONG.*

*GONG.*

*GONG.*

*GONG.*

*GONG.*

# Winnie Roach

IF WINNIE ROACH knew there was going to be such drama unfolding during happy hour, she would've *refused* to give up her phone. Her fingers itch to text everyone back in LA. I mean, goodness gracious—sticky fingers in Queen Manor? The gossip column practically writes itself.

Petey is currently emptying his pockets, revealing tiny marble figurines, a gold picture frame, and, most expensive looking of all, a ruby bookend in the shape of a goat, its horns made of diamonds that catch the dim light.

"Scandal!" Winnie hisses, restraining herself from clapping cheerfully.

"I w-w-wasn't really going to t-t-take them." Petey's face is awash of all color. "I j-just s-s-saw them and th-thought… Uh…"

Gia goes about the room, returning the objects to their rightful positions, before turning back to the group.

"You seriously were trying to steal from Mortimer Queen?" Scott shakes his head, looking disgusted. "He's *dead*. Not only is he dead, but he left you in his will. What is wrong with you?"

"I w-was only l-l-looking at them!" Petey squeaks, lifting his hands as if worried someone might hit him. Winnie can only dream. How juicy would that be?

"Your pockets were filled," Chester points out skeptically. "What were you planning on doing, having them polished?"

"Those bookends were Liotta's *favorites*." Crystal folds her arms. "And you were going to take them."

"Shall I run and get my phone to call the police?" Winnie asks Gia, trying not to sound too hopeful. *And maybe the local news?* She doesn't say that last part aloud.

"No, that won't be necessary," Gia replies calmly. "I believe Petey will learn his lesson soon enough."

If Gia is referring to some karma or cosmic justice, Winnie has to heartily disagree. She prefers to take destiny into her own hands. Stained with the shade Coral Number Two, Winnie's lips are the most dangerous weapon of retribution. The second she gets hold of her cell, she'll start spreading the word about Petey's maleficence. Sure, he doesn't exactly hold celebrity status among the public, but his book is taught in *schools*, for goodness' sake. How would the education system feel about including a criminal's work in their yearly curriculum? Maybe Oprah would do a segment...interview tearful professors, invite Winnie to sit on a plush purple TV set and talk about the moment they all knew Petey was a thief.

Gia pops this little dream when she opens a pair of French doors and guides them into the dining room, brushing past Winnie as she does so. She shivers and takes in the new room before them.

Without any windows to allow in even the silvery storm light, the room is lit by an abundance of candles flickering shadows across a long central table. At the far end, four ancient grandfather timepieces are crammed disjointedly on either side of the unlit slate fireplace in a way Winnie finds oddly disconcerting.

Above the mantel is a framed painting of Mortimer Queen much like Winnie always remembered him: in itchy-looking clothes and bland hues. She always thought of him as a walking Triscuit cracker, his dull attitude (grumpy, tasteless, crotchety) just as bland and dry as his style. And this painting is none the better. He's depicted in a too-large tweed suit, with tired lines around his eyes and that terrible, very *Mortimer* deep frown. *Yep, that's Mortimer all right.* She can't help but scoff.

He was quite elusive when they lived next to each other in LA, despite their nearness, their town houses suckled together like two lips kissing. Their proximity once had her assuming Mortimer would have the decency to say hello once in a while, while taking out the garbage, perhaps, or getting in and out of his archaic Cadillac, but he never so much as waved.

But *that* wasn't even the worst of their interactions (or lack thereof). That came later.

When Winnie learned she'd been included in Mortimer's will, though, she felt victorious. Perhaps he'd changed his mind about her. Maybe he even recognized her tenaciousness in ascending their shared social ladder.

*Unlikely*, she thinks now, pressing her fingers to her temple. She knows many people interpret her ambitious spirit for bitchiness. But she can't help it. She's worked hard to be seen as a threat. When she began writing back in the early eighties, so many publishers wouldn't even take meetings with her—because she was a woman who wrote scary books about serial killers and vengeful female protagonists, the industry was unkind. In fact, her first book was published under the name Win Roach, as advised by her agent. *It's nothing personal*, he said. *We don't have to explicitly say you're a man, but statistics tell us you'd sell more copies with a less feminine name.* Mortimer, she imagines, had no higher an opinion of her voice.

But what did Mortimer know?

At Gia's gesture, Winnie takes a seat at the stone table. She isn't particularly hungry for anything but information. What was she left in Mortimer's will? And why?

"Gia, I'd just *love* a tour of this beautiful house," she gushes, pressing her palms together. "Do you think it would be okay for me to skip dinner and take a look around myself?"

"No. Everyone must eat."

Sighing, Winnie settles in next to Crystal, who is still glaring at Petey.

"But Winnie, I'd be happy to share a little bit of the manor's history, if you'd like. I'm sure Mortimer would be pleased you've taken such an interest in it."

"I'd love to hear about it," Scott interrupts, taking a seat across from Winnie. "When was the place built?"

"In 1805. The manor has been in the Queen family for generations, starting with Waldorf Queen, who wanted a home close to the burial grounds of his beloved wife," Gia begins. "He built the home on top of her grave."

Winnie looks down at the floorboards, shuddering slightly. How wonderfully spooky.

"It is passed down from generation to generation, to every first-born son," Gia continues. "The manor is very important to the Queen's lineage. In fact, many people don't know that this house inspired Mr. Queen's most popular novel, *Monster House*."

Winnie hears "oohs" and "aahs" from the group. She's, of course, read *Monster House* cover to cover at least three times. It's a deliciously gory novel about a man who invites his downright-traitorous family over for dinner before poisoning each of them slowly and secretly throughout the night. Cut-and-dried murder story, right? Wrong, because the relatives come back to curse the house and the man within. Winnie had always wanted to tell Mortimer how much she admired the story, but… well, things became sticky between them.

"Does that mean it's haunted?" Buck asks, cracking a smile and lifting his hands in the air. "Are we in for a spooooky weekend?"

Everyone but two people laugh at this; Gia presses her lips together like she's holding in a good joke, and Petey is dabbing furiously at his forehead, still refusing to meet anyone's eye.

"Funny," Gia says. "Though Mortimer's father, Regulus Queen, didn't quite appreciate the book as much as you all do."

"Why is that?" Chester asks. "Not a fan of horror?"

"He wasn't happy that Mortimer so publicly spoke of the manor," Gia says. "As much pride as the family has for it, this house is guarded from the public. Regulus felt Mortimer was giving away a piece of their family history for profit."

"But it's not like he was spilling any big secrets." Winnie sniffs. "It's a work of fiction. What could possibly be wrong with that?"

"Hang on," Scott raises a hand. "I'm sorry to interrupt—but didn't Mortimer's parents die when he was really young?" He looks to the others for confirmation. "I've heard the stories before. He was basically an orphan by age eight, right?"

Gia flinches and, for the first time, appears nervous. She jiggles her jaw and it makes a clicking noise. "Per tradition, Regulus and the rest of the family is buried beneath the manor." She avoids Scott's imploring eyes.

"Including Mortimer?" Crystal looks at her feet.

She appears not to have heard her or has decided to disregard all questions. Winnie is rather curious about this as well, but she has the good sense not to ask again.

"We're standing on a plot of dead people," Chester mutters under his breath, his eyes wide with wonder. "Neat."

Winnie wonders, *logistically*, how a person could possibly be buried underneath a house. Perhaps that's where the tunnels lead to and Felix is going to stumble upon a graveyard. How *incredible* would that be to see? She flaps her hands in her face, cooling off the jealousy.

"Gia, you mentioned that the manor is passed down to firstborn sons," Scott raises his voice, perhaps so that he's sure to be addressed this time. "I wasn't aware Mortimer had any children."

"He doesn't," Crystal says quickly. "Mortimer couldn't have children. But he always wanted them."

Winnie suddenly wants to stab herself in the eye with one of Crystal's kitten heels. How has it taken her *this* long to see the obvious? Clearly, Crystal and Mortimer were having an affair. She wants to gag at how cliché it is. A beautiful young thing and an old mothball-scented man? *Please.*

"That's correct," Gia says. "Mortimer has no children."

"So, who will the manor get passed down to?" Chester asks eagerly.

She pauses and looks up at the ceiling, thinking long and hard. After a beat, she smiles. "Time will tell. Now, who's hungry?"

Gia lifts a hand and claps twice. Instantly, half a dozen servers in black uniforms bring out individual plates and set them in front of the six people at the table. Winnie is not only surprised to see them—where have they been hiding this whole time?—but disturbed by their matching bald heads and missing eyebrows. Beyond the sharpness of their jaws and cheekbones, it's nearly impossible to tell them apart. She stares at them, her fellow tablemates just as entranced by the sudden service. Just as quickly, the servers back toward the edge of the room, then stand as if in wait, and the group trades a final look before they tuck in.

Supper consists of a beautifully seared steak with a cranberry compote, buttery artichoke leaves, and a small truffle salad. There is no water—only wine. Winnie doesn't protest this, gladly swallowing a mouthful of cabernet.

"There ain't any walnuts in this, right?" Buck asks sternly. "I'm allergic to walnuts."

The servers ignore him. Their faces are blank, unmoving.

"Hello?" Buck waves his hand. "Walnuts? Big nut allergy here, and I left my EpiPen in the truck. Anybody there?" He looks at the others. "Anybody else seeing this? Am I speakin' English?"

"Just stick to the steak, Buck," Chester says. "Steaks don't contain nuts."

"And don't eat the salad," Scott advises. "You never know."

"Wasn't gonna." Buck shrugs, brushing the salad off his plate with disdain.

The servers all have faraway looks, their lips dry and flaking. Gia snaps her fingers, and they obediently glide out of the room.

"Enjoy" is all Gia says before exiting behind them, just as another clap of thunder sounds off.

Rain whips against the manor, the wind howling in the distance. Winnie glances at the barren, unlit hearth, thinking the room might not feel so creepy if a roaring fire were going. She rubs her goose pimpled arms, wishing she hadn't given Gia her coat. This caftan dress is made with the thinnest silk and doesn't offer much warmth. Without pleasant background music or chatter, the atmosphere is stiff. She decides to break the ice by turning to Crystal.

"So, you and Mortimer were good friends, hmm?" She unfurls a black cloth napkin and sets it over her lap. "Were you lacking a grand-father figure in your life?"

Crystal flinches, staring down at her empty plate. This comment might be too nasty, but Winnie can't help herself. She wants to shake Crystal's shoulders and shout, *Why are you crying over that old fart? Look at you!*

"I never noticed his age," she says with a hint of defensiveness. "He had a young heart. That's all that mattered to me."

Winnie watches her carefully, noting the rest of the table following their conversation like a tennis match. "How did you two meet?" she asks.

"I don't remember, really," Crystal answers. "It feels like such a long time ago."

"So you must've known Liotta too?"

Crystal grips her fork tightly, practically bending the stem. "I did," she says curtly.

Then Winnie opens her mouth, the question she's been dying to know for so long at the tip of her tongue. But before she can get it out, she stops. She *feels* Mortimer watching, like he's hovering inches away from her, so close that his cold belt buckle presses against the back of her neck.

"Oooh." She shivers, brushing her shoulders. "Sorry. I just got chills. Um, Crystal dear, did you happen to know…I mean since you were so close with them…did you know if Liotta was…was *happy* with their relationship? Did she seem, you know, all right?"

Crystal chokes on her bite. "That's extremely personal, Winnie. And I don't know anything about it." She narrows her eyes. "Why do you ask?"

"No reason," Winnie answers.

No one has a sniffer for affairs like her. She's exposed countless famous entanglements, and it really isn't even that difficult. It's all about listening. Watching. Betrayals sell as well as murder—and sometimes, even though she's a horror author, Winnie can't help but dip into the tabloid scene. She never saw Crystal nosing around the townhome, but, of course, most smart cheating men wouldn't allow their mistress to enter their real house. Winnie will keep an eye on this, see what else she can dig up.

Across the table, Petey is trying to convince Chester that he's not a bad guy. Winnie frowns at the conversation, one that only "bad guys" would ever have to start. Both men's faces are illuminated only by candlelight, making Petey look especially strained.

"I hope Felix makes it in time for dessert," Scott remarks. "Would be a shame if your friend missed out on all this, Winnie."

She picks up a giant spoon and waggles it at him. "Don't you worry about Felix. He can handle his own. Do you know what a gay man from middle-of-nowhere Arkansas has to endure to escape cow patties and Confederate-flag knitting parties? He'll be fine."

"Fair enough." Scott lifts his hands in surrender, a smile playing on his lips. He's always had that crooked grin, which makes him all the more endearing.

Quite honestly, if Felix doesn't show up for a while, she won't mind. When he arrived, she feigned exuberance that he was there, but secretly it was a shock to her, too. The other day, they had lunch, which really meant they had wine at 1:00 p.m. at Pazelli's Bistro. Felix asked her if she wanted to go to an art opening that weekend featuring some Harvard dropout with a fixation on charcoal circles. Felix assured her the artist was going to be the next big thing, but he always said that.

"In any case, I'm going out to Vermont on Friday, dear," she told him, swishing the pinot grigio in her glass. "So I wouldn't be able to attend even if I were interested in…black circles."

"*Charcoal* circles, doll," Felix emphasized. "What the heck are you going to Vermont for?"

Winnie hadn't told anyone about Mortimer Queen's will yet. Normally, this would be prime material to send forth into the community—*her* community—of CEOs, old-money families, real estate moguls, artists, writers, party planners, and more. But she didn't want to share with anyone quite yet. It was…complicated.

But she told Felix then, slipping it out like a swift second pour.

"Queen? You mean…*that* guy?" he asked, stunned. "The one who…you know… When you guys had that…what would you call it…confrontation?"

"Yes, yes, yes," Winnie said, hushing him and looking around to make sure no one had heard. "But I guess he turned over a new leaf, because he's left me something. And I have to go get it."

"Wow." Felix sat back in his seat. "I'd pay good money to see that. Think I could tag along?"

Winnie specifically remembers snorting into her wineglass and joking, "Sure, why not? I'm sure Mortimer, God rest his soul, would've wanted anyone and everyone to come gawk at his mansion."

They laughed at his. Chortled, actually. But apparently Felix took it as an invitation. Goodness, she doesn't even know how he got the address.

She can't really blame him. People tend to hear what they want to hear, believe what they want to believe.

*Huh.* Winnie keeps her eyes on her steak, where the bloody juices are pooling from the meat. When she first read the letter about Mortimer's will, she considered it an honor. But what if, just like Felix, she saw the invitation as she wanted to see it? What if being included in the will was a punishment, rather than a gift?

She lifts her gaze to Mortimer's portrait above the mantel, his eyes boring into her with more life than his human body had.

She was wrong. All this doesn't feel like an honor anymore.

It feels like an ambush.

# Petey Marsh

THAT STUPID RUBY goat would've fixed a lot of binds in Petey's life.

Not only was being caught stealing from a dead man utterly mortifying, but the realization that a few trivial knickknacks on Mortimer's shelf would have completely paid off his very overdue credit card bills brings him even more shame.

Fork in one hand and handkerchief in the other, Petey rakes through the truffle salad on his plate while reaching to blot the moisture off his forehead. He's so rattled by the last hour that he accidentally switches up the motions, dabbing the salad with the kerchief and nearly poking his eye out with his fork. He shifts his eyes around the table, checking to see if anyone noticed, but all the dinner guests seem to be trying hard *not* to look at him.

"C-c-can you pass the w-wine?" Petey asks Chester, who ignores him.

So he stands and reaches across the table, his fingertips barely able to touch the uncorked bottle in the middle of the table.

"Jesus, Petey! You'll catch fire!"

Quickly snapping back his warmed arm, he pats the smoke wafting from his singed sweater. One of the candles must have gotten too close to his sleeve. He feels eyes scorching into him now, hotter than the flame that nearly burned him. Maybe they wish it did.

"Here." Scott moves the cabernet within safe reaching distance.

"Thanks."

Petey pours himself a heavy glass and takes a sip. He then clears his throat and addresses the group. "Um, I j-j-just wanted to say that I'm t-t-totally embarrassed b-by what I d-d-did. I kn-know there's n-nothing I can s-say, but I'm sorry."

Scott seems to speak for the group, clearing his throat and talking with the same aplomb as a well-groomed politician. "It's not really our concern. And you gave it back, so what's done is done. Let's all just move on, okay?"

Petey bites his lip, grateful for Scott's grace. The wind picks up outside, thrusting itself against the house's groaning foundation.

"Guess the manor agrees with that," Melanie offers, smiling shyly.

People chuckle.

Petey wants to tell the group that he's actively trying to fix himself. He could tell them about the kleptomania support group he goes to every Thursday in the basement of Saint Lucien's. Maybe he could say something funny like, *They give us lunch, too, but it has to be bad enough so none of us slip a few extra sandwiches in our pocket, you know?* But he's not honest nor witty, so he simply ducks his head and wipes his palms on his corduroy pants, leaving damp fingerprints there.

God, he's so sweaty. Even his socks are soaked. Under the dining room table, he scrunches his toes and hears the squelching of wet cotton. He has a chronic condition—primary hyperhidrosis—otherwise known as overactive sweat glands. It's worsened by high stress situations. Like Mortimer and his creepy house.

Abandoning his sopping handkerchief and using the clean cloth napkin folded by his flatware, Petey wipes his forehead. He told himself he was going to blend in, and he's done the *opposite* of that, notably making himself a criminal jackass.

For years Petey has dodged Mortimer Queen at every turn. He's moved every year in fear of being found, changed phone numbers often, and rounded each corner with bated breath, expecting the old man to be waiting for him. Now, even with Mortimer dead, Petey feels like he has strayed straight into the belly of the beast.

"Chester, do you *have* to do that?" Crystal suddenly sighs, interrupting Petey's thoughts.

He looks over and sees Chester pressing a forefinger into the tip of his steak knife.

"Just testing the blade," he says, a blood droplet oozing from the spot where he's applying pressure.

"You're making Melanie sick," Crystal says, gesturing to her.

Petey agrees. Indeed, Melanie's cheeks are now a grayish green.

"I think that's just what she looks like all the time." Chester snickers.

"You're an *ass*." Crystal seethes, half standing.

Melanie smiles weakly at her, a nonverbal thank-you, and Crystal nods in return, settling back into her seat.

"Chester, please." Scott intervenes again, gritting his teeth.

"Scott, *please*," Chester mimics him and rolls his eyes.

The niceties are over with this group, that's for sure.

Across the table from Petey, Melanie pushes her food around with a fork, her face still appearing queasy. Her hair dangles dangerously close to her potatoes, the ends dragging along the melted butter on top. She's clearly the youngest in the room and has a buttress of blemishes on her chin. Petey is reminded of a younger version of himself—acne, giant glasses, and a fear of speaking to anyone. He watches her put down the fork, pick it up, then put it down again.

Petey isn't the only one who notices.

"I can help you cut your steak if ya want?" Buck asks politely.

"I'm actually a vegetarian," Melanie says softly from beneath her bangs.

"It shows," Winnie remarks and then goes red-faced. "I mean, not saying you're unsightly, dear. You're…you're quite pretty. Just very…"

Pale? Thin? Wafery? Petey would've assumed a writer could find the right adjective, but Winnie trails off in defeat.

"What is with you people?" Crystal slams down her fork, outraged. "Did all manners fly out the door when we stepped foot in this house? Since when do we say the first rude thing that comes into our brains?"

"Down, dear, down!" Winnie says. "I'm sorry. You're right. That was mean of me." She tries to catch Scott's eyes when she adds, "Someone has a guard dog!" But he is looking so intently at Crystal that he doesn't notice. He's been watching her the entire dinner, barely touching his food, a look bordering on affection in his eyes.

Petey's stomach sours. *Sure*, when Scott stares, it's okay. But if Petey does, it's leering and creepy. Not that he's able to have any kind of love life—he carries a secret too big to have anyone close.

"People need meat," Buck says, wolfing down his steak in large chunks. His salad and artichoke are untouched. "'Ss just natural. We're meant to hunt."

"Not all of us own Ruger rifles," Chester says.

"You should. Never know when ya might need it."

Buck reminds Petey of his father, whom he was required to call *Sir* from birth. Sir is a blue-collar man who has worked at a run-down welding plant for more than forty years, packing the same ham-and-cheese sandwiches in his tin lunch box, getting the same paycheck after clocking out at 5:00 p.m. sharp every day. Even when Petey made enough money from his book to pay off his parents' mortgage and move them into a nicer neighborhood, his father refused to quit. In fact, he acted like all the extra money was more trouble than it was worth. If Petey's mother weren't soft and kind where her husband was hard and surly, they wouldn't have accepted the help at all.

However, Buck exudes lightness and compassion. And he talks, too. Sir never uttered an unnecessary word. It was always *we need more milk*. Or *roof needs patching*. Or *amen*. It's why Petey thinks Sir never took to him, even as a kid. His stutter produced more words than necessary, took up valuable space in the home that could be filled with precious silence or the Willie Nelson songs coming from the living room record player.

*Who am I kidding?* Petey thinks bitterly, fussing with an artichoke leaf. *If I actually had managed to steal anything here, I'd have sold it and given all the money to Sir.*

Even with his stacks and stacks of bills sitting on his counter at home, he'd force the money into his father's hands. *Don't need it*, Sir would say, at the same time Petey's mother would respond, *You're too good to us, honey. Thank you.*

"We're all dying to know, Petey..." Chester says, chewing with his mouth open. "Why did you stop writing after *Shrieking with Shrinks*? That was years ago. Do you have anything in the works?"

Petey, in the middle of taking a shaky swig of water, chokes on an ice cube. His nerves feel like a collection of lightning bugs being rattled around in a glass jar.

"N-no." He tries to straighten, but his stomach ties in knots. "I—I don't know. I've been really b-busy. I mean, I'm actually w-w-working on something...s-soon."

*Lies, lies, lies.* They can all tell, and he knows it. Petey's agent has been asking the same question for years, begging him to write more. But he won't. No, he *can't*. Even though he's done everything he can to hide from Mortimer, Petey still receives his letters. They come every first of the month, like clockwork, regardless of where he is. If he's on vacation, one comes. If he moves, one comes. Even when he was on an author's cruise in Alaska, an envelope was left in his quarters, sealed with a bloodred wax crest. *I know what you did. If you ever so much as touch a pen again, I will find you, and I will end you.*

Pretty simple instructions that Petey dutifully followed.

More silence at the table.

"So, Buck." Winnie talks while simultaneously pulling lipstick out of her silky robes and applying it. "Is it true you used to work for Mortimer? That's fascinating. I bet you have plenty of fun stories to share, hm?"

Buck, who has finished his steak and is eyeing Melanie's, stiffens at this. "Yep," he says curtly. "I was his publishing assistant."

"You must know tons about him then," she continues, leaning forward. "Did you ever go through his emails? Eavesdrop during meetings? Kidding, kidding, of course."

"She's at it again," Scott says with an air of teasing. He speaks to the whole table now, making sure everyone is included. Petey wishes he had that kind of charisma—the ability to unspool tension with a charming grin "Winnie is the biggest gossip in the country."

"You're just buttering me up." Winnie winks at him.

"That's high praise," Chester says. "You must be very resourceful."

This pulls a chuckle from the table.

"No, really! Any rumor or nasty bit in the tabloids, she's probably responsible for it," Scott insists, making this sound like a compliment instead of a jab. "What is your role called? Oh, wait I know—you're a backchat correspondent, right? For Bunker Media."

Petey almost chokes. Bunker Media owns some of the biggest magazines in the country—possibly in the world. Winnie must have her filed fingernails in some of the most powerful people's personal lives.

"It's a part-time job," Winnie assures the table. "Call it a hobby of mine. I told Bunker that I was far too busy with my writing, but they insisted…"

They all nod along while Crystal and Scott share a smirk. Slowly the table recedes into further chatter. Minutes pass, and though dinner seems to be coming to a close, everyone's plates are far from clean, except Buck, who finally asks Melanie if he can have her untouched steak. He's halfway through this second serving when dessert is served: a dark chocolate mousse with a sweetened chipotle pepper cream. Petey eats his quickly, hoping that the sooner all their dishes are spotless, the sooner the will can be read.

*The will.*

Petey imagines that most people are here at the Manor because they're eager to hear what's been bequeathed to them—excited at the idea of taking home a rare item or Queen dollar or two. But he's been dreading the reading since his invitation came in the mail. Because there's no logical reason for Mortimer, who constantly threatened Petey, to have left him anything. He wouldn't have come if the letter hadn't been delivered to his agent's office instead of his home address. Franny did three things upon reading it: bought Petey a giant bouquet of sorry-for-your-loss lilies, wrongly assumed he and Mortimer were the best of friends, and booked his nonrefundable flight to Vermont.

Crystal, who is swirling a spoon in her mousse, suddenly huffs. "It's funny, Mortimer hated mousse," she says, bordering on wistful. "He pretty much loathed all sweets, though."

"What k-k-kind of person hates d-d-desserts?" Petey laughs nervously.

It was meant to be funny or rhetorical or just something to *say*, but Crystal stares at him with her scathing eyes and replies, "Um, Mortimer. I think I was pretty clear when I *just* said that."

He shrinks, pressing his shoulder blades against the back of the chair. Melanie tugs on her bangs. Winnie pretends to be fascinated by the butter dish. Chester picks at his teeth with a steak knife.

"Crystal," Scott warns. "Keep. The. Peace."

She folds her arms childishly. "I. Am." Then, as if she was chewing on the thought for some time, she asks Petey, "I'll drop it, but I want to know, did you steal anything else?"

"No! I swear!"

The candle nearest to him suddenly leaps from its sconce, toppling onto the table. Its flame licks across the cloth like a swift-moving snake and manages to catch hold of the napkin in Petey's lap. He screams and rockets to his feet as fire engulfs his chair.

The guests jump into action around him, panic sweeping the table. With his thick boot, Buck kicks the seat over and roars at everyone to bat at it with their cloth napkins. Together they manage to quell the flames, and then all that's left is a scorched, blackened chair.

"What the *h-hell*?" Petey gasps for air, clutching a hand to his chest. "H-how did that…? I didn't even…"

"It was an accident," Melanie says kindly, her face a little ruddy from all the excitement. "And no one got hurt."

"Yeah, these candles are a lawsuit waiting to happen," Scott agrees, his own much-broader torso heaving.

"Still! You should've been more careful!" Crystal hisses, slamming her empty glass back down on the table and putting her face in her hands. "Jesus! That could have been *so* bad."

Petey doesn't understand. Didn't they all see it, too? The candle… it *charged* at him. His arms, though they have a proclivity to whack into things, weren't even nearby.

Chester nudges the burnt chair with his toe. "Bet that was an antique," he says. "Must've been hundreds of years old."

"Probably why it went up in flames quick as a hiccup," Buck adds. "Old wood. Chances are it was hand carved. Damn shame."

*Oh God, oh God.* Petey leans down and rests his hands on his knees, taking big gulps of air. This couldn't be going worse.

"All right, I'm just going to say it." Winnie throws her hands in the air. "This place might be cursed. Now, don't look at me like that, Scott. I'm not some crazy old lady! Look at what's happened since we arrived!"

"A window breaking, a wall flipping, a chair catching fire…" Melanie lists lowly.

"I saw something weird in the bathroom," Scott confesses. "On the mirror was this handprint…"

"Terrifying." Buck smirks, and Scott laughs in chagrin, shaking the seriousness out of his expression.

"Okay, yeah. But also, Gia told me she hopes I 'make it.' What does *that* mean?"

"That she's hoping your career *finally* takes off," Chester sneers. "God bless your soul."

"It *is* a little odd that the Manor is sitting on a burial ground," Crystal concedes, glancing at the floor. "I…I never knew all that stuff about Mortimer's family."

"Okay, so it's a creepy place," Chester says, tossing back the dregs of his wine. "So what? If you don't feel comfortable, you can leave."

He stares around the room like it's one of his famous dares.

"Plus, ain't that just a little too classic?" Buck asks, settling into his chair with sigh. "It's a tired ole trope. Big spooky house. Freaky-looking butlers. Come on now. Can't we do better than that? Aren't y'all horror writers?"

*No!* Petey wants to scream. *No, I'm not!*

"I don't know." Winnie relaxes, too, grabbing a bottle of wine by its neck. "The chair catching fire is pretty fun, isn't it? Fictionally speaking, that is."

"It'd have been better if Petey had gotten stuck in place while it burned," Chester says, then grins. "*Fictionally* speaking."

"Now, that's what I don't like about the genre these days," Scott says, flapping his cloth napkin in the air to seemingly fan away the smell of burnt wood. "It's all about the worst imaginable ways to die. Trapping people in giant ovens, cutting off heads millimeter by millimeter…is that really what makes a good horror story? A gory death?"

"Right." Buck stabs a finger in the air. "What's important is the *journey*, makin' *that* scary."

Petey can't fully focus on the shoptalk. His heart still hammering over the whole fire debacle, and Chester's comment about Petey *burning alive* doesn't make him more at ease.

"I disagree." Crystal can't seem to help herself. "I find that the true root of horror is in its characters. They should be the scariest part of a book because the human mind is the most macabre protagonist in existence."

"But what about Netflix?" Scott raises his brows, and there's a united groan. Crystal giggles, and he grins even wider, as if proud of making her laugh.

"Streamin' services!" Buck playfully shakes a fist in the air. "It's all about what'll do well on TV these days."

"And none of the big platforms want a horror movie about the evil stuff 'normal' people do," he says, using finger quotes on *normal*. "They want the haunted houses, the freaky man in the mask, the sadistic killings. It's more entertaining."

"My publisher actually suggested I remove an entire plot point from my latest book," Winnie says mulishly. "Because it wouldn't play right on *TV*."

Outrage! Irritation! There's suddenly a wave of unity among the group that wasn't there before. Petey can feel it happening, but he's not part of the harmony as he scoops his burnt napkin from the ground. They all hate him for the same reason Mortimer hated him, and even if he returned the items he stole—*all* of them—the trust would remain broken.

Before he came to Vermont, Petey practiced confessing his crime aloud.

*I s-stole an unp-published copy of M-Mortimer Queen's m-manuscript from his house.* He never got further than that, couldn't imagine any scenario that would end in forgiveness.

While the others keep talking, their complaints growing louder and the synergy becoming stronger, Petey stares at his brittle broken chair on the floor. He could've been toast.

And he certainly will be if anyone finds out what he took from Mortimer Queen.

# Chester Plumage

G ONG.
    *GONG.*
    *GONG.*

The grandfather clocks clang seven times, their necropolis striking the next hour and quieting the group's momentary bonding. Chester feels the dissonance of the bells deeply, like his fingernails are being bent backward. He leans into the uneasiness, resisting the urge to clamp his hands over his ears.

*Feel the fear. Feel the fear.*

Chester repeats the mantra in his head until it's louder than the gongs. It's his motto splashed across billboards in New York City, LA, Phoenix, Dallas, DC, and even a few in Cincinnati, Ohio. He has a *big* following in Cincinnati. A few years ago, a sixteen-year-old tried to rappel down the Purple People Bridge to spray-paint FEEL THE FEAR along the metal side so that boats would see it as they passed. He managed to write FEEL TH before he fell and shattered six bones while hitting the Ohio River.

"Y'all really jumped at that sound." Buck laughs as the clocks silence. "No need to get all twitchy. Just tell yourself it ain't somethin' to be afraid of, and it won't scare you."

That's where Chester disagrees. In fact, his whole moral code revolves around feeling and accepting fear, not denying it. Being brave is one thing, but to be comfortable with the uncomfortable? That's the true making of a man—not to get all philosophical, of course. He writes scary books for a living, for Christ's sake. There's no need to be so serious about it.

Hell, the I Dare You to Scream series has become a brand thanks in large part to his blog, where he can chat back and forth with his fans, mostly young reckless *kids*. So he's not going to get too sanctimonious when his site is filled with self-submitted videos of youths cage diving with hammerhead sharks (dull, overdone), jumping the subway rails (fun, but lacking imagination), and sitting in a box of poisonous tarantulas for an hour (excellent). His brand sells—whether it be through book sales or plastic toys in kids' fast-food meals.

Chester sucks on a spoonful of mousse, trying not to breathe out of his nose too much. Petey's slightly burnt chair reeks of dank untreated wood.

*Crap.* Happy Meals. He rips the spoon out of his mouth and resists the urge to whack himself with it. He forgot to tell Quinn about the McDonald's call he received a few days ago. Quinn, a dominating force in the PR world, worked out a deal with the national restaurant chain so that with every new I Dare You to Scream release, Burger Mania would have a new toy relating to it in their kids' meals. But according to the rep on the phone, that wasn't happening anymore.

"We tried to reach Quinn but couldn't get through. They said the books have become less child-friendly recently. I'm sorry, but it's just not appropriate anymore," she told Chester. "You know that. I know that.

*Parents* know that. We agreed to this collaboration when the series was comparable to Goosebumps and Skeleton Creek."

"I understand," Chester said, though he could already feel Quinn's fury radiating all the way from her office in New York. "That's my fault. I'm evolving as a writer, and I get that not all my readers will evolve with me."

"Yes, well," the rep replied, giving a pregnant pause. "If I'm being honest, the last book was too gory, even for me."

"Fine, that's fine. Thanks for being transparent. I'll pass along the information to Quinn."

Then he forgot to do just that. It's obvious what she'll say, anyway. That these new books are destroying not only the brand but his image. *The blog has to come down*, she'll tell him for the umpteenth time. *It's getting bad, Chester.*

But the likes, hearts, favorites, reposts, comments—they're like *drugs*. Less important is what people think of him nowadays or what they say to his face. The pixelated thumbs-up emojis on his posts are like shots of endorphins being pumped through an IV.

Impatient and exhausted with everyone here, Chester cranes his neck and asks, "Should someone go get Gia? I think we're about done here. I want to get on with this."

He's eager to get his hands on whatever Mortimer left him. Chester wasn't sad to hear Mortimer had died—in fact, it was a relief. But part of him thought it was a tragedy that the two of them never sat down and broke bread. Mortimer, above all people, would have understood Chester. He wouldn't have scolded him for his gore, for his risqué writing style. That's why he was left in the will—Mortimer must have sensed they were two dark souls that never got the chance to connect.

But, of course, they could never have been friends. Chester knows that.

As if on cue, the doors leading into the entry hall are abruptly thrown open, their golden knobs crashing against the walls. Gia stands with her hands delicately cupped on top of each other.

"Did everyone enjoy their meal?" she asks, her face, a smooth gray, glowing against the dim candlelight. Chester has been dying to ask her age, but he can't stand to hear Crystal screech at him about "decency" and "manners" anymore. At the thought, he stifles a scoff. Like she wasn't curious, too.

"It was delicious, dear," Winnie says, pulling out a compact and dabbing her nose with powder. "The steak was a little undercooked, but that's a common snafu. Where was your chef trained? Italy? *Please* don't say Italy."

Gia either doesn't register this or chooses not to, turning her head toward Petey, who's standing near his spot at the table.

"We had a terrible accident." Scott motions to the destroyed chair. "A candle was knocked over, and the seat caught fire. We're so sorry."

Chester rolls his eyes at the apology. *We? I didn't do anything.*

"Oh my!" Gia says, her brows rising without wrinkling a centimeter of her forehead. "Is everyone okay?"

"It w-w-was my fault," Petey volunteers sheepishly. "I d-don't know what h-happened, but s-s-somehow—"

Gia interrupts this with a snap of her fingers, and three servers materialize and start taking away the chair carcass. They're freakish and offbeat; all their pupils are so big and black, they seem to overtake the irises. And Chester *loves* them. He's a fan of anything that makes people unsettled. It's fitting, really, that he gravitates toward things and people that are so often cast aside.

"How many people do you employ here?" Chester asks once they're gone.

"None."

He narrows his eyes, turning over Gia's words.

"They're volunteers, you might say," she explains. "I couldn't make them leave even if I wished to."

Chester slides his dubious gaze across the table and sees everyone else wearing a similar expression. He glances toward the door the servers exited through. Maybe he could go after them and propose an interview. Already he's spinning a novel in his head centered around the bald, alien-like servers bound to a dark old Manor.

Petey starts to apologize again for the chair—not that he offers to pay for it—but Gia is ready to move on.

"It's time for the reading of the will," she announces solemnly.

He's never been to a will reading before, but Chester imagines there should be a sort of court authority or a lawyer present. In all the books he's read involving a final testament, the family crowds around a giant mahogany desk as an older gentleman with the tiniest, thinnest glasses allocates the dead's belongings. Before Chester arrived at the Manor, he thought this whole thing would be wrapped up in an hour, tops, and he'd spend the rest of the weekend exploring the grounds, nosing around Mortimer's things, and garnering inspiration for his next book. If only he could slip away from the group and find another tunnel entrance, like Felix did. He envisions a tale reminiscent of Edgar Allan Poe's "The Cask of Amontillado." A man wanders those dark damp tunnels for weeks trying to find a way out, walking until his feet wear down to the bone… He's not even aware when he dies, leaving his body behind to rot as his ghost continues to wail through the underground passages…

*We can't talk about rotting bodies*, he can already hear Quinn say. *Parents don't want their kids reading about that.*

Screw that. Bodies rot. It's just a fact. And kids should know that.

Gia strides to the hearth before bending down to fuss with the unlit wood, the left side of her mouth twitching like she's withholding a smile. She seems…excited by the whole ordeal.

"Thank goodness," Winnie says, wrapping her flowy sleeved arms around her waist. "It's getting a little chilly in here."

But Gia doesn't light a fire. Instead, she pulls a box from the grate and brings it over to the table, then sets it down with some pageantry before pausing so everyone can get a good look. It's a jewelry box, the kind grandmothers might keep their pearls in.

"Oh…it's the box." Buck says, more surprised than Chester expected.

"The box?" Scott asks.

"Yeah, Mortimer's. He kept it on his desk at work."

Winnie takes in the ash smudging the gold, seemingly trying to keep the judgment out of her voice. "Sort of an odd thing to keep at the office."

Gia unclips the box's latch and flips open the lid. Inside is what appears to be a pile of black soil. She buries her fingers inside and withdraws a piece of paper folded into a tight square. Gia slowly starts to unfold it. With every crease, she straightens further, growing almost taller in the quiet of the group.

A thought suddenly parachutes into Chester's mind. Maybe Mortimer planned for this arduous process to drag out. Maybe it's all a big joke. This ceremony could be a farce. *And to Chester, I leave…absolutely nothing. The police are on their way, and you're under arrest.*

Jesus. He rubs at his slippery nose, all too aware of how oily it is.

Finally, the dirty piece of paper is undone, and Gia holds it in front of her face. Chester picks at a wart that's blooming on the side of his finger and frowns. Is she having a stroke? The clocks tick. His patience wanes.

"Wha—" Chester begins, confused. But then, it starts.

*"Know all persons by these presents that I, Mortimer Victor Queen, of Essex County, Vermont, being of sound and disposing mind and memory, and not acting under duress, menace, fraud, nor under the influence of any person whomever, do make, publish and declare this my last will and testament."*

A spindly spider lowers itself from the ceiling and lands in the center of the table. It scrambles toward the gravy boat and disappears. Scott exhales deeply, accidentally blowing out one of the candlesticks.

"My comrades," Gia continues reading. "It is with great pleasure that I inform you that I am dead, cremated, and placed in my intended urn."

All eyes fall on the box.

"Is that…?" Crystal lifts a shaking finger. "That's not his… That's not Mortimer's…"

Chester balks. They've been sitting in the same room as his ashes this entire time—they ate *dinner* with them. How creepily awesome.

*"This brings me joy, because if I'm dead, that means you all are surely sitting around my table, breaking bread together. I'm sure many of you are wondering why you are here tonight. And I shall leave you in suspense no longer, as I'm not a writer of thrills but of horror. So we bring on the fear."*

*Bring on the fear.* Chester keeps his spine as straight as he can, unwavering at the words. He's been afraid of this moment since getting the invitation. It was dangerous to even show up here today because for a long time, he's been waiting for someone—especially Mortimer—to ask about it. About *her.*

But the outcome was far too tempting to pass up.

Gia lifts her eyes and pauses, giggles. Chester scoots on the edge of his seat.

*"I give, devise and bequeath unto Scott Clay, Buck Grimm, Winnie Roach, Crystal Flowers, Petey Marsh, Chester Plumage, and Melanie Brown…a game."*

A loaded silence falls over the room. Gia's eyes flicker over the page and then at each of them.

"Uh, what?" Scott asks, somewhat politely. "I'm sorry, I don't understand."

Relief washes over Chester. It's like Gia finally ripped off the Band-Aid. A *game?* Of course, how very artistic of Mortimer. He must be rolling over in his grave, so pleased with himself. Chester's brain starts working on overdrive, laying out how he can spin this for his I Dare You to Scream blog. Readers will eat it up.

"I'm confused, too," Crystal says. "What does that mean?"

"That's not all, right?" Winnie frets. "There's more?"

"Oh, there's more," Gia says, but there's something in her tone that makes Chester hesitate. *"My fellow writers, tonight won't end as you expected. I can only assume most of you came because you believed I'd be giving you something of great value."*

Chester notes that most everyone looks at the floor at this, save for Melanie and Buck. He curls his lip at the ones who look guilty. None of them deserve to be here. Mortimer would have hated their falsity.

*"My Manor is quite special, if you haven't already realized. Through all my years here, it has given me quiet, comfort, and protection. In return, I provide it sustenance. Food, you see. I admit, I'm feeling quite theatrical as I put forth this plan, yet I can't help but want to bring justice to my life story. Very few horror novels end with it, no?"*

"This is the most verbose will reading I've ever been to," Winnie says, drawing her finger around the rim of her wineglass.

Scott scowls at her and then focuses on Gia. "I'm sorry, I don't quite understand. Put forth what plan?"

Gia only speaks louder. "I hope you've enjoyed your short time at the Manor thus far, because not everyone will leave. As I said, I provide it with sustenance, and what it craves is you."

If it were anyone else reading the will, Chester would expect a quippy *just kidding!* But Gia doesn't seem in on the joke. She's serene, still staring at the paper. At his right, Buck explodes into laughter.

"What?" he booms. "Oh man, Mortimer is a character until the very end, ain't he?"

Crystal's nose is wrinkled, and Petey's sweat has dripped into his wineglass.

"Why would he write that?" she says. "Did he think this is funny or something?"

"N-n-not everyone w-will leave?" Petey asks, still standing. No one has offered him their seat. "Wh-what's *that* supposed to m-mean?"

"Quiet!" Chester shushes, intent on hearing more. That's the problem with people—just when it gets good, they have to clutter up the moment with questions. *A game. A hungry house. Oh, this is all too good.*

*"You'll soon come to find that there is only one way to escape the Manor, and that's the widow's peak on the roof. No door nor window will allow you to leave. The only way out is up."* Gia looks at them again and smiles.

Chester beams right back, eager to convey his enthusiasm.

"In order to get to the peak, you'll need to get through seven rooms: the dining room, the great hall, the library, the greenhouse, the guest suites, the master bedroom, and the attic. Each is sealed with a riddle you must solve, and only then will the doors open so you can continue."

"All right, we get it—it's a joke." Scott gets to his feet. "I don't know if this was just a big 'fuck you' from Mortimer to us, but it was a huge waste of our time. We came all the way out here."

Gia's upper lip curls. "*Sit,*" she growls. "I'm not done."

Chester swears her eyes turn darker.

Scott lowers himself onto his chair. Chester relishes the moment. If you smushed all his high school and collegiate bullies into a ball of playdough and molded a man out of it, that would be Scott Clay. And Chester would love to crush him.

"I am not totally merciless, my dear writers, because I cannot stomach the plot of my final story to end in all-out bloodshed. I am giving you a chance to survive the night. All you need to do is move through my Manor and solve the riddle in each room."

For the first time in a long while, Melanie speaks. "Survive the night?"

Chester looks at her. She anxiously rubs at a mark on her forehead. He leans forward and props his chin up on his hands, waiting for more. Fear has settled over his skin, prickling, but that's okay. He takes a deep breath and welcomes it in like an old friend. He gauges the room. Does he stay for the games, or—now that he has inspiration for his next book—does he find an exit?

Gia is looking at them all like they're something to eat. Maybe she's more dangerous than he first believed.

"I'm leaving," Winnie announces, standing and heading toward the door.

"M-me too," Petey bobbles in agreement.

Chester gets up, but slowly. He tenses, waiting for Gia's reaction. She exhales loudly, lifts her hand, and snaps once.

All the candles extinguish, like a massive breath shot through the room. Even he yelps, adding to the chorus of screams as they're submerged in darkness. Chester feels like he's being swallowed whole, the air suddenly thick in his lungs. This is the definition of vulnerability. He strains desperately to see something, anything. He imagines being stranded miles off the coast, his legs kicking uselessly in the ocean while great white sharks circle just below.

Chester gropes around for the table, knocking over glasses and pushing aside plates until he finds his steak knife. Gripping the end tightly, he holds it out in front of him and slashes into the empty air. Dimly, he hears the cries of those around him, but he's focused on defending himself while visions of what could happen in the dark flash across his mind: a gun pointed at his temple, hands grabbing at his throat, his own knife turned on him and pressed to his Adam's apple.

Then he registers the undeniable *human* warmth of hot breath on the back of his neck. Before he can flinch away, someone whispers in his ear. "*Feel the fear.*"

Chester slices again, his knife cutting through nothing. He backs away and rams his tailbone into the corner of the table, shooting pain up his spine. A laugh unexpectedly bubbles up from his chest. He can't help it! All this—the lights going out, the whispering, the knife in his hand—is perfectly terrifying. Chester's soul feels split right down the middle, torn between fright and elation.

"I'm going to ask you all to calm down." Gia's voice is even, emotionless, everywhere. "I'll make the lights come back on as long as everyone behaves. Is that fair?"

An ensemble of agreements and pleas answers her. With a soft poof, every candle in the room is lit again, their flames dancing merrily. Chester blinks rapidly to clear the spots over his eyes. Around the room, everyone is suddenly exposed, like rag dolls strewn across a playroom. Petey has hopped onto Buck's back, scrambling up as Buck tries to pry him loose, Scott is crouched in wait near the door, and Crystal and Winnie are shoulder to shoulder, both holding up their fists, ready to fight. It takes a moment for Chester to spot Melanie; he finds her poking her head out from underneath the table, checking to see if the coast is clear.

All at once they spring into action. Scott leads the pack, attempting to wrench open the door that leads to the entry hall. Buck is at the French doors that go into the parlor, banging on the glass.

"Let us out!" Scott barks, spittle flying from his mouth. "Unlock them. This is fucked up, and we're *leaving*."

Chester moves across the room and takes a try at the doors himself. The knobs refuse to turn in his hand. With his heart pounding audibly, he whips his head around, searching for an answer in the others' faces. This is really happening. They're in real danger here.

"You need to let us out," Buck orders, pointing a large finger at Gia. "This ain't right. Whatever this is—some sick prank or joke—it ain't funny."

Gia simply grins. "Sit," she commands.

Scott opens his mouth to protest, but Chester hurries to shut him up.

"Just do what she says. You know that's where this is going anyway."

Scott reluctantly does as he's told, and the others follow his lead, their faces pinched and frightened. Once everyone is in their seats again, Gia raises the will once more.

"Where was I?" She trails her finger along the paper to find her place.

*"I advise you not to dawdle, though,"* Gia says. *"Every hour, the clocks will sound. If you have not written down your answer—anywhere will do—and passed safely through a room in an hour's time, my dear Manor will take one of you. There's no way to tell who it will be. The Manor is not particularly picky, only hungry. And a word of warning: for every wrong answer to a riddle, you will receive a punishment."*

"Gia, Gia, Gia," Winnie says, her smile wobbly and laced with fear. "Please. Be honest with us. What's this really about?"

"I've told you. Mr. Queen is allowing you the opportunity to live through the night, provided you can solve his riddles. If not, you'll be eaten."

Chester can't help it. Another laugh, incredulous this time, bubbles up. It hurts coming out, like chugging a soda and feeling a burp in your nose.

"What's so funny?" Scott demands, turning on him. "Are you part of this?"

Chester's shoulders shake, but he stifles the chuckling. Finally, he wipes his watery eyes and manages to say, "No...of course not. It...it just sounds absurd. Like it could be fun, no?"

Scott contemplates him for a moment. "You're actually insane."

This makes Chester chortle again. He grips his stomach; his body feels ripped in two, the more manic side taking control. Everyone's faces are just so damn *terrified!*

Seeming to give up on him, Scott directs his attention back to Gia and speaks intently. "So you're *not* going to let us out? You're keeping us trapped in here?"

"You'll be free to move through the rooms," Gia replies. Then she adds, "As long as you follow Mr. Queen's directions."

"Okay, that's enough. Let us go." Crystal's determined eyes are shiny with frightened tears. "You'll never get away with this. What, do you think our friends and family won't wonder where we are? How are you going to explain that? I bet my agent is freaking out as we speak since I haven't responded to his texts in an *hour*."

In another moment in time, Chester might've quipped that it's pathetic the first person who would care to go looking for Crystal is on her *payroll*. But saying it aloud would only make him laugh again, and people are already giving him mistrustful glares.

Gia sets the paper down and smiles at her. "Have you not been listening, Crystal? The Queen family has been feeding the Manor for many, many years. There's *always* an explanation."

"You're bluffin'," Buck says, gripping the table until his knuckles turn white.

"Even in death, Mr. Queen has connections, power. He can make anyone disappear like…" She lifts her fingers, ready to snap again.

Everyone collectively cries, "NO!" and Gia drops her arm to her side.

Chester's heart is body-slamming itself into his chest. And he's never felt so wonderfully alive. Part of him wants to bang his fists on the table and chant, *More, more, more!*

*Stop it!* his feeble logical side hisses. *This is bad!*

"Unfortunately, I won't be staying," Gia continues. "But I'll be eager to see who, if anyone, comes out alive." She tilts her head, her upper lip twitching. "Although, who knows? Maybe I'll pop in and see how things are…progressing. You're all quite fascinating." She gestures toward Scott. "Irritating at times, but aren't all humans?" She unfolds the paper once again.

"You may believe, my dear beneficiaries, that I am a monster. But I implore you to pose a question after facing my riddles. Then, and only then, should you look at yourselves and ask, 'Who is the real monster?' You might be surprised to find you are in good company this evening."

Finished, Gia moves toward the door, and Chester watches as Scott readies himself to launch toward her the second she opens it. Scott widens his eyes at Crystal, who nods back and Chester waits, hoping in some part they succeed.

Then, above their heads, the ceiling groans, as if lamenting the weight of something mighty. A lightning-shaped crack splits through the plaster, and a sprinkling of stucco dust powders the tops of their heads. After a moment—chaos.

The ceiling explodes, something hard and alabaster landing with a crash atop the dining room table. Chester's stomach shoots into his throat.

The body's been stripped of skin, muscle, hair—but its skull still sits cockeyed on a broken, mangled neck, its mouth ajar like it's screaming. Through the candlelight, Chester can see a diamond-studded tooth.

Felix.

# Crystal Flowers

**E**VERYONE ERUPTS INTO screams as the grandfather clocks at the end of the room, the four horsemen of the apocalypse, give eight resolute gongs. With every clang, the dining room shakes.

*GONG.*

Crystal is thrown to the floor, her hands raised uselessly to try and brace for the fall. Pain shoots through both her wrists, and she doesn't have a second before the next—

*GONG.*

The room shudders again. She hears shattering as all their wineglasses hurtle across the space and crash against the walls. Plates fly like Frisbees overhead, and the silverware whistles through the air.

*GONG.*

Crystal curls into a ball, thinking it's the most protective configuration. Instead—

*GONG.*

Another tremor comes along, quaking the room, and her left knee clips her mouth. She suddenly tastes rust.

Finally, the clocks fall silent and the room stills. Crystal waits a moment before lifting her head. She expects to see destruction, the crumbling walls, collapsed roof, and detritus of a high-magnitude earthquake, but all is just as it was.

No, not exactly as it was. There are a few slight differences. The hearth, for example, now houses a cheerful fire that crackles merrily, and as Crystal gingerly stands, she sees the dining room table is not only undisturbed but refreshed. Dome-shaped stainless steel covers have been placed over each plate, cutlery and goblets neatly arranged, clean cloth napkins folded in tight squares. The body is gone.

The ceiling is clean and patched, like Felix's skeleton didn't just…

"No!" Winnie laments, sitting on the ground while clutching her elbow. "Oh, Felix…Oh no…"

Crystal isn't eager to search the room for it, but his body is nowhere to be seen. Vanished, just like Gia. The others stir, groans and whimpers coming from across the room. Scott, who must have thrown himself on top of Melanie during the chaos, stands. Somewhere, underneath the layers of terror and confusion, a twinge of jealousy stirs within Crystal.

"Is everyone okay?" he asks, lifting Melanie.

"No!" Crystal doesn't mean to shout, but she can't quite bring herself to tame the volume. "Of course we're not! What just *happened*?"

Buck shakes his head, as if trying to rid himself of a crown of orbiting stars. Petey crawls out from beneath the table, muttering nonsensically, and Chester is already on his feet, staring white-faced at the place settings.

"Earthquake?" Buck asks, his tone begging, as if Crystal can confirm for him that this was simply a joke gone bad.

"What about the *ceiling*?" She points to it. "And the…"

Winnie, bordering on hysteria, clutches her pearls and moans.

Crystal moves a hand to her chest, tapping the fabric of her suit to solidify that her heart is still beating. *Don't cry, don't cry, don't cry,* she repeats for the hundredth time tonight, but she feels the familiar heat behind her eyeballs. She shouldn't have come this weekend. Hadn't Mortimer already caused enough turmoil in her life?

Petey leans over and vomits chunks of undigested artichoke while Scott tries for both doors again. Still locked.

"Help! HELP!" Buck cups his hands around his mouth and shouts, "SOMEONE HELP US!"

"This has got to be a…a…a prank or something," Scott says, leaning against the wall as his knees buckle.

"Seriously? A prank? You think a prank can shake a whole damn house?" Chester finally snaps his head up and cackles. Goose bumps prickle Crystal's arms. Why does he keep *laughing*? "You think that body was made of plastic? That it is all some elaborate trick? I guess you've never seen a corpse before because *that's* what they look like. Can you think of any explanation other than the fact this house might be—"

"Haunted? Alive?" Scott grips the back of a chair, looking queasy. "I…I don't understand how, but maybe it's a big performance or…or…"

"Or this is *the* house," Crystal says, the realization striking as hard as her knee did not moments ago.

*Monster House.* It's still, to this day, one of her tried-and-true favorites. Her love for it predated meeting Mortimer, and back then she never even considered that her feelings for the story would transfer to him. The first time he came over—a terribly awkward time—Mortimer gravitated toward the bookshelf in the living room, hovering and acquainting himself with *it* more than with her. He was so ill-suited for her home's ultramodern aesthetic, wearing loafers with that extra rubber padding for anti-slip assurance and an itchy button-up dress shirt. Crystal fretted that if he chose to sit on her chesterfield, fitted with a terribly uncomfortable upholstery, he'd break his tailbone. Not because he looked like some old man, but because he was…soft. Real. Well-worn.

Thankfully, though, during Mortimer's first and last visit to her house, he was more interested in browsing her library. She nearly fainted when he pulled out her copy of *Monster House* before flipping it open with an open pout.

"What's wrong?" she asked, standing a few feet away. Initially, this had been a *come over for wine and cheese* sort of invitation, but she felt more like a realtor showing around a prospective client.

Mortimer held up *Monster House*. "You dog-ear pages?"

"Only on books I really like."

"The spine is bent back, too. The edges are all dulled, and…here, is this a coffee stain? This book has been *abused*."

Crystal raised a brow. "I'd say it's been well loved."

"Ah. Sometimes it's hard to distinguish the two, hm?"

She didn't know what to say to that. And it didn't matter. Mortimer moved on to the next book on the shelf. Then the next, and then the next. He spent an hour there, going over the titles, asking her questions: "What did you think of Pamela's character arc?" and "Did you figure out the killer before the big reveal?" Then he left. They hadn't even *touched*.

The similarities between the man-eating mansion in *Monster House* and the Manor they're currently trapped in are undeniable, almost to hilarity. What did Gia say? That it would *eat* them, one by one, if they didn't answer the aforementioned riddles.

"Gia did say the book was based on this place." Chester squeezes his eyes shut for a moment. "Maybe it's a little more than loosely inspired."

Petey responds by lurching forward to be sick again, while Winnie reaches for Crystal, looking utterly lost. She shrinks back. By nature, she's not a touchy person, especially when it comes to strangers, a baffling quirk for someone in her line of work. All day she writes about people intertwining their limbs, touching every square inch of exposed skin. But Crystal herself is categorized as weepy, always hyperaware of everyone's sadness—exaggerating their pain in her mind, creating a story, a back-story, a whole testament to their woes.

Like, once, she saw an old man buying a single can of on-sale tomato soup at the grocery store. Crystal went into the parking lot after and cried, thinking of him returning to an empty home, sitting in a lonely living room, and prying open the discounted dented can.

It's more a nuisance than anything, a trait Mortimer thought was endlessly irritating. Once she started to take care of Liotta, he ordered her to keep it together or get out. She didn't cry for a long while after that.

"So this is real," Scott says on a breath. "We have to play this…this game."

A *game* is Chutes and Ladders, played with her niece and nephew over ice cream. A *game* is the back-and-forth eye flirting she and Scott have been doing since they met. If this is a game, Crystal doesn't want to play.

"We're all going to die!" Winnie screeches. "Just like Felix!"

The reminder of the bones immediately sends Scott and Chester into a panicked argument:

"It's obvious we have to find the riddle and solve it!"

"Should we be playing into this, though?"

"We should set the house on fire so the authorities have to come rescue us."

"Are you *insane*? We're locked *in*."

Crystal's knees won't stop knocking together, so she pulls out a chair and sits down. That's when she notices something strange.

"Hey, guys," she says. "Guys? Look at this."

At the spot she's chosen, there's a folded name card next to the set of new cutlery. *Winnie*. With a quick scan around the table, she sees every spot has one.

"Here's Buck's name," Scott says, argument forgotten as he moves around the table.

"And yours." Melanie points to another spot.

"Did we have these before?" Crystal frowns. "I don't remember any assigned seating."

"Why the hell does that matter?" Buck booms, throwing his hands up. "We gotta get outta here, people!"

But it's too late, the fresh mystery pulls at Crystal, finally giving her panic focus. She moves around the rest of the place settings, lifting one of the stainless steel covers to investigate what's underneath. The plain white china is no longer plain nor white. Thick numbers are stamped across it in bold red: **560,934**. Crystal raises the plate for Scott to see. Wordlessly, he reaches down and picks up the plate near Buck's name, flipping that one over, too, revealing **10,452**. Melanie overturns another, the one at Scott's place: **498,034**.

Crystal's mind is working furiously. "So the numbers must be associated with the name card."

Buck, frustrated with the lack of action, begins slamming his shoulder into the door again. Crystal resists rolling her eyes and focuses on the problem at hand while the others—minus Winnie, who has her knees to her chest, rocking back and forth on the floor—investigate between crashes.

"I bet you're right." Scott allows, speaking slowly. "Here's yours." He showers her the number **765,958**. "That mean anything to you?"

*How much my house costs…? No. How much debt my sister is in…? Nada. How many people have my photo as their phone backgrounds…?* Nothing comes to mind.

"I don't think so."

*Thunk, thunk, thunk.*

"Wait." She grabs her plate and stares hard at the number. "Yes, I think…I think this is how many Instagram followers I have." Her neck flushes. "Not that…I mean, it could be just a coincidence." She hopes no one thinks she's bragging about her social following, surely not in this situation. It's really just a graveyard of an app at this point—she recently hired some eager college student to post for her so she wouldn't have to look at the mix of lewd and insulting comments underneath her posts anymore.

*Thunk, thunk, thunk.*

"Huh." Scott looks at his number again. "Now that you say it, I think I have around this many, too."

Petey looks like he's trying hard not to appear downtrodden when he holds up his plate: **10,452**. If things were different, Crystal might feel bad.

"I d-don't really p-post m-much," he says, not that he needs to defend himself.

*Thunk, thunk, thunk.*

"Wait, that can't be it," Melanie says, holding a dish close to her face. "This says three million. What author has three million followers?"

*Thunk, thunk, th—*

"Can you please stop?" Chester admonishes, craning his neck to stare at Buck. "For the love of God, just stop!" He faces the others, his brows heavy with frustration. Apparently, he's through with the maniacal laughter, his expression simply testy. "I do. I have three million followers."

Crystal tries not to be impressed.

"Lotta impressionable kids," Scott mutters.

"I think this all has to do with the riddle we're supposed to find." Crystal reaches toward the last name card and plate. *No, wait, this makes eight. There are only seven people.* She stalls for a moment, counting the places. There's one more setting than before. Crystal clears her throat, the paper corner of the place card pressing sharply against her finger. "Who is…Mary McKinnon?"

Shrugs and darting eyes are exchanged around the table. She feels her frustration rise at the lack of legwork—or brainwork—the others are providing. Does she have to do *everything*? Maybe Mary was a guest who never showed up… Lucky girl.

"What's her follower count?" Chester asks, casually trailing a finger along the back of his chair. Crystal eyes him for a moment. His posture, his composure. Suddenly something feels…*off*.

She lifts the cover at Mary McKinnon's spot. The number painted on the plate is an unremarkable **1,342**.

"Okay, I'm confused." She sets it down. "Are the numbers the riddle? Or a math problem?"

From the floor, Winnie finally speaks. "You want to solve a *riddle* right now? A *math problem*? No. No, no, no. We need to get *out*. Can't we break down a wall or something? Shatter another window?" She stares at Buck's biceps.

"Please." Buck snorts. "Haven't you heard me tryin'? This place is solid."

"Well, that settles it. Everyone start looking for…for something," Scott says. "A riddle, I guess. Some sort of clarification."

"But these—" Crystal gestures to the table.

"We don't know if they mean anything," Chester snaps. "So just look around. Like Scott said."

She hasn't known him for long, but it seems strange that he's agreeing to do anything *Scott* says. Everyone remains where they are, trapped in inaction.

Then the room stirs again, shakes just enough to warn them. Their hour deadline is approaching.

They spring into action. The search is frantic, unorganized, and—if Crystal is being honest—a little useless. Melanie gets on her hands and knees, scouring the floor. Scott peers under vases and antique decorations, while Buck picks at the wallpaper, trying to see behind it. Petey does his best to help, though he, for the most part, just stands around looking green.

Crystal approaches the empty fireplace, then rests a hand on the mantelpiece as she shifts her gaze to the portrait of Mortimer. The eyes, thick brushstrokes of oil paint, seem to follow her. It's him, but it's not... *him*. The artist got his physical features right, but he's wearing them all wrong. Mortimer wasn't the surly man everyone saw him as, at least not to her. He'd never hurt her—at least not on purpose—until now. But *why*? Crystal feels the tears again and instead glowers at the painting.

"I didn't do what you think I did." She whisper-hisses, "*You* were the monster, not me!"

Mortimer's portrait blinks.

With a yelp, Crystal's hand flies to her mouth. But before she can wait for another move, a shout pulls her around.

"Petey, what are you eating? Hey... Hey! Don't!"

Scott barks the warning, and Crystal watches as his hands grip Petey's cheeks, pushing them together until his eyes bug in alarm.

"Spit it out! Spit it out right now!"

Petey might've had an easier time doing so if Scott weren't suddenly trying to force fingers down his throat. Petey manages to choke up a bright pink glob, spits it onto the floor, then rubs the sides of his face as he's released.

"What was that about?" Buck shoots Scott a disappointed look. "Don't be puttin' hands on another man."

Scott jabs his thumb at a crystal bowl set inconspicuously on the dining table, hidden among the fine dinnerware. Crystal can't believe she missed it before. The bowl is filled with bright pieces of candy—no, not candy. She makes her way over to it and plucks one from the pile. It's Jabba Jaw bubble gum, the chalky kind that turns into a tough old sock when you chew it long enough. She hasn't seen these since the nineties, when she and her friends would buy pieces for twenty-five cents, chomp on them for a few minutes, then hurl them at boys their age biking to the neighborhood pool.

"I'm s-s-sorry!" Petey fixes his disheveled glasses. "I thought c-chewing on s-s-something would m-make me less n-nauseous."

"Who knows what that could be?" Scott seethes. "It could be poison! You saw what fell from the ceiling, right? That wasn't convincing enough to be a little more cautious?"

Chester pipes up. "Relax. We just had a three-course meal, and no one died. I don't think the Manor plans on poisoning us."

"How do you know?" Scott's upper lip curls, a dog giving a warning growl.

"Because a smart predator doesn't contaminate prey before eating it." Chester waggles his wormy eyebrows at Crystal. She instinctively steps backward, bumping into the mantel. Crystal refuses to let herself think too hard about that horrifying sentence. Instead, she flips over the piece of bubble gum in her hand. That's when she remembers.

"There are jokes in these." She says, taking in blank stares in return. *Right, who the fuck cares about* that *right now?*

"Yes, there are. I remember," Winnie replies, her voice vacant. "They were discontinued after a few years. People kept swallowing the jokes before they could read them."

Crystal unwraps the piece she picked up, palming it like a die.

Scott rakes his hand through his hair, a whine catching in his throat. "Why are you touching that when I just said—"

The tips of her fingers turn white as she snaps the gum cube in half, procuring a tiny slip of paper inside. After some finagling, she unfolds it and gasps. She ignores the others' questioning looks and bends down to retrieve the half-chewed wad Petey spit out. There's a second piece of paper stuck inside the slobbery mass. Once she's cleaned both off as best she can, she slaps them onto the table.

1. I led a girl astray
2. Sought out to impress her idol

"This is it. This is the riddle." Crystal can barely contain her excitement, a thrill rushing through her chest. "I think we have to find them and put them in the right order."

Buck claps his giant hands so hard, everyone jumps. Then he clubs Petey on the back. "Good find, champ! Knew ya had some brains!"

"It was *Crystal* who figured it out," Scott emphasizes, then gives her a slow-blinking look, an apology for doubting her in the first place. Her cheeks warm. "Everyone, grab a piece. And be very careful not to rip the paper inside."

As it turns out, not every piece of gum has a part of the riddle inside. Some contain jokes (*I used to play piano by ear, but now I use my hands!* and *I tried to catch fog yesterday... I mist.*), while other pieces contain more strange misplaced sentences. Melanie is the most adept at breaking open the pieces, finding the right ones. Her frail fingers make quick work of each Jabba Jaw cube. Crystal can't help but watch her every few moments as the paper slips stack up in front of her. She may be quiet (always so damn quiet), but at least Melanie is the kind of person who jumps right in to help when it counts.

Once they're done, Crystal scatters the fragments along the table, pushing them around with her fingers, trying to arrange them correctly. Her brain starts whirring, blocking out the disjointed advice and ideas from the group around her.

Mortimer used to call her a bulldog. He knew how stubborn and determined she could be, how she had the innate desire to lock her jaws into something and see it through to the end. But he also saw how hard she tried to quell that aggressiveness, especially with the public. She played the part of the beauty, wearing baby doll dresses and false eyelashes that made her look wide-eyed and innocent. That's the part everyone—her agents, publishers, Instagram followers, readers—expects her to play.

But not Mortimer. Never Mortimer.

Mortimer would look at her seductive photo shoots and ditzy

marketing ploys and give her a stern stare. "This is not who you are. Stop dulling yourself so that you won't intimidate people, Crystal. If people fear you for your tenacity and determination, then so be it."

Mortimer did a lot of messed-up things to her, including trapping her in a man-eating Manor, but he did convince her that the real her was *enough*.

She huffs finally, shushing everyone around her before slapping Scott's hand for trying to move a piece. "Sorry, sorry. Just…don't touch anything. Let me think."

Her eyes scan the papers, bouncing from one to the other in rapid succession. *Come on, Crystal! You're a writer. You're good with words!*

"There!" she shouts. "Don't move. Nobody touch anything. This is it. It has to be."

The group leans in to read.

> *I led a girl astray,*
> *A child who dared to dream,*
> *Sought out to impress her idol,*
> *But I wasn't what I seemed.*
> *I sent her to new heights*
> *On the promise of my affection.*
> *I was not the hand that killed her,*
> *But I offered no protection,*
> *I knew the secret, knew my role,*
> *But still I did not stay.*
> *She was just a silly girl at best,*
> *One who won't be missed today.*

There's a pregnant pause as everyone digests the words.

Buck gives a low whistle. "And how much time do we have to figure this damn thing out?"

Right. They're being timed, a fact that quickly dampens any sort of celebration that stirred in Crystal's chest. She jerks her head around to look at the grandfather clocks, and her heart does a free fall. "Fifteen minutes."

"We w-wasted so m-m-much t-t-time!" Petey wrings his hands.

"Maybe if it didn't take you a hundred years to get a sentence out!" Chester retorts sharply.

"Stop it," Scott says. "Let's focus up. Anyone have any ideas?"

While the others talk over one another, Crystal watches Chester. He sinks away from her gaze, from the table where the rest worked, his beady eyes darting from the dining room table to Mortimer's portrait. She sees he's clutching something in his hand, a bit of it sticking out. Testing out a theory, she scans the place settings, counting.

There's one name card gone, and she bets anything it's currently balled up in Chester's grasp. Her spine stiffens the way it does when there's a knock at the door when you're not expecting guests. He knows something about the riddle.

Something about Mary McKinnon.

# Melanie Brown

MELANIE *GETS* MYSTERIES.

People? People defy the laws of logic. But she can crack a good whodunit open like a squirrel with a nut. Melanie loves mystery books, not that she'd ever admit that to a room full of horror authors. She appreciates the way they're woven with clues, how it's the reader's duty to turn the pages and pluck at each string until the whole thing unravels. She dreams of writing a story like that, a mystery so tightly wound that the reader forgets to come up for air. But all the manuscripts Melanie sent to literary agents and publishers were rejected.

Well, it's no wonder. All her English professors say the best authors write what they know, but all Melanie knows is what has already been written. Petra is always on her case about going out into the world, experiencing things, but Melanie prefers to spend her time in her worn reading chair at home. There she can sit with the quiet and not worry about filling a silence, coming up with something to add to a conversation.

Petra always says Melanie is too worried about what people think, that Melanie truly believes no one will think what she has to say is worth listening to.

Maybe Petra is right.

But aren't people the worst kind of mystery? Sherlock Holmes, Nancy Drew, Alex Cross—these, Melanie can wrap her head around. At their core, they're predictable. The inciting incidents, clues, red herrings, suspects, twists, and resolutions. She has this formula memorized like her mother with the recipe for low-fat, low-sugar pudding. But what's laid out on the dining table right now—plates painted with Instagram followers, Jabba Jaw bubble gum, a riddle about a "silly little girl"—Melanie can't quite make sense of it. It doesn't follow the formula; it's all too *human*.

She doesn't want to be the one to say it, but the group only has thirteen minutes left to solve the riddle before—what exactly? The image of Felix flashes in her mind, how his body went *splat* onto the table, spraying clumps of mousse and red wine in its wake. Was that one of their destinies in thirteen—no, now twelve—minutes?

"This doesn't make any sense," Scott says after the tenth time repeating the riddle aloud.

"Even if we had an answer, who would we give it to?" Crystal keeps nervously tugging at strands of her hair as she stares at the papers, pulling them out of her bun like the strings of spiderweb.

"Maybe we jus' say it out loud," Buck tries, his face red with concentration as he broods over the riddle.

"There are too many goddamn variables here!" Winnie brays. "None of us have a clue what's going on!"

Melanie's focus sharpens at the word. Clues. Right, where are the clues? The plates, for one thing, boasting everyone's Instagram followers. Why is that important? Who sincerely even *cares?*

Her gaze hops and skips between Chester, Crystal, and Winnie.

Well, *they* do. Melanie doesn't know them all that well, but she knows that, within the industry, popularity on social media is just as valuable as dollars.

Okay. What else is there? Bubble gum. Could be meaningless, simply a medium to give them the pieces of the riddle. But if it could have been anything, why a discontinued candy?

Scott is right—this doesn't make any sense. Mortimer was a *horror* writer through and through, so why would he leave them a mystery to solve? Sure, the genres slightly intersect, but at the end of the day, they always lean one way more than the other. If he were staying absolutely true to himself, Mortimer would have trapped them in the Manor with a bunch of monsters—ghouls, cretins, demons, bogeymen. And even though she didn't know him beyond their one strange, hazy meeting, Melanie thought he valued his integrity, his *readership*, more than anything. She pictures him like an old ship boarded by explorers and pioneers to traverse oceans: impressive, weathered, and very difficult to steer off course.

"No one take any guesses unless they're sure." Chester speaks for the first time in a while. He's been devoid of sarcastic jabs or comments over the past forty minutes. "Remember what the will said? For every wrong answer, we'll be punished."

"Let's b-b-break it d-down," Petey says. "P-piece by p-piece. Maybe it m-makes more sense like th-that."

They all stare at the scraps of paper.

Then Scott clears his throat and starts reading aloud. "'I led a girl astray, a child who dared to dream.' *I*. So that means the answer is a person."

"Not necessarily," Winnie counters. "It could be an object. You know, 'the more you take, the more you leave me behind. What am I?' That sort of thing."

"Footsteps," Melanie murmurs in answer.

"That's right. Footsteps."

Melanie checks the time. Nine minutes. She starts to open her mouth but feels the rap of an invisible hairbrush across the back of her hand. *Tell Mrs. Maudlin "thank you"! Say you're sorry to your sister! Tell Mr. Hardwick to have a merry Christmas!*

As much as Cynthia hated the fact Melanie was a painfully quiet, shy child, it seemed she also loathed when her daughter spoke. Melanie lived every day in thick, toxic contradiction. When she would pad into the kitchen on Sunday morning and ask if she could please have a bowl of oatmeal, Cynthia would look up from her coffee, her fingers pressed against her temple. *Oh, would you shut up!* she would growl. That very same day, if her mother had the ladies over for bridge, Melanie would stand quietly at the bottom of the stairs and watch them come through the front door. Cynthia would hiss, *Are you dumb? Say hello!*

"Sought out her idol, but I wasn't what it I seemed," Scott reads. "Okay, it sure sounds like a person. *Her* idol"

They go through the rest line by line, but it doesn't help.

"Maybe we should just forget it." Chester kicks at the Persian rug below their feet, his tone clipped. "How do we really know something bad is going to happen?"

Winnie straightens, her nostrils flaring. "Was seeing my dear friend *dead* not proof enough?"

"Maybe...maybe he got what was coming to him. Just because it happened to him doesn't mean it—"

"*Don't* finish that sentence," Scott warns, stepping in front of Winnie and intercepting her ring-studded hand before she can slap it against Chester's greasy face.

"Chester." Crystal speaks slowly, carefully, her eyes sharp. "Why does it seem like you're so against us solving this thing? Is there something you're not telling us?"

For a man with millions of followers, Melanie thinks, Chester squirms when more than one pair of eyes is on him.

"I'm not against the riddle being solved, obviously!" he says with an off-putting smile. "I'm saying it's not *going* to be. It's a waste of time, and if you haven't noticed…" He gestures to the clocks and chuckles between words. "We—we have *very* little of that!"

When Melanie was seven, Cynthia lost an eyeshadow palette, more specifically, her Clé de Peau Beauté Eye Color Quad. It was a four-square palette with the colors Warm Ocean Sunset, Sand Dune, and Caviar Pearls, and apparently it was *very* expensive. Cynthia was distraught about misplacing it, enlisting both Melanie and Petra to turn the house upside down looking for it. Petra was always less enthusiastic about following their mother's orders, but she was particularly reluctant during the days of searching.

"It's just makeup!" she whined. "You can always buy more! What's the big deal?"

Cynthia never found the palette, but Melanie did. It was stuffed inside Petra's dresser drawer underneath all the frilly socks she refused to wear, and it was snapped in half, the packed powders now broken pieces in their trays.

Right now, Chester is doing an excellent imitation of Petra.

"No, you're acting off." Scott is locked in on Chester. "You know something."

To his credit, Melanie thinks *everything* about Chester's personality is a little off—shifting from inappropriate cackling to sour and stern silence. In her opinion, the word Scott should be using is *guilty*.

"I'm acting *off* because we're stuck inside a madman's mansion!" Chester half shouts, a manic look in his eyes as he waves his arms in a frenzy. "Oh no! The crazy is catching! What are we going to do? You know what we do? We feel the fear. We wait for our fate and face it."

Crystal moves to stand beside Scott, her arm pressed against his. An unimpressed look on her impressive face.

"Cut the bullshit, Chester. Who is Mary McKinnon?" Crystal asks again, impatience forcing the words through clenched teeth. "If you know who she is, then you might know what the riddle is about. Don't give us this 'feal the fear' bullshit. You're just as scared as us, but you're hiding something, and I'm sick of it. Why aren't you telling us?"

"*What* aren't ya tellin' us?" Buck joins in, his stature most intimidating of all.

"Who says the riddle is about her?" Chester lifts his arms into an exaggerated shrug. "Maybe she was just a guest who didn't show up!"

Crystal shakes her head. "No." She narrows her eyes. "You're lying. I can tell."

"What are you, an expert or something? What lies are you hiding, Miss Flowers?" Chester shoots back. But the barb doesn't land. The group moves closer to Chester until he's backed up into a corner.

Melanie's anxiety thrums. She hates conflict, can hear her mother and Petra's arguments through the walls. She walks over to the table to get some distance, hovering beside Mary McKinnon's place. *If she were here, would she be like…them? Or like me?* Melanie thinks. *What would you do if you were here, Mary?*

*Brring! Brring!*

She stiffens, the rest of the room going quiet.

"Was that…? Is that your phone?" Melanie asks Chester, whose brows form a prominent V.

"No. I gave it to Gia. Just like the rest of you."

The chirps continue, coming from all sides of the room. Now, though, they're quicker, more urgent, a cacophony of likes and comments. Melanie cups her hands over her ears, the pings becoming overpowering.

"What is that?" Winnie howls over the noise.

"My ears!" Crystal shrieks.

But no one is more overwhelmed, Melanie realizes, than Chester, who is now the color of rancid mayonnaise. He spins around to look for the source of the chiming, but it's ringing from the room itself. Melanie presses down hard on the sides of her head, her eardrums pulsing in pain.

And just as suddenly, it stops. Nobody moves nor speaks.

Somebody new has joined the group.

Seated at her place at the table is a young girl wearing a blood-soaked *Feel the Fear* sweatshirt, her neck bent, her arms twisted every which way, the side of her skull flattened and caked with brain matter. She stares straight ahead, her eyes a milky blue.

The loudest scream comes from Crystal, who sinks to the floor and hides her face. Scott topples backward, and Buck repeats, over and over, "What the hell? What the *damn* hell?" Winnie runs to the door and futilely pulls on its brass knobs, while Petey attempts to shield himself with a chair.

But Melanie, so close that she can smell rotting flesh, can't bring herself to move. A plate on the table rattles, drawing her eyes. It's Chester's. The number starts to slowly tick down until it's moving so swiftly, shaking the plate so violently, that she can hardly see the digits anymore. At last, it stops, and what remains looks like a bloody zero smeared on with a finger. The dead girl screams, and the plate cracks in half. Then she disappears.

Melanie doesn't realize she's holding her breath until her lungs start to protest. She lets out a long wheeze and whips around to look at the grandfather clocks. She assumed the girl was their punishment for not answering the riddle in time. But no, they have three minutes left, and the girl, Mary McKinnon, is gone. In fact, Mary McKinnon appeared to be dead.

"Someone for the love of God, help us!" Winnie pleads to no one.

Chester gawks open-mouthed at where the girl sat. He moves toward the chair, laying a hand on the back. "She…she was really here."

There's clear recognition in his voice. *She.* Mary.

Melanie looks around, desperate for someone else to have made this connection and do something about it. But the others are in a tailspin—she's the only one with any sense left. She speaks to Chester in the strongest voice she can muster.

"Did you…did you do something to her?" Her voice cracks and she clears it. "Are you the answer to the riddle?"

He says nothing for a moment, and she worries he can't hear her over the shouting, yelling, and banging on the door. Finally, Chester tears his gaze away from the empty chair and looks at Melanie with desperation. She feels like he's searching her face for any signs she might let this go.

"I…" He opens his mouth, and she can see his tongue, which is patchy and white with dehydration. "You don't understand. I didn't mean to…I never meant to…"

Her suspicions confirmed, Melanie turns—to tell the others, to shout it at the Manor, to provide the answer they so *desperately* need to survive this room—when Chester lunges. He catches her hair and yanks her down, her skull hitting the floor with a *crack*. Melanie's vision blurs for a moment, and when it clears, Chester is standing over her, his face slick and determined. He leans down, places his hand over her mouth, and whispers, "Please. Please don't. I'd rather die."

*GONG.*

*GONG.*

*GONG.*

Melanie is too late.

The clocks start their dirge.

From the fireplace, an arm of flames shoots out, dexterous and unapologetic, and grabs the leg closest to the hearth.

Petey.

Melanie gasps. *No, it's not him. He didn't do it!*

He screams, his skin sizzling, producing a rank, inhuman smell. Melanie can't see if the others are leaping away from the danger, but she's so close, she can feel the heat on her cheek. The arm drags Petey across the floor, his wails raw and primal. He digs his fingers into the carpet and kicks with his good leg, but the flames don't let up.

Buck leaps, his arms outstretched, and grabs Petey's right hand. He digs his heels in and pulls, making animalistic yowls as his face grows red with effort. Somewhere in the back of her mind, Melanie wants to help, too, but she can't remember how to move.

"D-don't let g-go!" Petey screams.

"I won't!" Buck howls back. But his grasp slips, and he falls onto his back.

Petey is sucked into the hearth, the entire structure imploding into a fireball as his body is eaten by flame. Melanie feels her eyebrows singe. That's when the fireplace's opening curves, its bricks bending, the stones of the hearth moving, turning into sharp points.

Teeth. It opens and closes.

Chewing its food.

And as it opens again, Petey's body is gone. A slow cheerful crackle of fire is left in his wake. As if nothing happened.

And the door into the entry hall creaks open.

They are free to continue to the next room.

# Short Story #1

### Chester Plumage

Chester Plumage stands in the lobby of the Seattle Marriot, his mouth tacky from falling asleep on the plane. The flight from Columbus, Ohio, was five hours nonstop, and he and the stewardess (he knows the term is outdated, but the woman was a bitch, so Chester will call her what he wants) squabbled the entire trip because he refused to turn off his cell phone ringer.

"I paid the five dollars for Wi-Fi," he said extra slow, to emphasize the ridiculousness of it all, "so I could get on my Instagram. What's the problem?"

The stewardess stood next to his seat—he bought all three in his section so he wouldn't have to accidentally brush knees with anyone—and leaned down low.

"I'm only asking you, sir, to turn off your sound. It's disrupting and, frankly, quite rude to the other passengers."

His phone chimed five times in a row, another round of

likes on the latest post he put up while eating a shitty slice of Ohio pizza in the airport terminal. It was a submitted video of a group of guys putting their friend in a giant Yeti cooler and tossing him off a bridge. Chester thought it was wonderful, and apparently so did the rest of his fans.

"I like the sound," he insisted. "And you can't tell me what to do."

Apparently, she could, because the plane would not budge until Chester complied. And even after that, she refused to take his drink order. He couldn't even get a plastic cup of damn tap water, let alone a cocktail.

This, among other reasons, is why he hates promotional tours. They require too much in-person time with his fans, whom he prefers to communicate with via social. There's something about seeing their sweaty, round, too-eager faces that makes him nauseous. They can gush, as he scribbles a vague slash of an autograph in their book, about how much they love his work and how awesome it is to meet him, but for some reason, digital hearts and likes give Chester a bigger thrill.

"You do realize I can reach millions of people online," he'd told his publicist before leaving on this most recent book tour. "I can go live on Instagram and do this, no hassle, no flights, and no terrible hotels."

"What's wrong with the hotels?" Franklin asked, completely missing the point. "We can book whatever place you want, Chester. Just let me know, and we'll make the changes to your itinerary."

"Do you not hear me? Millions. How many people do you think show up to a book signing on average? A few hundred?"

"Not true. Phoenix attracted thousands."

"Yeah, but I'm not really counting the protestors rallying to have me chucked out of the city."

But he'd lost the battle, and now, after finally landing (and shooting the stewardess a dirty look), here he is standing at the hotel lobby desk for the second time that day, ball cap tilted down to hide his face. The willowy clerk was nice enough when he checked in fifteen minutes ago and even offered him complimentary water, which was more than the bitch on the airplane had done. However, he spent approximately three minutes in his designated room before marching right back down to speak with her again—and not because he particularly enjoys the conversation.

"Hello, sir," the clerk says, still smiling. Did she ever stop? "Can I help you with something else?"

"Yeah, see, I have little problem." Chester drums the desk with his knuckles. "The room is nice, the bedsheets look clean—but the mini fridge…it only has three of those tiny liquor bottles."

The clerk blinks. "Yes, sir. That's the standard amount we stock the fridges with."

"Well, it's not enough," Chester says, louder now, leaning forward so the clerk takes a tiny step back. "Three little bottles? Three. That wouldn't even knock a kid out for the night."

There are people in the lobby, staring. He can't see them, but he knows they're there. They're always there, everywhere he goes, glowering at him. Sometimes they scowl; other times they hiss and boo. *You're disgusting!* and *Go to hell!*

Chester is fine with these comments for the most part, but the ones that dig into his skin and tug like fishhooks are from well-intentioned people, usually parents: *Aren't you ashamed?* and *Don't you understand the harm you're doing?* He swears he would hear those remarks in his sleep, if not for the steady stream of comments and likes he consumes each night before tucking himself in bed.

"You know what?" Chester slaps the counter, making the clerk jump. "Never mind. Don't worry about it."

He strides out of the hotel, pretending not to see the cell phones held up, not-so-discretely filming him. The February air is frigid, and he's only wearing sweatpants and a loose long-sleeve, but he trudges across the street anyway before entering the fluorescent gas station aptly named Gassy's. The cashier grunts hello while flipping through the channels of an ancient TV, and Chester pulls two cases of beer out of the glass fridge. He'd prefer something harder, of course, but this will do.

While the cashier swipes his card, Chester feels a light tap on his shoulder. He turns to find a girl with short fringed chestnut hair, tattooed arms, and a nose piercing. Her jaw is working overtime, chewing a baseball-sized wad of bubble gum—the smell wafting from her molars is overpowering.

"Hi. Chester Plumage?" She chomps, looking him up and down. "My name is Mary. Mary McKinnon. Huge fan."

*Smack, squish, pop. Smack, squish, pop.*

The sound is entirely irritating, and Chester decides then and there that this girl can kick rocks.

"Yeah?" He takes his credit card back and carries the beer out. Mary follows. "I appreciate that."

"I read your books. All of them. And follow you on Instagram," she tells him proudly. "Have for two years. I'm a Chesterfile."

The Chesterfiles—a stupid name for a club—is a group formed to follow the I Dare You to Scream mantra: *If you're not afraid, you're not alive. Feel the fear.* His website has been taken down twice, his Instagram profile often banned for weeks on end. But still, the Chesterfiles are there, waiting for his return, his next dare. Franklin hates his involvement online, especially because of all the lawsuits, but it's the only thing Chester really enjoys these days. He's going to fire Franklin soon anyway. Fuck these book tours.

"Thanks for all your support," Chester says, waiting at the crosswalk.

"Do you want to grab a drink?" Mary asks, blowing an egg-sized bubble.

*Smack, squish, pop. Smack, squish, pop.*

He laughs, taking a good long look at her. "How old are you?" The walk sign glows green.

"I'm…I'm twenty-one," she says, jogging to match his long strides across the street.

"Yeah right. Sorry, but you better take off. I have an early morning."

"Doesn't look like it." Mary has to puff a little to keep up with him. "Want company?"

"No thanks."

"Please? I won't even drink, okay? I just want to ask you a few—"

Chester stops in the hotel parking lot and narrows his eyes at her. "Listen," he says, his patience waning. "I appreciate your readership, but I really want to be left alone. Just go home."

He thinks he's made his point clear and walks into the lobby, but then he hears that awful gum noshing and realizes Mary has followed him. She's too goddamn close, and people are staring even more than they were before. *Chester Plumage and an underage girl? And we thought he couldn't get worse!*

The girl is oblivious, bouncing on her toes and swinging her arms.

"You know how you always say to feel the fear in life? A few weeks ago, my best friend and I got on a back road late at night and drove eighty miles per hour with our headlights *off*. It was pitch-black. I swear, we couldn't see *anything*."

"That's not facing your fears," Chester says. "That's just stupid."

"Feel the fear!" Mary punches the air and whoops, unbothered by his lack of enthusiasm. "Hey, you want some gum? It's this old kind my uncle gives me every year for my birthday."

"No."

"You sure? It's got jokes inside."

"Yes."

He wants to head toward the elevator but doesn't want to risk anyone videoing the girl going upstairs with him. The police are always looking for reasons to arrest him, but he has an expensive team of lawyers to keep him out of legal trouble. They're becoming more and more frustrated with him, though, as he pushes the limits of what's acceptable. Last week, he posted a submitted video of two teenage boys leaping into a silverback gorilla pit at the zoo, shouting, "Feel the fear!" It did not go over well. He needs to be scandal-free for a bit, at least until these lawsuits cool off.

"Mary," Chester growls between gritted teeth. "Please go home. I can't have you following me up to my room."

"Then there was another time." Mary ticks on her fingers, disregarding him. He'd be mildly impressed at her ability to chew gum while talking so fast—if he weren't furious. "I climbed up a billboard and hung from it for a full three minutes. My legs were just dangling in the air—it was totally awesome. Oh, also—"

*Smack-squish-pop-smack-squish-pop-smack-squish-pop-smack-squish—*

Chester has no other option but to lean down and hiss into her ear with enough venom to kill an elephant, "I don't give a rat's ass about you or your stupid little stunts! I told you to fuck. Off."

*Smack.*

*Squish.*

*Pop.*

The elevator door dings across the lobby, and he takes the opportunity to beeline for it, shoving a man out of the way to stab the Close Doors button until his finger aches. Thankfully, Mary was stunned stupid and didn't come after him.

In his hotel room, Chester cracks open a beer and gulps it down so fast, the hops barely brush his tongue. He sits on the edge of the bed and breaks the seal on a second, fingering the tab. He's itching to turn on the TV and watch a rerun of *Friends* or whatever else is on, but Chester can't bring himself to split the silence that fills the room.

Because silence is terrifying to him. So he must face it head-on. *Feel the fear.*

He takes a moment to consider how his outburst might negatively impact him. Even if the girl were to take to social media and complain about how rude or awful of a guy he is in real life, Chester is confident the other Chesterfiles wouldn't take her side. *What do you expect?* they'd write under her lengthy whiny Instagram post. *You know who he is, right? You probably deserved it. Go jump off a roof!*

That last make-believe comment is one Chester has seen many times. His fans are *vicious* to one another. It's not concerning to him—it's entertaining. He wouldn't want his readers to be anything but cruel; it's part of his brand, part of what fuels his characters to face their fears. Everyone he's ever been close with has been callous, real. That's the truth of people, and Chester's books are about the truth.

Just as Chester is polishing off his second drink, there's an urgent knock at his door. Thinking the clerk sent up an apology in the form of a few extra liquor bottles, he goes to receive it.

Instead, it's the girl, Mary. She looks much older now that she's fuming, her hands planted on her hips. "You're an *ass*."

She blows a giant bubble, and it pops with a *crack*. Then she flashes her cell phone in front of Chester's face, so close to his nose that he can't see what's on the screen.

"See? Do you see?" Mary says, triumphant. "You're not hot shit, you know."

"No, actually, I don't see," Chester stands back and squints. "What am I looking at?"

"I have four million followers, ass wipe."

He registers this, chewing on it for a half a second before realizing how bitter it is. A sarcastic, basic white girl with piercings and forehead acne has more of a social following than he does.

"Okay." Chester feigns like this doesn't bother him in the slightest. "And? So what?"

Mary slips him a smug smile. "I don't *do* anything," she says. "People just follow me because I exist."

"Oh yeah, and why is that? Because you're *so* interesting?"

She rolls her eyes.

"I'm Gen Z. It's what we do. A freaking newborn baby could get fifty thousand subscribers in a day. Half my friends have reached a million, and they don't even *care*. None of us do." Her finger pokes his chest. "But you do. I know you care more than anything. And what's even more pathetic is that you try. You really, really *try*, don't you?"

The spot where she's touched him burns. Taking a step back into his room, he puts one hand on the door, ready to slam it.

"Yeah, well, at least I don't hang off billboards and think I did something worthwhile," he sneers. "Here's a news flash: I don't repost all those stupid videos you guys send me because I think they're impressive. I'm *laughing* at you. All of you. Now leave me the hell alone. Jump off a roof for all I care! Maybe *that* will make you interesting."

Only after he shuts the door does Chester allow his face to crumple. After peeling off his pants and T-shirt, he crawls underneath the bedcovers with the remaining beers nestled in the crook of his arm. He types an email to Franklin, explaining what just happened. At the end he writes, *Is this something I should be worried about?* At the last second, he saves the message as a draft and exits the screen. If Chester sends it now, Franklin will immediately call him to talk things out, and his eyelids are heavy with sleep.

It seems like mere minutes after he falls asleep that he gets woken up to screaming.

Chester bolts upright, a crunchy piece of gelled hair falling onto his forehead. He cocks an ear, thinking the scream came from a dream. But there it is again, a collection of horrified wails outside his window. He tears out of bed and stumbles across the room to shove apart the curtains. Pressing his nose to the glass, he can see a group of people gathered around the hotel's front entrance. He squints to try and decipher what it is they're surrounding, but it's hard to tell. A few minutes later, an ambulance and three police cruisers arrive.

Finally, Chester decides to investigate. He pulls on a pair

of sweatpants and a sweatshirt, then hurries down the hallway. Some people have their heads poked out of their rooms, asking one another what's going on. Chester takes the stairs, dashes through the lobby, and bursts into the cold air outside.

People are crying—guests in bathrobes, raggedy T-shirts, and slippers. Paramedics are ushering them out of the way; the ambulance doors open, ready to welcome a person—a body. A woman in a tight flashy dress is being consoled by a young cop. She's sobbing, her false eyelashes barely clinging to her lids as she sobs.

"I—I w-w-was getting out of m-my cab when it h-happened," she blubbers.

"Where were you coming from before that?" the cop asks, one hand on the woman's shoulder.

"I w-was out!" The woman sniffles. "At the b-b-b-b—"

"The bars," the cop finishes for her. "Right. And you started walking toward the entrance and…"

"I heard a noise a-above m-my head," the woman says, shaking. "And th-then…then…she landed r-right there! Right in front of me!"

The woman wails even louder, burying her face in her hands.

The cops are instructing the small crowd to go back inside. Chester sees they're already lining the area with police tape. In the shuffle, he gets nudged to the side. He trips over something and barely manages to right himself before hitting the pavement. Disgruntled and still a little drunk, he bends down to pick up whatever it was.

It's a purple Converse.

Chester immediately drops the shoe like it's made of hot metal.

"What a fuckin' shame," a cop mutters.

"You think she jumped?" a second officer asks.

"Maybe. Or fell," the first cop says. "God. What a mess."

"Hey, sir. Excuse me, sir?" Chester realizes the second cop is talking to him now. "We're going to have to ask you to move along with the rest of the hotel guests."

Chester's mouth is so dry, it feels coated in cobwebs. He points to the shoe on the ground.

"You...you guys probably want to bag that up," he says.

"Shit." The first cop grunts and waves a few people over. "All right. Please go ahead and move inside, sir."

"It's a girl, right?" Chester can't help but ask. He has to be sure it's Mary.

The cop frowns. "Yeah. Did you know her?"

"No. Definitely not," Chester says quickly. "I overhead you a second ago. It's a shame."

He moves into the lobby, past an even bigger crowd of guests waiting to hear more. The hotel staff is trying to keep things calm, shouting orders and urging everyone to return to their rooms. It seems no one really wants to oblige except for Chester, who heads straight up, lies on the bed, and stares at the ceiling until the sun comes up.

Not having slept, Chester gets out his phone and calls his publicist to cancel his book signing, claiming he's hungover and will puke all over the store's children's section if Franklin makes him go. It works.

A few hours later, he's rolling his suitcase back through the lobby, snagging a coffee by the continental breakfast. As he passes, a TV playing a grainy news update snags his attention.

"Good morning, I'm Christina Vallee with Channel 9, WLTV," says a blond woman on the TV. "More today on the death of seventeen-year-old Mary McKinnon. Police are officially ruling the death as an accident. The family asks for privacy during this hard time."

Chester closes his eyes and takes a deep breath, trying to calm himself with the bitter notes of hazelnut-roasted beans.

"We also learned here at Channel 9 that Mary McKinnon is the niece of celebrated horror author Mortimer Queen. He has yet to comment."

Hot liquid scalds Chester's hand. He releases the cup he's squished, grabs his suitcase, and sprints out the hotel's side entrance. His Uber is still eight minutes away, but he can't stand being anywhere near the hotel for another minute.

*She was Mortimer Queen's fucking niece?* His suitcase boggles along the marred pavement.

"This is not your fault," he repeats to himself. "This is not your fault. This is not your—"

Except he told her to jump off a roof. He *said* the words aloud. Why? Why the hell did he do that? He's never uttered that phrase once in his life, and he chose to do it then? To a teenager?

*It's not like you pushed her off the ledge, though.*

But he goaded her. Just like she goaded him.

Of course, there have been others like Mary. The girl who stabbed her roommate, the boys who were injured on the railroad tracks, the group of kids who messed around in a factory after hours and were permanently scarred. But Chester has never faced the evidence himself. He hates to admit that it's shaken him.

*Brring! Briing!*

There's that sound. That glorious, sweet sound of followers blowing him kisses and chanting his name. *We like you, Chester!* they sing.

Someone exiting the hotel says to their companion, "Christ, did you hear about the girl who fell off the Marriot? She was just a *kid*!" At the same time, Chester leans his nose closer to the cell phone screen and watches the likes roll in.

# Scott Clay

**W**INSTON CHURCHILL ONCE said, "Fear is a reaction. Courage is a decision."

It's been mere moments since Scott witnessed Petey being swallowed by the mouth of the Manor's fireplace, and yet Scott is thinking of the goddamn sixty-second prime minister.

Maybe because his dad was a vocal Churchill fan, a man so obsessed, he kept stacks of World War II books and autobiographies in their living room like he was building a replica of London circa 1940. Scott's brush with death forced him to think of the one person who might greet him at the pearly gates of the afterlife—God, he hoped it wasn't Dad. Even with twenty-two years to think about it, he still has no idea what he would say to him.

Regardless of why the quote comes to mind, Scott subconsciously proves it to be true. In the moments following Petey's death, he has no control over his movements. He tries grabbing Crystal to get her far away from the now-merry fire, but she yanks her hand away and rebukes him with "I'm fine! You get Winnie; I'll get Melanie!"

Buck stands at the open door waving them along screaming, "Move! Move! Move!"

Scott tugs on Winnie's long flowy sleeve. "Come on, Winnie, we have to go! Can you stand?"

She doesn't respond. He's sizing her up, debating how possible it would be to scoop her up and carry her out, when she finally nods and extends an arm. He takes it and guides her out of the room.

Once he knows everyone is safe in the entry hall, Scott moves to slam the doors behind him. He waits a beat, his chest rising and falling, only turning away when he's sure they won't fly open in retaliation.

The entry hall is a completely different space than the one Scott walked into only a few hours before. It's dark save a few candelabra, and the once-grand chandelier is unlit, making it look like a looming aquatic monster instead of a light fixture. This is too big a space to have such little light; an abundance of shadowy corners now lurk, and Scott has the sinking feeling of something lying in wait. Even the spiral staircase, a part of the room Scott thought was striking when he first saw it, now feels ominous.

The most obvious disparity from the hall then compared to now is that it's humid and hot, the air so soaked with moisture that the walls are literally weeping. Thick droplets fall from the chandelier, splashing onto the giant checkered floors. Scott's shoes, with their smooth soles, squeak and slide along the surface. He almost slips but manages to balance himself before he does.

Worst of all are the clocks. Though he can't see all of them through the dimness, Scott once again hears the ticking. And to the beat, his brain repeats, *Petey is dead. Petey is dead.*

Scott scrambles to find the right word to describe what just happened, like he's arranging magnetic words on a fridge until the sentence makes sense. Saying Petey was killed implies it was an accident—car crash, falling icicles, lightning strike—but calling it *murder* doesn't fit either, because there was no hand that pulled the trigger nor drove the knife in. No, Petey was eliminated. He was removed. He was destroyed.

Everyone huddles on a square rug at the hall's edge, terrified to take another step. Scott's eyes, done scrutinizing the room for danger, land on Chester. Unbelievably, the slimeball has a smile tugging on the corners of his mouth, like he can't believe he's unscathed. It's the last straw. Scott's blood feels hot in his veins, and he winds back his fist before smashing it into Chester's greasy face.

The thud reverberates off the high ceilings. Chester staggers backward, holding his jaw with a look of bewilderment. His feet move at lightning speed, slipping and sliding in place on the wet floor. Unfortunately, he doesn't fall.

"What the hell was—" he begins to protest, but Scott won't let him say another word.

"I saw you! Why the hell were you putting hands on her?" He points to Melanie, who flinches. Immediately he feels bad, which makes him even angrier. "I should bash your head in."

No, he should be following his therapist's orders, counting to ten and taking deep breaths, but it feels good to be angry right now. His fury is a burning, all-encompassing sensation. And it's better to be engulfed in that heat than face the terrifying reality of what he saw in the dining room. Sure, there are more pressing issues, but this one can at least be solved with fists.

"Stop it! Scott, what are ya doin'?" Buck's hulking body steps between them, his boots apparently immune to the slippery tile.

"Get out of the way. I'm gonna make him swallow his own teeth!" Scott snarls. "He attacked Melanie!"

Buck stops barricading Scott, his brows shooting upward. "Melanie? Don't you mean Petey? Petey's the one—"

"I saw what happened to Petey! But I also saw Chester throw Melanie to the ground beforehand!"

"You did *what*?" Crystal, who is pressing both hands on either side of her skull, snaps her arms down.

Chester massages his face, opening and closing his mouth like he's testing if it still works. "Are you serious?" he complains, though there's still a glint of panic in his eyes. "We just saw a man burned alive by a living, breathing fireplace, and you're attacking me?"

"Please," Winnie groans, holding her stomach and tilting forward. "Please don't...don't talk about it. I'm going to be sick..."

Scott tries to take a step, but Buck bars him from getting closer once again. He isn't the only one to worry about anymore, though. Crystal flies forward, her fists pounding against Chester's chest. He yelps like a dog getting kicked, holding up his forearms in protection. She stops before Buck can intervene, her angry breaths hissing through her teeth.

"You don't touch a woman!" she shouts at him. "Do you hear me? You don't *touch* her!"

"I didn't!" Chester insists again. "I might point out, though, that you're touching *me*."

Scott feels his muscles bunch up at Chester's blasé tone, ready to lunge again.

"Scott." Buck holds him back. "Hang on now. Just hang on—"

"What's your deal?" Scott shouts, ignoring Buck. "Were you trying to attack Melanie like you attacked that girl in the riddle? Were you the answer?"

"Of course not!" Chester answers quickly, any sign of humor vanishing from his expression. "The Manor took Petey, not *me*. The riddle was clearly about him. How could you not put two and two together?"

Scott pauses, reliving the fire wrapping around Petey's leg, dragging him into the hearth... It might even be easier to accept this death if they knew why, but like the will said, if the riddles aren't solved within the hour, the punishments will be handed out at random.

His faltering conviction must be obvious on his face, because Chester speaks again, insistent. "I swear, it wasn't me. I didn't *do* anything to that girl. Why the fuck would I? I'm not some fucking mental case with anger issues."

The blow lands. But how could Chester know his secret? He looks to Winnie, her face surprised, guilty. Of course, she'd whisper about him. Gossip. Scott shakes his head. Fuck it. He focuses again. Where to put the second punch. The nose? The stomach? But before he can, Buck shoves him back with his protruding belly.

"Hey, stop it, everyone stop it!" he barks, then turns to Melanie. "You okay, honey? Did he do somethin' to you?"

Scott waits for her to nod, to cry, to confirm what he witnessed in the dining room amid the chaos. Chester had yanked her to the ground—hard. Christ, the back of her head bounced off the floor.

"Melanie?" he prompts.

Her gaze flickers to Chester for a second before clearing her throat. "I'm fine."

"See? She's fine." Chester slaps his bony thigh. "Jesus Christ. I didn't touch her."

"You better not have." Crystal glowers. She's positioned herself slightly in front of Melanie, a guard dog.

Scott's nostrils flare. He stares at Melanie expectantly, silently pleading for her to speak up. *Tell them! Tell them he came after you!*

But she doesn't. Instead, she regards Scott for a moment longer and then looks away defiantly.

Christ. What the hell? He didn't imagine the attack on Melanie. Why isn't she saying anything? His frustration redirects from Chester to her, and he grinds his teeth. She's making him look like a liar, a hothead. But what can he do?

"There." Buck nods like an accomplished moderator. "Ain't no harm done. Now shake hands like men."

Scott glares stony-faced and is about to refuse when Chester surprises him by sticking out a hand. They shake, their hands making a suctioning sound from the moisture in the room. Scott still isn't convinced Chester didn't push Melanie down in the previous room, but time's wasting, and they need every second to get out of the hall.

"All right, fine. I won't waste any more time, then," Scott says with a pointed look at her.

The others get quiet again, looking around the room with stiff necks and wide eyes, the heat making them flush and fidget. That's when he notices what else is different about the hall. "Look there!" He gestures to the far end of the room, where a marble pedestal sits beneath the glow of a candelabrum. "That wasn't there before. Has to be something to do with the riddle, right?"

Atop the pedestal is an open book, too far away to make out.

"All right, go see what it is," Winnie says, poking him in the back.

"Yea, go ahead, Scott," Chester adds, a look of innocence on his slick face.

"Oh, and now you want to participate in the riddles?" Crystal challenges. "How convenient."

"Well, maybe seeing a fireplace chewing on one of us changed my mind!" he quips back.

Scott feels his irritation rise. "All right, all right! Enough! Before we do anything, we need to set some ground rules," he says authoritatively. His eyes move to each of them. *Look at me. Listen.*

Winnie fans her face with her flapping hand. "It's sweltering in here. Oh God, do you think that's the second punishment? Being boiled alive?"

"*Ground rules?*" Chester repeats like it's a dirty phrase. "Are you serious?"

Scott nods. "Dead serious." He winces. Too soon. "Think about it.

117

This, all this?" He waves his arms in a big moon shape. "It's the beginning of a horror story. Who knows a horror story best? We do. So we should set some parameters to help us get out of here alive."

"Like what?" Crystal hugs her waist, folding in on herself like origami.

"What's the biggest mistake our characters make in our books?" He swings around to look at everyone. The answer should be obvious, but maybe they're not thinking straight. It would be a miracle if they were. "Splitting up. The one who breaks away from the group always dies first. So rule number one? Stay together."

"Golly, maybe we should write these down." Chester rolls his eyes.

Ignoring the sarcasm, Scott continues. "Rule number two?" he asks the group.

"This seems like a waste of time." Winnie brings a thumbnail to her mouth and drops it suddenly. "Oh, wait, I know. Play the game."

"What does that mean?" Scott crinkles his brows.

"Sort of like…do what the killer or monster wants you to do. For a little while, at least. I feel like characters always try to get away with stuff or escape."

"Run fast," Buck reluctantly adds. "If you see somethin' in here comin' after you, run. And not some half-assed jog. Sprint like your life depends on it."

Scott doesn't point out that there aren't many places to run to within the confines of the Manor, but he adds it to the list anyway. He's not wrong. The futile attempts people make to get away—especially displayed in horror *films*—is infuriating. How many times has he screamed at the screen, *Run! Run, God damn it!*

"Don't be an idiot." Chester pipes up, a lilt in his voice now that he has something to contribute. *Not such a dumb idea anymore, hm?* "The biggest mistakes characters in horror stories make is choosing to do stupid things. So don't be stupid."

"How about, 'Don't take unnecessary risks'?"

"If you want to sugarcoat it, sure."

"Anything else?" Scott can't help but look to Melanie. She stares back at him, her hands going up to tug at her curtain bangs.

She flashes a glance at Chester, then murmurs, "Rule number five: trust no one."

A chill crawls up Scott's spine. Everyone nods in agreement.

"As long as we stick to these rules," Scott continues, "we might have a chance of getting out of here alive."

"What rule did we break that made Petey die?" Chester snaps.

"Play the game." Scott surprises himself with how quickly the response comes to him. "Not *everyone* was willing, so we lost time."

"Okay, okay!" Winnie tussles her fingers through her hair, a concerning number of strands coming out on her ring-clad fingers. "We have rules. Can we *please* figure out that book thing now?"

Obliging her, Scott takes a single step, his foot landing directly in the center of a square tile. Instantly, a growl vibrates from beneath his brown Oxfords. He retracts his foot, feeling the ripple slowly dissipate. He used to have a Doberman who, if she wasn't in the mood to be pet, would make the same throaty warning until you took your hand away.

"What's wrong?" Crystal asks, finally peeling away from Melanie's side.

Scott stares at the spot, a droplet of moisture sliding down his temple. "I…I don't know. I don't think it's going to let us cross that easily."

"It." Melanie nods. "The Manor."

"Fuck what the Manor *thinks*." Chester bumps Scott's shoulder and strides straight out toward the middle of the floor.

He doesn't make it far. The second tile he steps on drops, and he shouts, his left leg follows it through the floor.

"What the—Help! Help me!" Chester yells, his right knee trying to get purchase to bring his dangling leg out of the hole. Scott can't fathom how slick the tiles must be for Chester not to be able to pull himself out, and now he's dangerously close to falling below to…*where?*

"Don't move a muscle!" Buck shouts.

"I'm not!" Chester replies, trying to use his arms to hoist himself up. "What do I do? I'm in a hole. I'm in. A hole!"

"Oh God, oh God." Winnie's hands fly to her mouth. "It's happening again! It's taking someone!"

For a moment Scott thinks she's right, and his chest tightens so violently, he presses his hand against his sternum, trying to release the tension. But then it clicks into place. The Manor isn't attacking Chester. This isn't their punishment. This is the game.

"I'm coming to help you, just hold on!" Scott says, assessing the floor.

That's when Chester laughs, and Scott freezes.

"Eh, don't need you being the hero, Clay," Chester replies, easily swinging his leg up to stand on the tile. "'I'm coming to help you.' Jesus. You really think you're the main character here, don't you?"

The group stands in stunned silence, and Scott's insides burn as Chester glances into the hole and whistles, chuckling again. "Ooooh, to be fair, I could've been toast."

Finally, the others shake off their shock.

"Jesus, Chester! That's not funny!"

"What in the darn hell, man!"

Scott wants to club him again. Wants to push him off the tile completely and let him be taken. But one sentence saves him.

"Oh, hey, there's something on this tile."

Scott was right—this is the game.

"What does it say?" he asks, crouching to investigate. The floor is slick with the same moisture that clings to their clothes. Thick and putrid. Scott reaches an arm out and presses a palm on a tile, feeling an immediate growl. He keeps his hand there and wipes at the surface and realizes there's a word there he hadn't noticed before.

"Pilferer," he reads. "This one says 'pilferer'"

Buck moves forward, wringing his beard out, and Winnie gags. "I don't wanna interrupt, but should we be frettin' about the heat and the… whatever this is? It ain't poison or somethin'?"

"I wouldn't worry about it. Don't you see?" Chester chimes in from his tile. "It smells like a locker room in here." He bends down and swipes a finger across the tile. Before Scott can protest, he sticks it into his mouth and makes a popping sound as he pulls it out. He then laughs gleefully. "Yep, that's sweat."

Scott won't admit it, but it's that kind of unhinged behavior that makes Chester terrifying. Still crouched on the ground, Scott can't help but think of Petey. It's an awful way to remember somebody, but having only known him for a short time, a huge part of his personality was… well, perspiration. But Petey was the answer to the first riddle, so he couldn't help solve the current problem at hand.

"Chester. Focus. What does your tile say?"

"Let me see… It says 'lesser.'"

"Is that helpful?" Crystal asks him, pulling close.

Scott stands. "Not yet, but I think it will be." He rubs his chin and then, without waiting for someone to tell him it's a bad idea, steps directly onto the tile carved with 'pilferer.' It falls almost immediately, and he pitches forward, landing on another square that, thankfully, doesn't budge.

"So we're just shootin' through this? No plan?" Buck demands, his hands on his head like someone just missed a field goal. "What the hell was that? Talk to us!"

Scott, who is almost side by side with Chester now, reads the word on the one tile between them, "This one says 'artists.' And the one you're on says 'lesser.'"

*Think, Scott, think.* He wishes so badly that any of this information flipped a switch in his brain, but he can't get his thoughts to align. And suddenly he's flooded with fear. And not of the Manor-punishing kind.

What if, when they get out of the Manor, the others go home and spread the news that, in the face of danger, he's a teeth-chattering phony? An idiot who can't solve a stupid riddle? What if Winnie sits across from Barbara Walters, twirls her pearls in front of the camera, and says, *Who can we credit with our escape? Oh, definitely Buck. He was so wise, so courageous, and so handsome!*

Okay, the last bit would *never* happen—Scott was on *People*'s Sexiest Men of All Ages issue—but still. This could happen if he doesn't snap out of it and get across this goddamn floor.

When he's writing, Scott often puts himself in the headspace of his characters: What would they do? What are their motivations? How would they solve a problem? So he tries doing the same thing, but with Mortimer. If he were Mortimer…*I'd be a sadistic psychopath.* Yes, that's definitely true. But Scott thinks he wouldn't create any kind of challenge or game for them that's unbeatable. He's the kind of man who would want even his victims to be *impressed* by his ingenuity.

"Artists…Lesser…" He thinks saying the words aloud will make them make sense, but it doesn't. Scanning the rest of the floor, he sees that each tile has a word—seemingly unconnected, unrelated, and unhelpful.

"Melanie has an idea!" Crystal calls, and Scott turns his head to look back. She elbows Melanie, who coughs and takes a beat to speak.

"The tiles that are safe to stand on might spell out something, like a phrase or quote. So…you have to pick the words that complete the sentence, and maybe it'll give you a clear path to the other side."

"And the ones that fall?" Scott asks.

"Meaningless, I guess."

He brings his gaze back to the floor, realizing how simple it was. *Idiot. You couldn't think of that sooner?*

"But we don't know the quote in question," Winnie says.

Scott extends his arm to tap at the square in front of him. The floor shudders—another *hands off* warning. "Here. This next one says 'borrow.'"

Chester points to the space directly in front of him. "And that one says 'write.'" He lifts his head and grins at Scott. "You have to admit. This is sorta fun."

"You and I have different definitions of fun." Scott grunts.

"Oh!"

The gasp brings unrestrained joy to Scott's heart because it's not the *I just thought of something terrible* kind, but the *I just remembered* kind. And it comes from Melanie. While, again, he wishes he were the one having these revelations, their time is ticking.

"T.S. Elliot!" she whisper-shouts. "It's his quote! 'Lesser artists borrow; great artists steal.'"

"I thought Pablo Picasso said that." Winnie frowns.

"Nah, it was Igor Stravinsky, wasn't it?" Buck argues.

Christ. It doesn't matter *who* the quote is accredited to. Scott takes a step onto the word *borrow* and holds his breath. This time, instead of a grumble, the floors creak, and Scott sucks in a breath. But it settles and stays still.

"Yes! Yes! That's it!" Scott can hardly contain his excitement. "So the next word would be..." He looks to Melanie, already forgetting the rest of the quote.

She says something, but it's too quiet. Of course, the one person who might actually know what's going on is a *door mouse*.

"Speak up, I can't hear you!" he insists, trying to keep his voice from reaching angry-shouting territory.

"*Great!*" She enunciates louder this time. "The next word is '*great*.'" Her entire face shape changes when she speaks like this—boldly, proudly. It's like her muscles are finally stretching after a long period of neglect.

A moment later, Scott finds the correct tile. It's a few squares away, a big leap for him, but he manages. There's a great whoop from the group, and even Chester is nodding with respect. He's suddenly back in the room with Barbara and Winnie, who, this time, is gushing about him. *It was all thanks to Scott! He was so heroic. We would have been lost without him!*

He hates to agree with Chester, but something about this *is* a little bit invigorating. Scott remembers playing a game of the floor is lava when he was little. Along the edge of his childhood home were thick, unruly woods filled with old stumps, branches, and fallen trees. He and Dad would traverse out like brave explorers and leap around them, pretending they were surrounded by molten heat. This brings the same adrenaline— leaping and not knowing if you'll make it.

Then Dad lost his job, started drinking more, and stopped coming into the woods with Scott. He heard his mother's anxious phone calls behind doors: "He's going to drink himself to death!" and "I've never seen him so depressed."

So he spent hours alone in the woods, jumping from stump to stump, wondering, in that innocently dark way kids do, if his father was really going to die, and if he did, could Scott go with him?

After leaping onto the last tile with the word *steal* on it, finishing the quote, Scott reaches the other side. He resists the urge to pump his fist in the air and approaches the pedestal with the book, his entire body buzzing so forcefully that he has to blink three times to focus on the word written in tiny letters on the leather-bound cover.

Scott's stomach sinks.

This isn't the riddle. It's *Shrieking and Shrinks*, by Petey Marsh—the now-late Petey Marsh.

How does *this* help them? Petey is dead! Was he supposed to be here to explain why his book was left behind as a clue? Scott considers tearing it in half. Chucking it at the wall. At Chester's head, just because he can. There's nothing Scott can't stand more than being made to look a fool—and Mortimer keeps doing it. They've wasted all this time getting here. And now what?

Before he can open his mouth and deliver the news, Crystal's warbled voice rings out.

"Guys…what's that sound?"

# Buck Grimm

**H**ERE'S A COMMON misconception: those who write horror like scary things.

Buck doesn't correct people when they assume this; he hates to burst their bubbles. It's like when he went to his annual physical, where his doctor preached to him about the importance of eating more cruciferous vegetables. Sitting atop the examination table (though his feet still managed to be flat on the floor, so was that really sitting?), he'd been so motivated by her words that he went straight to the grocery store and bought a whole bagful of something called arugula. Then, two days later, he saw his doctor in the Burger King parking lot, a triple-decker cheeseburger in one hand and a cigarette in the other.

The straight-up truth is people aren't always what they seem. Comedians are often the saddest people Buck knows, psychologists definitely do *not* have their shit figured out, and the best chefs in the world go home at the end of the day and eat bowlfuls of cereal.

Except for Mortimer Queen. Buck had him pegged for a twisted genius from his first day as a publishing assistant at Deacon's Group. There was no "Burger King parking lot" moment, only a sick confirmation that every preconceived notion he'd had about his boss based on his novels was right.

As Buck watches Scott finally make it to the other side of this chessboard, he represses the desire to scream. A *real* scream. Not the kind men do when they're around their buddies—a low-pitched holler so no one thinks they sound like a woman—but a full piercing screech.

Because Buck is terrified. Of *course* he gets scared just like everyone else, even if he is a horror author. Intruders wielding rusty cleavers, a man in a rubber mask standing outside a bedroom window, a demonic woman who can turn her head all the way around and spit beetles from her mouth, a fireplace that can gnash a body between its brick teeth— these are the things that can keep him up at night.

The entry hall's windows are blackened now, like thick tar has been painted over the glass. They're not even allowed to glimpse outside. He wonders, dazedly, if he'll ever see the sky again. If he'll ever sink his teeth into a rare, juicy burger again. If he'll ever visit Nan back in Oatmeal. Every week he leaves a plate of hummingbird cake on her gravestone, and every week when he returns, it's gone. Seemingly taken by the cemetery groundskeepers.

Would they worry when the cake stopped coming? Or, even worse, would they assume that he stopped caring?

"Guys...what's that sound?" Buck tilts his good ear upward, straining to hear. Years ago, before he was sober, he drunkenly shot a hunting rifle without ear protection and went deaf in his right ear. He's never minded much until now because he's never had to listen this hard for danger before. Cars honk loudly. People are clumsy and noisy. Mountain lions are pretty stealthy, but Buck has become so well-read on the animal that he can predict what they're going to do before they do it.

This is unknown danger. And it's coming from the holes in the floor. *"Help me! Help me!"*

It's faint, but he can hear the cries. Winnie lurches, her feet reluctant to leave the safety of the rug.

"Felix? Felix! Is that you?" she shouts back at the voice. "I think it is! I think it's him! He's down there!"

Buck feels his forehead wrinkle with skepticism as he listens harder. *"Help! Someone help me!"*

"I ain't all that sharp in the ears, but that don't really sound like—"

"He's my friend." Winnie paces and clutches her pearls. "I know what he sounds like, and that's him. He's *alive.*"

But the voice ceases instantly, leaving behind the chorus of ticking clocks.

Scott hops his way back across the floor, picking up Chester along the way. The two rejoin the group on the edge of the room, the book clutched in Scott's hand: *Shrieking and Shrinks.*

"It's *not* the riddle?" Buck takes the book and flips it over, examining the front and back. "Why the hell did we go to all that trouble for Petey's book?"

"Are you sure?" Crystal snatches it from his hands and flips through the pages so fast, her hand blurs. "It's blank? All the pages are empty."

She lowers the book to show the proof. Indeed, the pages are bare.

"Did you not think to open it?" Crystal asks, her eyes tracking Scott's.

"I knew it was blank." Scott straightens, but his nose twitches like he's holding in a sneeze.

"Men." She rolls her eyes. "I know you're bad at noticing fresh haircuts and new dresses, but *seriously*? What is it with your gender?"

Buck notices Melanie smirk the tiniest bit at this, looking up at Crystal with something resembling awe, like a younger sibling watching their big sister gave their mother sass.

Before Buck moved out of Oatmeal, a woman like Crystal would make his traditional Southern roots quiver. But moving to LA forced him to recognize that the folks in his hometown were in a bit of a bubble and that his understanding of gender roles was *way* outdated. It was always clear to him that women were strong; Nan raised six boys all on her own, ran a sewing business from her house until her fingers were worn to the nubs, volunteered at Oatmeal's hospital, and always managed to have the most delicious food in the whole county on her dinner table at six o'clock sharp. Then she started the whole thing all over again when she took Buck in.

However, the women outside Oatmeal—particularly the writers he's met—are another kind of strong: Brazen. Fearless. Undaunted. And always simmering with this pervasive sense of discontent, like they've never quite forgiven men for holding them down for so long. Mortimer complained about female authors all the time, griping about their recent popularity within the horror genre like it personally offended him.

That's why it surprised Buck when he found out Mortimer was having an affair with Crystal Flowers, the physical representation of everything he despised.

Even now, standing in such close proximity to her makes Buck uncomfortable—and not because he's seen her half naked on Instagram. After the will reading, it was clear why he'd been invited to the Manor, and though Mortimer set the trap, Crystal is the reason.

"Why isn't anyone listening to me?" Buck feels a thwack on his lower back as Winnie continues to go on about the sound from below. "I. Heard. Felix!"

"It's not Felix." Crystal continues to flip through the pages, frowning.

"How do *you* know?"

"Because Felix is *dead*, Winnie. And we will be too if we don't keep our heads. Hey, look. It's not completely blank. Some of the chapter numbers are still in here. I wonder why…"

"Let me see. I'll figure it out." Scott tries to grab the book from her hands, but Crystal moves away just in time.

Buck would like to raise his hands and soothe Scott, who is practically steaming out of his ears, just like he used to do with overbearing horses. It's called gentling, and Scott needs a hearty dose of it by the way he seems to be itching to be in control.

"I'd say those numbers mean somethin'," Buck offers, knowing it's less than helpful but still wanting to try. "Like a…a code. What are they?"

"Chapters one, two, three and…seven." Crystal reads them off and looks up expectantly at him, like he should be reacting to this.

"Er…Well, those add up to thirteen, don't they?" he suggests.

Chester slow claps, his hands making a horrible suckling sound from the sweat.

"Oh, fuck off," Scott snaps.

"What?" Chester asks innocently. "I'm applauding his math skills. Now more than ever, shouldn't we be boosting one another up instead of—"

"Be quiet, you!" Winnie flicks him on the nose like a dog, and he yips, likely still a little spooked from his encounter with Scott's fists. "Thirteen is an unlucky number. Is it meant to be a warning?"

"Maybe." Crystal thumbs at her chin. "One could represent the letter 'A,' then two is 'B,' and…but no, that's not anything."

While she thinks aloud, Buck eyes the clock nearest to him to check how much time they have left. But his eyes pull instead to the largest grandfather clock in the room, just a ways down the wall. He had noticed it earlier and thought that it stuck out just like he did, in an odd way. A large physical presence, impossible to ignore. Buck peers closer, trying to make it out through the darkness. The pendulum isn't swinging. The hands aren't ticking either. He skirts along the edge of the room, staying off the falling tiles. *Odd*, he thinks, sticking his finger in the clock's face and moving the long metal hand in a circle.

"Buck! Be careful!" Scott barks, finally noticing him.

"Wait, look at what he did!" Crystal points to the grandfather clock. Buck frowns. "I didn't mess anythin' up. It was broken already."

"No, no." She shakes her head, stepping closer to the clock. "What time is it here?"

"Twelve thirty," Scott says a little too quickly, determined to have his voice included in the mix. "Why does that matter?"

It clicks right then. Buck snaps at Crystal excitedly, and she nods eagerly in return.

"Move the big hand between the twelve and the one, and the little hand between the eight and seven."

He does, and almost immediately he hears the cogs click from within the clock's body. A flap opens, and out pops a black wooden bird, its beak wide. Without missing a beat, a throaty voice sounds:

> *"Every man has his word,*
> *But it's hard to keep.*
> *It can be broken,*
> *To buy it isn't cheap.*
> *This man stole mine*
> *And tarnished his in turn.*
> *I invited him here tonight*
> *So hopefully he would learn.*
> *Can you tell me who is lying through their teeth?*
> *Think hard, my dear friends*
> *And reveal the thief."*

Buck has never been good at puzzles. But Mortimer was a whiz. He'd leave them all throughout Deacon's Group—on the fridge, computer monitors, file cabinets—and if an employee solved one, he'd name a character in one of his books after the lucky puzzle savant. Mortimer was always particularly generous with leaving sticky note riddles on Buck's desk, front and center for everyone to see. But he never could answer any of them, and Buck always figured Mortimer was taunting him with his own stupidity.

"I got *nothin'* from that," he says the second the cuckoo bird finishes and retreats into the clock again.

"That was so wonderfully creepy." Chester approaches and cocks his head at the clock, seemingly fascinated by its engineering. "I wonder how he…" He moves the hands away, then back to 12:37, and the bird pops back out to recite the riddle again.

"We can do this. Come on, guys," Scott claps twice like he's pumping himself up. "'I invited him here tonight.' So, again, the answer has to be one of us."

He gestures to the men of the group. Chester flinches, probably worried about receiving another blow to the face.

"Well, the book and the sweat. That's *Petey's* book. He has to be the answer," Winnie chimes in, crossing her arms.

"No, we decided Petey was the answer to the *last* riddle, remember?" Crystal says. "That's why the Manor took him."

There's a beat where no one speaks, and Buck feels the reality sink in, dark and deep in his bones.

"We were wrong." Melanie speaks up, her words reflecting the look on everyone's faces. "Someone else must have hurt that girl in the poem. Someone here killed Mary McKinnon, and they let Petey die in their place."

Scott snaps his head over to Chester, who he's obviously decided is guilty. Before another fight breaks out, Buck feels his mouth moving, his arms up in a calming gesture.

"That makes sense. Petey tried to swipe that damn crystal goat. He's a thief. It fits."

"But Petey only did that today," Melanie says, fidgeting with her sleeves. "Why would that be in a riddle Mortimer supposedly wrote before he died?"

Buck's patience has fully worn through. He wants to give their answer, even if it might be wrong. That's been his attitude since birth: he scribbled all wrong answers on his high school tests and turned them in early because he couldn't take the pressure; he took a shot while hunting even if it was a bad one because the tension of the gun in his hand was too much; he gave his publisher *Blood Bath* without copyediting a lick of it because it was burning a hole in his desk.

"Why are we splittin' hairs? We got the answer! Look, you want to talk about clues? That's his book, that quote on the tiles is about stealin', and this room is sweatin' just as bad as he does—did."

Scott narrows his eyes at Chester with a sort of *I'll deal with you later* look, then says, "Okay, are we all in agreement?"

No one argues.

"Just write the name," Crystal implores. "Do it on the floor or something."

Buck bends down over the nearest tile, tracing the letters through the sweat.

"I don't see how this is going to work," Chester says from above Buck's head. "How will it know what—"

But the second Buck finishes the *s* in *Marsh*, the sweat dissolves into the floor, disappearing completely. There's a horrible howling sound that cuts through the air so cleanly that Buck thinks that whatever's responsible for it *must* be right there in the room with them. Three heartbeats later, the door at the top of the spiral staircase makes an audible *click*.

"We did it!" Scott bellows, pulling Crystal in for a hug. "I can't believe it! We really did it!"

She allows him to whirl her around once before pulling away and tugging at her clothes, her face pink. Buck draws his brows up at the show of affection. There's no romance in a horror story—unless it's two teenagers making out in an old Cadillac right before someone comes and slashes them to bits. But to each their own, he supposes. And honestly, he gets the comradery. He's in such high spirits, he slaps Chester's back—a little too enthusiastically, by the way Chester yelps—and gives Scott a firm handshake like they're old college buddies. It feels good to celebrate, even if only for a second, and try not to think about the five more rooms they have to get through.

"I'm going down there."

The words are almost lost in all the giddiness, but Buck soon realizes he's not the only one who heard them. They track the voice, and his heart lurches. Unbeknownst to the group, Winnie has leaped from tile to tile and now finds herself standing on an island surrounded by darkness. She points downward, her mouth set determinedly. No one is smiling any longer.

"What are you talking about, Winn?" Scott asks, raising his hands.

"I said I'm going. Felix could be down there, and if I don't…if I don't at least try and save him, I'll hate myself forever."

"Okay, do you not understand what just happened?" Chester coughs out an incredulous, nervous laugh. "We solved the riddle. We. Did. Good. Now we get to live another hour. What you're doing? Right now? That's the *opposite* of playing the game, remember?"

"I heard Felix. I'm going to go get him and bring him back."

"Winnie, he's not—" Crystal starts to say.

"Shut *up*, girl! I'm not an idiot! I know he might not be there. I could burn alive or get chewed up or…or…whatever! The point is, someone is here because of *me*, and I'll do anything I can to make up for that."

"Doing something stupid doesn't mean you're brave," Scott says. "And killing yourself won't make him come back. Winnie. Please. You don't have to do this."

She hesitates, takes a deep breath, and jumps.

Buck's own shouts blend with the rest, as a wave of panic shoots through them all. Scott gets down on all fours and starts calling into the darkness, asking if she's okay, if she's alive, if she can hear him. There's no reply.

"Is there…is there a lick of a chance that…?" Buck murmurs, not wanting to finish the sentence.

Scott stands, a somber, angry look pinching his face. "She's dead."

*No.* This is too sudden—too final. Petey's death is something Buck knows he will lie awake at night reliving again and again. And now Winnie? Winnie just…left. He's not used to it all, to deaths like this. Nan was dying for months before she finally went. Buck spends years raising pigs, preparing them to be slaughtered. But this is too quick. Too immediate.

Too out of his hands.

"Now wait just a minute!" he protests, gripping Scott's arm. "She… she could be at the bottom! She coulda made it and…and knocked herself out or somethin'. That's why she ain't answerin'. We could—"

Scott wrenches away. "She's. Dead. We have to keep moving."

The floor doesn't pulse beneath their feet anymore, so Scott decides it's safe to walk across the tiles. He tests them out for himself before extending a hand for Crystal to take. She looks over her shoulder at Melanie, then at Chester and Buck. There's a level of distrust in her eyes.

"What is it?" Scott asks her.

"She doesn't want me alone with Melanie," Chester mutters, even *his* chipper demeanor soured by Winnie's decision. He passes Scott to cross the room, starting up the stairs.

"And for good reason." Scott glowers. He leans close to Crystal's cheek and murmurs quietly, so Buck can barely hear, "Don't worry. I'll keep an eye on him."

Then they follow Chester up, their hands brushing against each other as they climb.

When Buck reaches the first step, he digs into his pocket and pulls out his lighter. He drops it into the closest fallen space, waiting to hear it strike some kind of bottom. But it never does. It was meant to be helpful, so that Winnie could use it for light, but the thought of it bouncing off her lifeless, broken body makes him wish he'd never done it. He turns and sees Melanie watching him closely. It makes him uneasy, how easily she blends into the surroundings here. She fits. She belongs, somehow, like a ghoul hovering in the haunted house.

"Have you ever had hummingbird cake?" he blurts, then almost adds, *And do you think it'll taste just as good if we get out of here?* But he doesn't want to scare her, especially with the strong *if* in the question.

Melanie shakes her head. Buck swings his arms back and forth. He should be climbing the stairs with the others, but part of him thinks Winnie is going to shout any minute now and tell him she's okay.

"My mom makes a sugar-free butterscotch pudding," she says.

"That sounds awful."

"It is."

There's supposed to be a laugh there between them, but Buck doesn't think either of them is capable.

"You knew Mr. Queen well, didn't you?" Melanie asks.

"Maybe a little too well."

Her eyes widen, the ivy green a stark contrast against the fringe of her black bangs. "Do you…? Did he ever mention me? In his last months of life, did he talk about meeting me, or…?"

"I haven't spoken to Mortimer in years."

"Oh." She deflates. "I guess I was just thinking…I've been so focused on what he's been doing to us, but now I'm wondering what *we* did to *him*. And I can't figure out what I could have done to make him so mad…"

Buck sucks in his gut like someone punched him, and he thinks back to that day in Mortimer's office. It had gone so wrong, so quickly.

But was it bad enough to kill over?

# Short Story #2

## Petey Marsh

It's Petey Marsh's first day as a mover.

He sits in the passenger seat of a great truck while a man named Beckett drives with one hand on the wheel and another elbow-deep in a bag of gas station sunflower seeds. When he sucks salt from his dirty fingers, Petey has to roll the window down to keep from getting nauseous.

The truck's thermostat says it's 90 degrees in LA today. The front of Petey's MOO-VING CITY uniform T-shirt is already soaked, and all he has to dab at his face with is a thin fast-food napkin he found on the seat.

"So what made you want to get into the moving biz?" Beckett asks as he takes a left-hand turn and nearly flattens an older woman walking a Chihuahua.

Petey says plainly, "I n-needed a j-job." One that he could keep for more than a month. He's been fired from Staples, Olive

Garden, Electric Mart, and Fun Land—every time has been because he was caught stealing.

Not copious amounts of money or anything, but stealing, nonetheless. At Olive Garden, he smuggled ten boxes of frozen breadsticks over the course of his time working there. When his manager saw the security footage of him struggling to squeeze the load into his beat-up Chevy, she fired him on the spot.

"I'm not even going to call the police," she told him. "This is just too pathetic."

Electric Mart caught him slipping batteries into his pockets. Fun Land discovered he'd been hacking into the claw machine and stealing the prizes inside (a fake Rolex watch, digital camera, and iTunes gift cards) and Petey doesn't even want to think about what happened at Staples. It's too embarrassing and involves about a thousand paper clips.

"Sorry it's just us two today," Beckett says. "Stu has the flu, and Pedro's kid got into a fight at school. But we'll be okay on our own. I'll show you the ropes and teach you everything you need to know."

Petey stares out the window. He struggled to choose between this moving gig and a job as an assistant behind the deli counter at Piggly Wiggly, and he chose the former because he didn't think his stomach could handle the meat grinder. Plus, there's something titillating about fondling a parcel of someone else's things. His kleptomania support group leader, Terry, has warned him not to put himself in any situations that might tempt him. But Petey only goes to those meetings because his parents threatened to kick him out of the basement if he didn't.

Beckett pulls up in front of a line of beautiful brick town houses and accidentally drives the tire up the curb before finally parking. Petey is grateful when his feet touch the ground. He and Beckett walk up to the front door and knock on the grandiose door. A minute later a woman with a tight bun and even tenser expression allows them inside.

"Afternoon, ma'am," Beckett says cheerfully. "We're here to move ya."

"Great, great," the woman says, tapping her phone distractedly. "Start with the living room, the dining room, and the office. Then you can handle the upstairs. Don't ask me what's fragile and what's not—it's all fragile and very valuable, so please don't drop anything."

"Of course!" Beckett gives her the *okay* sign with his saliva-and-salt riddled fingers. "Where are you moving to?"

The woman glances up, annoyed. "This isn't my house. I'm just the assistant. Do I have to sign anything?"

"Yes, ma'am." Beckett pulls out a clipboard. "Petey, why don't you start in that room over there, and I'll be right there."

He gestures to two French doors to their right. Petey shrugs and does as he's told.

"Are you sure he's qualified to do this?" the woman asks Beckett. "He's a little…short?"

Petey pretends like he doesn't hear and gets to work. It looks to be an office—or *was* an office. It has empty bookshelves, scratched wooden floors, and dozens of taped-up cardboard boxes that prove to be heavier than he thinks. He carries two out to the truck and returns to the office winded. Taking an extra-long time to adjust his glasses, Petey contemplates how much effort a fake asthma attack would be.

"Hey, I'm going to start in the living room," Beckett says, sticking his head in. "You good here?"

"Yep," Petey lies. "All g-good."

When Beckett leaves, Petey lifts another box, and the bottom suddenly bursts, its contents spilling onto the floor. Heavy books, folders and papers fall at his feet with a thud.

He's torn between irritation that he'll have to clean up the mess and giddiness over his luck. *Technically* he wasn't snooping because he didn't open the box himself; it was just a happy accident. A layer of drool spills over his bottom lip as he crouches to paw through the pile, pocketing a few expensive-looking ballpoint pens, a stapler (which is so big he has to shove down the front of his pants), and an emerald paperweight.

His fingers brush against a thick stack of papers bound together. The cover reads *Shrieking and Shrinks: Mortimer Queen*. The name rings a bell. Was he a celebrity? Has Petey seen him on TV before? No, that's not it...

Beckett returns yet again with a goofy grin on his face.

"Want to hear something cool? This is Mortimer Queen's house!" He uses the kind of loud whisper airhead robbers use in comedy movies before getting caught in the act. "He's, like, a millionaire. No wonder it smells expensive in here!"

"Wh-wh-what does he do for a l-living?" Petey asks, still holding the bound papers.

"He writes books." Beckett shrugs. "I don't read, but I've seen the movie versions of his stuff. They're really scary. Uh-oh, you got some spillage?" He gestures to the floor. "No worries. We can tape the box back up. Want help?"

"N-no. I'm g-good."

Once alone, Petey thumbs through the manuscript's pages. On the last page, he finds a date near the bottom. It's marked eight years ago. He wonders if this could be valuable if he sold it online to a superfan. Without thinking too hard about it, Petey slips the manuscript into the back of his pants and tugs his

T-shirt over it. There. Now he's counterbalanced the stapler. He then spends the next three hours lugging boxes back and forth until his lungs feel like they're about to burst.

When Beckett signals that they're done, Petey could sing, he's so happy.

"What time will you be back tomorrow?" the woman asks as they go to say goodbye.

"What!?" Petey blurts.

"We'll be back to move the furniture at eight a.m.," Beckett answers, sending Petey a pointed look. "Not a minute later."

"Good. I'll see you then."

Beckett drives Petey back to Moo-ving City headquarters to lock up the truck with all of Mortimer Queen's boxes for the night. Beckett explains that they'll deliver them to his new address in the morning, then go back to the town house to pack up his furniture.

The minute Petey gets into his car, he reaches around his back and tugs the manuscript out of his pants. To his disappointment, the pages are damp and wrinkled. If it's worth anything, the damage will surely reduce its value.

He drives forty-five minutes to his parent's average one-bedroom house. When he walks through the door, his mother, Trudy, is putting plastic wrap over a plate of meatloaf, green beans, and a roll.

"I was just about to put this in the fridge for you! How was your first day? I want to hear all about it."

Petey's foul mood permeates the room along with his stench. He wordlessly moves past her and yanks open a cabinet, rooting around for a box of Cocoa Puffs.

"I made meatloaf," Trudy protests when he pours the entire box into a bowl.

"I don't *want* your meatloaf." Petey sloshes milk on top of his cereal.

"Your shirt looks dirty." Trudy is never very bothered by his attitude. "Throw it in the hamper, and I'll wash it tonight so it's clean for tomorrow."

"I don't even know if I'm going in tomorrow," Petey says through a mouthful of chocolate.

"What do you mean?" She places her hands on the counter like she's bracing for a blow. "You didn't get fired already, did you? What's all that paper in your hand?"

This time it's Petey's turn to ignore her. His appetite spoiled, he tosses the bowl into the sink, brown milk splattering. He marches downstairs into the basement, where he's been living for the past six months. The space is dark and smells mildewy; the only light Petey keeps on comes from his archaic desktop computer, which he now plops in front of.

He quickly does an internet search of Mortimer Queen's net worth. The number sends him into a spiral. Then he searches *Shrieking and Shrinks* but can't find a trace of it anywhere. So this was an unpublished edition the guy tucked away in his office?

Petey hears the couch scraping against the floor upstairs and knows Trudy is about to turn on her go-go dancing workout DVD. He'll hear nothing but thumps and grunts for the next half hour. Groaning, he slides forward and hides his face.

A worse sound, however, is the front door opening and slamming.

His father, Bruce Marsh, is home.

Bruce wastes no time barreling downstairs and confronting Petey. He's what Petey thinks he'd have been if he hadn't stopped growing at thirteen—tall, broad shouldered, and permanently pissed looking—but they still share the receding hairline.

"So?" Bruce thunders, his arms folded. "Did you last the day?"

"Y-yes." Petey plays with the computer mouse, shaking it aimlessly across the screen.

"You're not fired?"

"N-no."

Bruce scrutinizes him and uses a thumb to wipe a yellow crust from the edge of his mouth. His work shirt is stained with unidentifiable marks and stitches from where Trudy fixed up small tears.

"Color me surprised." Bruce grunts, turning away. "Maybe you can actually pay some rent this month."

"D-don't c-count on it. It's my m-money."

Bruce lingers on the stairs, his shoulders sagging. Without rotating to look at Petey, he murmurs, "I sure hope that one day that someone teaches you some respect. Because I clearly failed."

It would have been less hurtful if Bruce had struck him across the face, but Petey doesn't give him the satisfaction of replying. He waits for his father to go upstairs and then stares down at the manuscript in his lap before looking back up at his computer screen. Mortimer's net worth blinks back at him, practically sparkling. Maybe this is the answer: writing.

He's never written before, but he has read plenty of science fiction. Maybe he'd be good at it if he tried. He could work days, moving boxes in and out of rich people's houses, and come down here at night to write. If he's dedicated, it might take three or four months.

Wiping his hands on his shirt, he looks up Mortimer Queen's net worth again. The number stares back at him through the screen, taunting and teasing. He imagines rubbing that kind of money in Bruce's face, dangling it front of his face and then yanking it away when the geezer tries to reach out and take it. Maybe if Petey had this much in the bank, the itch to steal would go away. If he wanted something, he could just buy it.

Nah, who is kidding? You can't put a price on that kind of thrill.

Petey returns to the computer and does one last internet search. He pulls out his cell phone and dials a number. Two rings later, a voice answers, "Hello, Black & White Publishing, how can I help you?"

"Yeah, h-hello." Petey licks his lips. "How do I g-go about s-s-submitting a m-manuscript for c-consideration? I'm looking to get p-published."

# Chester Plumage

CHESTER THINKS PEOPLE, in general, are incredibly stupid. This is evident throughout history. Take the Emu War of 1932, for example, where members of the Royal Australian Artillery were sent to combat the overgrown emu population and instead were beaten by these flightless birds. Shortly after discovering they were under attack, the animals broke their herds up into smaller groups, assigning each one with a lookout to warn the others before gunfire broke out. After the soldiers failed to shoot the birds down, they actually tried to use *trucks* to run them over, which, of course, didn't work either. To this day, it's widely accepted that the emus won the battle and the war.

However, he hadn't pegged Winnie as unintelligent. That's why her suicidal leap is especially rattling. Her grating personality and lascivious humor were somewhat reminiscent of his own, and he appreciated that she stuck to her word so reverently, even if the information or story she was telling wasn't always true.

As he walks up the entry hall's winding staircase, he feels Scott's and Crystal's eyes boring into his back. They know now that Petey wasn't the answer to the first riddle, which poses quite the problem for him, especially with Scott's proclivity for violence. Truly, he hadn't *wanted* anyone to get hurt, but Petey just happened to be the sacrificial lamb.

Guilt is not a feeling he often bumps elbows with, yet he's been doused with bucketfuls since he got here. He's managed to avoid thinking about Mary ever since *it* happened, so being forced to face it has been as painful as Scott's punch. And now not only is Petey's blood is on his hands, but Winnie's might be, too.

Because he heard the voice calling from below. It didn't sound like Felix. It sounded like Mary. She was taunting him, coaxing him into the blackness, where she must think he belongs. The trap *must* have been set up for him, but Winnie took the bait. For the second time in his life, a woman jumped to her death, and he's responsible.

*Damn you, Winnie. Damn you, Petey.* If they hadn't died, then maybe he'd be able to enjoy the brilliance of Mortimer's Manor. It's hard to be angry at a man who designed such a fascinating plan for revenge. Chester's always thought about what he'd do if he could get back at all those who've wronged him in the past—public humiliation (caught naked in the middle of Times Square), punishment (stealing someone's precious pup—leaving it unharmed, of course, as he's not a *monster*). But nothing comes *close* to this. It's the *Mona Lisa* of vendettas.

Before Chester can open the door leading to the next room, Scott shoves in front of him and puts an arm out, clotheslining him.

"Ow." Chester rubs his throat. "I didn't know we were so eager to be first. Don't worry, Scotty. Everyone gets a turn to be line leader."

Scott glares, and in return, Chester gives his sweetest closed-mouth smile.

Scott ignores him and addresses Crystal. "Normally I would hold the door open for you, but I think I should go in first." He sounds genuinely apologetic. What a load of crap. "Just to make sure everything is…"

He can't say the word *safe*. Nothing about what they're about to step into is going to be safe.

"Well, go on!" Chester flaps his hands. "Go check to make sure everything is neat and tidy for us."

His blond hair disappears through the doorway, and Chester swears he can see steam pouring from his ears. *Good.*

"Why do you do that?" Crystal asks, disgusted.

"Do what?"

"Antagonize him. It's unnecessary and quite frankly astounding that after all we've been through together."

He places a hand on his chest in mock appreciation. "You think I'm astounding? *Thank you!*"

She crosses her arms and sets her mouth in hard line. This is a normal reaction from women toward him. And men. And children. Come to think of it, dogs don't particularly care for him either.

Scott returns a moment later, beckoning them along. He walks inside, and Chester is immediately overwhelmed with the familiar scent of well-loved books. The comforting smell forms a lump in his throat. *Don't get soft now*, he orders himself. *You've never been sentimental before, so don't start now.*

In any case, the room doesn't exactly match the happy memory of his home library nor the many libraries before it.

Rows and rows of shelves extend down long, dimly lit corridors. Each one labeled with a gold plaque: thrillers, slashers, gothic, supernatural, monsters. The shelves go on for a mind-boggling length, and Chester is again impressed with Mortimer's talents. The architectural engineering it must take to squeeze a room of this size into the width of the Manor… Or perhaps it isn't the work of human hands. After all, this isn't *just* a house.

At the forefront of the shelves, strung across the wall is a banner with the words CONGRATULATIONS hanging limply. A dozen balloons float, less from the waning helium and more like they're fixed in time, frozen in the stiff air. Two velvet reading chairs have been tossed on their sides, books are haphazardly strewn about the shag rug, and an easel holding a poster-sized photo of Mortimer's infamous author headshot is snapped clean in half. Chester rubs his hands along one of the oak bookshelves, rich and carved, but it's hard to appreciate the magnificence when the room itself is such a wreck.

Oddest of all is the one thing *not* disturbed in all the mess.

"Is that a *cake*?" Buck asks as he and the others crowd around a desk in the middle of the library. He, for some reason, exchanges a glance with Melanie, who almost smiles.

"I don't think I should have to say this, but don't eat it," Scott says darkly.

It's a huge five-layer cake, nice and thick. The frosting is virgin white—probably buttercream—and the red piping on the top reads, *Happy release day, Mortimer!* Chester resists the urge to swatch a finger through it. Why not? Could be his last chance to have something sweet.

Where one would expect serving plates or cutlery, an ink bottle and an old-fashioned feather quill lie.

The group is silent, taking it all in, their steps echoing as they tentatively explore the shelves. Chester appreciates the sound because it drowns out the uninvited ones that replay in his own head:

*Brrring! Brrring!*

*Smack, squish, pop. Smack, squish, pop.*

He's been hearing these for years, ever since his encounter with Mary McKinnon. Not their unfortunate reunion in the dining room—he's still trying to convince himself that was a trick of the candlelight—but the day she approached him in Seattle.

*I was not the hand that killed her, but I offered no protection.*

Melanie accidentally brushes up against him as he steps away from the cake; her frame is slight, and her steps are so silent that Chester, not realizing she's standing there, jolts.

"Sorry," he mutters, giving her a wide berth.

"It's okay."

He can't understand why she didn't let Scott beat him to a pulp, why she didn't come out and recount how he'd attacked her. What she *knows*. For this reason alone, he's frightened of her. A woman who is brazen with secrets, like Winnie, is intimidating, but one who harbors them quietly, that's far more terrifying.

"Do you think Mortimer really threw a book-release party here?" Crystal asks, gazing up at the stiff balloons. Their strings brush against her head as she walks about the room.

"No." Chester eyes the banner. "I think it's for us. A reenactment, maybe."

"A reenactment of what?" Buck asks. "A bull bein' let loose during his celebration? It looks like hell blew through here."

Scott scowls about the space, his hands on his hips. "I have no idea what it could mean," he says. "Melanie, you're good at this. What are the clues here?"

Chester watches this compliment land as gracefully as a beesting on Melanie. She fidgets uncomfortably, but then she focuses her gaze around the room.

Two air vents on either side of the library walls suddenly make a hacking sound, and before anyone can react, streams of colorful confetti come coughing out. This, of course, makes Chester burst out laughing. The others tighten together, trying to stay away from the vents as the confetti piles up around them. *Please.* They only need to fear if their next punishment is drowning in a roomful of bad decorations.

But the coughing finally stops, and he brushes his shoulders off before grabbing one of the pieces and finding that it's not confetti at all but a pastel-pink business card. One look at the ground confirms that they're all the same card in shades of blue, purple, yellow, and pink. Hundreds of square photos of a young brunette man beaming up at Chester.

"Carl Badsman, L&P Management. Isn't that the PR firm in New York?" he asks.

"Good lookin' fella."

"Buck, while it's *entirely* unhelpful, I agree with you." Chester flaps the pink card. "He's indeed handsome. But why did we just get his business card vomited all over us?"

Scott bends down and picks one up, pushing a tongue against the inside of his cheek while he thinks. "I feel like I've seen this guy before," he says. "He's got a familiar face. And I live in New York, too, so maybe… maybe we've met? I don't know."

"Melanie, stop! Don't!" Crystal's scream disturbs the thick contemplation in the air.

Chester spins on his heels and almost lurches forward. Melanie has her hands wrist-deep in the cake, her jaw determined. He waits for something to happen—her skin peeling off or her hands melting before their eyes—but she grits her teeth and yanks a potato-sack-sized lump from the cake's center, sending sponge flying everywhere.

Melanie shakes the sleeve of a dress shirt, cake and frosting falling away. As her thumb brushes away the buttercream, a rust-colored fabric is revealed.

"I saw it peeking out of the sponge," she explains.

Inspired by Melanie's courage, Chester goes to take the shirt from her, and their fingers touch. She immediately offers it up to him, no questions asked. Her willingness causes pinpricks of shame to ripple up his arms, and the memory of grabbing a fistful of her stringy hair flashes in his mind. It hadn't been intentional, really. More of a panicked reaction, like whacking someone when they try to tickle you. Should he…should he apologize? Now? The words are on the tip of his tongue: *I'm sorry.* But what if she doesn't accept an apology? What then?

He clears his throat and croaks, "Good eye, Melanie. You're very perceptive."

She twitches again.

"You don't like compliments, do you?" he asks while wiping more icing off the shirt.

"I'm not used to them," she says quietly. "But thank you, that's nice to hear."

A glob of icing plops onto the floor with a *smack.* His trepidation around her is peeling away. It's something about how she looks at him, like he's not a monster. "Maybe it's better you don't experience that a lot, though. It can get addicting," he says, thinking of his Instagram, all of the likes.

That's when he notices what's happening to the shirt. The more icing that comes off, the more the true color is revealed—a baby blue. The red is really...

"Blood!" he cries, pinching it between his fingers and holding it away from his body. "It's covered in bloodstains!"

"Drop it! Just drop it!" Scott orders, his hands in his hair. "This is bad. This is very bad."

Chester wipes his sugar-caked hands on his shirt. "Noooo, really? I think finding a blood-soaked shirt in cake is quite a *good* omen."

There's no point in standing around any longer, he decides. The only thing to do is to tear this room apart looking for the next riddle. For some reason he feels inclined to let the others know where he's going, like this is suddenly some fucked-up little family.

"Fine, but take someone with you," Scott says, playing the role of the strict father. "We'll stay and turn this area upside down."

Chester can't believe the name that pops from his mouth, like a grape was lodged in his throat for a few minutes before being catapulted across the room. "Melanie, will you come?"

Scott blinks rapidly, his mouth downturned at the suggestion. He clearly doesn't want Melanie anywhere near Chester after witnessing his aggression in the dining room.

"I'm not going to hurt her!" he insists.

"The fact you have to say that is reason enough for us to be worried." Crystal folds her arms. "Take Buck."

"I don't want Buck."

"Okay. Then I'll go with you."

"No thank you."

"I'll go," Melanie pipes up. She registers Crystal's displeasure and adds, "It's fine, really. We can't be afraid of one another when there's already so much here we have to be scared of."

"Scott! Do something!" Crystal demands.

He looks between Melanie and Chester for a minute, then nods decisively. "All right. Go on."

"But—" Crystal starts.

Scott holds up a hand. "They said they're fine."

Chester knows Scott is only allowing this because he doesn't like to be told what to do—and if he gave in to Crystal's barking orders, it would make it seem like her decision and not his. But, regardless, he's pleased to walk undisturbed back into the shelves with Melanie, a comfortable silence settling between them.

Chester should feel bolstered by their success with the last riddle, but Winnie's quick exit has crushed his confidence. He walks down the monster section with Melanie gliding behind him, yanking books out one by one. *You can tell a lot by the contents in someone's library!* Mortimer Queen once said in a podcast interview. If that were true, Mortimer's collection wouldn't scream, *I am dusty, I am archaic, I am predictable.*

*The Island of Doctor Moreau, Dracula, Frankenstein, Beowulf.* The deeper Chester walked, the fewer titles he recognized. *Emberfang, The Shadowspine Crawler, The Banshee of Toulouse.*

"Can I say something?" Chester asks, his eyes toward a weathered copy of *The Mummy*.

When Melanie doesn't answer, he turns around to look at her and realizes she's nodding to his back.

"I'm…I'm sorry about hurting you. In the dining room."

"It's okay."

He balks, stunned into momentary silence. He's said sorry for much less, and it's always rebuked. People online clamor for his apologies, but when he gives one publicly, it doesn't matter. He's never forgiven. For a while, he didn't know what that even felt like. And now?

It feels…gross. Like putting a wet bathing suit on your dry body.

"It's not," he says, bordering on irritation. "And I wouldn't have blamed you if you outed me back there." He flicks a spider off a yellowed book and absently flips through it. "Why didn't you say something?"

"It didn't seem important."

"Well, that's fair. In a ranking of tonight's important events, me grabbing your hair has to be at least fourth or fifth, way under Petey getting eaten and Winnie jumping down a black hole, but still." The sarcasm comes so naturally that the words are out before he can regret them. But Melanie doesn't flinch. Maybe she's not as weak as she looks. She further surprises him by what she asks next.

"Did you really kill Mary McKinnon?"

"No." He answers without delay. "But it's still my fault she's dead."

Melanie goes rigid in the middle of pulling a book from its place on the shelf.

"It was an accident. I was on a book tour. She found me at the hotel and was…clingy. She wanted to show me all the dangerous things she'd done, to try and impress me. She—"

"Mary," Melanie says. "You can say her name."

Chester licks his cracked lips. The truth is, he's afraid saying her name will conjure her again. Seeing her at the dining room table nearly killed him, and encountering her among the dark, dusty bookshelves would finish the job. But he inhales shakily and nods. *Face the fear.*

"*Mary* was young. Too young. It looked bad, especially with my reputation. I'd *never* touch an underage girl, just to be clear. So, to make her go away, I was cruel. I practically dared her to go up on the roof and…" He's surprised to hear his voice crack. "Mary was Queen's niece. His late sister's daughter. She was his only blood relative left. And I…I never wanted anything to happen…"

He feels a tiny hand on his shoulder. After being tossed into such horror and violence, the gentle touch makes him want to crumple.

"It's okay. I believe you." She turns away, facing one side of the bookshelf. "Can I ask you another question?"

Chester wipes furiously at his eyes, which were, mortifyingly enough, threatening to fill with tears. *She's giving you a chance. Don't mess this up.*

"Sure." He returns to the search, shoving aside the complete collection of Monster Files lined up in chronological order.

"The last riddle claimed Petey was a thief, right? And yours was…"

Chester stiffens again and forces his shoulders down from his earlobes.

"I think Mortimer left these riddles as reasons why he brought us here."

He nods. She's spot on. Mortimer's punishment is both physically and mentally torturous. It's brilliant, really. When a riddle is read aloud, like his was, the person it centers around will know it's about them. It's just up to their discretion whether they want to reveal their darkest secret or take a chance and hope someone else will die for their sins.

Twisted. Sick. But still impressive. Part of him is slightly giddy to hear what the others' crimes against Mortimer are. He steals a glance at Melanie, who is scrutinizing the book titles in the dim light. What could *she* possibly have done?

Her quick gasp pulls him out of his thoughts. "Whoa, look at that!"

She points to a section of the shelf that's empty, save six books propped up on display. They stand out among the rest of the Mortimer's musty collection, not just because they look new and clean but because of what's on their covers.

Their names—Chester included.

Attached to the shelf is a plaque. This one also reads MONSTERS.

Melanie stands on her tiptoes to pull down a pale blue book embossed with Crystal Flowers's name in dripping gold letters.

"What the fuck?" Chester takes it and flips through the pages. "All blank. Great. First Petey's, now these, too? For an author, Mortimer did *not* seem to appreciate words."

They work together, leafing through to find any sort of clues as to what they are, but find nothing.

"Weird," Chester breathes, running his hands down the letters of his own name. It's off-putting to see it on a book that wasn't written by him. "You...you don't have one."

A question plays on her pale lips, one that she doesn't have to say aloud: Is that good or bad for her?

He stares down the corridor, the silence somehow audible, like the sound a conch shell makes when held up to an ear. Being singled out, regardless of the situation, doesn't seem to be a good omen within these walls. It also makes him feel like maybe Mortimer made a mistake by inviting her here—Chester has found issue with every single guest today, but Melanie is an outlier. He might deserve punishment. Hell, everyone else probably does, too. But her? For the first time, he starts to doubt Mortimer's brilliance.

Determined to solidify Melanie's safety, he reaches into the back of the monsters shelf and roots around for her book. Instead, his fingers brush something small and cold. He flinches at first, and then his hands close around metal. He withdraws his arm and opens his palm, staring down at a knobby brass key with jagged teeth. This *has* to be important. In every mystery he's ever read, every crime-solving show he's ever watched, finding a key is always a good thing. He grins excitedly and, after showing it Melanie, slips it into his pocket.

"Scott's going to be so pissed that I did something right." He beams, and Melanie gives a halfhearted smile. She still must be thinking about why she wasn't given her own book.

"It's funny he put us in the monster section," Chester says humorlessly, tossing his book back onto the shelf. "Bet he's sending us a message. Thinks *we're* monsters? Like he's innocent?"

He's hoping this will make her feel better and serve as a reminder that being part of the collection is not a good thing, but Melanie just shrugs and says, "We should go back. Show the others the key." She pauses, deep in thought. "Should we tell them about the books, you think?"

"I… No. I don't think so. It'll just make them worry." *About you*, he can't help but think.

"Right."

They turn around and start walking back. The sound of their footsteps intensifies, bouncing off the shelves loudly. Suddenly Chester halts.

"Listen," he hisses.

A third pair of footsteps is coming from behind. He remembers the rule, remembers Buck saying it in his Southern drawl.

"Melanie, *run*."

Chester takes off, Melanie following close behind. There is someone else—*something else*—in the library. He accidentally knocks his pumping arms into a few books, shooting pain up his knuckles. But he doesn't stop until they reach the main section of the library. He sees the group ahead huddled in discussion, but they spring apart with terror when they spot them coming in full steam. Buck squares up, his eyes narrowed over Chester's shoulder like he's preparing for whatever's chasing them.

"What happened? What's going on?" Crystal shrieks. "What's wrong? Melanie? Are you okay?"

Chester gulps for air and turns his head, looking at where they came from. He's going to pretend like his name being absent from her question doesn't hurt a little. "Footsteps." He pants.

"Footsteps?" Scott, whose knees are bent, ready to run, groans. "You thought you heard footsteps? You almost gave me a heart attack. What the hell is wrong with you?"

Chester feels his face get hot. "Nothing! We heard footsteps, so we ran! Pretty natural response, if you ask me." He stares in the direction they came from, but nothing appears. "I guess…I guess we were wrong."

"You think?" Scott rolls his eyes. "While you were busy back there being wrong, we actually found something."

He gestures to a cleared-out section of the bookshelf. Upon further inspection, Chester realizes there's a keyhole in the very back. The key practically thrums in his pocket, and he's bursting to rub it in Scott's face.

"This ain't exactly good news," Buck adds. "What are the chances of finding a key in all this mess?"

Chester clears his throat loudly, forcing the attention to himself. He clasps his hands behind his back and rocks back and forth on his heels. "Oh, I don't know," he says in singsong. "What are the chances? Someone would have to be very keen to find it. Very detail oriented. Smart as a whip. Handsome, probably."

Melanie palms her forehead. Scott's expression transitions from confused to incredulous.

"You didn't," he says.

Chester tugs the key out of his pocket and holds it up. "Oh, but I did. Can I get a thank-you or maybe a kiss on the—"

Scott cuts him off. "I cannot fathom how you can possibly joke about this. Put the goddamn key in the lock."

There's some risk in being the one to do this—in every horror story Chester has ever written, it's always the character who instigates action who gets killed off. The one who investigates the strange noise. The one who tests the waters. The one who opens the suspicious door.

But, as always, he thinks, *Feel the fear!* He reaches through the shelf, jams the key into its slot, and turns.

Nothing flies out at him—no screeching demons nor swarm of flesh-eating moths. A small flap opens, revealing a neat stack of laminated note cards strung together on a key ring. The top one reads, **ANSWER ME**.

"They look like...like questions." He flips through them. "About Mortimer."

Scott looks over his shoulder, his brow furrowing. "They're trivia questions," he says.

Chester groans. In the room they have one hothead, one wallflower, a teary bulldog, a gentle giant, and Chester, the most hated man on the internet. They're like the Australian soldiers running around and shooting aimlessly at beasts much smarter and bigger than they. If trivia is really the only way to receive the third riddle, they're royally screwed.

Because like he said, people are incredibly stupid.

# Crystal Flowers

**C**RYSTAL IS FACING the question every woman ponders at least once in her life: *How well do I know him?*

A woman might find a stash of felt puppets in her boyfriend's closet, leading him to finally admit he's "into that sort of thing"—*sexually*. Or maybe he shouts at her when she drops the tray of lemon-encrusted tilapia as she's taking it out of the oven and that's when she realizes how short his temper is. Or perhaps he goes into convulsions at dinner and has to be rushed to the hospital because she had no idea he was allergic to garlic.

When it's revealed that they must play trivia and that the topic is Mortimer, she feels a rashy hot flush moving up her neck. She looks around at the others, wondering if they have any idea how close she and Morty were—she hasn't called him that, even in her mind, since they split. If they did know, no one would have that worried, stricken look on their face. Because they would assume, for the most part, that she'll have all the answers.

One tends to learn a lot about a person when they're in a relationship with them for three years, even if it's a secret one.

They first met in New York City when they reached for the same order at a cozy hole-in-the-wall café, Fox in the Snow. "Venti pour over with a sprinkle of cinnamon!" an overworked, underpaid barista called out.

When Crystal's and Mortimer's hands met, they did the awkward dance.

"Ope, I think that's mine."

"Ope, you're right. Guess we have the same taste!" Ope, ope, ope.

Funnily enough, she'd been clutching a copy of *The Rise of Bartholomew* to her chest, one of Mortimer's books. When he introduced himself to her as the author, Crystal gushed and asked if he wouldn't mind sitting and allowing her to pick his brain until their coffees went cold. They spent hours tucked in the corner of that café, ordering two more rounds of black coffees with cinnamon, a coincidence Mortimer adored right away.

It was the perfect meet-cute. And of course it was, because Crystal executed it as such.

She'd read in a *Writer's Digest* that Mortimer spent his winters in his home in New York City—something about how the brutality of December and January inspired him. Then she dug around in his mentions on social media, and though he never posted anything on his page other than book promotions (which was probably managed by his PR agency), he was tagged in several photos taken inside Fox in the Snow. So Crystal staked out the café every day for a week, clutching a copy of *The Rise of Bartholomew* (which she hadn't had time to read) and finally caught the trout she was setting the bait for.

Initially, the plan had been to coerce him into helping her get a publishing deal. Three dates—four, tops—and maybe some kissing. She vowed she would not sleep with him; that's where the line was drawn.

But the coffee date went well. Too well. So she invited him over to her apartment the next day for wine and cheese. And then she wanted to see him again. And again.

She shared her dreams of being a writer, not because she wanted to use his connections, but because she felt comfortable doing so. Mortimer had this way of listening, like trivial sounds—a car honking, a phone buzzing, a waiter bringing by more waters—were *criminal*, because they kept him from hearing her for even a second.

And then Crystal got published on her own accord, without having to use Mortimer's persuasion to grease the wheels. She could've stopped seeing him—he was thrice her age and married for God's sake—but she didn't want to. And yes, she knew about Liotta before making her plan.

*Liotta.*

Crystal inhales and tucks her hair behind her ears. This is not the time to think about her. It's time to focus on trivia about her evil, much older, dead ex-boyfriend.

"Let's get crackin'." Buck claps his hands together like cymbals. "Read the first question."

Scott has the note cards and starts reading: "'What's Mortimer Queen's cocktail order?' This has to be a joke. We're trapped in here being picked off one by one…and he wants us to guess his favorite way to get pissed? I should—"

"Orange mocha espresso martini," Crystal and Buck say at the same time.

A gunshot fires, and her body convulses so sharply that she feels like she might be sick—but once the shock settles, she realizes it wasn't a gun at all. Melanie scoops down and roots through the latex corpse of a balloon.

"Here's part of a riddle!" she says, waving it like it's the world's tiniest flag. "Keep going!"

"Well, can't we just pop the balloons ourselves if the clues are in there?" Chester points out.

"Do *you* want to try bending the rules?" Scott flips to the next note card and gives him a hard look. "Because I bet you anything, if we tried, we'd be in trouble."

"*Bet*, you say?" Chester thumbs his chin.

"God, stop it you two." Crystal's patience wanes. "Scott, can you just try to ignore him? We need to hear the next one."

"Okay, okay. Christ… 'Which side of the bed does Mortimer sleep on?'"

She can picture it. His side. He was always up before her, so she'd wake up to an empty space. The weird thing was, he'd try to make his side up—pull the sheets taut, set the comforter up, and get the pillows fluffed and in place—so it was almost like he were never there. Sometimes she'd lie in bed all morning, wondering if him being there was just a dream.

Sometimes she wished it were.

"The left," she replies, her stomach knotting. Her eyes go to Scott's, and she suffers another bout of pain seeing the disgust there. He tries to hide it by clearing his throat and looking away, but it's too late.

A second balloon pops, and Melanie collects another piece of the riddle. It's suddenly much quieter in the library.

"So you guys were…" Scott clears his throat again. "Um, you were… close? You and Mortimer?"

The back of her neck prickles. *Why? Why do you need to ask that? Can't you leave it alone?*

"Is that the next question?" Crystal retorts, finding it far easier to be angry than vulnerable.

"Well, no…but I just think it's odd that Mortimer would bring you here, considering you were his…um…"

"Mistress?" she hisses, the hairs on her neck spiking like a cat on the defense. "You can say it. Mortimer and I were having an affair. Big deal."

"He was a little old for you, wasn't he?" Chester smirks.

Crystal doesn't want to look at Melanie because she can't stand to see the disgust sketched there. She reminds her so much of Liotta, it makes her *sick*, which explains the desperate desire to protect her. Maybe she can save her this time.

That's how it felt when Liotta greeted her for the first time in their New York home. Crystal walked in with Mortimer like the floor was made of needles. The house had always been off-limits during their relationship, until now. It felt like ducking underneath caution tape or the velvet ropes of a museum.

"Don't be nervous," Mortimer had whispered to her, squeezing her hand once. "This is going to work."

"I'm still really uncomfortable about this!" she'd said, her words barely audible.

"Think about how nice it'll be to spend so much time together. Come on. Liotta is waiting in the bedroom."

At first, this made her think they were about to walk into a sexy scene—Liotta splayed out on the bed, wearing a silk bathrobe—but, of course, it was starkly different. She was in bed, sheets tucked up to her chin and the long-sleeves of a blue nightdress fanning out. What hair she had left lay flat on her head in soft, delicate wisps, and her face was the color of the stark-white duvet. Crystal had never seen someone who displayed the history of their beauty so well. Though she had wrinkles and age spots, the features that would have made her gorgeous in her youth were still there: strong clean brows, a sharp jaw, and a tiny nose.

Crystal hated that Liotta forced herself to sit up in bed to say hello. It was an even worse feeling when she smiled at Crystal—she could tell it hurt to do so.

Mortimer crouched at the side of the bed and took his wife's small hands into his own, pressing them to his lips. Though she was supposed to be jealous that the man she was seeing was being so sweet to someone else, Crystal was oddly grateful he was gentle with Liotta.

"Honey? This is Crystal, the caretaker I was telling you about," he said in a lulling tone. "She'll be living here for a while and will help with all your medicine, chemo, and whatever else you need."

Liotta gave her another smile so bright, Crystal had to turn away and pretend to swipe dust off her dress. "I apologize in advance for being such poor company! A gorgeous girl like you deserves more than being locked away with a dying old lady."

Crystal cringed and tried to speak but couldn't come up with anything save a tight nod.

Mortimer rescued her by planting a kiss between Liotta's eyes and getting to his feet. "I'll show you around the house, Crystal. Give you a tour."

She was about to follow him out of the bedroom when Liotta grabbed her wrist and held it with a surprisingly strong grip. Her brows were slightly slanted, and her mouth twisted to the side. It was almost... pitying.

"I hope we can be good friends, regardless of your affair with my husband."

Crystal would have yanked her arm away if she thought it wouldn't snap Liotta's clean off. "I... What do you...? I..."

"It's all right, dear." She patted her, and Crystal felt her chest expand. "Really, I don't care in the slightest. I just wanted to get that out of the way so we can be real with each other. Is that fair?"

"That's...fair."

"Good. Good." Liotta nodded and leaned back into a pillow, her small head fitting perfectly within its indent. "Because we're going to need each other. You and me."

Chester's grating tone is only marginally more pernicious than the memory it drags her out of.

"Did it end poorly?" He's pressing. "Is that why you're in here with us? What did you do to piss him off?"

"What did *you* do?" she fires back, her tongue lashing with venom.

He snaps his mouth shut.

"We have fifteen minutes left," Scott concedes. "Let's move on."

Crystal wrings her hands, wanting so badly to dig into his thoughts. Part of her wants to defend her relationship with Mortimer so that Scott will understand, but what would she say? How would she even begin to explain?

Scott avoids her eyes and continues, "'What was the last book Mortimer released before he died?'"

Crystal looks to Buck, but his face is blank, just like hers must be. She has no idea.

"Jeez, I should know this…" Buck scratches the back of his head. "I guess I sorta stopped payin' attention to what he published when I came up as an author."

"It was sort of a flop, wasn't it?" Chester shrinks inward, his eyes darting around like lightning is going to strike him down. "I mean, I don't remember anyone talking about it."

It's an awful feeling to be clueless so often in one night. Crystal peels a Carl Badsman business card off the bottom of her heel while she thinks.

"Oh! I know!" Buck slaps his thigh. "It was *A Hundred Ways to Die*."

Immediately it's clear that is the wrong answer. The ground starts twitching, and after a short breath, a clear, steaming liquid starts to gurgle from the cracks in the floorboards.

"Climb!" Crystal has the good sense to scream. "Climb now!"

She leaps onto the middle bookcase shelf as the floor floods, the foul-smelling water rising quickly—colorless, but with a film of mustard-yellow vapor hovering just above its surface.

"It's nitric acid!" Chester shouts, clinging to shelf across from her.

"Are you sure?" Scott demands—a stupid question, really. For once, Crystal is on Chester's side. If someone tells you something is acid, you don't question it.

"My dad worked in a steel mill," Chester responds to the skepticism anyway. "They used this stuff to strip their old materials."

"What in God's gravy!" Buck struggles to keep his massive boots wedged onto the bookshelf. "Does that mean it'll strip *us* if we fall in it?"

Crystal hugs the bookcase, trying not to think about how it smells of Mortimer: wet wood, peppermint, and cigars. She gags and turns her head away to speak to Scott, who is the closest to her. "Do you still have them?"

She worries he dropped the trivia questions until he lifts a finger, the key ring hooked there. With one hand, he flips to the next one and groans. "'When was his last book *released?*'"

"Nobody read your goddamn book!" Chester shouts to the ceiling. The acid hisses, as if in reply.

Her feet killing her, Crystal kicks off her shoes. They hit the floor, and the acid turns Kelly green, sizzling angrily. She can see the heels lowering as the material corrodes away. It's then she realizes that the bottom of the bookcases they're all clinging to like life rafts will soon be eaten away, too.

"October thirtieth!" Scott shouts the date with enough confidence to shake an innocent man on trial.

With a gurgle akin to a regurgitating toilet bowl, the acid rescinds ever so slightly, but not enough. There's a sharp *crack* and *pop*—the sound of wood slowly collapsing in on itself. The bookcase on the front wall, where Melanie and Buck are perched, teeters forward before lurching to a halt. Crystal's stomach clenches watching Melanie's grip slipping, and she barks, "Buck! Help her!"

"Hang on, Mel!" he orders, leaping from one end of the shelf to hers and wrapping his arms around her like a seat belt.

"How many questions are there left?" Melanie asks from under him. "We have to keep going!"

"One," Scott strains. "But I…I don't really get it. 'What's the term for a minor head injury with a brief loss of consciousness?'"

"A concussion!" Crystal manages to say.

Suddenly she hears the most beautiful melody—liquid being slurped down the drain. Peering over her shoulder, she sees the acid receding until the floor is visible again. The desk in the center of the room has lowered, all four legs eaten down so that it's slightly cockeyed. Somehow, the celebratory cake has gone undisturbed.

"There's writing," she announces as the acid retreats. "There's writing on the floor! The riddle!"

"Forget the riddle—is it safe to come down?" Chester squeaks.

"I don't know. Let me check." Scott descends, putting a single leg out and testing the floor. "Yeah, it's fine. The acid is totally gone."

There's no time to be relieved, however, because just as Buck descends from his perch, he collapses, grabbing at his foot.

"What happened?" Scott demands, kneeling and prying Buck's hands away so he can see.

Crystal can't help but hiss when she sees the injury. The tip of his shoe is gone, singed at the edges. And poking out is what looks like a shaved, white nub—his big toe, burned down to the bone.

"Oh God." She wants to look away but has never seen anything so gruesome.

Buck clenches his teeth into a chimpanzee-like grin, shaking his head over and over. "'Mmm fine. Just…just skimmed my foot a little, that's all. Ah…" He bats Scott away and inspects the wound. "Looks like I got lucky. It's already cauterized, so no bleedin'. Oooh, that hurts somethin' bad, though…"

"We should wrap it," Crystal says, though her experience with medical emergencies stems from sexy-nurse scenes in her books.

The obvious choice is Chester's ascot, which he willingly offers. Scott tries to tie it around the nub, but Buck insists on doing it himself. Crystal, remembering they're on a time limit, jerks her head toward a clock and finds they have eight minutes left. She stands and angles herself to get a better look at the writing on the floor while massaging her tender palms. They have hard dents in them from where she gripped the bookcase. The others follow her lead, cocking their heads while trying to decipher the charred words that have appeared in the wood.

Buck attempts standing, too, but Scott shoves him down. Crystal can tell that even though he was the first to go to Buck's aid, he's slightly gratified at being able to overpower such a big man now that he's impaired.

Unwilling to wait a second longer, Crystal reads the riddle aloud:

> I took a man into the alley,
> Ordered him to do as I said.
> A little competition threatened me,
> So I kicked him until he was nearly dead.
> Don't be fooled by my charm.
> I don't care about peace.
> If you see me, I implore you to ask,
> "How was your latest book release?"

As always, there's a delay as the words sink in. Chester is the first to speak.

"You know, Melanie had an idea when we were in the stacks…"

Crystal grinds her molars together. She's still not pleased Melanie went back there *alone* with him, but disagreeing with Scott seemed… unwise. She eyes him now, his hair damp with sweat and his face lines deep. He's calm now, but she can almost feel the heat bubbling beneath his skin, and she isn't sure whether to be attracted to or frightened by it.

Melanie festers underneath everyone's eyes before Chester steamrolls on.

"She said that all these riddles allude to us and what we did to make Mortimer pissed enough to lock us in here. It can't be a coincidence that Petey was the previous answer."

Crystal stares at the words on the floor not because she needs to reread them, but so that she doesn't instinctively look to Scott. If the riddle really is about one of them, this one has his name written all over it. She's wondering if anyone else is thinking the same when Buck speaks.

"We're all thinkin' it. Might as well come out and say it." He looks to Crystal. "'Sss about you."

Her knees buckle, she's so caught off guard.

"Me?" She gasps. "You think I beat up a guy? How could I? Why would—"

"'Don't be fooled by my charm'?" Chester points out. "Sure sounds like you. And all those questions about Mortimer, you were the one who knew them. Did you get jealous of someone Mortimer was close to? Do them in so you wouldn't have to share your weekly allowance?"

Her head is abuzz with a thousand insults she wants to spit at him, but her tongue is tied. She looks to Scott for help, but he's staring at the ground. Betrayal strikes her like a whip, and she turns so he can't see the hurt in her eyes.

"It's not me" is all she can muster, feeling her bulldog energy Mortimer loved so much deplete. "I...I never did anything like that."

Melanie clears her throat, bringing the attention back to her. Crystal can tell this is something of a sacrifice for her—like whooping and hollering so a bear diverts its attention to someone else until the original victim can get away.

"Actually, I have another theory," Melanie offers softly before clearing her throat and speaking louder. "The riddle refers to a book release. Scott..." She looks apologetic. "You knew the date. October thirtieth."

Crystal catches Melanie's eye and gives a slow blink in thanks. Melanie returns it with a barely noticeable nod.

Scott's ears turn amber red. "So the riddle is about me because I saved our asses by knowing a trivia question?" He scoffs, shaking his head.

"We're not accusing you," Crystal says, though two seconds ago, that's exactly how she felt. "It would be a good thing if we could figure out the riddle's answer, regardless of who it's about."

"It can't be me. I've never done a *thing* to Mortimer!" Scott protests, straightening to his tallest posture.

"Why did you know Mortimer's release date, then?" Chester asks, tapping his fingertips together. Is he *enjoying* this? "Was it just a coincidence?"

"I only remembered because it was the same date *my* new book came out," Scott insists. "Caused quite a kerfuffle with my publisher. They called me in for, like, three meetings that week alone because they were worried his release would overshadow mine."

"Did it?" Crystal isn't sure why she's asking, but the answer seems like it matters.

"I… No, actually." He shifts his tone with her so that it's no longer angry, just confused. "Now that I'm remembering, I didn't hear anything about the book I was competing with."

"Maybe because you did something to make it that way," Chester says in the same cadence someone would use while playing Clue.

Crystal glares at him—but it's too late. The fire in Scott's eyes is back.

He turns on him, his nostrils flaring. "Don't be stupid! Of course I didn't! In fact, I went to a L&P Management Halloween party the week before just to show face. My agent told me it would look good if I played nice."

It seems they've run into an impasse. If Scott denies it's him, then there's no point in risking putting his name down. Crystal shudders to think of what the punishment would be. More acid? Or something worse? What's *worse* than acid?

But then she catches Scott's eye twitching, a dawning realization spreading across his face. He grabs a handful of business cards off the desk and stares at the image of the smiling young man.

"Holy shit. I remember now. I saw this guy that night at the

Halloween party. I saw him! I—" His breath hitches. "Oh God…I hit him."

There's an explosion of "what?" and "how?" and "why?" and one "of course you did" from Chester.

"I didn't mean to!" he says quickly. "I mean, I definitely didn't take him in the alley and kick him until he was…whatever the riddle says. I'd never do that!"

Crystal can tell he's frightened—of them, of Mortimer, and maybe of himself. She reaches over and interlaces her fingers with his, squeezing. "It's okay. Tell us what happened."

Just as she knew he would, Scott relaxes. Men like him are creatures of touch, like dogs that whimper and whine until they're scratched behind the ear.

"I went to the L&P Management Halloween party," he starts slowly. "My agent said the company had extended an invitation to any of his clients and that it would be good to go. Make connections. See people. Talk up my own book release. All that stuff."

Crystal dares to glance at the clock. Six minutes. He has to make this quick.

"It was an open bar. And I was so fucking nervous that I drank—a lot. And everyone else was drinking. The details are fuzzy, but toward the end of the night, some guy was talking shit about my last book. Kept calling it 'derivative.' You know *using* that word is derivative in itself? Anyway…I shoved the guy. And he pushed me back. Then I swung and he ducked, and I hit someone else in the back of the head. He went flying over the bar. The last thing I remember is being kicked out and staggering home."

"And the guy you accidentally hit was Carl Badsman?" Chester confirms.

"Yeah, I'm pretty sure. I tried calling their offices the next day to apologize, and someone front the front desk answered. She was real mad.

171

Told me, 'Carl has suffered a concussion' and that I was lucky he wasn't pressing charges."

"'Course they wouldn't." Buck snorts and then winces. "L&P would've done anything to keep the police out of their business. Heard they were into some shady tax stuff." He sits up slightly, as if struck by something. "Hey, you know what? Carl Badsman. That was Mortimer's lead PR rep. Headed all his book launches. What if…what if Carl got hurt so badly that the launch got fucked up? And Mortimer blames Scott because of it?"

"But wait, wait, wait." Scott holds up a hand. "I didn't do it on purpose! I had no idea who Carl was in the first place! It's not like I was plotting to destroy Mortimer's life! He's…he's telling it all wrong!"

Crystal lurches forward at the realization. Her stomach clenches, and the roof of her mouth goes as dry as baked clay. She remembers the day she walked in on Liotta dabbing makeup on a plum-colored bruise, her fingers shaking so badly that the foundation was all streaky.

"We have to tell someone!" Crystal pleaded then.

"*No!*" Liotta whisper-hissed. "Don't you get it by now? It's what he does best. He takes the truth and turns it his way."

Crystal buckles at the memory and claws at the air, desperately feeling for Melanie's hands—the ones that remind her so much of Liotta's. Cold and fragile but also strong and safe. Melanie holds tight as Crystal moans, "He's…he's rewriting."

# Short Story #3

### Scott Clay

Scott untangles his naked legs from the lavender sheets and rolls out of bed, rubbing his face and trying not to vomit. The room is dark and smells heavily of vanilla perfume—God, he hates the artificial sugary scent. He envisions women taking long soaks in tubs of frosting and marshmallow whip, marinating so they're tantalizing enough to eat. It's ridiculous. He wants a woman to sleep with, not to serve with coffee.

A feminine voice murmurs from beneath the covers. "Where are you going?"

Scott is about to open his mouth and give an excuse as to why he's slipping out so early when last night, amid pillow talk, he promised they'd make pancakes and watch *Pride and Prejudice*.

*Think. You're a writer. Get creative.*

He's rescued by the ringing of his cell phone.

"I've got to take this. It's my publicist," he says and pecks her lips impersonally, ignoring the morning breath. "I'll text you."

He won't. She's a beautiful woman, maybe even a nice one at that. But he doesn't have the time, nor the emotional capacity to see her again. She approached him at a bar last night, recognizing him from an interview with Conan O'Brien. The recognition and attention made him horny, and he went home with her. Done and done.

He pulls his pants and shirt on, pressing the cell between his ear and shoulder while slipping on his shoes.

"Yancy?" he says. "A little early for a Sunday, huh?"

"Scott, I've got bad news."

He grabs an apple from a bowl on... Is her name Katherine? Hannah? Stacy. He grabs an apple from a bowl on *Stacy's* kitchen counter and takes a massive bite before slipping out the apartment door. The hallway to the elevator is empty and narrow, so his voice bounces off the walls.

"Good morning to you, too. What's up?"

He's not concerned by this phone call, Yancy has a bad habit of overreacting. Last week she called him bawling because his author portrait for the back sleeve of his book was in black and white and not charcoal and white. Apparently, there's a difference.

"It's bad," she says, and he can practically hear her gulp. "*101 Ways to Die* is coming out next month."

"Mortimer Queen's next book?" He slaps the Lobby button in the elevator. "Seriously? Shit. When exactly?"

Yancy lets out a moan. "August 11," she says. "The same day as your book."

Scott squeezes the apple so hard, it pops in his hand, juice running through his fingers. He drops the remains and slaps his palm against the elevator wall.

"Fuck!" he swears. "How badly will this affect the release?"

"It's…It's not great," Yancy says. Scott can imagine she's popping nausea tablets while she's talking. "It's always difficult competing with book releases in the same genre, but competing with Mortimer Queen is…"

Scott strides into the apartment common space and out the front doors. It's warm and muggy outside with the sun slowly rising. A man wearing tiny yellow shorts speeds by on the sidewalk checking his watch.

"Why are you telling me this?" Scott snaps, such urgency uncomfortable so soon after waking. "What the fuck am I supposed to do about it? You're my publicist. Do something!"

"We—we could move your release date," Yancy says quickly. "It'll be tricky and definitely cost more, but at least it'll be—"

"Hell no!" he says, still standing on the sidewalk. "He can move *his* date!"

"Yeah, see, here's the thing. I doubt he would do that."

Scott supposes he could, in theory, move his date. But he can't afford to. Deals are in motion. The schedule is set. Refunds will not be given. And more importantly, he refuses to yield to an old has-been who *used* to be brilliant.

"Just fix this!" he orders and ends the call.

Scott needs this next book to work out. He hasn't exactly been conservative with his spending and has driven himself deep into debt.

"Fuck," he says while calling an Uber from his phone. "Fuck, fuck, fuck."

A woman pushing a stroller past him scoffs. "Watch your language!" she scolds.

Scott resists telling her that her baby is as ugly as she is. He strains to keep his blood pressure steady when his ride pulls up.

The driver, thankfully, isn't one for small talk, so he's left alone to sit with this bad news.

Once he's home, Scott staggers into his apartment and takes a long cold shower. When he's through, his head feels clearer, his boiled blood cooling like defrosting chicken. He makes a cup of coffee in the kitchen and pulls out his laptop, doing a quick Google search of Mortimer Queen's representation.

"Carl Badsman," he reads aloud.

His phone rings again—Yancy.

"Yancy, what do you know about Carl Badsman?" Scott asks her before she can start to speak.

"Carl? From L&P Management? He's Mortimer's publicist. Why?"

"Hang on," Scott says, clicking on a pop-up adorned with a flurry of animated balloons. L&P's Fifty-Year Anniversary Celebration. "Have you ever been to Baxter's Pub?"

"Yeah, I've been. It's on Eighth." She pauses. "Good black bean burger, if you care."

"You know I don't. What's the dress code like?" He scribbles down the event's date and time on an old take-out receipt. "I'm headed there on Thursday."

———————

Scott shows up to Baxter's Pub in a sports coat and T-shirt. The place is already packed with people, and a large banner hangs over the bar welcoming guests and employees of L&P. Waiters meander around with trays of champagne flutes balanced on their fingertips. Scott grabs one as he walks in, surveying the scene.

He's looking for Carl, but all he has to go on is his name. An extensive internet search produced nothing of substance, and even his LinkedIn profile picture was blank. He's a phantom of the web, an oddity in this day and age. It was poetic that he would be Mortimer Queen's publicist—a weirdo representing another weirdo. Perfect.

Scott struts to the bar, where a woman in a black romper is sitting alone on a stool. She's nursing what looks like a cranberry vodka through a short straw.

"Do you mind if I sit here?" He pats the seat next to her and gives the most dazzling smile he can procure.

"No, not at all." The woman flaps her hand. "Go ahead. I'm just being antisocial over here."

"I'm not judging. These kinds of things are overwhelming."

"Aren't they?" She stirs the drink. "But we get a ton of shit if we don't come." She studies him. "Who are you?"

Scott extends a hand. "I'm Paul Richards," he says. "I just started at L&P last week, so we might not have met before."

"What department?" the woman asks curiously, not necessarily suspicious but perhaps panicking that she doesn't have a good handle on the company's staff.

"HR," he lies, praying she's not in the same sector. "You?"

"PR. I'm Regina Hawthorne. Nice to meet you, Paul. Welcome to the rat race."

"Oh, so you must know Carl?" Scott widens his eyes. "He's a friend of a friend. I was told I should meet him."

"Carl Badsman." Regina nods, taking a long sip. "He's over there, if you're feeling brave enough to introduce yourself."

She jerks her head toward a man near the buffet table stacking sliders on a plate. He has reddish hair, tiny eyes, and a sort of hump over his brow. Scott thanks Regina and dips away, blending into the mesh of people to watch Carl from afar. He mingles for an hour before losing his nerve and stepping outside. He leans against the building and sighs, running his fingers through his hair.

Just as he's about to tuck his tail between his legs and go home, Carl stumbles out of Baxter's, calling over his shoulder. "I can drive just fine, assholes! I had two beers."

"Yeah, and twenty sliders!" Someone laughs.

"See you tomorrow!" Carl says and passes Scott without a second look, heading down the street.

Scott follows on the opposite side, keeping his head low. Carl whistles as he walks, eventually stopping at a meter and pulling out his keys.

"Carl Badsman?" Scott asks, and he jumps.

"Holy shit, you scared me." Carl laughs nervously. "I don't have any cash on me… Sorry."

"I'm not trying to ask you for money." Scott frowns and looks down at his attire. This jacket is *new*. Does he look homeless? "My name is Scott Clay."

Carl squints and then says, "Scott Clay, the author?" He brightens. "Pleasure to meet you! Again, sorry about before. A little bit jumpy is all. I read far too many horror novels."

Scott jams one hand in his pocket. "I wanted to talk to you about something," he says, shoving thoughts of his charred apartment aside. "About Mortimer Queen's next book release."

"Sure!" Carl says. "We're very excited about it. His last book ever, he says. We're really going out with a bang. Have you been invited to the release party yet? If not, you're of course—"

"No, you misunderstand," Scott says, shuffling his feet. "You see, my book comes out on the exact same day."

Carl blinks, his smile fading. "Ah." He winces like his shoes are too tight. "That's an unfortunate coincidence, I suppose."

"I was hoping you might be able to switch your date," Scott

says. "Push it to next month or the month after. You can see how Mortimer's book might overshadow mine."

"I'm really sorry." To his credit, he does sound genuinely upset. "But I can't move the release date. Everything is set in stone."

Of course. Scott feels like an idiot thinking a face-to-face conversation would change anything. He scratches the back of his neck.

"I'm asking you…" He takes a big breath and closes his eyes for a moment. "No—actually, I'm begging here. You have to know what this will do—"

Scott halts his words when he opens his eyes and sees Carl on his phone, texting. *Texting*, while he pleads for mercy. His molars gnash so roughly, he swears he loses a few inches of enamel. Heat rises from the bottoms of his feet to the hair cuticles rooted in his scalp.

No, no. *Control anger before it controls you.* He thinks about what his therapist says about practicing cognitive restructuring. *Whenever you find yourself getting angry, think, "It's frustrating, and it's understandable that I'm upset about it, but it's not the end of the world, and getting angry is not going to fix it anyhow."*

Carl finishes shooting off another text and looks up. "Sorry about that," he says, but he doesn't appear to be very apologetic. "Anyway, I really wish I could help you, but I can't. Things like this happen."

"But this could ruin me," Scott says, surprising himself with how honest he's being. He realizes how dangerous this is—what would it do to his reputation if Carl told people in the industry how he came groveling to him?

"Look." Carl sighs. "I'd like to help, but I can't. I'm sure you'll be fine?"

The question mark on the end of the sentence doesn't scream confidence.

"Right." Scott shoves his balled-up fists into his pockets. *Getting angry is not going to fix this*, he repeats in his mind. "Thanks anyway."

He turns and walks away, feeling both entirely defeated and proud for controlling his temper.

"Yeah," he hears Carl say and then chuckle. "It was worth a shot, right?"

As quick as a trigger, Scott turns and barrels toward Carl. He yelps and hurries to open his car door, but Scott immediately slams it shut and shoves him onto the ground.

"What the hell is the matter with you?" Carl exclaims fearfully, his hands covering his face.

Scott sees black specks in his vision. He's most dangerous when he blacks out completely and can't remember what he's done or who he's done it to. He grabs Carl's shirt and hoists him up so they're nose to nose. His breath reeks of burgers and mustard.

"You're going to do everything you can to fuck up Mortimer's release campaign," he growls.

"Wh-what?!" Carl appears not to be a fighting man, because his arms hang at his sides. "I…I don't know… Please let me go—"

Scott slams his fist into Carl's face, his knuckles sinking gloriously into his mouth and knocking out a few teeth. He hears them hit the pavement and strikes again, this time in his stomach. It's soft and plushy, like pizza dough.

"I don't care how you do it," Scott says as Carl writhes on the ground, bleeding. "Fuck up the announcement. Delay book shipments. Forget interviews. Do what you have to do to make sure my book rivals his."

Carl groans and tries to pull himself along the road.

Scott draws his leg back and kicks him, a crack splintering the alleyway. Another kick. Carl spits up blood.

"I'll do it!" he finally gargles, his mouth oozing. "I'll do what you want!"

The compliance assuages further stress building in Scott's lower back. He rubs it, internally setting a reminder to schedule a deep-tissue massage. Crouching next to the crumpled, whimpering man, Scott grips the back of his neck.

"I swear. I swear I'll do it," Carl continues. "And I—I w-won't tell anyone about this. Just let me go home to my wife and kids!"

A screw loosens in Scott's skull, jarred by these words. With a grunt, he gives one last punch to the head, and Carl stops whining. He checks his pulse—still alive. Perfect.

After stealing his wallet (it has to look like a mugging, right?), he quickly stalks away from the scene, wiping his hands on his shirt and cringing at the blood smeared there. Great. It's one of his favorites. His knuckle aches, and he knows it'll be bruised and swollen tomorrow. He'll tell people he slammed it in a car door or something.

The last hit wasn't necessary, but it was prompted by Carl bragging about his darling wife and children. It wasn't just the fact he had loved ones to go home to, to eat meals in front of the TV with, to kiss good night—but it was that Carl was capable of wanting all that junk.

Scott never has. Never could, even if he wanted to.

All he will ever care about is his career, which is why he came inches from killing a man tonight just to save it.

# Melanie Brown

**M**ELANIE'S HANDS ARE being crushed, the air pockets between her knuckles popping like hot kernels or corn. Crystal is gone—present physically, but by the glassy sheen that's fallen over her irises, she's far away.

There's no time to dig into what she's just sai, because the minutes are ticking down. She tries to wrench out of Crystal's grip but can't break free.

"Someone needs to write the answer!" she says to anyone who will listen.

"With what?" Chester asks, his hands outstretched and empty.

She's filled with irritation. "How about *the quill on the table*!" Surprise blooms in her chest at the intensity in her voice, but she quickly tucks it away.

Scott, for once, is useless. He's visibly shaken at the prospect of Mortimer dragging him to the Manor under a false story, like the audacity of it all is too jarring to go on. Or perhaps, she thinks, he's faking being in shock. She has no reason to trust he's telling the truth, though Crystal seems to have formed a...*bond* with him. For her sake, Melanie hopes he's being honest.

Chester dashes for the quill, ink dripping off the pointed end. He hits the floor and starts scratching out the letters *S* and *C*. Scott chooses this moment to shake from his stupor and raise his hand out.

"Stop! Don't write my name! It wasn't me! I didn't *do* anything!"

To Melanie's surprise, Chester stops writing and looks to her expectantly. Not Buck. Not Crystal. *Her.* His eyes widen in question, and when she nods, he goes back to writing. *S...C...O...*

The clocks scream in protest.

*GONG.*

*GONG.*

*GONG.*

They're too late.

Chester finishes the name anyway, muttering softly at first then full-on shouting, "No, no, no, no. We got the answer. We got it right. You can't *do* this! We got it right!"

If only there were some way Melanie could at least pretend to protect herself—a hiding place, a shield. No one speaks. Buck hoists himself to both feet, glaring at the surrounding walls with unnecessary boldness. The Manor will take one of them; there's no fighting it.

And then the books come.

They fly off the shelves in a thick swarm, opening and closing like snapping mouths. A swirl of them dances above their heads in a circle, creating a gust of wind that almost blows Melanie over. Then they dive.

Melanie feels her cheeks and arms pepper with cuts as the books shoot past, slicing her skin. But they don't come for her. The swarm descends on Chester, who kicks and spits like an angry yowling cat. A book near his leg opens its mouth wide, and Melanie can see a hundred tiny razor-sharp teeth before it chomps down into the flesh. He howls and begs for help, but it's difficult to even see him through all the leather binding and pages flying loose in the air. Within a minute, Melanie hears a horrible wet choking sound, and a splash of hot liquid sprays across her forearm. *Please, just die already,* she prays as Chester emits another tortured splutter.

Finally, the mass of books starts to calm, flapping back to their positions in the surrounding shelves before falling still. Melanie feels a wiggling beneath her foot and looks down to see a thin paperback struggling to get out from under her shoe. She lifts a toe, and it rockets upward, flying lopsided as if injured, until it's nestled back into place. The shelves ooze blood, a thick stream of it cascading, then vanish into the floorboards.

On the ground where Chester once was is now a smattering of bloodied pages, the casualties of his struggle. There's not a piece of him left, and Melanie can't help the small slice of hope that blooms at the thought of him getting away, disappearing into the house. A small, stupid part of her.

Scott leans over to rest his hands on his knees, gagging. Buck is swearing loudly, dragging his fingers along his chest and pacing in a tight circle.

She's not sure when Crystal let go, only that Melanie suddenly has access to both hands. She leans against the bookshelf behind her in an attempt to keep the room from spinning.

Near her white-knuckled hand is a globe, the kind from long past—with outdated names and soft borders. Seeing it, with its light-purple and orange swatches of land, Melanie is yanked into a memory, unbidden.

It's dank. Sticky. Her feet are dangling, and in the distance, she can hear glasses clinking. Someone is talking close to her ear—Mortimer. He smells of smoke, whiskey, and something medicinal. Sterile, like the sheets of a hospital bed.

"I bet you want to travel the world," he says. "To get out of this town.

I have the money to do it. I could close my eyes, point to a spot on a globe, and be there by tomorrow afternoon. There's a theory out there, a *theory*, mind you, that there are advanced beings out in the galaxy. That they could spin our earth like a toy. And you know what would happen? The centrifugal force would become so extreme that one side of the planet would be plunged into darkness forever. Can you imagine? Half the earth plunged in eternal blackness."

Melanie's vision swims. Mortimer's skin ripples like crests in the sand dunes. Why is he telling her this?

"That would be awful," she slurs.

"No, it would be wonderful!" He laughs, the hoarseness so clear, like he's right here. "I recommend you try it, Melanie. Take the world into your own hands and add a little darkness to it."

When the memory fades, all that's left is a pricking sensation on her forehead. The scar there demands to be recognized. She presses a finger to it, feeling a pulsing heartbeat under the puckered line. This is the first time she's recalled that night so clearly, and as much as forgetting scared her, remembering is even more terrifying.

Faintly aware that someone is calling her name—Scott, Buck, Chester—no, Chester is dead—she reaches out and places a hand on the dusty globe, letting it slowly spin it.

*Half the earth plunged in eternal blackness.*

As the globe spins for the third time on its axis, a sharp *click* comes from behind the shelves, and the bookcase before her suddenly creaks open on a hinge.

"Melanie." Scott approaches from behind. His voice is ragged. "What did you do?"

He says it like it's a bad thing, as if she's broken a piece of the room. Without waiting for further scolding, she grips the edge of the bookcase and pulls so that it swings open. A doorway stares back at them, its stone walls lined with flickering torches.

"It's a hidden passageway," she says.

"Come on," Scott urges, turning away from it. "The door is open. We can go to the next room. Buck, do you need help walking?"

He gives a swift "I'm fine," then stands.

But Melanie stares into the passageway, her fingers itching to reach up and tug on her bangs. Instead, she folds her arms, tucking them tightly in place. Felix went through a passageway similar to this, and he wound up dead. She should be afraid of stepping another inch closer, but instead, she feels drawn. Like she's meant to go inside.

"I'm going through here," she decides aloud.

"What?" Scott whirls around. "You can't be serious."

"This could be a way out. Mortimer probably never thought we'd find it."

"Yeah, see, you're saying 'could' like it's no big deal. It also 'could' be a trap. You can't seriously be considering—"

"I'm not considering." She's startled by the firmness in her voice. "I'm going."

Crystal wipes her eyes and pats her cheeks, as if trying to get herself together. "I'm going with you." Her chin juts out, though it still trembles.

"You don't have to. I'll be fine alone."

"I know that." Crystal sounds unsure and then repeats with more believability, "I *do* know that. But I want to go."

"Absolutely not," Scott orders. "No way."

Crystal takes both his hands in hers and looks up at him, unsmiling. The touch is barely affectionate, but the intensity in her eyes makes Melanie turn away.

"Please don't," he whispers to her.

She lets go and moves to stand next to Melanie, waiting to follow.

Scott splutters in protest, looking to Buck for assistance. He limps over to Melanie until she has to hitch her neck up so she can see his face clearly. Thinking he might throw her over his shoulder and carry her to the next room, she tenses.

Buck leans down and wraps his massive arms around her. She stiffens at first, then sinks into the hug, warmth spreading across her body like a thick coat of paint. When he releases her, his eyes are wet, but his mouth is set in a firm line.

"Do what ya gotta do" is all he says before hobbling over to Crystal and doing the same.

Scott practically implodes. "You can't just let them go! This is Winnie all over again! You're going to die, don't you guys get it? You're going to die, and I can't save you in there!"

A strange unbridled laugh escapes Melanie's lips as she gestures to the four of them left. "You clearly can't save anyone here either."

Then she walks through the passageway. She doesn't have to glance over her shoulder to check if Crystal is following; she can hear the extra footfalls and smell the vanilla perfume.

"Come back! Please, Melanie! We have to stay together!" Scott pleads, his voice echoing. "Crystal! Crystal, turn around! Come back!"

Melanie squeezes her eyes shut, willing herself to keep going. She thinks fleetingly of the last time someone other than Petra wanted her to stick around. Never. And only here, in this cavernous mansion of evil and death, she's met someone who is begging her to stay.

But Scott's voice vanishes the deeper they go. Water drips noisily from the ceilings, and a mixture of moss and spiderwebs hangs like curtains that Melanie has to push through.

She's not entirely sure why she needed to deviate from the set path. It was more than just a feeling, more than just wanting to escape the strict cadence of death, the rules Mortimer has laid out for them. Even though she hates him for what he's doing to them, Melanie has this carnal desire to learn more. Maybe then she'll uncover why he's doing this. It's an instinct, like a cockroach sensing danger.

She certainly feels like a bug walking through the moist passageway, the walls becoming narrower and the torches farther apart. Crystal must've thought Melanie couldn't hear her cry over the dripping water, but the soft sobs echo down the chamber.

"You don't believe him, do you?" Crystal suddenly asks, breaking the silence between them.

"Who?"

"Scott. You think he did what the riddle said."

Melanie wasn't expecting this to be a topic of conversation, but she allows the question to bounce around in her brain.

"I don't know what to believe," she says carefully. "It seems unbelievable that Mortimer would make up a reason to take revenge."

Crystal sighs. "That's the word for him. 'Unbelievable.' If you'd known Mortimer like I did, you'd understand. He sees reality as…well, as a first draft. Plenty of space to edit the truth the way he likes it."

Melanie nods before remembering she probably can't see her do so in the dark. "Why did you come with me?" she finds herself asking.

"I think you're right about there being more than one way out of here. All of Mortimer's houses had these secret passageways. A hatch that led down to the cellar and out the back door, a bookcase that led around to the front of the house…I used them whenever I needed to slip out unnoticed."

Crystal's tone lowers as she finishes the sentence, like she changed her mind halfway through and hopes Melanie doesn't hear.

"But I wasn't the only one who used them to escape," Crystal continues quickly. "Liotta. She started using them when things got…worse."

"Worse?" Melanie repeats, but Crystal doesn't offer an explanation.

A high-pitched whining rattles through the tunnel, and Crystal yelps. Melanie waits for a beat, standing perfectly still, until she's sure nothing is coming after them. Then she starts walking again.

"You are fearless." Crystal shudders, speed walking to catch up to her.

Melanie can't help but laugh. "No one has *ever* called me that."

"Well, you are. Own it."

This makes Melanie smile, even in the dark, damp space they're in. If

Cynthia heard Crystal say this, she'd probably grip her wineglass (which is in her hand 99 percent of the time) so hard that it would shatter.

"Watch your head," Melanie tells Crystal as a dank plant, one tendril skimming past her forehead, hangs down.

It all happens so fast. One minute Melanie is smiling, and the next everything goes wrong.

Crystal lets out a strangled scream, and Melanie whirls around to find her ensnared in the ivy, the vines slithering around her neck. Her legs flail as she's lifted off the ground, her hands clawing at the constraints. Melanie rushes forward but is lashed in the face with a vine. Hot blood drips down her cheek as she rights herself. But before she can do anything to help, Crystal's body drops onto the ground in a heap.

"No!" Melanie crawls over, her shaking hands hovering over her body.

"She's alive, you know."

With just a turn of her head, she comes nose to nose with Gia Falcone.

Melanie extends her hands protectively over Crystal, taking in the groundskeeper's haunting glow, a wispy light emanating from her skin. Her eyes, which were already dark when she first welcomed them, are now two inky eight balls blinking back at her.

"Hello, Melanie." She smiles, her lips stretching far too wide for the expression to be comforting. "I'm glad to see you."

Melanie stares past Gia toward the other end of the passageway, briefly wondering if she can make a break for it. Every muscle in her body twitches, urging her to flee. *Go. Go. Just go!* But Gia extinguishes the idea as quickly as a live match pinched between two cold fingers.

"I'm not here to hurt you, Melanie, so there's no point in running."

The muscle twitching stops. She stops looking down the tunnel and recenters herself on Crystal. For some reason, she believes Gia. She won't hurt Melanie—as long as she behaves. And trying to escape will only make Gia angry.

"B-but Crystal…she's alive? How do you know?"

"She is. The Manor wouldn't dare disobey Mortimer's orders. No, you are to be granted an hour in each room before it can feast. Those are the stipulations."

Melanie stares down at Crystal, not realizing until then how precious her company was in the tunnel. She wills her to open her eyes and stand up—facing Gia alone is too much. But then she remembers Crystal saying, *You're fearless, you know.* With great effort, Melanie looks back at Gia.

"Are you going to kill me?"

"Do you *wish* to die?"

"N-no."

"I assumed so. Most people don't."

"Then…why are you here?"

"To help you, of course."

"Why would you want to *help* me?"

Gia throws back her head and cackles, her neck bending unnaturally before it snaps back into place. She lifts a hand, snaps, and Crystal's body rises from the ground, a plume of gray mist supporting her spine. "That's very humorous of you. Mortimer did not mention you liked jokes," Gia says in singsong. "Shall we go on together?"

Melanie wavers, unsure if this is a guise to lure her further. She takes her chances and, keeping one eye on Crystal, begins walking. "Where does this passageway lead?"

"Don't you know?" Gia frowns. "You are the one who found it after all."

"Well…sure. But I'm…" Melanie clears her throat. "I'm just having trouble remembering the way."

Gia flutters forward, her toes now suspended inches in the air. When she brushes against her, Melanie's stomach plummets, a physical reaction to undiluted dread. Gia must be made of the stuff, her muscle fibers and skin cells stitched together from all the evil of the house—death in many different textures.

"Of course," she says. "I quite understand. The Manor is vast, and the secret tunnels often shift. Follow me. I was dying for a chance for us to be alone."

Melanie can tell Gia means for these words to be not only comforting but encouraging, and yet she's even more afraid than before. *Alone? Why does she want to be alone with me?* Kindness coming from a black-eyed phantom doesn't feel warm nor inviting—it feels like a trap.

But still, she follows Gia's flowing body for a moment, then, afraid of the silence, Melanie forces out a question. "Why do the tunnels shift?"

"Oh, growing pains. The Manor has become much larger over the years. I swear, it adds a story for every dozen people it consumes."

At this, Melanie is overcome with dizziness. For a moment she's able to step outside of this moment and look at the bigger picture. If ghosts and monster houses exist in real life, what else is real? What other terrible things mingle among them? She thinks of the house she grew up in, picturing the light-gray front porch, the big chestnut door and bright, cheerful lemon-scented entry hall. What if *it* was alive, too?

Although, if Cynthia owned a man-eating house, Melanie has no doubt a few of the "unfavorable" neighbors would have "disappeared" by now.

"Are you all right?" Gia stops and turns. Earlier this would have sounded like a caring inquiry. But as she is now, it comes like a taunt.

"I'm fine," Melanie manages to gasp. "Just…tired."

"Understandable. How is your head?"

"My…what?"

"I heard it was quite the fall. Mortimer is never shy about blood, but he said the amount you spilled took even him by surprise. Head wounds, I suppose. Always the worst."

Melanie grazes a finger over the mark on her forehead.

It dawns on her that Gia must know exactly what happened that night between her and Mortimer. She could ask. But something makes her think she's supposed to already know. Gia acts like the two share a secret—and that secret is the only thing keeping Melanie safe.

"Here's the doorway." Gia stops and snaps her fingers.

The grating sound of metal scraping against stone indicates she's telling the truth. A door reveals itself, opening so that a sliver of bright light is revealed. The mist under Crystal evaporates, and she hits the ground, her white hair cascading over her face as her head lolls to the side. Melanie drops on all fours.

Gia sounds bored. "Don't worry about her. She'll wake when I go."

"You're not staying?"

"No, I'm afraid not. Mortimer warned me not to meddle. That's your job. Now go and bring *her* back."

Without warning, her skin peels back like the skin of an onion, flaky and translucent. She stands smiling as her body is torn apart layer by layer until she's completely gone.

"Wait!" Melanie calls to the empty air. "What do you mean, that's my job?"

Suddenly, Crystal gulps and sits up, her chest heaving.

"You're okay! You're fine!" Melanie calms her as best she can.

"Am I...? Am I...?" Crystal touches her chest, face, and arms, like she can't believe she's still there.

"It's okay! You're..." Melanie starts to say, *You're safe*, but she stops herself because that would be a lie. "You're okay." When Crystal's breathing evens out, Melanie quickly explains what just happened.

"Gia was here?" Crystal jerks her head around and then rubs the necklace of black-and-blue bruises around her throat. "What did she mean by 'bring her back'?"

"I don't know." Pausing, Melanie admits, "I thought you were... gone. Really, I wasn't... I didn't know if... I'm really glad you're okay."

Melanie has always favored being alone, even in the worst times. It was something Petra never understood about her, always offering to *be there* for Melanie after a Cynthia blowup when Melanie just wanted to hide alone.

But now Crystal's presence is a warm relief. Melanie never thought she'd feel this way, especially about someone like Crystal. But maybe the manor changes things; maybe it's already changing her.

Crystal sags back onto the ground and stares at the ceiling. "I don't know if I can keep going, Mel. It's like…what's the point? Wouldn't you rather just die here and now rather than jump through a hundred more horrifying hoops? I—Why are you smiling?"

*Mel.* It's the most ridiculous thing, but hearing it feels like having a warm blanket draped across her shoulders.

"I… It's stupid."

"What's stupid?" Her palms touch her cheeks, feeling them heat up.

"I've never had a nickname. Not even from my own sister. And you guys keep calling me 'Mel.' It's…nice."

For a minute, Crystal stares at her like she's crazy. Then she, too, cracks a smile. "All right, *Mel.* Let's keep going, I guess."

After pulling each other to their feet, both of them grip the cold iron handle and tug. Metal scrapes against concrete before Melanie is nearly blinded by what she sees.

It's a large room filled with fluorescent lights overhead; the walls are so white, she has to cup a hand over her brows until her eyes can adjust. Along the glossy floors are massage tables, plushy chairs with footbaths, a rolling cart of nail polish, rubbing alcohol, clippers, and cotton balls, and there's a massive marble granite tub in the center of the room. It's slightly raised, sitting over a coal-filled fire; flames flirt with the edges of the bath, skirting up the sides.

In it, Winnie Roach is all but submerged, her head resting against the lip of the bath, two cucumbers on her eyes.

*Is it really her? Winnie? No, she's dead. She jumped… She…* Melanie stares hard, considering that this might be a trap. Back when she entered the secret passageway, she was so sure of herself. Now she doesn't know what to do. Among the Manor's strange decrepit rooms, the modernity of this one is terrifying.

"Winnie?" she whispers hoarsely, making her way to the tub.

"Is she…?"

The same horrifying thought crosses Melanie's mind too late as she extends a hand to shake Winnie awake. What if her skin is cold to the touch? What if the cucumbers fall off, revealing a blank, vacant stare? What if she's…?

Winnie screams, bolting upright and splashing hot lavender suds on them. She stares wide-eyed at Melanie, then glances down at her naked bright pink chest.

"What am I doing in a bathtub?" she shrieks.

"I don't know!" Melanie matches her volume.

"What are you doing here? What's happening?" Winnie continues to screech.

"We don't know!" Crystal has two hands over her ears. "Please stop! You're freaking us out!"

Winnie's eyes bug so big, Melanie thinks they might pop out and bob in the bathwater. "I'm freaking *you* out? Good lord!"

Melanie grabs a magenta robe hanging on the wall and gives it to her, and Winnie burrows in its soft material.

"Where am I? What happened?" She pats her face, chest, waist, and knees like she's taking inventory. "I don't…I don't understand."

"You jumped through the floor!" Melanie reminds her. "In the entry hall. You said you were going to look for Felix. We tried to stop you…"

"Oh." Winnie's breathing evens. "I… Right. I heard his voice." She swallows. "And then I…I remember being led here. And someone…the walls…the walls told me to take a bath."

"The walls?" Crystal repeats, exchanging a glance with Melanie. "Was the Manor talking to you?"

"I think so. I don't remember anything after that." Winnie looks toward the tub. "Where is everybody else? Are they...?"

"Scott and Buck, they're still alive."

"Chester is...?" She swallows. "I see. What do we do now?"

Melanie remembers Gia's last words to her and gestures to the door at the other side of the room. "We bring you back."

# Scott Clay

"Y A SHOULDN'T TAKE it to heart."

"I'm not."

"They were gonna do what they wanted to do, regardless of what we told 'em. Nan always said, 'People are gonna ride their own river no matter the current.'"

"Buck, I really can't stomach another one of your grandma's proverbs."

It's been exactly eight minutes since Melanie and Crystal abandoned them, striking into the secret passageway without any regard for Scott's warnings. He stares into the darkness, waiting and watching for a sign that the girls are coming back.

"I'm just sayin', this ain't the Mystery, Inc., and you ain't Fred Jones."

"Since when does Fred have a last name?"

"That ain't the point. I know you see yourself as the leader of this group, but—"

"I'm not leading anyone," Scott snaps. "I wanted to give them a chance to change their minds, that's all. And it looks like they're not coming, so…" After lingering a moment longer, he finally tears himself away and stalks toward the door.

This is why Scott doesn't stay connected with his family nor hang around friends anymore. No matter how much you try, you can't make people stay. Can't *make* them do anything, really. People don't do as he says, they get hurt, and he gets angry.

He opens the wooden door, the top rounded in an arch. All these entrances and exits are different styles—some massive and metal, and others, like this one, smaller and cabin-like. Back when his novels were raking in cash, he considered himself somewhat of an architecture enthusiast and spent thousands of dollars at old estate sales. There's an obscure neighborhood on the outskirts of New York City designed in the nineteenth-century Beaux Arts era being torn down. It's a style based on grandeur and authority. Some of the greatest buildings in the United States fall in that category: the Library of Congress, the Met, Grand Central Terminal. When he had the funds to do so, Scott collected bits and pieces of these old neighborhood houses. He has an entire room in his apartment dedicated to festoons, slabs of stone, sections of broken pillars, and chipped statues of Roman gods and goddesses. It doesn't matter what it is, as long as it falls within the parameters of the Beaux Arts style. Consistency gives him room to breathe.

And these doors are definitely *not* consistent.

Beyond the archway are stone stairs unevenly set like rows of crooked teeth. Just to prove a point, Scott starts climbing without waiting for Buck. *Fred Jones, my ass*, he thinks. But then he hears the clomp, clomp of the large man limping and remembers he's down one toe, he offers an arm with a sigh.

As they get closer to the top, he leans down to inspect the stone, which is now covered in thick green moss. *What the…?* The door at the top is draped in foliage, and Scott barely finds the doorknob through a tangled clump of ivy.

When he shoulders through to the other side, he starts to think Melanie and Crystal had the right idea.

"Well, I'll be a possum in a persimmon tree," Buck exclaims. "I ain't never seen anything like this."

Scott is too stunned to respond. Because he's now face-to-face with shrubbery at least nine feet high, tended and trimmed so it's flat and neat. On the ceilings, heated HID lights stretch as far as he can see, and there's a gap in the center of the shrubs—an entrance.

"It's a maze." Buck bemoans, shaking out his injured foot.

To their left is a collection of garden tools hung on the wall, along with mud-caked boots and a rusty metal sign reading NO SNAILS ALLOWED.

Unlike the other rooms, Scott is confident on what to do here. He's just not sure he wants to.

"Well?" He glances over at his lone companion. "Are we ready?"

"Yeah, only, I wish I knew what we had to be ready for."

Taking a bracing breath, Scott and Buck enter the maze. It's well lit, for the most part, though there's not a lot to see. As they walk down the straight narrow path, the ground slowly transitions from concrete to hard packed dirt, eerily smooth, like no one has walked along this route in ages, if ever.

"Mazes give me the creeps." Buck shivers. He's slow, but Scott doesn't mind the pace. It's probably best they take it easy, keep a sharp eye out for anything strange—like more acid or flesh-eating books. "Every October, Oatmeal has this big fall fair—hayrides, pumpkin patches, funnel cakes, that kinda thing—and of course there was always a cornfield maze."

"You get lost in it as a kid?" Scott says absently, his eyes combing up and down the walls. "Scar you or something?"

"I wish that's all it was." Buck snorts. "Some kids blindfolded me, dragged me in the middle, and then kicked the crap outta me. Left me out there bleedin' and dizzy as hell. Took me ages to crawl out."

"You weren't...um, as large as you are now, as a kid?"

"No, I definitely had size. Towered over most everyone in town by that age."

"I don't understand. Why didn't you fight back?"

"Don't have much of a fightin' spirit. Never did. It's actually why I started reading—I'd hide in the Oatmeal Public Library so no one would pick on me. Kids didn't think I was smart enough to read, so they never looked there."

Scott brushes a hand against the shrub wall, guilt rising within him. Because even though he can hear the stale hurt in Buck's tone, he can't help but think that if he had a son who refused to fight back, he'd be disappointed. And what does that say about him?

Realizing he's waited too long to respond, Scott clears his throat and keeps his voice light. "Well, Buck, that sounds like it was pulled straight out of an uplifting commercial. Like the one where the kid is crying at the breakfast table because he doesn't want to go to school, and his dad pours him a bowl of Cheerios to perk him up."

"Oh yeah. I always hated that kid. And Cheerios."

The two grin at this and keep walking. They come to a fork in the path, and Buck pauses, waiting for Scott to decide. He moves them to the left.

"We should *not* be laughing." Scott sighs, a trace of a smile still playing on his lips.

"Yeah, well, we are. Hey, what was your childhood like?" Buck asks.

"Really?" Scott cocks his head at him. "You're asking about my childhood? Now?"

"Good a time as any."

"Okay...I guess it was good. I wasn't bullied. Had friends. Did well in school. Always had presents under the tree at Christmas." He pauses. "I guess the pebble in my shoe was my dad."

"Classic."

"Right. He, uh, he lost his job when I was young and then started drinking. That wasn't the issue, though—the drinking, I mean. If anything, that's the only reason he stayed around for as long as he did. It's just that he lost interest in stuff. In life, I guess."

They come to another fork, and wordlessly, Scott opts for the left path again. He appreciates that Buck doesn't give him a withering look or say something stupid like, *I'm sorry that happened to you.*

"He leave you and your ma?"

"No, he killed himself."

"Sorta the same thing."

"I guess you're right."

Buck gives a contemplative sniff, and Scott arches his brows.

"I assumed ya got your temper from your daddy," Buck explains. "Most men do. Their dads beat on 'em, so they beat on other people. But it wasn't like that for you, was it?"

"Not at all. Dad was great when he was all there."

"Then why do you think you're so angry?"

Scott chews on this, his gaze set on the fork in the pathway fast approaching. "I honestly don't know. Chemical imbalance probably. I feel like we blame our lineage for too much these days. I know the damaging effects of trauma and all that, but at some point, I think I took ownership of my temper. My shit is my shit, and that's just how it is."

"Mm. Good man."

"But," Scott continues, "if you wanna know why I'm angry now? That's pretty obvious." He gestures around. "And, not that it would make things better, but I might even be less pissed off if Mortimer had a good reason for doing it." He gauges Buck's expression, which his hard to read beneath his beard and bushy brows. "You believe me, right?"

"Does it matter if I do?"

"To me it does. If I die in here, I want to go out with a cleared name."

Buck's left eye twitches—probably trying to hide how much his foot hurts—and says, "The *Times* printed an article a few days ago about Mortimer's upbringing. Did you see it? Sorta a tribute piece."

Scott wishes Buck would stay on point, but he nods. "Yeah, I read it."

"So you know all about how his parents died. He was just eight. They were hiking in the Appalachians when, not just one but both his parents got bitten by a deadly spider. Died within minutes, leaving him out there in the mountains alone."

This is old news to Scott, who heard Mortimer recount it in tons of interviews. After realizing his parents were dead, he climbed up a tree to get a better vantage point but wound up getting stuck because he was too afraid to get down. He stayed there throughout the night and heard a grizzly bear wander over to his parents and... It was a gruesome, horrifying story. Even now, Scott feels bad for eight-year-old Mortimer.

"Yeah. Terrible," he says, then remembers calling this out when they were getting a history lesson from Gia. "Wait—yes. This morning... Remember when Gia said that Regulus was pissed off about *Monster House* being published? I knew that was wrong, but she just skimmed over it."

Buck snorts. "Yeah, noticed that too, did ya? Guess demons can fuck up, too, because she let the truth slip. The story is made up. Not real."

"*What?*"

"I mean, they did get lost in the Appalachians. For a few damn hours. But Mortimer decided on an alternate endin' that worked better with his disturbed-writer brand. His dad died of colon cancer when he was sixty-five, and his mother passed away at the ripe ole' age of a hundred. He was payin' for a cabin in the Alaskan bush up until the day she croaked."

"How do you know? How has no one else caught on?"

"I was his assistant," he says, as if it should be obvious. "I saw everythin'. And I'm sure some people knew—but the ones who did probably preferred this lie 'cause it sold more books. So, yeah, I believe you didn't do anythin'. But I also believe Chester and Petey didn't deserve what they got either."

Scott stiffens. To be grouped in with those two feels wrong. But at least it secures his innocence. For now.

They stop at the point where the path converges left and right. Both look identical, so there's really no good way of picking which one to go down.

"Should we split up?" Buck asks. "Better odds?"

The rock that's already sitting in Scott's stomach somehow sinks lower. He shrugs.

"I'll stay if ya want me to."

"You'll stay?"

"Didn't I just say I would?"

In agreement, they turn right, and the path becomes narrower, the hedges less kept. The leaves thin out and are replaced by twisted, gnarled branches covered in thorns. The air thickens with the stench of rotting roadkill, and Scott is forced to walk with a permanent nose wrinkle. They take a left, a right, and another left.

Scott halts, his heel digging into the dirt. "Oh God." He gags. "What *is* that?"

They've come to a dead end, which would be disappointing as it is, but there's something more disturbing for them where the path ends. A deer carcass speared with a stake stands before them, its arms manipulated so that a wooden sign is propped in its arms. Clumps of fur are missing, along with sections of ribs.

**CAN'T PUT IT DOWN! BUCK GRIMM'S**
*BLOOD BATH* **IS A MUST READ.**

—Agatha Bentley, *New York Times*

"Shit, shit, shit." Scott grabs Buck's shoulders and forcibly moves him back, putting as much space as he can between them and the animal. "Nope. Absolutely not. We're leaving. We. Are. Going."

He wants to brush off what they've seen as a sick prop, a fear tactic by Mortimer Queen, but then they meet another dead end and another deer arranged on two legs, a swarm of maggots swallowing one empty socket. There's a second wooden sign.

**BLOOD BATH IS A MASTERWORK OF BLOOD-POUNDING TWISTS, TURNS, AND RELENTLESS SUSPENSE.**

**—George Harrold, *The Boston Globe***

Buck moans and crouches, letting his head fall into his hands. "It's me this time, ain't it? It's gotta be."

"Hey, hey." Scott tries to yank him up, but it's like pushing a baby elephant back onto its feet. "This is a good thing. Now that we know how this all works, when we find the riddle, we don't have to waste a bunch of time thinking of the answer."

"'Cause it's me."

"Well, yeah. From context clues, it looks like it's gonna be you." Scott hesitates. "What did you do to Mortimer?"

A buzzing ripples through the air, like an old-fashioned timer sounding when the oven is done. Before Scott has even dropped his hands from his ears, the lights above them shut off, plunging them into darkness.

It's a curious thing what the dark makes you do when it comes so abruptly. Even though he's lost his sight, Scott's knee-jerk reaction is to run. Blindly. Maybe it makes him feel less of a target if he's moving, or maybe, subconsciously, he thinks he can outrun the blackness. Either way, he's wrong. He crashes into the wall of branches, and thorns tear through his flesh like it's wet paper until he's fixed in one place like an animal snared in a hunter's trap.

"Help!" He tries to yank himself out but feels the thorns dig deeper into his thigh.

"Hold still, hold still!" Buck commands from somewhere behind him. "I'm gonna remove ya limb by limb. This is gonna hurt, but no more than if you tried to rip yourself out all at once."

Scott feels hot tears rush down his cheeks, the salt stinging fresh cuts there. He momentarily surrenders, allowing Buck to carefully maneuver his limbs around the brambles. "Hurry," he whimpers. "Please."

A few minutes feels like eons, but finally he steps out of the thorn trap and falls to his knees. He can't tell what part of his body is hurt and what was spared because it all radiates with pain. His legs and arms are slick with hot liquid—his own blood.

"C'mon," Buck grunts in his ear. "I'm used to huntin' at night, so I can see a little bit. You hold on to me, and we'll get through this."

Scott staggers to his feet and tries to ignore how bending his skin—moving his legs, swinging his arms—makes the cuts split open even more. They move along, quickly stumbling upon a three-way intersection. Despite the walls and lack of windows, a chill wind has picked up, confirming for Scott that nothing about this place follows the laws of logic.

"Wait, I just remembered something," he says, though they don't stop hobbling forward. "God damn it. I'm an idiot. The right-hand method!"

"Eh?"

"It's a kind of algorithm. If you follow the wall to your right, only making right turns, you're bound to get to the exit of the maze."

"Why is that?"

"No idea. But I've been making left turns this whole goddamn time."

It takes him three more right-hand turns to remember that he got that tidbit from one of his dad's old presidential autobiographies. Who was the avid puzzler? Bill Clinton? Regardless, the method is working.

They haven't run into a dead end in at least fifteen minutes. Hope, an unfamiliar feeling, creeps up Scott's spine. Maybe, against all odds, they can escape.

"I see it!" Buck crows. "I see the end!"

"Thank God!"

Scott feels Buck lurch to a stop.

"What? What's wrong?" Scott paws at the air. "Why aren't we going? I thought you said—"

The ceiling screams with an explosion of light, and Scott has to cover his eyes. But even when his vision has returned, he's sure it's been damaged somehow because what stands in front of him can't be there.

A huge deer with bulky, muscular shoulders and milky-white eyes blocks one of the two pathways before them. It has a massive crown of antlers with bloody strips of deer skin hanging off the sharpened tips. Past the animal—if it is really still an animal and not some kind of demon—Scott can see the end of the maze, a clearing, a door. The other pathway is clear, but it's obviously the wrong choice.

The deer stamps a foot and slowly turns its head, cockeyed. Then it stands. Not in the kind of wobbly, humorous way a dog might get on two feet, but in one confident, swift movement. The deer straightens, towering over them. On its belly is a wooden sign nailed into the skin.

**DOESN'T FEEL NICE TO BE FORCED
INTO SOMETHING, DOES IT?**

"He never wanted us to finish the maze." Buck bows his head. "We're going to die in here. And it's all my fault."

"What are you—"

"Blackmail, Scott. Mortimer thinks I blackmailed him. That's why I'm here. I stopped by the office after hours to pick up somethin' from the printer and walked in on him and Crystal."

Scott can't take his eyes off the deer as he processes this new information. "So you blackmailed him with his affair?"

Instead of appearing defensive like Scott expected, Buck's face bunches up with hurt and horror. "No! I would never do somethin' like that! I...I told him later on that Liotta was a lovely woman and that... and that he should shit or get off the pot. Somethin' like that."

"Then how is that blackmail?"

"I...It was jus' bad timin', that's all. I asked him for help with my manuscript later that week. There was a deal he needed to sign." His eyes bulged as something visibly clicks in his brain. "Dear lord, I actually said, 'I would love your help so I don't have to seek other options.' To him, that probably sounded like a threat. But I never meant it. I could never..."

The dirt beneath Scott's feet seems to soften and drag his shoes farther into the mud. But it's not another trick sucking him through the ground—no, what's really weighing him down is the realization that time is almost up and there's no way out.

One of them is going to die.

# Winnie Roach

ONCE IN A blue moon, Winnie will lock herself in her townhome, hide her car keys, cell phone, and laptop, and drink an entire bottle of pinot grigio.

Most of the time she wakes up in bed with a splitting headache, a sweating glass of ice water mercifully waiting on the bedside table (she always remembers to leave one for her hungover self), but other times she ends up strewn across the living room couch like a drunken teenager who came home late from a high school party.

She read somewhere that making mistakes in life is inevitable, so she'd prefer to make the most common one among women her socioeconomic circle—drinking to excess—on her terms. Because blacking out in public is not only embarrassing, it's dangerous. Not because doing so is bad for your liver and all that, but because when you get to that level, you lose control. People who drink so much that they forget what happened the night prior are usually the ones who let secrets slip, and she has too many of those to risk.

So, even when Winnie gets shaken awake, practically boiling in a tub full of lavender bath salts, she's confident she didn't black out. Not from drinking, anyway. She nursed a single glass of wine at dinner, bringing it to her lips and letting the wine sit there without truly sipping. And in the entry hall, she felt fully alert, if a bit dazed from all the insanity happening. She was sharp and clearheaded even when she dropped below the floor to find Felix.

But now her mind is an empty void. Her last memory is a stomach flip-flopping sensation as she leaped into the abyss. Now here she is, standing underneath a ladder in a fuzzy magenta robe, Melanie and Crystal on either side of her with grim expressions. She rubs the back of her head, finding the tips of her hair damp with bathwater. There's no aching nor bump on her skull that would explain the lapse of memory from point A to point B.

She bunches her toes in the fur-lined slippers Melanie found back in the salon. When the three women walked out the door, the first thing they saw—the only thing—was the ladder. Winnie trusts it as much as the belt around her robe, which she tightens yet again as it slips loosely around her waist.

"We have to go up this way? It doesn't look like it leads anywhere." She gulps, rubbing the remaining lipstick off her mouth. Even knowing the color is there irritates her. Why did she put on so much makeup before coming to a will reading in the first place? She'll never wear this color again as long as she lives—*if* she lives.

"Yes," Melanie says. Winnie doesn't remember her being so confident. "I bet there's a trapdoor that'll take us to the next floor. Maybe we'll find Scott and Buck."

Winnie has nothing. No ideas, no memories, no clothes, and no Felix. And at this point, no pride, because she simply nods at Melanie, who starts the climb.

Crystal follows. And when Winnie grabs the first rung, her hands shake on the wood, orange dust staining her palms. What if no one had found her? Woken her up? She would have stayed in that tub, shriveling until she became a dead, old raisin.

"Crystal," she starts while she climbs. "I just wanted to….to apologize to you. Before I jumped, I…I believe I was unkind to you. And you were right after all. It was stupid of me."

Above her, Crystal replies, "Maybe not. You didn't have to go through the acid, which is a huge bonus."

Winnie's foot almost slips on a wrung. "The *what?*"

"You don't want to know more than that, trust me."

Melanie's voice comes from farther up. "I found a door!" She bangs on something—metal? And she rattles what sounds like a latch.

Light pours over them. Winnie doesn't stop climbing until her head is through the ceiling, poking up into a completely new room. Her nostrils are filled with the pungent smells of dirt and greenery. A second later, she's scooped from beneath her armpits and whisked into the air by a pair of strong arms. Her chest practically bursts as she's squeezed.

Buck's beard scratches against her cheek. "Mercy sakes alive! I never thought I'd see you again!"

He eventually sets her down, her slippers sinking into cold, moist earth. He's beaming at her, his hair matted with dried sweat and dirt. Overall, though, he looks thrilled.

Scott, on the other hand, resembles Carrie after a bucket of pig guts gets dumped on her at the prom. Winnie hisses through her teeth at the sight of him, and he stares back with just as much astonishment.

"You're alive!" he utters. "I can't believe it! What happened to you?"

"I could ask you the same question!" She goes to touch his blood-slick arm but can't bring herself to make contact. "Are you…? You're not okay."

Even though she hasn't even brushed his skin, he winces. "I've been better. Got caught in the thorns." His eyes fall on Melanie and Crystal, who are being smothered by Buck's bear hug. "I'm so glad to see you all again. I wish we had better news to give you, but we're currently… stuck."

Crystal rushes forward and throws her arms around him. He clenches his teeth, pain etching his face, but returns the hug, placing a hand on the back of her head to hold her there. When he removes it, Crystal's white hair is stamped with red.

*Love. At a time like this?* Winnie thinks dizzily. Looking at Scott now, she finds the silly infatuation she had for him has dried up. Instead, all her focus is drawn inward to her *own* safety. *I'll get us out*, she promises herself. *I'll take care of us.*

Scott jerks his head behind them, and that's when Winnie turns to see a mammoth deer standing on two legs, its eyes glazed over with a milky foam. While it doesn't seem to even be considering coming at them, she tries to run, her feet slipping in the mud. She skitters cartoonishly in place, Buck holding her before she falls.

"What the hell is *that*?" Crystal takes three steps back, her face ashen.

"*That* is Mortimer's idea of irony." Buck is calm, like a man accepting his own fate. "We can't get past it, and the exit is on the other side."

Winnie almost wishes she were still lying in the tub. A clump of the animal's skin falls off like a handful of clay, revealing a rib cage. A sign is nailed onto its stomach, but the words are nonsensical to her. How she can be expected to *read* when this…this *thing* is standing in front of her? A bitter taste rises in the back of her throat. Why couldn't Buck and Scott have figured this all out *before* she got there?

The only time she tears her gaze away from the deer is to survey their surroundings; they're walled in with tall thorny branches, an open path leading into a hovering murky mist. The other path is…not so open.

"Did you find Felix?" Buck asks, his eyes wide with pure intentions, even though the answer to his question should be obvious.

"No." Winnie brushes her hands anxiously against the robe's soft material. "I don't remember anything, in case you were going to ask. Melanie and Crystal found me. Felix is... You all were right."

"I'm real sorry, Winnie."

A lump forms in her throat. She knows she deserves no sympathy. Felix's death is on *her* hands. When she gets out, the press will have a field day. His photo will be thrown up everywhere, splashed along shiny pages of magazines right next to the latest tax-evasion scandal. She's monetized tragedy before and never thought twice. But Felix? Her friend? It's too much to contemplate.

"I'm sorry, too." Her eyes still track the rotting deer until Scott's voice pulls her away.

"Are you okay? Did you get hurt at all?" He leans close to Crystal's face so their foreheads are practically touching. Her shoulders sag, and Winnie can tell she's refraining from crying.

"I'm fine," Crystal whispers. "I...I'm sorry for leaving."

"Don't apologize." He gestures at Melanie. "You made a good choice."

"Scott, we saw Gia—I mean, I didn't, but Melanie did."

He swings his head, looking at her for an explanation.

"She didn't say a lot," comes her reply. "I think she was checking to see who was left. I don't know. She didn't tell me anything."

Winnie blinks rapidly. What jars her more than hearing Gia reappeared is how rushed Melanie's answer is. Since when does she ever respond so quickly and with that much...gusto?

She's hiding something.

"Great," Scott growls. "Well, I hope she comes back. I'd love to wrap my hands around her neck—"

Winnie tunes out the rest of his threat. She looks at the hot lights above; a long humming noise comes from their bulbs. Suppose there's faulty wiring and an electric fire starts? This room is a tinderbox waiting to ignite.

People underestimate fire. They play with it so freely, lining precariously hung shelves with candles, leaving roaring hearths unsupervised, and cranking up stoves until flames lick dangerously up the sides of pots and pans.

A town house is especially susceptible to fire. Winnie's, for example, is part of a long row of homes wedged together. If one goes down, it's likely the others are soon to follow. It's this fact that made her knock on Mortimer's door that one fall day. She'd just come home from a lunch with the girls when she saw smoke coming from his town house's front window, which was slightly cracked open. It wasn't an alarming amount, but it was enough to cause concern. When Mortimer didn't answer the door, her alarm turned to full-blown panic.

"Mr. Queen? Mr. Queen, are you in there? It's Winnie, your neighbor. I see some smoke. Is everything okay? Hello?"

The doorknob twisted easily in her hand, and she breezed into the house, continuing to shout. Her lungs filled with smoke, and she hacked violently into her curled fist, her eyes streaming as she blinked through the haze. The town house was set up identically to her own, its living room and kitchen open concept, so she could see everything: A woman fussed at the stove, her back to Winnie. A blackened pot overflowed with a terra-cotta-colored sauce. A burnt casserole sat in the oven, illuminated by the peekaboo light. A trail of smoke snaked through the kitchen and out the front window.

Before Winnie could call out louder than the overhead fan, the woman turned, spotted her standing there, and dropped a tray of sliced red potatoes.

"I'm so sorry!" Winnie said, rushing forward and scooping them up. She doubted the woman would want to serve them, but it seemed like the polite thing to do. "I didn't mean to barge in! I saw smoke, and the door was unlocked and… Are you all right?"

The woman, still standing, put a hand to her mouth and chewed her fingernails. She shook her head. "It's no use... I've gone and ruined it. I don't know what I thought... That I could rescue this...this pathetic excuse for an evening..."

Her eyes glistened with tears, and when she moved her hand, Winnie saw a busted lip and a dandelion-yellow bruise.

Abandoning the potatoes, she stood and touched the woman's arm gently. "Hey... Hey...it's going to be okay. Although I—erm—I might put this out. Hang on." She removed the angry pot from its spot on the stove and turned off the oven. Then she flapped a hand towel about, ushering some smoke away. "Why"—*cough*—"didn't your"—*cough*— "smoke alarms"—*cough*—"go off?"

The woman bit the inside of her cheek. "I turned them off. They wouldn't stop *beeping* while I was trying to *fix* everything, and it was distracting."

"That's rather dangerous, you know!"

"I know." The woman began sobbing, and Winnie drooped the towel to rush to her side again. "My h-husband is g-going to be s-so angry with me!"

Winnie eyed the woman's bruises. "Are you Mortimer's wife?"

She rubbed the back of her hand against her nose and straightened, as if the name spurred her to collect herself. "I'm Liotta Queen. I'm sorry for all this. You must think I'm crazy."

"No! Well, maybe a bit crazy about fire."

"I was in the middle of making dinner when he called and yelled—I mean, he... We just got into a bit of a spat over the phone. It rattled me some, and I lost control of everything." She bit her lip, which seemed especially painful, considering it was scabbed over. "I can't believe I let it get this bad."

Winnie wondered what Liotta was referring to: the dinner or the marriage. "I'm sure he'll understand," she said with unrequited confidence. "It was an accident."

Liotta gripped the kitchen counter. "*No*. You don't get it. He'll kill me for this."

"Then I'll help." Winnie pushed up the sleeves of her Calvin Klein kaftan blouse. "Tell me where to start."

"I couldn't do that to you… You're a perfect stranger, and I—"

Ignoring her protests, Winnie bent down and continued scooping up the potatoes.

From there they cooked wordlessly together for the next hour, Winnie trying not to think about the fact she was helping prepare a meal for a man only so he wouldn't beat his wife. In the same way a blacksmith would build his knight a shield with plenty of strong steel, Winnie spiced and salted a new eggplant casserole to perfection. *No* man could be angry after having a slice.

She left Liotta mere minutes before Mortimer got home for supper—she knows because she was peering through her own window and watched him walk up his front steps, a deep-set frown carved onto his gray face. On four separate occasions, Winnie picked up the phone and debated calling over there (the HOA had given out a directory with all their numbers in case of emergency), but she chickened out every time. She saw Liotta again only one other time, at a French restaurant a block away from the townhomes. Felix and Winnie were waiting for their table as Mortimer and Liotta were walking out, bellies probably full of bouillabaisse and hazelnut dacquoise. The two women exchanged looks, Liotta smiling warmly before her husband grunted at her to hurry along. She looked like a dog whose collar was being tugged just a bit too tightly.

That was it. Liotta was dead a few weeks later when her pancreatic cancer made a surprising and aggressive reappearance, according to the *New York Times*.

Although Winnie's memory of the past hour is gone, this one is as vibrant as ever.

"I can't believe we got this far," Crystal says, still lingering with Scott. Winnie spies that their hands are interlaced. "We're so close. It's so...so frustrating that we might...we might..."

Winnie half expects Chester to finish with, *die? in a chiding tone,* before remembering he's already gone.

Scott looks down at Crystal, biting his lower lip. Winnie can see the gears turning in his head. He turns to address them. "When you see an opening, you need to run," he instructs firmly. "If I don't follow, then leave me behind. Do not come back."

Crystal scowls. "What are you—"

"Do. Not. Come. Back," he orders. "You have to do what I say."

Without a moment of hesitation, he runs headfirst toward the deer. Crystal screams, but it's not loud enough to drown out the thud as Scott's body collides with the animal. It kicks and roars as he pulls it into a headlock, dragging it aside until there's an opening in the path. Beyond, a few feet away, is a large copper door.

Winnie shoves Crystal's back and shouts, "Go!" which sets the group in motion. Buck leaps on one foot, his face red with concentration, while Crystal and Melanie charge forward. Winnie's arms flail as she runs. *God, is this how exercise feels?* She fleetingly frets that her heart might burst from pumping. When the four of them reach the door, the search begins for a handle. But there's none in sight. Winnie drags her nails down its metal, determined to inflict pain on the Manor for all this.

A howl of pain ripples through the room, and she whirls around to see Scott on his back, the deer spearing its antlers into his chest. She screams, watching as he grapples at the animal's neck before giving it a hard jerk. The snap is audible. When the deer collapses in a heap, Scott pants, drops his arms to his side, and stares up at the ceiling.

Crystal, Melanie, and Buck race to his side, but Winnie can't stomach getting any closer. She can smell Scott's blood—rusty and warm like old pennies left in a car cupholder.

When Buck hoists Scott up, maneuvering his arm so that it slings over the back of his neck, relief settles over her. Until she sees his slack face, an ill grayish hue. The color is even more startling against the deep-red blood blossoming on his chest.

Seeing her shock, Buck addresses her, his voice tight. "He'll be fine. I can help him the rest of the way."

"That's... He's... There's no way he'll make it through—" Winnie stammers.

Buck glares into her so fiercely that she stops midsentence. "He'll. Be. Fine."

"I'm okay," Scott wheezes, taking them all by surprise. "I can walk. Lemme go."

Crystal, rather than dissolving into tears like Winnie expects, charges forward like a bloodhound, searching the area around the door.

"Where's the riddle?" She demands, like one of them might be hiding it from her.

After a few minutes of searching, Buck readjusts Scott's weight and says, "Ya know what I think? I think the maze *was* the riddle. And I already know the answer." Scott grimaces, his eyes glazing over for a moment before blinking rapidly. "It's me. Mortimer thought I black-mailed him. 'Sss why I'm here."

"We need something to write with." Crystal scans the ground, doing everything she can not to focus on Scott. "Why are you all just standing there? *Help* me!"

The smell of blood is making Winnie's head spin. *Wait. That's it.*

She takes two steps toward Scott, and with an apologetic grimace, she presses a finger onto his wound. He screams as the fresh liquid pools, dripping down Winnie's wrist. Buck yanks him away, roaring indignantly. Winnie ignores him, approaches the door, and drags a finger along its cool metal, writing Buck's name in huge dripping letters.

She stands back to survey her work.

And from somewhere in the center of the maze comes the only consistency they've experienced since stepping foot in the Manor:

*GONG.*

*GONG.*

*GONG.*

*GONG.*

# Short Story #4

### Buck Grimm

"This ain't right."

Buck Grimm stands at the Starbucks coffee counter with a grimace hidden by his beard. He holds two paper travel cups, trying to force one back into the teenage barista's hands.

"Sorry?" The girl—Tabatha according to her name tag—itches her head underneath her green uniform visor and steps away from Buck's arm extending over the counter.

"I ordered a venti dark roast with half decaf," he says, shifting his bulky frame. "This is a light roast."

Tabatha purses her lips.

"I recognize the smell," he explains, reading her thoughts. "I need you to do it over—and do it right this time."

She sighs and takes the drink back, then sets about making a new cup. It could just be the wee hours getting to him or the sound of the coffee grinder triggering a migraine, but he thinks

Tabatha is copping an attitude—slamming things around and stomping to and from the dark roast pot. Irritation fiddles with the wires in Buck's brain, which has yet to be kickstarted with whiskey yet.

Buck turns his head and apologizes to the growing line behind him for making them wait, even if it's not his fault. A few people huff, and one man checks his watch. Buck usually steers clear of confrontation and public scenes, but a line of caffeine-starved young professionals is nothing compared to an enraged Mortimer Queen when his order is wrong. The last time Buck made that error and brought him a latte with soy foam instead of almond foam, Mortimer made him respond to fan mail for twenty-four hours straight, by hand. His wrist has never fully recovered.

Tabatha reappears with the correct drink (he inhales the steam rising from the lid just to be sure) and puts a hand on her hip, as if getting impatient with *him*. "Please move out of the way."

"It's pretty indecent of ya not even to say sorry." He grits his teeth. "Ain't you never heard of common courtesy? Now you're whole attitude nearly ruined my mornin'."

"Mm-hmm. So sorry. I really hope things get better for you."

Buck can't help but huff, his Nan's voice in his ears. *Lousy city folk got no manners.* He storms out of the Starbucks and gets into his truck, then sets all four mismatched wheels moving into reverse. He hastily drops Mortimer's order in the cupholder, ignoring how it splashes over the sides, and pulls a silver flask out of the center console. After checking out the windows first, he tilts it into his coffee and takes a quick sip. The liquid runs down his throat and settles into his belly with a warm purr.

A lot of people think drinking and driving is dangerous because it dulls the senses, but those people can't handle their liquor. He's more alert than ever as he peels out of the parking lot, drumming his fingers against the dashboard as the radio blares "Workin' Man Blues" by Merle Haggard.

He doesn't consider himself an alcoholic, but he's self-aware enough to know that he should be ashamed of the two shots of Buffalo Trace in his morning coffee. *Should.* But certainly isn't.

His mother's many addictions drove her to the grave: booze, pills, gambling—you name it. It would be logical to fear replicating her life, since they share the same genes and all, but dying isn't what bothers him. Being a coward does, because that's exactly what he is. He's terrified to be sober, because it's then that he starts pondering life and the meaning of it and how much time he's wasted being a nobody. He could quit drinking at any time; he knows that for a fact. Booze doesn't call to him like it did to his mother.

Nah, alcohol isn't his demon; it's merely a crutch. Ever since he accepted a job as Mortimer Queen's assistant, life has been like a rodeo bull with its balls tied too tight. So he drinks. A lot.

He pulls into the parking lot of Deacon's Group where Mortimer has his very own office. It's a bit unheard of for an author to claim territory at their publishing house, but Buck is pretty sure no one is fearless enough to tell Mortimer no. Sure, this is partly because of his wealth, but it's also just…Mortimer.

The front desk attendant nods at Buck as he hurries through the DG lobby toward the elevator. He presses the Up button and checks his watch while struggling to keep his shoulder bag from sliding down his arm and jostling the coffee around. By the time he gets to Mortimer's floor, his palms are pink with small burns.

The fifteenth floor—known in the building as the Crypt, a

excruciatingly long moment before turning to face the window again. "We'll discuss repercussions at the end of the day." Even the back of his head glowers.

"Sir, I'm real sorry—"

"Go. Now." His voice rises a few octaves.

"Yes, sir," Buck says quickly, drying his clammy hands on his beard.

He sets the whiskey-free coffee on Mortimer's desk and snatches the tainted one before running out of the room, tripping on his own massive loafers. He feels the rest of the Crypt dwellers watch as he hurries, keeping his head down, to his cubicle. He squeezes himself into his chair and hunches over his computer, practically smothering the mouse with his giant hand.

"Oh fuck, oh fuck, oh fuck," he mutters in a hushed panic and presses two fingers into his eyelids. The pressure feels like it could pop his eyeballs out of their sockets like peeled grapes, but the pain is a good distraction. "Jesus Christ. Oh lordy. Nan, help me."

He's got to be fired. Mortimer is just dragging out his suffering for an entire day, the sadistic bastard. There's no way around it—no one survives being caught drinking at work. It's a dumb rule anyway. In Oatmeal, everyone drank. He once saw Father Obermeyer crack a Hamm's beer at Sunday service. Maybe if Mortimer threw back a shot or two during the day, he wouldn't walk around like a stick is shoved up his ass.

*Cool it, Buck*, he thinks. *Settle your engines before you go and start a fire.*

He ditches the coffee in the garbage, but not before he chugs the rest of it. Sure, he could get in even more trouble, but there's no way he'll be able to stomach an entire day without more

whiskey in his system. He leans back in his chair, his back cracking in three different places. Should he retaliate before Mortimer
can strike? Shit in his office? Draw a penis in the bathroom?

A voice behind his shoulder makes him jump. "Hey, Buck?
You got a second?" It's Georgia Deerwood, an associate publisher for Deacon's Group.

He wheels his chair around to face her and stands. He does
this whenever a woman enters the space. "Mornin'," he says
nervously. "How are you, ma'am?"

"I've told you, Buck, you can cut the 'ma'am' bit." Georgia
smiles. "It makes me feel old. Am I interrupting anything?"

"No! I mean, no." He lowers his voice, knowing he gets loud
when he's nervous. And drunk. Is he nervous or drunk or both?
"What can I help ya with?"

"It's about your manuscript," Georgia says. "I got a chance
to read it over the weekend and...well, Buck..."

He fidgets with the button threatening to pop from his
collared shirt.

"It's amazing. Truly, I couldn't put it down."

"Thank you so much." His spirits soar. "I truly appreciate
that."

"We want to publish it," Georgie says outright, not beating
around the bush. Her grin is wide and genuine, like she's just
offered a kid a trip to Disney World. And she might as well have.

"I... Oh my God." He laughs, pressing his palms together
as if he's praying to Nan again and holding them to his lips. "Are
you serious?"

"Dead serious," she says. "I can't believe you've waited this
long to bring this to me. It's going to be a hit, Buck."

In truth, Buck had tried to show his manuscript to Mortimer
the first day he started working for him, but he was turned away

immediately. *If you only agreed to work for me because you thought it would give you a leg up, I'll fire you now*, Mortimer chastised. Buck tucked his tail between his thick thighs and never brought it up again. *Of course* he only agreed to be an assistant to get a leg up! Why else would he do this?

"I've gotten the go-ahead from everyone on the upper floors," Georgia says, lifting a packet that looks like a contract. It's filled with tiny text and signatures scrawled on the bottom. "All we need is Mortimer's ink, and we're set to get started."

Buck blinks. "M-Mortimer's? No disrespect, ma'am—I mean Georgia—but just out of curiosity, why does he need to sign off on this?"

"Well…" She looks around and leans forward. "This is strictly confidential for now, but Mortimer just bought sixty-six percent of the company." She winks. "Funny, I thought you'd be the first to know."

Buck feels the room swim, and he grabs the cubicle divider for support. But his weight is too much for it, and the wall tumbles down, crashing into Rita Billing's desk. She leaps up from the wreckage, her mouth agape in outrage.

"Sorry! Sorry!" He pulls the slightly bent cubicle wall back into position. "Wow, Georgia. This news is crazier than an over-fed hare at a shooting range."

She keeps her smile, but her eyebrows slant like she's not sure what he's saying.

"Oh! I'm sorry!" he explains quickly. "It's a Southern saying. It just means… It's stupid. Sorry."

When he gets nervous, he gets loud. When he's frantic, he starts spouting Southernisms. When he drinks, he does both these things at full speed, like an inebriated train with a broken whistle.

Georgia hands the paperwork to him. "You should be the

one to tell Mortimer the good news," she says. "I'm sure he'll be thrilled for you. If you could get me his signature by the end of the day, that would be amazing."

"Right." Buck licks his parched lips, wishing he'd brought his flask into the office in his pocket. "That's... I can do that. And thank you again. This really just dills my pickle."

He winces as another one of Nan's sayings slips through. Georgia laughs, repeating the phrase under her breath as she walks away. He's left to stare at the paperwork—his future typed out in black ink—and knows he might as well shred the documents here and now to put himself out of his misery.

And then he remembers.

His last and only ace.

For the rest of the day, he does nothing but stare at his computer and move back and forth from the water cooler to his desk. At lunch he forgoes food and sneaks down to his truck to finish the rest of the whiskey in his flask. When 7:00 p.m. hits, he's the last in the office besides Mortimer.

Buck sends a quick prayer to Nan and heads for Mortimer's office, then knocks twice before entering.

Mortimer sits with his elbows on the desk and his fingers laced together.

"Sir?" Buck asks, though he knows he should just stay quiet until directed to speak. "I don't know if ya heard, but...the other editors on the floor would love to publish my book, *Blood Bath*. I reckon they think it's good and need your signature."

His heart is thrumming in off-kilter beats as he awaits a response. Depending on what Mortimer says, he might have to do something not only incredibly risky but incredibly stupid. The alcohol still burning through his blood helps, though, and he stands firmly in place.

"The truth is," Mortimer begins, not even giving Buck the benefit of eye contact, "you've been a great disappointment to me. I feel cheated. Cheated that I've given you so much opportunity and that you've squandered it to be a worthless drunkard."

*Ouch.* Buck winces, feeling like his chest is being slashed with the iron claw.

"You know, of course, that I'll have to fire you," Mortimer continues flippantly. "You'll receive no pay for today. You can return your passwords and building key to—"

Buck clears his throat. "Actually, sir, before you…*decide* on anything…"

"Decide?" Mortimer chuckles, rubbing the one item on his desk lovingly—a gold box. Buck assumes he keeps it there as a silent message to the rest of the Crypt: *I have trinkets worth more than your soul.* "I've already made my decision."

"I just wanted to give you your messages."

"What are you—"

"Two messages, really. A *Crystal Flowers* called, sir," he says, before Mortimer can cut him off. "She wants to know if she can pack a second checked bag for your trip to London this weekend. She also mentioned that she'd like it if you could book the same couple's massage as last time."

Finally, Mortimer meets Buck's gaze. His pupils take up most of the real estate in his eyes, making them deep pools of tar.

"Now, ain't that the girl who was in here the other night?" Buck can't believe the words coming out of his mouth. "The one half naked, bent over your desk right there?"

"You slimy oaf—"

"Oh, and Liotta called. She just got back from the hospital. Got her stitches out today. Heard she fell down the stairs in that fancy LA home? Ain't it *nice* to have a *nice* wife and *nice* things?"

Mortimer stands, his nostrils flaring. "Don't you dare talk about her! Don't you draw her name across your disgusting hill-billy tongue!"

Buck wobbles a little. Normally, the insult would graze against him, but he's drunk, and the word *hillbilly* has always carried more weight to it than it should.

The two men stare at each other, neither speaking for a long time.

Buck finally hitches his belt and clears his throat. "Look, all I'm sayin' is that I would love your help so I don't have to seek other options."

There. He's said it. The threat hangs there in the air between them like a gutted pig leaking warm blood from its throat.

Mortimer glares, his lips set in a hard line.

"So…" Buck twirls his beard with a finger, getting it momentarily stuck before ripping it out. "What will it be, Mr. Queen?"

A tingle runs down his spine after he says the words, the same kind of sensation he gets after slamming a shot glass down on the bar.

"As I was saying…" Mortimer's growl is no longer threatening, but *threatened*, like a cornered beast. "Congratulations on your book deal."

Buck's eyes bulge before he very gently places the paperwork on the desk in front of Mortimer. Without breaking eye contact, he reaches into his drawer for a pen and slowly carves his signature onto the required line.

"I'm not going to lie, Buck, I didn't think you had it in you."

Buck holds Mortimer's glare, not daring to blink. "I surprised even myself, sir. But people do all kinds of things to get what they want."

He turns and walks out without giving Mortimer an inch of space to reply. The signed contract is purring in his hand, and he caresses the pages lovingly while standing in the elevator. Hell, with the shit he knows, he practically *owns* the most powerful man in the publishing industry. Why stop here?

For some reason, he procures an image of Tabatha standing behind the coffee counter, surveying him with biting disinterest.

This day may have started out rocky, but it got a hell of a lot better.

He'll have to swing by Starbucks tomorrow and let her know.

# Buck Grimm

SOMETIMES PEOPLE DIE for no rhyme or reason. One minute they're walking in the park on a July day, and the next they're keeled over on the dog-poo-littered grass.

The difference is, no one is going to find their bodies here, their missing person cases will go cold. He's not sure exactly how their disappearances will be explained, but Mortimer has proven he can pull strings even from the grave, so Buck doesn't doubt it'll be easily taken care of.

At this point he feels like he's walking through the Manor on a strange high. He tells himself that the things he sees—the upright zombie deer, for one—are merely presented to him as ill side effects of too much cold medicine. That's not the case, and he *knows* that, but the lie is the only thing keeping his feet on the ground. His feet *and* all nine remaining toes.

When the door swings open before them, he debates staying put.

Last winter he was sitting at a bar, drinking a Coke, when a movie started playing on one of the boxy hanging TVs. The bartender told him it was a Christmas classic and seemed offended when Buck admitted he'd never seen it before. It was about a little kid who gets left at home during the holidays and has to protect his house from two clumsy burglars. Honestly, Buck felt empathy for the robbers as the kid led them through a house of blowtorches, hot irons, nails, swinging paint cans, and a tarantula.

After his third Coke, Buck roared at the TV with sugar-fueled indignation, "Stop followin' the kid! That's what they gotta do! He's only leadin' them to more skull crackin'!"

The bartender laughed and gave him another soda on the house. "That wouldn't make it a very good story, would it?"

But this isn't a Christmas movie, and they don't owe the viewers an entertaining plotline. He could stop right here, and no one could do anything about it. Sure, they might plead with him for a minute or so, but eventually, survival instincts would kick in, and they'd leave him behind. He could wait the allotted hour and get chewed up by the prickly branches. Might be a kinder death than what awaits in the next room.

As Crystal and Winnie dart through the copper door, Scott tries to wriggle out of Buck's hold.

"Hang on there," Buck warns. "You better let me—"

Scott pushes him away—weakly, but Buck doesn't fight it.

"I…I can walk." Scott grunts, a hand pressed to his wound. "If I can't walk, I can't…I can't get through this. I need to move."

He hobbles through the doorway. Just as in the entry hall, Melanie lingers behind so that it's just her and Buck left in the greenhouse.

"Prideful idiot," he complains when Scott has gone. "He'd rather die than depend on someone else."

Melanie's response isn't one he expects. "I think I can do it," she murmurs. "I know it seems hopeless, but we've come this far. And…I really think I can get us out of here."

It's incredible Buck can be startled at this point, but he feels his stomach flip in response. Melanie steps a little closer to him, her blue veins pulsing more clearly underneath the harsh greenhouse fluorescents.

"Whaddya mean *you* think you can do it?" he asks. "Why is it up to you?"

She takes a deep breath. "I guess it's just a feeling. Like I'm meant to help."

"That's nice and all, but you're here because Mortimer wanted you dead, just like the rest of us."

"I'm not so sure." She frowns, her hand fluttering like it aches to travel from her side.

Buck suddenly wonders if Melanie really believes him when he said he didn't blackmail Mortimer. It will bother him, he realizes, if she doesn't. Somehow, they've developed a friendship through this. Like a tiny oxpecker plucking ticks off a rhino's back, Melanie has unknowingly kept him grounded, her simple, uncomplicated presence reminding him of reality, which he's dangerously close to losing grasp of.

"All right," Buck concedes to his little oxpecker. "Let's go, then."

She leads the way through the door before shutting it behind them. They're presented with a tall skinny hallway of scratched hardwood. Buck parses through the room list Gia said hours before. (Had it only been hours?) This must be the hall to the guest suites.

"Lookit," Buck says, rubbing a hand across the peeling flowered wall. "Do you see the outline there? It's a tiny door."

"Another secret passageway?" she says warily. "I just got through the last one…"

When Buck finds the brass knob, he opens it and pokes his head through. When he's sure he can fit his whole body in without getting stuck inside (it would be ironic to get trapped within a house he's already trapped in), he ducks through the small opening and stands up on the other side.

He finds himself in a room only slightly bigger than a walk-in closet. It boasts the same wallpaper and contains only a rusty iron bed frame, a chest, and a cracked chamber pot.

"What's this space supposed to be?" Melanie has followed him.

"Bet it was the servants' quarters."

"It's horrible."

"I don't know. Sorta the least awful of all the rooms we've been in, right?" He squints at the wall and, playing detective again, finds a seam in the paper. Curling his fingers underneath a long edge, he pulls and uncovers yet another opening, only this one has spiral stairs winding down. "They liked to keep servants as invisible as possible," he explains to a stunned Melanie. "Wouldn't even let 'em use the main stairs. Bet these lead all over the house."

"How do you know so much about servants?"

"I lived in *Texas*. All our old houses have this shit. Everyone I know has theirs boarded up or demolished. Think it makes people sick to think about."

He takes two steps down before Melanie exclaims, "You're going? Just like that?"

"Might as well. Just to check it out."

"I'm coming," she quips back.

He shrugs and starts down the stairs, finding the air noticeably colder. It's unlit, and they have to walk (or, in Buck's case, hobble) along before finding the exit cracked ajar.

"Is this...?" Melanie gasps, stepping through the doorway after him.

"The cocktail parlor. Yep. Hard to imagine we were in here enjoying drinks just a few hours ago."

They've emerged from the wall behind the bar, which is frozen in time. Buck's whiskey glass is still sitting out, along with Chester's gin and tonic and even a napkin of cherry stems from when Crystal was nervously snacking on them straight from the jar. He only realizes how dry his throat is until he sees all the discarded glasses. Taking the soda gun in hand, he presses the Water button and squirts some into his mouth. It's deliciously cold. The simple act of nourishing his body after enduring so much darkness makes him almost want to cry. He's about to offer some to Melanie but hears her first.

"She's gone!"

"Who?" He pivots on his good foot.

Melanie is standing on the opposite end of the room, close to where Felix disappeared, her eyes fixed on the painting hanging there. "Buck. The woman in the painting. She's gone."

His memory jolts as he joins her in front of the now-empty frame; its canvas is a simple backdrop of deep browns. "Someone said it was Liotta Queen, right? How could she just…disappear?"

"I don't know." She shifts her gaze. "Did you know her? Liotta?"

"Only by name. Sometimes called the office asking for Mortimer and I'd patch her through."

"Do you think she was as awful as him?"

The back of his neck is getting increasingly itchier the more they talk about this. "No. I don't think so. She was always real polite to me over the phone. And when I got my book deal, she sent flowers. Bluebonnets, native to Oatmeal, where I'm from."

Melanie nods like his words are solidifying what she already assumed. "Why would she stay married to a monster?"

He pushes a long stream of air from his nose. "Sometimes monsters are the people we love the most."

Her upper lip twitches, and he can tell she doesn't like that. Making the decision for both of them, he tugs on her elbow. They stop at the bar to grab one more drink from the soda gun and head back up the stairs.

After moving through the servants' quarters and down the narrow hall, they emerge into the guest suites—into chaos.

Winnie and Crystal are grappling, their hands snagged in each other's hair as they bend over, head-to-head like angry rams. Scott is lying on the suite's filthy king-size four-post bed, his arms splayed out in a T. His eyes are closed. Not good.

Buck beelines to Scott.

"Hey, bud. Scott? Can you hear me?" He pats his cheeks and finds them icy. After sticking two fingers on his neck and finding a pulse, Buck adjusts Scott so that he can remove the dirt-caked sheets from the mattress and tear them in half. He does his best to beat the filth off and wraps one around each bleeding arm, then knots them into makeshift tourniquets. Scott's legs have sustained a few gashes, too, so Buck makes a few pillowcase bandages for those.

Buck's focus is so narrowed that when he's through with tending to Scott, the women's screeching almost bursts his eardrums.

"You ruined everything!" Crystal yanks a fistful of Winnie's red hair. "You loudmouth bitch!"

"Let go of me!" Winnie howls. "You're the one who slept with a married man, you whore!"

Melanie stands a few feet away, two hands pressed to her cheeks. Before Buck can do or say anything, Crystal throws Winnie against the wall, following after. They bounce off, hit the ground, and immediately start clawing at each other. Winnie gets atop Crystal and starts slapping, her face bunched up like the back of a basset hound's neck.

Initially, Buck assumed the floor was a dark chestnut hardwood, but upon further inspection, he realizes it's a layer of dirt, just like what was on the bedsheets. And the women are now covered in it.

With a great heaving sigh, he yanks Winnie off, careful not to grip her arm too hard. He keeps a close eye on her sharp nails, recognizing their danger by the strands of Crystal's hair caught under them. Thankfully Winnie doesn't fight against him and, with a scowl on her face, allows herself to be dragged away. Crystal leaps to her feet, her legs caked in fresh dirt.

"You don't know!" she screams at him. "You don't know what she did!"

"Can y'all just cool it for one flippin' second?" He raises a hand to her like he'd do to a raging mother cow pissed off at a farmhand. "What in the damn hell is goin' on here? And do you not see a man bleedin' to death over there?"

The fire in Crystal's eyes cools to a slow burn as she turns toward Scott on the bed. It's like she's just remembered he's there. "Oh God—I didn't even… Is he going to be okay?"

"Did the best I could, no thanks to you. Lost a lot of blood. When did he go unconscious?"

"I…I don't know! We came in here and started looking around… and then I found the magazines and—"

"She attacked me!" Winnie points a quivering finger. "Like a…a… demon!"

Crystal rolls her eyes. "You whining old hag! Tell them what you did, or I will!"

Buck has only a few seconds to take in his surroundings while the women exchange insults a safe distance away from each other. Beyond the uncleanliness, the room has a grand coffered ceiling and elegant glass light fixtures hanging on either side of the bed. There are the necessities—a wardrobe, a desk, a chair—and the walls are, of course, decorated with clocks.

Crystal gestures toward the desk, and Buck puts a finger on Winnie's shoulder, telling her to stay put while he checks it out.

On the desk is a stack of magazines, their pages smeared with dirt. It looks like Crystal has managed to clean a few of them at least, evident by the one thrown on top. A full-page shot of a woman in a string bikini straddling a man on a pool lounge chair. They're in passionate lip-lock.

**Spotted! Ava Walker and Dylan Carter getting hot and heavy. Thanks to our always-in-the-know source, Winnie**

Roach, POP Weekly has the scoop. Walker, newly married to
heartthrob Logan Hayes, has been seeing Carter for at least
six months. Gasp! The shock! Thanks for the dirt, Winnie!

Beyond the editorial being ridiculously stupid, Buck doesn't understand why it's reason to get into a catfight with Winnie. Crystal is suddenly at his side.

"And this one!" she spits, forcing another magazine into his hands,
the cover folded over.

She puts the busty in busted! Thanks to a tip from our
gossip guru, Winnie Roach, our photog snagged this picture of Cameron Stewart and her fresh boob job walking out
of Lily Baker's LA home. That's right, the Lily Baker: gay
icon, queer rights advocate, and CEO of the marriage brand
Making It Work. Cleary, she's not making it work, because
our source says the two women have been sleeping together
ever since Baker's wife, Syndey Evans, left to go shoot her
Bollywood movie. You gotta keep us in the know, Winnie!

Crystal tosses a handful of magazines into the air, their pages fluttering loudly before landing on the floor. "There are dozens more! All
about Winnie exposing secret affairs. 'Thanks for the dirt, Winnie!' And
this room *happens* to be covered in dirt?"

Scott groans a little from bed, and Buck moves over to check his
pulse again.

"Listen, I don't know what any of that means for this here situation,"
Buck says to Crystal. "And there ain't a point in—"

"She told the tabloids about Mortimer's affair!" She bares her teeth.

Winnie wipes a smudge of mud from her face but only smears it in
further. "I didn't even *know* Mortimer was having an affair until today. I

never would have dreamed someone would be desperate enough to sleep with a molding gargoyle until I met *you!*"

Buck catches Crystal as she dives at Winnie, her fingers bent into claws.

"Stop it! A man is dyin', and ya'll are fightin' like a bunch of hornets in a jar! Have you two even looked for the riddle?"

The two women avert their gazes, both going a different shade of pink.

"We started," Winnie says petulantly.

"I'm sorry I got so distracted after learning she destroyed everyone's lives!" Crystal snarls.

"Hang on." Buck bears down on her. "I *always* knew about you and Mortimer. In fact, I walked in on y'all in his office. You might not remember because I opened the door and all I could see was your bare behind before I fled."

Crystal's entire face goes from pink to red, the kind of color Nan would've seen and called the doctor for a house call. "I…I didn't… That's not…"

"So, all that to say, I don't reckon you're a saint either." Buck folds his arms. "You think *Winnie* destroyed lives? What. About. You? Look what you did to Liotta."

The lights cut out as quickly as a blade across a pig's throat, and he suddenly feels Crystal cling to him, her body shaking. The suites were already cold, but now it feels as if the entire room has been cupped by frozen hands. He's attacked by an onslaught of emotions, each one a deep lash against his soft underbelly: fear, jealousy, envy, regret, disgust. He's never felt them so physically before, like they are poisons he can hold in his hand and touch to his lips.

A throaty voice slices through the darkness.

The lights clap back on.

Crystal screams.

# 17

# Crystal Flowers

IN THE CORNER stands an old woman in a nightgown, its lacy ends dripping over her bare spidery feet. She has hollow, bruised cheeks and short sprouts of hair blooming from her balding head. Bludgeoned red eyes fix on Crystal.

"Liotta," she utters, barely able to get the words out. "How are you...? What did...? Is it really...?"

It's been years since she's seen Liotta Queen in the flesh. Though that might be the wrong way to phrase it, since Liotta doesn't seem to *have* flesh. She's broken down, sagging, decaying like her body has lain dormant for years. Her eyes are the only part of her that move.

No...this can't be Liotta. She was beautiful, even just before death. Crystal's lungs curl at the memory, her jealousy stale but still lingering even now.

Oh God, is she here to punish her?

"Melanie, don't move!" Buck speaks calmly and firmly.

Crystal doesn't register until then that Melanie is the closest to Liotta, standing only a few feet away from where she looms. Like Crystal, she's frozen in place. No one seems to want to move, just in case they startle the…her.

"What do you think she wants?" Winnie whispers, reading her mind.

"Me…" Crystal whispers, her eyes locked on the apparition.

Liotta has reason to seek revenge, but she couldn't have cared less about the affair. No, sleeping with Mortimer was the lesser of Crystal's evils.

"Look," Buck says, "this could be just like the deer situation. We just need to…to be delicate. No matter the reason she came, we still gotta find that riddle, or else we're dead."

But Crystal can't focus. She takes a step forward, her breathing shallow and noisy.

"Don't, Crystal!" Winnie shrieks, but Crystal keeps going.

"You need to know, I never wanted this to happen. I'm so sorry—"

"Loooooooooookkk!" Liotta's rasp is so visceral, it brings Crystal to her knees.

"I know!" she wails, hot tears gushing down her cheeks. "Look at what I did to you! I…I never thought… I didn't know… You have to believe me! I didn't know!"

Buck comes from behind and tries to pull her back, but she yanks herself away.

"Stop it! Leave me alone!" she shrieks.

"Quit talkin' to it! You'll make it madder!"

Her blood boils with so much hatred—for Mortimer, for herself, for Buck because he called Liotta an *it*—that when he reaches a hand out again, she sinks her teeth into it, tasting salty blood. She spits onto the floor, a dribble of it dripping down her chin.

Buck howls and staggers backward, swearing colorfully. She half anticipates a blow to the back of the head in retaliation, but none comes.

"Crystal." Melanie's voice teeters on the edge of accusatory. "What did you *do* to her?"

"Loooooooook!" Liotta screams again, sounding dry and mutant.

A low grumble vibrates from the floorboards. A sleeping giant stirring awake. Crystal snaps her head toward the clocks, thinking they've run out of time—but there's still fifteen minutes left.

The Manor has apparently come early.

With a great splitting crash, a grouping of hardwood planks near Winnie's feet break apart, forming sharp wooden molars. They crack against one another like gnashing teeth, the floorboards splintering into pieces with every chomp. Winnie screams and tries to leap out of reach, but the surface bends every time she takes a step so that she starts to slide toward the gaping mouth.

Buck picks up the desk chair and hurls it into the wooden jaws, which shreds the furniture long enough for Winnie to sprint to the other side of the room.

"Loooooooook!" Liotta implores again, either unable or unwilling to react to the chaos.

It's the voice that spurs Crystal to move. She swears there's a glint of the human Liotta flashing in her eyes. She's still in there—she has to be.

"Liotta," Crystal pleads, crawling on her hands and knees until they're only a foot apart. "Please. You have to help us."

"Crystal! Don't!" Buck shouts as he dodges a sharpened shard of chair that's spat from the mouth like a toothpick.

Liotta's eyes follow Crystal, watching as she reaches a trembling hand out.

"Please…" she murmurs one more time before making contact.

A second later, her chest tightens. It's unlike any ache she's ever experienced, and Crystal fleetingly wonders if she's having a heart attack. Salty tears rush from her unblinking eyes as the real world blackens and she wakes in an entirely different room.

She's lying in a king-size bed with four iron posts and an overhead canopy. The room ripples like it's made of water, her heartbeat thudding in her ears. Everything throbs, and her face is slick with cold sweat.

The bedroom door swings open, and here comes—*herself*. Crystal. Dressed in a knee-length dress and fur coat she bought from a boutique in Paris. She went with Mortimer. It's not visible, but there's a tiny red wine stain on the fabric. She knows this because *she* was the one who dribbled it there.

Crystal lurches and throws up on the puffy white duvet. She's watching herself. But how? Crystal's head spins.

The Second Crystal, the crown of her hair smattered with snow-flakes, lets a black backpack slide off her shoulder and hit the ground so she can rush over and rub her back. At the sensation of being touched by her own hand, Crystal wants to vomit again, but her stomach is empty. Up close, she can see all the details on Second Crystal's face—*her* face—that she never noticed before: the tiny mole hiding beneath her hairline, the scar behind her ear, the peach fuzz along her cheekbones. Her hair is in an elegant knot with a few wisps framing her face—Crystal knows those wisps. *She* stood in front of the mirror and hand selected which pieces would be free of the rubber band.

"Are you ready for your medicine?" Second Crystal says, her face pinched with bitterness. God, she never realized how ugly she is when she's angry.

*I'm Liotta?*

Then her mouth is moving of its own accord. She doesn't fight it. "Hopefully one of the last doses. Doctor says I can come off these injections soon."

These words. She remembers now. This is the day it happened.

Second Crystal nods and, from a plastic case, withdraws a syringe and a vial stamped with tiny print. Her hands are steady as she pierces the vial's lid and pulls the plunger. Amber liquid draws up into the syringe.

There's more conversation. It's bleary, like they're speaking underwater. Second Crystal brings the syringe close to her arm, a brown teardrop dripping from the tip of the needle. But she pauses, her lower lip trembling. There's so much anger etched across her face, it's a wonder her features don't crumple from all the weight.

A numbness settles over her lips, tongue, trickling down her chin…

A strangely distant voice shouts: "*Look out!*"

Then it's over.

Crystal is ripped from the scene and thrust back into the Manor's guest suites amid Buck's and Winnie's terrified shrieks. Rubbing her thundering chest, she touches her face, shoulders, and arms, confirming that her body is truly hers again.

Someone has stepped in front of her: Scott. He's wobbling, his knees buckling, but he stares into her eyes, inches from her face. She blinks, confused, and then registers the large syringe jammed into his neck. Before she can scream, he topples over. Liotta stands there looking like her regular human self—the woman she once recognized: simple but pretty, quiet but sharp.

Scott wheezes, gasping for breath as he stiffens like a board. His lips turn blue.

Just like Liotta's did that day.

"No!" Buck bellows, racing to him and falling to his knees. He rips out the syringe. Blood spatters the dirt-coated floor.

Crystal *wants* to move, to lean over Scott and beg him to stay alive, but when Liotta steps even closer, Crystal whimpers with fear. Liotta's lips curve softly, and her eyes, haloed with lines, sparkle. Crystal inhales orange blossom perfume, fresh linens, and chamomile tea. A teardrop heavy with regret and love spills across the bridge of her nose.

"Loooook," Liotta whispers in her ear, her voice laden with milk and honey. She points to a space on the floor.

Crystal, who almost can't bear to look away from her lost friend for even a moment, follows her gaze.

In one corner along the hardwood, dirt has been disturbed, and beneath it she glimpses a word.

Without hesitating, she quickly scrapes her hands along the floor, sending muck flying. Melanie appears by her side, following her lead. Only a few feet away, the Manor has cracked its floor mouth open even wider, stretching it toward Buck and Winnie, who are cowering in the corner. Scott continues to make awful suctioning sounds, his lungs failing him. Crystal can't allow herself to think that he'll die. It's not a possibility—not when they're so close to the end. She just has to figure this out.

After a few moments of frantic wiping, they find a faint crimson scrawl painted on the floor. The riddle.

> *I am a person who dug the dirt,*
> *Spread the rumor, and shouted the news,*
> *Killing a marriage that was never hurt*
> *All because I saw a bruise.*

It's unnecessary. This riddle is simply Mortimer relaying a final message from the grave: *I know what you did, you bitch.* Crystal knows what it means, but she has to be completely sure.

"Winnie," she commands, ignoring the goose bumps peppering the back of her neck due to Liotta's unrelenting gaze. "Come read this. Hurry." Their fight seems exponentially less important now, with Buck now throwing more furniture into the gnashing teeth to keep it away from Scott. With her hair still bedraggled, Winnie staggers over. Melanie joins, unasked.

"You know the answer's me, but I'm innocent. I didn't—he—" Winnie stammers above the roaring, chewing floor.

"He did some revising," Crystal finishes quickly, moving her finger through the dirt on the floor. "I know, I know."

*WINNIE ROACH*

The Manor whines. Crystal knows now when it's disgruntled. Unsatisfied. Hungry. The floor stops chomping, going still. Warm satisfaction pools in her belly. Even under these circumstances, it feels good to get something right.

"Scott? Scott! Come on, man! Breathe!"

She snaps her head up to see Buck pumping on Scott's chest. He listens closely to his nose for breathing and, apparently finding none, blows air into his mouth.

Five excruciating minutes later, timed by the ticking of the clocks on the walls, Buck falls back, his face in his hands. Scott doesn't move. Winnie wails, dragging herself over and begging him to say something, to lead them out of here, but he's gone. The morphine, Crystal realizes numbly, killed him just as fast as it killed Liotta.

She can't speak. Her blood has gone icy, her emotions sterile. Why should she cry? She hardly knew him, and he certainly didn't know her. They were nothing, and even if they'd both gotten out of the Manor alive, they'd still be nothing.

Buck leans over Scott's body and mutters, "Goodbye, Fred." Some inside joke between them? She can't believe closeness has grown within these walls. Nothing can flourish here; it can only die.

The door out is there, unlocked and waiting for them. Crystal can't bring herself to leave, but Buck limps away, Winnie close behind. She's crying yet remains close to his back. Mourning, but not enough to stay behind and risk more attacks from the Manor.

Crystal hovers there, unable to register that Scott's body is just that—a body, with nothing left inside.

Melanie stands beside her, and Crystal surprises herself by suddenly desperately needing to be touched. She searches anxiously for Melanie's hand. It's cool, soothing as ice on a sunburn.

"You loved him," she says softly, not as a question.

"I didn't know him." Crystal chokes on the words. "I had no idea who he was."

"He was a good person."

"What if he wasn't?" The words come out unsolicited. "I'm sorry. I don't know why I... But what if he wasn't a good person? What if he really did what Mortimer accused him of? Would it be just as sad that he's...?"

*If you knew what I did, would you still mourn me?* she wants so badly to ask.

"I don't know. Maybe?" Melanie lingers on the question mark. "Were you sad when Mortimer died?"

"Yes," Crystal admits. "I didn't want to be, but I was."

"Hmm." Melanie takes a long breath. "Maybe it's just as sad when bad people die, because they never lived long enough to redeem themselves."

Crystal turns away and starts heading toward the door, her upper lip twitching. "No. *Monsters* deserve to die the way they were born: unredeemable."

# Short Story #5

### Winnie Roach

It's called Ozempic, and everyone who's anyone is using it. But no one is supposed to *know* when someone is doing it.

Take Laura Cleary, for instance. She shows up to Soho House for the girls' weekly Wine and Whine (all subjects are on the table) with a brand-new body so fresh, it still has the price tags on it. All throughout lunch, she's gabbing about how the palm hearts and kimchi diet "seriously saved my life," as she rubs her new flat abs and cuffs her thin wrist with a finger and thumb.

"Well, *whatever* you did, it looks great." Someone at the table nods into their pinot.

"The palm hearts and kimchi diet," Laura repeats fervently. "I swear. Kate Hudson did it!"

"Right, dear. Right."

Winnie isn't interested in jabbing herself with a needle of

medication meant for diabetes patients—she's skinny enough without even trying. Nothing tastes as delicious as a fat, salivating piece of gossip. And that's zero calories.

---

"I'm telling you, Betty," she says, sitting in her LA townhome, just having returned from Wine and Whine. "She's taking it."

Her good friend, Betty Truman—editor at BCA News—is on the other end of this call, clicking her tongue. Winnie can hear phones ringing in the background and knows she's in the BCA office, as usual. Probably working on a hard-hitting story about what politician is embezzling what money from which fund.

"Laura Cleary is *not* taking Ozempic," Betty says, and Winnie imagines she's rolling her eyes. "She's a titan in the fitness industry. She has abs on her abs. There's no way."

"She just went through a breakup with that guy from the Batman movie," Winnie says, leaning on her kitchen counter in an eggshell-white bathrobe tied at the waist. "And her new app isn't taking off like she thought it would. I talked to the coder who wrote it, and she gave me all the dirty details."

"I have her new app," Betty says, sounding offended. "It's good. My glutes are still sore."

"I'm telling you this is a good story," Winnie insists.

"I told you last week I can't run any more gossip columns." Betty sighs. "My boss is on me for more hard-hitting stuff these days. Give all your dirt to those rags *POP Weekly* and *Goss Central*. And call me when you hear something serious."

"You're no fun." Winnie frowns and hangs up.

She stares around the town house with one hand on her hip. It's official. Winnie is bored. Her latest novel, *The Cobweb*

*Killer,* is selling phenomenally after a swell of interviews and press trips. Now that the excitement is over, she's left feeling empty.

Writers have different reasons for choosing authorship: love for the written word, the desire to tell stories, passion for creativity… Winnie writes so she stays out of trouble. When she's elbow-deep within a manuscript, there's no time to linger in the lobby of Local Honey Salon, listening to women spill secrets to their most trusted hairdressers.

When she's on book tours, there's barely enough time to browse through her email inbox, chalk full of anonymous tips people send her about the bigwigs of LA:

Eleanor Geiger's Chinese crested dog that was, according to Eleanor's dogsitter, snatched by a hawk while she was out in the backyard, is still alive!! I saw it being walked by a gay couple in Malibu last weekend. The dogsitter might have sold it for $$$!

The mud used in the Soho House mud bath treatment is 60 percent elephant poop!! Look into it!!

Rodger Hammerfield, founder of the nonprofit Let Us See, is not blind! He's faking it to hold the position. At least six eyewitnesses saw him almost drop an almond scone at a Let Us See lunch, and he caught it in midair!

But there are currently no books to write, no ideas to latch on to, and no press tours to go on. So, instead, Winnie walks around the kitchen counter and moves toward the wall, pressing her ear there.

Her townhome is hugged by two others, so she shares walls with each of them: Dave and Susan Baker on the left and Mortimer and Liotta Queen on the right. The former—whitebread people with so little pizzazz, they think untucking their shirts is naughty—are terribly boring. They don't fight, have vanilla sex (from the regularly scheduled low thumping she's heard), and talk about the weather, *Game of Thrones*, and what they plan to eat for dinner. It's usually fish with asparagus.

The Queens, though quiet for the most part, are at least mysterious, which keeps things interesting. Mortimer makes an excellent antagonist in Winnie's life, scowling at her when they bring the trash to the curb at the same time and ignoring her friendly hellos. She enjoys the game, even if she's the only one playing.

A knock at Winnie's door forces her to peel away from the wall and answer it.

"Oh God!" She brings a hand to her chest; the beaming faces of Dave and Susan are so corny, it almost knocks her backward. "It's you two."

"Howdy, neighbor!" Dave waves, even though he's standing. Right. There. "Wanna Boggle?"

"Excuse me?"

Susan laughs and holds up a box Winnie didn't notice right away. "We were wondering if you wanted to play Boggle! Crack open a bottle of wine, get some fancy cheese out…"

"Oh. Um, no. I'm sorry."

The Bakers seem to be waiting for an explanation beyond that, and when nothing comes, they deflate and walk down the two steps that lead up to the door.

"Err. No problem. Next time!"

Winnie starts to close the door when she stops and inhales. "Do you smell that?"

"Yeah. Smells like the Queens are cooking up something delicious!" Stupid Dave and his stupid comments.

Winnie frowns. "They never cook. They always order in."

"How do you know that?" Susan laughs. "You keep an eye on them or something?"

"Yes. Don't you?"

Susan and Dave exchange glances and head back into their townhome, then shut the door behind them. Good. Maybe now they'll leave her alone. *Boggle.* Goodness.

The Queens do. Not. Cook. They either go out to eat or get takeout. It's like a practice within their religion—Winnie has *never* heard a single pot clang nor kitchen timer go off. This is worth investigating.

She knocks on the door but gets no answer. This could be taken as *we're not interested* or *come back later*, but Winnie chooses to think they just can't hear her. Twisting the knob, she lets herself in.

Liotta is in the kitchen, her back toward Winnie. She's humming "Fly Me to the Moon," chopping a red onion with nimble precision. A small pot of tomato sauce simmers on the stove, acting as percussion to Liotta's song. She scrapes what's on the chopping board into the pot and wipes her hands on a kitchen towel, turning slightly—

"Oh my!" Liotta jumps, stepping backward into the counter's edge. "Goodness! Who are you? What are you doing here?"

Winnie holds up two hands. "Sorry for scaring you! I'm Winnie Roach, your next-door neighbor."

This procures no response. Liotta watches her, wide-eyed.

"I smelled something, um…burning. And I worried that there was a fire," she lies, like whatever Liotta is cooking doesn't make her mouth water. "Just checking to see if everything is okay."

Liotta doesn't buy it. She wrinkles her nose and sucks in her cheeks. "Oh. Well. It's, uh…it's nice to meet you. I'm Liotta Queen. I can assure you, everything is fine. No fire here."

"What are you making?" Winnie glances around the space. "Is Mortimer home?"

"Eggplant parmesan. And no, I'm surprising him with dinner." Liotta clears her throat. "But he's due any minute, so…"

It's a more-than-polite way to usher out someone who barged into a house uninvited, but Winnie stands firm. Because she's spotted a swatch of mauve along the corner of Liotta's eye. Moving closer, Winnie can see another dark blue bruise poorly covered with matte powder.

"I can't help but notice…" She gestures to her face. "Looks pretty bad. What happened?"

"Clipped myself with a kitchen cabinet, actually. Silly of me. I can be a bit of a klutz."

Winnie nods and narrows her eyes. "You know, if it was… *something else*, you can tell me."

Liotta stares at her.

"Women have to stick together, don't we?"

"Okay, this is getting inappropriate and, quite frankly, intrusive. I would like you to go. We'd be more than willing to get together for cocktail hour at some point… Dave and Susan come over at least once a month, when we get our Wine of the Month Club."

A snort trumpets from Winnie's nose, and then she quickly gets serious. "If he's hitting you, Liotta, you should confide in someone."

Fire flashes in her eyes. "Get out. Leave my house, right now!"

Winnie spins around and marches out, calling over her shoulder, "Maybelline has a fantastic full-coverage concealer that'll keep that bruise nice and covered!"

The next day, she finds an extra wrinkle stretched along her forehead that wasn't there before. The confrontation with Liotta must have been more stressful than she thought.

Thank goodness it's Caesar day at Soho House. All the "girls" will be there (because even though no one is younger than forty, calling themselves a gaggle of "women" is far too formal), and the gossip will be flowing as abundantly as fat-free dressing. To Winnie, soaking up the latest dirt is like getting collagen injections—it keeps her young.

Around noon, she drives four blocks away to Soho, an art museum turned prestigious luxury restaurant, resort, and spa. Anyone who is anyone comes here. Last week, Winnie spotted the CEO of Weight Watchers getting a hot-oil massage. The governor's wife and boyfriend play squash here—it's a playground for scandal.

With her oversize sunglasses snug on the bridge of her nose, Winnie saunters through the club's glass front doors, inhaling the fresh smell of class. Her cortisol levels immediately lower as she clicks across the glossy marble floor toward the elevators. The restaurant is on the third floor.

"Ms. Roach?" someone calls out to her.

She stops on her heel, turning to find the club manager, William Fullerton, rushing toward her with his hands clasped together. He's a short man with a well-moisturized face and neatly gelled hair. Sometimes he stops by their table on Caesar day and offers the ladies a complimentary bottle of champagne, but other than that, Winnie doesn't interact with him.

"Hi, William," she says, looking him up and down. "How are you?"

He smiles and crinkles his nose, looking sympathetic. "Ms. Roach...I'm so sorry. I...I don't know how to say this." He rubs his palms together. "I'm going to have to walk you out."

"Walk me where?" Winnie asks, baffled.

"Out." William gestures toward the door. "Ms. Roach, your club membership is under review. Under these terms, you're temporarily banned from the premises."

"WHAT?" She gasps, the blood draining from her face. "What are you talking about? Under review? For what?"

A few women walk by in short white tennis skirts, gawking at her. She reddens and ducks her head, feeling faint.

"A few Soho members are concerned about your behavior," William tells her. "Well…I'm afraid it's more like one particular member: Mortimer Queen."

Winnie blanches. She hadn't even known Mortimer was part of the club. She's never seen him anywhere near the squash courts nor the shared office spaces nor—

"He says you are stalking his wife."

"I am not! That's…that's crazy!"

William winces. "Please lower your voice, ma'am. For the safety of Mr. Queen, I will ask you to leave for the time being until we get this sorted out." He leans forward. "I would remind you that Mr. Queen is not only a generous donor to Soho but also funded the new LA Library. Harassing him or his wife is, quite frankly, deplorable."

Winnie feels the color drain from her face and fall all the way to her toenails.

"You can't kick me out!" She cries while being hustled out the front door. "YOU CAN'T DO THIS! IT'S CAESAR DAY, FOR GOD'S SAKE!"

But through her protests, Winnie knows it's futile. William gives her a feeble pat on the shoulder and returns inside, leaving her standing outside like a stray cat begging for scraps. A handful of club members sidestep her on their way in, craning their necks back to catch a glimpse of her public and humiliating unraveling. She might never be trusted again with groundbreaking news, rumors, or dirty details.

Winnie is ruined. And it's all because of that bastard Mortimer Queen.

———————

For a whole year, Winnie is cast out of practically every social circle. The worst bit is, very few people even know the real reason why she was kicked out of Soho, just that she was and it was humiliating. She's heard speculation that she went broke and couldn't afford the fees or that she slept with one of the Soho board members and things got messy. Mortimer Queen's name is never mentioned among the rumors.

She barely clings to her sanity, scouring glossy magazine columns for gossip and feeling heartbreak reading information she's the last to know. It's an excruciating period, though she muddles through it with sheer grit, determination, and hunger for revenge.

Finally, one summer day, Betty invites Winnie to get lunch at Pepper, an unassuming café in the city. They haven't spoken in ages, which she assumes is because Betty feared being canceled by association.

At Pepper, both women order sparkling waters and share a bowl of green olives. Winnie wears massive sunglasses and a Gucci scarf tied around her head, a look she's grown accustomed to donning out in public.

"It's good to see you," Betty says earnestly. "I'm sorry it's been so long. You must hate me."

Winnie glowers over her shades. "Yes, well. I wasn't going to come at first." She takes a long sip of sparkling water.

"And…what made you change your mind?"

Winnie reaches into her purse and removes a folded newspaper, slapping it onto the table between them.

"Page six," she tells Betty, who flips the paper open and scans it.

"Liotta Queen is dead?" Her eyes crinkle. "That's the wife of that horror writer, right? The one who lives next to you?"

Winnie leans closer. "I think he killed her."

"It says she was sick."

"Right. That's what he wants everyone to believe. Listen…"

She then recounts the day she walked into Liotta Queen's townhome, exaggerating just a bit of the details like, *"Her arms were covered in bruises!"* and *"I could always hear him shouting at her through the walls!"* and *"She told me she was afraid of him!"* By the time she's finished talking, Winnie is certain Betty will be drooling over the gory details.

"So?" She presses. "Will you write the story?"

Betty rubs a finger along her lower lip, looking less enthusiastic than Winnie had hoped. "I'll admit, that sounds exactly like what my boss wants me to cover these days. *'Serious news.'* I mean, accusing a husband of murder? That's a far cry from nip slips and petty shoplifting. But…Winnie, there's just no evidence to back up those claims. And not only that, it's unethical."

"Oh. I see." She sits back and folds her arms on the table, thrumming her manicured fingers. "Do you remember when that young woman accused your husband of sexual harassment in the workplace?" she asks pleasantly.

Betty splutters, chokes on the olive, then hacks it up into her palm. "Wh-what? Yes, of course, I remember that! Why would you bring that up?"

"Because I made that go away," Winnie says. "I did you a favor and paid the woman off. You remember that as well, I'm sure?"

It was a $100,000 bribe to keep the girl from talking. Betty's husband got to keep his job as president of a Fortune 500 company, and Betty got to keep her lavish lifestyle. Because a journalist's salary certainly doesn't buy Prada bags.

"I've said over and over again that I owe you everything for that," Betty says in a hushed tone.

"Yes, you have," Winnie nods. "I'm cashing in that favor right now. Write the story about Mortimer Queen possibly killing his wife."

Betty narrows her eyes and purses her lips. For a long while, she says nothing.

Eventually, in disbelief, she asks, "Are you...are you threatening me?"

"Winnie...we're friends."

"Some friend. You shut me out for a year," Winnie snarls but takes a breath and smooths out her frown lines. "But you can make it up to me. I value our relationship, I really do. I'd like to keep it."

There's a starchy silence between them. Somewhere at another table, a baby gurgles as a mother stabs her arugula salad with a golden fork.

When Betty finally speaks again, she sounds terrified yet awed. "I know you're not doing this because you're a concerned neighbor. You don't give a shit about what happened to his wife. So I'll only ask this once." She sets down her fork and stares into Winnie's eyes. "What the hell did he do to you?"

She smiles broadly, knowing this is as much of a yes as Betty will offer. The article will be written. Mortimer will be ruined.

"He messed with me," Winnie says simply. "And no one messes with me."

# Melanie Brown

SCOTT IS DEAD.

Chester is dead.

Petey is dead.

The men are being picked off, one by one. Perhaps Mortimer wanted it that way—maybe he had a sentimental side and hoped the three women he invited would somehow make it out alive.

*I have a soft spot for people like you.*

He told her that, sitting at that sticky bar, the stools hiked up to sky-scraper standards—at least it felt that way. She's remembering more now, which doesn't make sense. It's been weeks. Nancy Grace (who Cynthia swears is the wisest woman on the planet next to Judge Judy) says investigators usually bring victims of crime back to the scene to elicit context rein-statement, a fancy way of saying their memories are triggered by the familiar.

That's how this feels. The closer she gets to the end of the game, the more familiar the manor, the more familiar it gets, and that makes her remember more about the day she met Mortimer. In fact, as she walks through the guest suite's Jack and Jill bathroom, she already knows the toilets there are onyx. Why does she know that?

Buck and Winnie are waiting for her and Crystal to catch up. Their bodies angle away from each other, stiff as boards. Mere moments ago, they were embracing over the loss of a friend. Now they return to survival mode. *But still*, Melanie thinks. *They waited. They care.*

Winnie clears her throat. "Not that it matters, but I wanted to make sure you all were clear that…even though I was the answer to that last riddle, I didn't do what it said I did."

"So you *weren't* an informant in all those gossip magazines?" Melanie asks skeptically.

"I… Well, yes. People like reading scandal, regardless of if it's true. A few magazine editors told me I single-handedly saved them from going under. You could say I saved an entire staff of people their jobs. So, yeah, I've done some bad things, but does the good I provided make up for it?"

She is answered with heavy silence. Buck's injured foot makes ascending to the next floor slower than expected, but no one complains. Lingering in the stairwell is an escape from the repeated onslaught of each room.

It was like Winnie's words were written from the biblical text of Cynthia herself. Neither Petra nor Melanie ever outright confronted their mother with a list of complaints about their childhood, but they didn't need to because Cynthia listed them herself.

*Sure, I might've yelled at you some, but I sent you to good private schools, didn't I?*

*I made you lose a few pounds before you went to Myrtle Beach for spring break—big deal. I paid for your hotel! I called you every single day to check that you were okay.*

*Stop looking at me like that! I might've smacked you with a brush here and there, but that's nothing compared to what your father would have done if I'd let him. No, instead I was the punching bag so neither of you got it! And I never get a thank-you for that, do I?*

That last one was the most startling. They never spoke of their father, who left before Melanie could even remember his face. Did he have the shadow of a beard peppered over his chin? What did his aftershave smell like? Was his laugh a low bellowing or a soft chuckle? Petra remembers him, though she mostly recalls sounds. Arguing. Screaming. Skin hitting skin.

"Hey." Crystal's hands land on her arm. Both her touch and tone are gentle. "Are you okay?"

Melanie exhales and shakes her head. "No."

Crystal nods. "Me neither. But we got this, okay? Together."

They finally make it to the top of the staircase and waste no time moving through the iron door. The novelty has worn off, and they no longer pause at the top before barreling inside.

The smell of sickness almost knocks Melanie off her feet. It's the kind of scent that lingers in the carpet, the bedsheets, a person's clothes. Purple grape medicine, latex gloves, lukewarm Gatorade, and a weak air freshener barely rivaling remnants of stale vomit.

The master bedroom would be, by all accounts, normal, if not for the addition of medical devices. The four-post bed is made of pointed iron rods with arrows at the top, the old duvet a deep red with gold stitching. The faded wallpaper contains strange cherub babies—another creepy oddity—and, of course, more cuckoo clocks are hung around the room. But there's also a beeping ventilator with blinking red lights, a rusted wheelchair, a blank-screened monitor, and a rolling IV pole with bags of bright yellow liquid attached to a collection of tubes dangling like spider legs.

Melanie hears Crystal gasp.

"It's...it's exactly like his room at home! An exact replica...minus the clocks."

"What's with this wall?" Buck asks, sounding repulsed.

"Don't ask me." Crystal shrugs. "I told Mortimer I thought the baby wallpaper was freaky, but he—"

"No, *this*," he clarifies, pointing to an entire section of the wall made entirely of chalkboard.

"Oh. He got his best ideas from dreams," Crystal explains, "so he'd wake up in the middle of the night and write them down on the wall."

Buck kicks it with his good foot. "Couldn't have used a journal?" he grumbles critically.

"There's no door!" Winnie announces frantically. "Does anyone see a way out?"

Melanie looks around and sees that she's right—they're closed in on all sides.

"It'll reveal itself," she promises with more confidence than she feels. "If we get the riddle right, it'll appear."

"Can't we just write the name down now?" Crystal asks, exasperated. "We know this one's me—it has to be."

Melanie approaches the bedside table. Perched there are three orange prescription bottles alongside a glass of water and a dirty gold candelabra, its candles burned down to short stubs of wax. A piece of paper is neatly folded in front of them with READ ME on the front. She retrieves the note before flipping it open.

"Identify the poisoned pill. Good luck," Melanie read, then sighs. "No, Crystal, I don't think writing your name will work quite yet."

"I can't take this anymore!" Winnie explodes. She tugs on her pearls so hard, they break, spraying the tiny white beads everywhere. "Now he's making us play Russian roulette with poison. No. Screw the riddle!"

The water in the glass ripples unsteadily, a tremor beneath their feet. The Manor doesn't like that plan.

"And screw you!" Winnie shouts, waving her fist at the ceiling. "Screw all this! You know what? I was right the first time! We never should have gone along with this!"

Crystal and Buck exchanges glances, darting their eyes Melanie's way. She knows what they're thinking. It's not surprising that one of them finally cracked; they're just surprised *she* wasn't the first to break.

"Remember rule number two?" Crystal offers, a false lilt in her voice. "Winnie? Calm down. Hey, listen to me."

"Don't!" Winnie snarls. "Don't you dare talk to me about the rules. Look where they got us! Three people are *dead!*" Winnie stamps over and grabs the stick of chalk from the chalkboard's ledge, waving it around like it's a loaded gun. "I'm done playing *his* game!"

She avoids saying *Mortimer*. Perhaps, Melanie thinks, she can't bring herself to. Melanie tosses Buck a pleading look, but he's far away now, his eyes glazed. He sits on the edge of the bed, his face occasionally twisting in pain.

"Maybe she's right," Crystal says under her breath so that only Melanie can hear. "I mean, fuck it." Before Melanie can protest, she clears her throat and says, "Winnie, write my name."

"But—" Melanie starts.

Crystal cuts her off. "Just do it." Her shoulders sag. She's close to giving up, too. Melanie suddenly feels abandoned, the only lucid survivor left on a sinking boat.

Winnie stands on her tiptoes and picks up the chalk:

*CRYS—*

Out of nowhere, a bird begins to sing.

Outside, among the trees, the lilt might have been comforting. The song, however, has no place in the Manor. It's a collection of skin-crawling off-key notes before silence descends.

Melanie prays for the serenading to return. Instead, the clocks on the wall shudder, their cogs and gears rattling disconcertedly.

Dozens of cuckoo birds burst from their faces with indignant cater-wauling and shoot like bullets through the air, their beaks sharpened to painful points. Melanie's screams are lost as she claws at the air.

"We regret to inform you"—a calm woman's voice echoes in the tornado of birds, like it's coming right from a beak—"that after reading your manuscript, we've decided it's not a good fit."

"It's not a good fit!" repeats another bird, grazing her ear. Hot liquid trickles down to her earlobe. "We sincerely appreciate you giving us a chance to read your manuscript!"

"But your voice doesn't reflect our agency!"

"We regret to inform you!"

"You're not a good fit!"

"You're not good!"

Her body sustains cut after cut—arms, legs, neck, face—and she tries to escape instead of fight back.

*Rule number three: Run. Fast.*

Melanie pumps her arms and drives her knees, the sudden burst of athleticism unfamiliar to her body. Birds continue to swarm, but instead of wasting precious momentum waving her arms, she grits her teeth and sprints as fast as she can toward a closet door. She throws herself inside and slams the door behind her, and a raid of tiny wooden pellets drill into it with sharp pops. A few birds have managed to get inside the closet with her, so she has to strike them down, then crush them under her feet. Under the dim closet light, she's startled to see crimson splattered on their splintered wooden bodies.

Then she realizes it's her own blood dripping from their jagged beaks.

Catching her breath, Melanie presses her ear to the door and tries to hear signs of life on the other side. She should come out and check on the others, but safety, even in the bounds of a musty coat closet, is deliriously tempting. *Just for a minute*, she thinks, self-preservation forcing her limbs to yank down a burgundy peacoat and a black fur jacket. Exhaustion settles over her. Nestling into the coats on the ground, Melanie lies on her side and stares into the back of the closet. Underneath the clothes is a row of shoes and hatboxes, their shapes only just distinguishable beneath the shadows. A coat has fallen from the hanger, lying in a crumpled heap.

*No.* Melanie blinks feverishly through the dimness. Too big to be a coat. *I dare you to move,* she thinks, pretending she's a small child in her bed, testing a shadow at night that turns out to be a coat hanger.

Except, this time, the shadow smiles.

Melanie tries to shriek, but nothing comes out. Gia pokes her head out from under a jacket sleeve and cackles, her mouth so large that it consumes the entire lower half of her face. She floats up, her eyes now black holes; the empty sockets have collected strings of spiderweb. Her evolution—or regression—is advancing with every appearance.

"Did you think you'd find a skeleton in Mortimer's closet?" She snickers, and her head bobbles wildly, threatening to topple from her neck.

"You...you scared me," Melanie responds.

"Of course I did," Gia says matter-of-factly, her tongue darting through her gapping teeth. "I came to see how you're coming along."

"You killed Scott," Melanie croaks. Being confrontational with Gia is certainly not a safe behavior, but she can't quell the furious fear bubbling in her blood.

"Me?" Gia puts a hand to her chest, and it sinks in like her skin is porridge. "I didn't do that. Why are you so angry, dear? Aren't you getting inspired?"

"Inspired?" Melanie spits. "Are you insane?"

"There's no need take that tone with me," Gia says reproachfully. "Don't tell me you've grown *fond* of these people. They're not like you, Melanie. They're not your friends."

"Yes. They. Are."

Gia stares at her closely and then glowers, a long hairy spider leg inching its way out of her socket. "Be careful, Melanie," she says plaintively. "Your survival is not guaranteed, regardless of Mortimer's wishes."

A barrage of banging comes from the other side of the door. Crystal's voice is pinched with worry. "Melanie?" The doorknob jiggles. "Are you okay? Can you hear me?"

Turning away from Gia, she wrenches the door open and practically falls into Crystal's arms. The two grip each other for a moment, surveying the damage. Cuts are slashed up and down their bodies, but they're shallow and clotting now.

"She's... Oh, it's awful... She's..." Crystal chokes, a sob lodged in her throat.

Over her shoulder, Winnie is splayed out in an X against the blackboard. The edges of her skin are pierced by dozens of wooden birds, their beaks drilled into the wall to crucify her there. Even her earlobes are penetrated, locking her head into place.

Her eyes are empty.

Melanie waits for something to happen—the floors to quiver, the walls to inhale, the ceiling to collapse—but it's still. She looks to the others, who seem to have the same thought: one of them is dead, and generally that means the Manor will come to feast. But the clocks, now absent of their chirping occupants, report that they have thirty-three minutes left. The hour is not up, and there's no sign of feeding. They have to keep going.

Wordlessly, Buck picks up the prescription bottles. He twists each one open and aligns the designated pills in front of their containers. One red, one green, and one blue. Three paths that exist only as a reminder that they're trapped in Mortimer's story, wedged between paragraphs and indentations, with plots unfurling from each one. Everything that's happened, everything the Manor has done, has been spun the way he always wanted.

"So the challenge"—Crystal swallows audibly, addressing the rainbow of capsules—"is that we have to find the one poison pill. Like *The Princess Bride*. And then we'll get the riddle."

"What the pecan sandy is *The Princess Bride*?"

"A movie. You've never seen it? I—never mind."

Buck snatches the note from the nightstand and flips it over a few times, trying to find more instruction. Melanie can't focus, her chest humming with outrage. Gone is the notion of skipping the riddle altogether, even with the right answer. The Manor can never be cheated.

"Don't look at it," Buck tells her, reading the strain sweeping across her face.

She gasps in reply. "'*It*'?"

"That ain't Winnie anymore. You gotta separate her soul from her skin so we can remember her as she was and not…not that." He loops an arm around his skull and tugs so that his neck cracks, much like a fighter prepping for another round in the ring. "Now, you recognize any of these? We could narrow it down by anything that looks familiar."

Crystal picks the green one up, letting it roll around in her palm.

"How would we possibly be able to tell?" She holds it up to her nose and sniffs. "I don't know why I'm doing that—you can't smell poison, can you?"

"You sure can." Buck takes the blue one and pokes the very tip of his tongue on the outer casing. Both Melanie and Crystal cry out in alarm, but he waves his hand. "It's just the coating. No need to worry." He smacks his lips. "A little sweet. Sometimes that's 'cause they're tryin' to mask the smell or bitter taste."

Melanie is reluctant to touch the remaining pill still lying in wait. "Then do you think that's the poison one?"

He tests the others with the same tentative lick, then strokes his beard.

"Honestly, gals, I ain't got a clue. Some are sweet, and some aren't. Could mean absolute bubkes."

"If we guess, our odds are one in three, obviously," Crystal says. "What if we break them open? Maybe see what's inside?"

Melanie shakes her head. "If we don't recognize what they are from the outside, what are the chances we can identify their insides?"

Her logic is sound but sour, and Crystal momentarily falls into a dejected slump. Surprise slowly hits her. Because Melanie knows exactly how Crystal is feeling, like she can read into her very body language as Crystal shifts her eyes. She's never been clued into social cues, but now—*here* of all places—she's discovered that every eye twitch, breath hitch, scratching of the skin can say something. And she's not sure she likes what Crystal is saying. Uneasiness nettles up Melanie's arms as she watches her pull a fake pout. She knows it's fake because it's too pretty— her lips purse seductively, her lashes are drawn down, and she subtly leans forward so that her chest is exposed.

"One of us could risk it and take one," she says with a voice dripping in syrup. "It would be, like, the ultimate sacrifice."

*Oh God, no.* Melanie has never seen bedroom eyes, but she is confident that's exactly what Crystal is giving Buck. Her stomach curdles— not only is it a revolting tactic but a disappointing one. It was foolish to think she knew who Crystal truly was in the short time they've known each other.

Thankfully, Buck isn't the slightest bit interested. In fact, he hasn't even noticed the doe-like display.

"Takin' one ain't enough, though," he muses. "If you survive it, that just means we gotta choose another pill, and we're back in the same hog-tied situation."

"But—" Crystal squirms, and Melanie, unable to withstand another bout of failed seduction, interjects.

"We should all swallow one. That way we're all taking the same risk with the same odds."

Crystal squawks out a laugh, but it's laden with more incredulity than humor. "I'm sorry, but that's insanely stupid. Why would we dole out the danger among us when one person could take the risk?"

Melanie steels her gaze. "Does that mean you're volunteering?"

Crystal goes rigid. "No, of course not—"

"Right, because no one person should have to do this. We all take the gamble."

"This seems in direct violation of rule number four." Crystal narrows her eyes. "Remember? 'Avoid risk.' Or, how I would put it, 'Don't be stupid.'"

Melanie knows Crystal is trying to send wavelengths through their locked glares. *Go with my idea, dummy! We could get this guy to do the dirty work if you let me speak!*

"This is the best option," Melanie announces firmly.

"I agree," Buck adds. "What's good for the goose is good for the gander."

Crystal sneers, her smooth forehead lining with scowl marks. "Fine," she finally relents, shooting Melanie a contemptuous appraisal. "I just hope my goose isn't the one that's cooked."

# Buck Grimm

**B**UCK THRIVES ON rules. *Always bring the tractor to a complete halt before dismounting. Never place yourself between a sow and its piglets. Get your peanut harvest off the ground before the first frost.*

And as much as the rhythm of the Manor's eating schedule repulsed him, it was also a rule he could tangibly count on. Someone dies, the Manor sups, and the door unlocks. But Winnie's lifeless body, crucified by wooden birds, remains untouched, and they're still required to follow through with the riddle. He supposes he shouldn't hold a thing made of drywall and scaffolding to have much integrity for protocols. Plus, *they* tried to bend the rules first—he's not surprised the Manor responded in kind.

He zones in and out of the conversation unfolding before him, the razor's edge in both women's voices grating his skull. Nan always said men fight with their fists while women torment with words. He always thought this was one of her old-fashioned, sexist ideologies, but he should've never second-guessed her.

"How do we decide who takes what pill?" Crystal challenges.

"It doesn't matter. We can do it at random," Melanie replies evenly.

"Ha! You want to decide who lives and dies at random? Great." The sarcasm cracks like a whip.

"Better than tricking someone into dying so you stay alive."

Ouch. A branding iron flush to the skin.

"Are you suggesting *I* tried doing that? That's ridiculous! When did you get so mouthy?"

"The same time you got manipulative."

In a futile attempt to salvage his crumbling mental state, Buck forces himself, yet again, into a warm daydream.

He thinks of sitting on Nan's wraparound porch in a hand-carved rocking chair, its seat woven with dried hay. The screened-in front door bangs, and she emerges with a soda, ice chips still encrusting the lid from when it was stowed in the cooler, and a paper plate adorned with a ham-and-cheese sandwich and potato chips. He eats with the plate sitting on his lap, rocking back and forth while watching a few older boys across the street throw a football to each other. The sun beats down on Oatmeal today, but the breeze cools his skin and smells like summer.

Nan tussles his burnt-red hair, then plants her hands on her hips. She opens her mouth, but the indignant cry that comes out does not belong to her.

"Buck! Hey! Hello? Are you listening?"

Melanie is in his face, so close that he can see the white puss within a few chin pimples. He refocuses his glazed vision and clears his throat.

"Hm?"

"Which pill do you want?" she asks, an edge to her tone like this isn't the first time she's repeated the sentence.

"Hang on, hang on!" Crystal inspects each one closely, her tongue waggling out of her mouth with concentration. "I'm still deciding!"

Melanie closes her eyes like she's dealing with a pup that won't stop whining at a closed door.

"Hurry up and pick," he grumbles to Crystal, who blows a distracted raspberry with her lips.

She brings the green pill inches from her eye, inspecting every millimeter of its smooth round body.

Buck sways on his feet, willing himself not to return to the sanctuary of Nan's porch.

She used to take pills—though none resembled brightly colored sprinkles like these. If they had, maybe Buck wouldn't be so scared of them. No, Nan took plain white chalky pills for her arthritis, liver, pancreas, you name it.

Oatmeal's aggressive rumor wheel (*It's a factory that never shuts down!* Nan would say) churned out rumors that she was dealing OxyContin, but Buck never wanted to believe that. His own mother had been so plagued with addiction that Nan opted for tea over coffee, wary of caffeine. *I don't need that bean juice as a reason to wake up every damn day! I got more important things to be alive for,* she'd squawk at breakfast—wheat toast dunked in runny eggs and spiced sausages.

But now that he thinks about it, no one ever accused Nan of *taking* the drug, just *selling* it…

No, he'd rather not pick at the wound. Not when Nan is dead. He might even see her in a minute or two, depending on his luck. He'll ask for the truth then.

"I want the red one," Crystal announces, then lays her palm flat so he and Melanie can pick.

"It doesn't matter," they say simultaneously.

"You choose." Buck nudges Melanie, and she selects the green pill. He's left with the blue, its shade reminiscent of a near-perfect blueberry.

They stand in a half circle, staring at one another.

"So…one of us is gonna…" He tries to say more but is too chicken to continue. *Is gonna what? Keel over on the spot? Foam at the mouth? Sprout festering boils?*

"Let it be known that I didn't want it to go this way," Crystal declares.

Melanie looks on like she'd love nothing more than to rip out her windpipe and play a little tune with it. He's never seen her wear anger before—it oddly suits her.

"On the count of three?" Buck pinches his green pill between two fingers. "One."

"Two," Melanie says.

"Three." Crystal grimaces.

They throw their pills into their mouths, no one bothering to reach for the glass of water on the bedside table. Buck's goes down with a bit of a fight, the rubbery shell of the capsule catching in his throat for a moment before he swallows.

Maybe it's an ominous sign that it fought back.

Like it knew what it was capable of.

He watches Crystal and Melanie's faces, analyzing every nose crinkle, eye twitch, and brow flutter while also taking into account how he feels. When his stomach growls, he slaps a hand over his belly and thinks, *This is it. I'm dying.* But the minutes drag by, and he realizes he's just hungry.

"How long do we have to wait?" he asks, breaking the silence.

"I don't know." Melanie reaches for the pill bottles. "Maybe the labels say—wait a minute. The riddle! It's here now!"

She holds the bottle up to his face, and he sees, in the smallest font, a riddle typed onto the label.

Melanie's momentary elation dissolves into a frown. "So we must've found the poison pill. But I don't understand why one of us isn't dead."

He shrugs, his excitement dampening. "Maybe it's a slow death and the poison won't take effect until later" is his suggestion.

"That would make a bad story."

Buck twists his beard until it's a thick, mangled rope. "Why in Dolly Parton's name would *that* matter?"

"Because it's Mortimer Queen," she explains thoughtfully. "It's like he's outlining a book. The clichés, the challenges, the riddles... You heard what he said in the will. This is his final story to tell."

He eyes her with appreciation and hesitation. "I thought you didn't know him that well."

Melanie bites her lip. "I think I know him better than I wanted to."

"Can we read the riddle already?" Crystal snatches the bottle from Buck's hand.

*"I'm the one who did it.*
*I have the poisoned pill,*
*But in this instance, a shot went in,*
*And the wife was my first kill."*

With a snort of disgust, Crystal whips the bottle at the ground. It bounces and rolls underneath the bed, out of sight.

"Don't bother. It's me," she says when Buck moves to retrieve it. "The answer is me. God, he really did start getting lazy. Didn't even *try* to make that one difficult."

He narrows his eyes. "You killed Liotta?"

A trace of uncertainty flashes across her face.

"Yes. It's my fault she's dead."

Instinctively, he takes two steps back. Melanie follows suit, her expression crumpled with disappointment. He'd always figured Crystal was a woman scorned, but to take someone else's life... And for what? *Mortimer?*

"You don't understand," Crystal rushes to say, saliva flying from her mouth. Her eyes are dry, though. Maybe she has no more moisture left to cry. "I'm not a murderer."

Buck weighs this. He looks at the clocks. "We have ten minutes left. Use two of them to tell us the truth."

"Winnie was right," she says quickly. "Liotta was being abused. She knew about Mortimer and me but hardly cared because it kept his attention off her. Because he was so focused on me, she actually recovered faster from pancreatic cancer. It helps, you know, when your husband isn't kicking you in the ribs or throwing you down the stairs."

Buck winces.

"I helped her with her medicine most days," she continues, refusing to meet their eyes. "She went to the hospital for her chemo and radiation, but Mortimer brought in a nurse to teach me how to administer her painkillers. Morphine. She needed less and less of it as she got better."

Melanie gulps, her cheeks sucked in so they're sallow.

"It was an accident. I…I wasn't paying attention. I messed up and gave her double the dose. I left to let her nap, and when I came up later to check on her…" She finally brings her gaze upward; it's wide and afraid. "What, you guys don't believe me?"

"So you killed her…" Melanie starts suspiciously.

"By mistake," Crystal hurries to say. "A terrible, fucked-up one, I know. But I…I *liked* Liotta. Why do you think I stayed with Mortimer even after I realized what he was doing to her? Because I couldn't bear to leave her alone."

Her words sound rehearsed and formulated. But if he questions her story, Crystal might start doubting his own, too.

There's a short, sharp *ping*, like a button falling loose from his pants. He looks along the floor, his brows knit. It doesn't take long to find the source, as it's rolled against his foot, right by the charred, bloody stump where his toe should be.

The red pill.

The one Crystal *pretended* to take.

"What is that?" Melanie's tone is dangerously flat as she sees it.

Crystal backs away, her mouth opening and closing. It's like her brain knows she owes them an explanation, but there's none to be had.

She duped them.

"You…you faked taking the pill," Melanie blinks rapidly and then widens her gaze. "You let us almost kill ourselves, but *you*…"

"And thank God I did!" Crystal finally manages to splutter. "I had the tainted one! I would have died! Aren't you glad I didn't take it? You're not going to stand there and say I should have…should have…"

"Yes. Yes, I *am* going to say that." Melanie takes a step forward and cocks her head. "I don't know if I believe you now."

Crystal shrinks away, her back now against the iron bed frame. "Wh-what do you mean?"

"That story you just fed us," Melanie shifts her eyes toward Buck. "She could've made that whole thing up. If she lied so easily about *this*, well, then…"

"No! No, I didn't! I would never lie about that!"

Buck has felt betrayal—when a trusted editor leaked his manuscript before it was done, or when he slept with a nice woman and woke up to see her half naked and rooting through his wallet—and it's always hurt in that same predictable way.

But this is different because he and Crystal share a common goal: survival. And so even if he doesn't want to, Buck understands.

"Hey, hey, calm down." Buck lowers his arm to block Melanie's advances. "Ain't no point in this. It happened. It's over."

Guilt pricks his chest when hurt smears across Melanie's face as clearly as goat cheese on a bagel. She expected him to have her back and now probably feels even more deceived. Sliding in front of her so his back is to Crystal, he speaks directly to Melanie in a hush.

"She don't matter. I'm here for you. You're here for me. We're in this together, ya hear me?" He pushes a finger against her shoulder. "Forget her. When we all get outta here, she'll have to live with what she did. Best punishment ya could give her."

"I can *hear* you," Crystal says frostily.

Buck can't read Melanie's expression, but she offers a faint nod. He turns away and walks to the blackboard. Fighting not to look directly at Winnie's body, he picks up a piece of chalk and moves to a clean section of the wall. For a beat, it's so silent that the only sound he can hear is the scraping of the chalk while he writes Crystal's name.

Before he can finish, the Manor grumbles, then coughs so roughly that dust falls from the ceiling. What follows is unexpected: a simpering giggle.

Suddenly, a scream pierces the air, and the chalks snaps in half beneath his fingers. He whirls around and his heart plummets. It's crazy that among all the cries he's heard over the course of the night, he can still pluck from the lineup whom this one belongs to.

"Nan?" he calls out, certain that it was her pleading shriek.

Another scream splits the air, and this time he can tell it's coming from the stairwell from which they came. Without considering alternatives, he races out of the room. The bedroom door slams behind him, locking with an audible *click*. He stands, his chest heaving, straining to hear Nan's voice again. Only a minute later does the stupidity crash down on his shoulders. His grandmother is dead. No one, not even Mortimer, is powerful enough to yank her from beneath the soil where she's buried.

From the other side of the door, he can hear Crystal suddenly pleading, "No, no! Please no!"

He grapples with the doorknob and pounds, roaring superficial phrases like, "I'm here!" and "I'm comin'!" and "It's gonna be okay!"

There's a sickening *thunk*, and he recalls images of his axe driving into a wet tree trunk.

"Crystal! Melanie? Can y'all hear me?" His fists are aching from hitting the door.

The quiet is just as bad as the screaming. He smashes his shoulder once, twice, three times before the door crashes open.

Melanie is bent over Crystal, who is lying face down on the ground, her arms peacefully at her sides. Her white-blond hair, the first thing Buck noticed about her, is unrecognizable now that it's matted with dark blood. While her head is facing away from him, the crown of crimson is proof enough that she's dead.

"Oh God... Oh no..." Buck breaks down, his knees wobbly.

It's not just that she's gone but that he could have helped if he hadn't been enough of an idiot to follow a false trail. Responsibility weighs heavily on him as he sags to the floor, gingerly touching Crystal's smooth arms.

"Wh-what happened?" he utters, feeling like he's just come upon a mangled doll.

"She...she tried to run..." Melanie gulps. "But she wasn't fast enough."

Before he can ask for more details—though why does he want them so badly?—the walls begin to curdle. Winnie, her body still nailed to the wall, is pulled through as the chalkboard bubbles like black tar. The cherub wallpaper peels into thick strips, curling into snakelike bodies that slither toward them.

Buck yanks Melanie to her feet and tugs her to the far corner of the room, away from Crystal's body. It's clear what's coming next, so he pulls Melanie behind him. He shudders at how her body is slick to the touch with blood. Blood that does not belong to her.

The ribbons of wallpaper converge upon Crystal's body, swarming like maggots. Buck squeezes his eyes shut, pretending the noises they make are innocuous: wet newspaper shredding, homemade applesauce ladled into a bowl, dry branches snapping under his boots.

A sharp bang sounds next to them. A hatch swings open from a patch of ceiling, and a ladder unfolds. That's their escape. Buck hoists Melanie—who can't stop whimpering—onto his back and tells her to wrap her arms around his neck.

"Don't look back," he tells her as he climbs, pain shooting from his injured foot into the rest of his body.

"I won't," Melanie deadpans.

Her voice, he realizes with a disturbed curdle of his belly, is eerily complacent.

# Short Story #6

### Crystal Flowers

Around Christmastime, Mortimer Queen's wife, Liotta Queen, starts to beat pancreatic cancer.

And Crystal is *pissed*.

What should be a season of new cashmere mittens, cozy evenings spent at the Plaza, and peppermint mochas from Eleven Madison Park (they put real flakes of gold in their whipped cream) is now a month focused on all things Liotta. Tiffany boxes are scattered under the trimmed tree with her name scrawled on every tag. Crystal's favorite snacks have been replaced from the kitchen: low-sugar chocolate-coated almonds from Dylan's Candy Bar turned into dried mango leather, fresh raspberries became sliced apples soaked in lemon juice, and oat milk was replaced by organic whole milk.

Crystal no longer dines at the grand mahogany table for supper since Liotta is now well enough to eat again. Mortimer thought it would be "inappropriate" if Crystal joined them. Now that he's stopped whisking her off to romantic excursions in Paris and lavish shopping trips on Park Avenue, Crystal wanders around the house with an excessive amount of time on her hands. She writes a lot, but her editor has noted the pages she's submitting are less sexy than usual.

"What's going on with you?" Carol Guttman asks over the phone one day after calling about Crystal's recent chapter. "You know I'm your biggest fan, but this is garbage. And I can say that, because it's not you. Who wrote this? Because it wasn't my fun, flirty friend Crystal, that's for sure."

Crystal, sitting in a velvet swivel desk in her room—her room in *Mortimer's* house—chews on the end of a pen and watches herself spin in a hanging full-length mirror.

"I don't know what you mean," she parrots—the same thing she's said the past two times Carol called with complaints. "I think this is some of my best work."

Her hair is getting stringy, hanging limply along her shoulders, which are fuller than usual. She lifts an arm, inspecting it. Is she getting fatter? Has Mortimer's neglect led to a neglect of her own appearance? A flicker of panic forces her to put the phone on speaker and get on the floor for some crunches.

"I know you don't really think that," Carol says, dismayed. "Look, your genre is horror erotica, and this is giving…sad and scary. Or maybe scary sad. What sells your books is sex. Are you going through a dry spell? Is that it?"

Crystal's abs clench at Carol's guess. She *did* just eat a whole box of buttercream sugar cookies this morning. They were delivered this morning, addressed to Mortimer with a *Happy Holidays!* tag, and she intercepted them since he was out for brunch with *Liotta*. He didn't deserve them anyway.

"Totally get it," Carol continues. "Happens to the best of us." Big sigh. "Okay, here's what you're going to do. Buy some crotchless panties. A leash. A whip. Do whatever you have to do to drum up some inspiration. I've heard melted chocolate feels great on—"

"Nope, nope, not necessary. I'm good. I get it."

"I want fresh, hot pages by Monday, okay? I'm serious. You're a star, but things have got to change, girl."

Crystal hangs up and hugs her knees to her chest. Carol's right. Things have got to change.

There's a knock at her bedroom door, and she starts. Mortimer steps inside, his black peacoat dusted with snow. His gray hair is neatly combed back, and his eyes, lined with crinkles, are sparkling. Most people look best in the sunshine, but he's stoically handsome in the cruel cold weather, like he was made for the brutality of the winter.

"Hi, honey," he says softly, always worried Liotta might hear, regardless of what wing of the house she's in. "Would you care to have dinner with me tonight?"

"Really?" Crystal wiggles her toes. "I'd love that."

He winks and leaves her with a crooked smile. She's always loved his grin—his canine teeth are extra sharp, like he has fangs.

As giddy as the first day they met, Crystal hurries to her closet to plan the perfect outfit. Something sultry but poised. Who knows? Maybe after tonight she'll get her groove back after all.

———

Later, Crystal finds herself perched in her old spot at the head of the dining table, Mortimer on the other side. Snowflakes swirl around outside the stained glass windows, and a fire crackles happily in the hearth. She takes a deep breath, relishing in the opera music drifting from Mortimer's vintage record player— Bach's *Christmas Oratorio*. It's been playing nonstop in the house, especially during the evenings.

She spears a seared scallop before popping it into her ruby-lined mouth. This lipstick shade is the one she was wearing the day she met Mortimer. He, unfortunately, has barely looked up from his plate, focused intently on the pomegranate-glazed baby potatoes.

Crossing and uncrossing her bare legs under the table, she decides to broach her least favorite topic. "Where is she tonight?"

There's no need to say her name. Mortimer understands.

"Her friend is throwing her an extravaganza of sorts." He grins into his potatoes. "A welcome-back party, if you will."

"Is that such a good idea?" Crystal can't keep her tone from bordering on icy. "Her being out late? I know she's getting better, but surely she can't be completely..." She sees his exuberant grin. "What?"

"That's why I asked you to dinner," he says, taking a swig of red wine. The wrinkled loose skin around his throat bobs while he swallows. "Liotta is officially cancer-free!"

Crystal drops her fork.

"Wow!" she manages to say, twirling the diamond earrings Mortimer got her. "That's...that's amazing!"

"The doctors are wowed. She responded to the chemo much better and faster than they anticipated. It's astonishing—her body rejected it for the first five months, and only recently did it really kick in! Can you believe that? The miracle of modern medicine."

She clicks her nails on the table, having just been to the

salon that afternoon. The color she chose? Lovesick Lavender.
"Mmmm. So she's made a complete recovery?"

"Indeed." He's mind-numbingly delighted. Can't he see
how this is affecting her? The fact Liotta is no longer dying is
*killing* Crystal. "Although the doctors say she needs three more
weeks without incident to be considered in remission."

There it is. It's as if he's given Crystal a deadline for when
this will all end. No more unfettered adoration. No more heat-
seeking attention. No more diamonds, allowances, trips to Italy.
She has to act fast. After getting to her feet, she slinks down the
table and sits in the seat directly next to him. She'd try to nestle
herself on his lap, but he's a bit breakable, and she can't stop
thinking about the box of cookies she binged this morning.

"You know what I was thinking?" she purrs, putting a hand
on his thigh and pouting seductively. "We haven't been on a trip
in forever. I read about this new resort in Norway. Hot springs,
mud baths...naked morning meditation..."

Mortimer takes Crystal's hand and pats it. Just the slightest
touch leaves her skin scorched with wanting. "Now isn't a good
time, honey," he says. "With Liotta feeling better, I should be
here."

Crystal pulls away, her eyes pricking with tears. She feels
white-hot rejection burn in the back of her throat so painfully,
she could scream, but instead, she makes the walk of shame back
to her seat, picks up her fork, and eats another potato.

"Except"—he dabs at his mouth with a cloth napkin—"I
do have to take a trip to London. They want me on a panel over
there. Are you free?"

She perks up. "I certainly am!" Her grin tingles with eagerness. How could she have doubted his affection for her? Nothing
will change between them. Nothing.

"Fantastic, because I need you to stay here with Liotta. Help her with whatever she needs: fixing lunches, organizing her medicines, driving her to appointments—your usual tasks."

Her fingers clench around the fork before she stabs the prongs through a baby potato that resembles Liotta's unsightly bumpy skull. It's the only way she can stop herself from plunging it into Mortimer's heart.

Like he just did to hers.

---

While Mortimer is away, Crystal is left alone in this massive New York mansion with a personal driver at her disposal, an allowance for shopping, and a spa gift certificate left for her on the kitchen counter—and she's absolutely miserable. It's sterile and cold and full of things Liotta likes: crystal chandeliers, cream-colored daisies, horse figurines, and long-stemmed feathers in tall vases. It's been three months since Mortimer sold the town house to put some distance between himself and LA, and Crystal still can't forgive him for it. Sometimes he took her there for weeks at a time, and while he attended meetings in the city, she drove out to Malibu and took long walks along the beach. Plus, it was as far away as she could get from Liotta, who wasn't well enough to travel.

"The gossip there has become too much for me," Mortimer explained to her. "It's such a negative thing to be surrounded by all the time. Everyone is in one another's business, hounding the next big story like addicts sniffing out a score."

She's dreaming of the soft Malibu beaches as she carries a tray of wheat crackers and chicken broth up to Liotta's bedroom. It's her usual lunch—*was* her usual lunch. With more energy, she's been going out more often lately.

When she enters, Liotta is sitting in bed, reading a paper-back. Her hair has started to regrow into a clipped pixie cut, and her color is less wafery than usual. It's odd to familiarize yourself with someone when they're at their worst, because any sort of improvement or recovery makes them unrecognizable. Liotta is now a woman who has been given another chance at life, and the contentment that surges from her being is both intoxicating and gut-wrenching.

"Oh!" Liotta perks up when she sees Crystal. "Lunch? That's so sweet of you." Her enthusiasm is half-baked.

Crystal moves to the bedside table, where the medication village resides, a space cluttered with prescription bottles, vials, and aluminum wrappings with itty-bitty pills inside. "Have you taken your medicine?"

"Which one?" Liotta's thin brows crinkle.

"Any of them?" Crystal sighs. "All of them?"

"I believe I forgot."

Crystal opens the prescription bottles one by one, a task she's essential for since Liotta has aching arthritis after the chemo. While lining up the mismatched order of chalky medi-cines, Crystal notices Liotta's troubled expression.

"Is everything okay?" Crystal asks with a twinge of hopeful-ness. Is Liotta in pain? Is the cancer coming back?

"I... Yes." She shifts, as if sitting on a lopsided pillow. "I'm thrilled to be getting better, but it's bittersweet, no?"

*Extra bitter, like dipping radicchio in espresso. But sweet? No.*

"I have to admit something to you," Liotta says.

Crystal fumbles with a few pills, and one rolls onto the ground. Her back aches as she scurries under the bed after it. "Sorry about that. Um, what were you saying?"

"I've grown quite fond of you, Crystal."

"Oh." That's unexpected. "Really?"

Liotta laughs. "Of course. You've been such a help, tending to all my old-lady errands. You're a gorgeous girl. You have a very pretty complexion and lovely hair. I'm sure you'd rather be out dating."

"I'm a writer," Crystal bursts like an angry pimple after it's been poked too much. "I've published twelve books, a few of them landing on the *New York Times* bestseller list." Humiliation blushes the apples of her cheeks, and she wishes she could suck the words back up with a straw.

"That's so wonderful. Good for you, dear."

The response is pandering, as if Crystal just told her she ran a local 5K.

"Anyway…" Liotta puts a buttery-soft hand on Crystal's arm; it feels like The old woman soaks them in lotion. "What I was saying is it's bittersweet that I'm cured because that means you'll be moving on."

Crystal pinches a pill so hard that its waxy coating cracks, and it dissolves into dust. "Oh, I can stay. I don't mind helping out around here," she says, an attempt at casualness. "You'll have plenty of things to do now that you're back on your feet, taking care of the house and Mortimer should be the last thing—"

"I'm his *wife*," Liotta says coolly. "It's the first thing on my mind. No, I'm afraid we won't need your services anymore."

"Have you spoken to Mortimer about this?"

One of the worst things about Liotta is that she shows no mercy when it comes to eye contact. She keeps her eyes trained fearlessly on Crystal's, even when the conversation steers into tense terrain. "Of course. He was the one who brought it up."

Crystal's heart twists in agony, writhing beneath this lethal blow. "Got it. I absolutely understand," she squeaks and clears her throat. "I'm sorry, I'll be right back. I totally forgot your tea." *Laugh. Laugh, Crystal!* "Can't take pills without something to wash them down!"

"Good point." Liotta bends the spine of her book back, delving into its pages once again. "Thank you, dear."

Crystal heads straight outside through a foot of snow to the gardening shed, where Mortimer keeps his rakes, mower, potting soil, and other lawn-care essentials. After pawing around for a moment (she's never watered the garden a day in her life), she finds a red container of Weed Stop.

Crystal hoists it inside and throws the jug on the kitchen counter. She stews a hot cup of Liotta's young pu-erh tea—a foul-tasting drink recommended for the toughest digestive issues—and pours a helping of Weed Stop in before mixing the liquids with a spoon. While stirring vigorously, she sends up a prayer that Liotta isn't going to deny this tea the same way she did her broth. *Please, just drink it! It's the last time you'll ever have to!*

As Crystal carries the mug up the stairs, the liquid splashes against the ceramic's sides and dribbles onto her hand. Her tongue is halfway out, ready to lick up the small swatch of tea, when she remembers. *Shit. Poison. Right.*

"Tea delivery!" She nudges the bedroom door open with her shoulder. Her voice sounds cartoonishly joyful, but she can't help it. Her nerves are throwing an unbridled dance party in her chest while wearing sharp heels and heavy loafers.

"You are a doll and a half." Liotta smiles. "Listen, I'm sorry about being so crass. About the broth, about your time with us... You've done so much for me, and I can't thank you enough."

The rush of fondness glazes over Crytal's skin like an

oatmeal-honey scrub at the spa, and she stops in the middle of the room, steam wafting from the tea in playful twirls.

"You don't have to say that, really…" Doubt lingers in her throat.

"I mean it," Liotta insists, throwing her book aside. "And you want to know something? I think you're what did it. You saved me. Don't look so shocked! Mortimer is a wonderful man, but he didn't have time to care for me when I was ill. You being here, tending to my every need…it's what healed me. You practically carried me right back into my husband's arms."

Crystal pushes the mug into Liotta's hands. "Drink up!" She bares her teeth, hoping it can pass for a smile.

Liotta is especially thirsty. She not only swallows all her pills with gulps of tea but tilts the cup back so she finishes the dregs.

"Gah." She hands the mug back to Crystal with a disgruntled grimace. "That's so wretched. I think I'm done with young pu-erh. Maybe I'll try licorice root." Liotta smacks her lips and shudders. "I hope I never have to drink that stuff again."

Crystal could leave. She could escape the ghastliness of watching Liotta die—and it would not be a painless exit. There would be pleading, retching, gasping, and quivering fingers. It would be easier to avoid all that, but she stands over the bed like the sandman, watching Liotta slip into a panicked stupor as the minutes roll by.

Because Crystal wants to be the last thing Liotta sees.

The "gorgeous girl" with "lovely hair" also happens to have the guts, the gall, the drive, to take what she wants.

# Melanie Brown

**D**YING USED TO terrify Melanie.

Every new suspiciously shaped mole brought about a nervous breakdown, showers were strictly forbidden if it was remotely drizzling (she read lightning can travel through pipes), and she had her car engine checked every other month to make sure the thing won't implode while she's driving. Even the *thought* of life being over—one minute she's there, and the next she's gone—would send her spiraling.

But now, lying in the Manor's dark, dusty attic, Melanie fears living more than death.

"We're almost out," Buck says. "We're so close."

She registers the words, but the vibrations of Crystal's screams still linger in her ears. *No! Please, no!*

"It doesn't matter," she whispers. "I don't think I'll ever escape this."

She wants to tell Buck to leave her there, that she can't handle any more of this nightmare. As she squeezes her eyes shut, the world becomes what she wants it to be for only a moment. Soft green hills, fresh air, the sky—what color is the sky? It seems like ages since she's seen it, and now she can't secure any color for it other than plain old blue.

"We've got to keep going, Melanie." Buck shakes her. "Come on, we can do this."

"Remember when you asked me if cake would taste the same once we leave?"

"Yeah."

She rolls over to look at him. "Do you think the sky will look the same? Or will it be…terrifying?"

He pulls her to her feet, where she stands like a marionette left hanging on a hook. "Nah, it won't look the same. It'll look better. Because there was a time when we thought we'd never see it again."

It's a good answer, but not enough to bolster her spirits. She takes the tiniest of glances about the room, finding it the least interesting and yet the most frightening out of all the Manor. There's nothing here but cardboard boxes and dusty furniture, everything half covered with sheets and plastic. The only light in the room is a dangling naked bulb on the low ceiling. Buck has to bend so that his head doesn't knock into any of the bare beams crossing above.

The worst bit? There's a single echoing *ticktock, ticktock, ticktock* coming from all sides of the room.

A hidden clock is taunting them.

Buck feels around the walls, mumbling about a light switch. Meanwhile, Melanie approaches an oddly shaped rectangle covered in a tattered white tarp. She clenches the fabric in her fingers and pulls. Once the dust settles, she finds a glossy bar made of finished redwood. Brown leather stools are nailed onto the floor just beneath the lip of the drip-edge top.

"Found a switch," Buck calls from the outer shadows of the room. "Think it's safe to try it out?"

"Yes? No. Yes. Do it."

A second later, four pendant lights are revealed hanging over the bar, and the wall behind the counter is suddenly aglow with neon signs—an arrow encompassing the words BAR OPEN, a stag head attached to a household beer brand, and a bright green happy hour announcement.

She's almost knocked backward, not by the abrupt presence of light but by the déjà vu. This is the bar she's been having flashbacks to.

Sitting waiting for them, like a welcome present, is a bottle of whiskey and two glasses. Buck takes it in his hands, frowning.

"You know anything about this?" he asks, rubbing the label with this thumb before setting the bottle down. "Think it's a clue about your riddle? Or a farewell token?" he adds hopefully.

*Her* riddle. He's right. It's the last one, and Melanie is the only person who hasn't had a room dedicated to her. One would assume knowing that the answer is her own name would make things easier, but like last time, they must still play the game. Not only that, but she's starving for answers. Everyone else has an explanation as to why Mortimer threw them in here—and whether they're true or not, they don't have to wonder.

She doesn't explain, mostly because there's not much information she can offer yet. She doesn't answer and instead sniffs the air. It's pungent: hard liquor spilled and dried over a wooden bar, stale popcorn, a dirty bathroom.

She suddenly remembers. Only a week ago, she was sitting at a bar very much like this one with Mortimer. The memory dries up there, and she draws a blank. Why? What did they talk about? What did she do there to upset him enough that he put her in the Manor?

"What do you think it's about?" Buck asks, reading her mind. "Your riddle."

"Are you asking me what I did to Mortimer? Or what he thinks I did?"

"Both."

The question hangs in the air.

"I don't know," she admits. "I wasn't sure at first, but now I think it's something worse than all of you."

They don't say anything for a few minutes. Maybe Buck doesn't really want to know, because he doesn't ask again. And for this, Melanie is grateful.

"This is the one room with no clocks in it that I can see," Buck says. "I can only guess we have about forty-five minutes left."

*Tick, tock. Tick, tock. Tick, tock.*

Melanie sighs and sinks into a dusty reading chair. It's too much time. She can't be here for another forty-five minutes—she wants to die *now*. She can't stop seeing flashes of the Manor killing everyone...Petey, Chester, Scott, Winnie...

Crystal.

Melanie swallows audibly, her stomach twisting.

Something stirs along the dark edges of the room, and she swears she can see tall shapes looming there: a stretched torso...stringy hair... thin slinky arms with knuckles that drag on the floor...

Gia is circling her. Waiting.

Melanie stares at the wall, thinking she might remain here in this position until the hour closes. *Then* Gia can take her.

But Buck suddenly cries out, "Aha!"

Melanie jumps.

"Look! The label has writin' on the back!" he says, peeling the thin sheath off the whiskey bottle. He unfurls it, his eyes quickly scanning the scrap. But Melanie sees what little light was left in them dim, like the final curtain call.

"What is it?" She stands. "Is it my riddle?"

He slowly shakes his head and utters, "No. It's much worse."

*To whoever receives this note: congratulations.*

*I had my doubts any of you would succeed in making it to the attic, but if you're reading this, then I can only assume you've survived.*

*As you must know by now, my Manor is an intelligent being. It is also an obedient one. It's been commanded to open the hatch to the widow's peak only when the final will recipient is in the room. If that is you and you alone, you are free to leave.*

*If you are not the sole survivor and have managed to bring others with you, then I'm afraid I've left you with one last decision. My Manor will not allow both of you to go alive. While there's more than one beating heart in the house, it remains locked. There's no more hour deadline, no more waiting until time runs out. My Manor will not kill again.*

*But one of you might. The choice is yours.*

*Good luck.*
*Mortimer Queen*

Bile gurgles in the back of her throat. It had been ignorant to think if they jumped through Mortimer's hoops, they'd get out of here alive. This note is his last bit of revenge, like a shark snagging a helpless foot before the person is plucked out of the ocean. But in their case, rescue isn't an option. They'll drown here instead.

*My Manor will not kill again. But one of you might.*

Or maybe *Buck* is the shark.

She feels his hand on her shoulder and jerks away; his heel clips a box of empty picture frames. Instinctively she tenses, slightly crouching and readying to leap away the minute he attacks. But only stares at her.

"What are you...? Do you think I'm gonna hurt you?" Realization settles into the lines on his forehead. "God, no! Melanie...I couldn't do that."

*Right*, she thinks, watching his baseball-mitt-sized hands and imagining them crushing her head like a watermelon.

"I would never hurt you." Buck is practically ripping out his beard with distress. "Even if it means savin' my own life, I'd never do that. Please believe me."

There's a long string of silence between them. It dawns on her how little time she's actually known him. What, seven hours? She doesn't even trust a cup of coffee that's sat out for that long.

"I trust you, and you trust me," an echo of her sentiment.

Melanie crumples the note in her hand. "Okay," she agrees, because what else can she do?

They stand silently among this truce; neither of them knowing what to do next.

Melanie presses her palms into her eyes, this realization settling into her skin like heavy lotion. She hears the hissing *crack* of a bottle being opened for the first time followed by liquid splashing into a glass.

Even if Buck doesn't kill her, they won't last without food and water. Sure, they have access to whatever they can find here, but eventually these resources will run out. She doesn't know what's worse—a gruesome death by the Manor or having to live out the rest of her life inside its walls.

# Buck Grimm

IT'S FUNNY, ON the red-eye Buck took this morning to from LA to Vermont, the flight attendant asked if he'd like a beverage.

"You seem like a beer man." She grinned cheekily. "Can I get you one with a cup of ice?"

Having been sober up until the Manor, Buck politely declined. That was beer—light beer. Watered down with *ice*.

And now he's ready to chug a whole bottle of what smells like cask-strength whiskey. This stuff is hard, completely undiluted, with an ABV over 60 percent. It's so strong, a drop could burn his second big toe right off. For God's sake, he had a *green juice* for breakfast.

The liquor is warm, which makes the burn tenfold, like tossing blistering oil into a frying pan. Whiskey used to generally lick down his esophagus and settle comfortably in his stomach, but this time it goes kicking and screaming. It doesn't matter, though. Anything to make him sleep. Make him numb. Make the time pass so he can forget that he's trapped here for as long as he can stay alive.

Melanie is turned away from him. They haven't spoken in an hour, which he was perfectly content with at first. But now a slight tipsiness is rolling into him, and he finds his lips are looser than before.

"You want a drink?" he asks her back.

She doesn't reply.

"We...we could talk a little? Good distraction."

He hears her snort. "A distraction? From dying?"

"Got anythin' else to do?"

She turns and hesitates before scooting closer to him and crisscrossing her legs. With a dejected, slack face, she reaches over and takes the bottle from his hands. She waterfalls a stream of liquid into her throat and coughs fiercely.

"That's...awful!" She gags, wiping her mouth with the back of her hand.

He glances at the bottle, his mouth downturned. "Actually, I think it's pretty well aged. Which is a good thing," he adds at her confused expression.

"I haven't had much experience, so I guess it would've sucked either way for me." Her face flushes. "You don't get invited to many college parties when people don't know you exist."

Buck swipes a hand in the air, batting the words away. "Ah. You're not missing much. Just a bunch of asshole kids funneling cheap beer like idiots. You're smarter than that." His throat is ablaze, every breath coming out like steam.

She gestures for the bottle again and takes a bigger swig this time. She puckers her mouth and leans over into a pre-vomit pose, but she levels herself after a guttural groan. "Ugh. If I'm so smart, why did I waste so much time writing crappy books that'll never get published instead of going out and making friends?"

Buck pauses. He recalls Melanie mentioning that she was trying to be an author—was it during introductions at cocktail hour? His cheeks go warm with shame. How could he have not asked her about it at dinner, before this all went to shit?

"I'm sure you're very talented," he says lamely. "You'll get there."

"That's what Mortimer said," she replies slowly, like the words are stuck to the roof of her mouth. "Said I needed inspiration." She pokes her tongue out with a *thpppppt*. "I think I might throw up."

"Do it." A whiskey burp barrels up from his stomach. "You'll feel better. Trust me."

With his blessing, she leans over and vomits into a cardboard box. Buck hopes it's the one with Mortimer's trophies inside. Then she slumps over, snoring loudly. He knows she'll feel like crap when she wakes up, but at least her drunken dreams are a respite from this hellhole.

With a grunt, he gets to his feet and traipses around the room, whiskey glass in hand. He considers the walls, wondering what the rest of their lives will look like here. If the running water works indefinitely, he guesses they won't die of thirst. No, it'll be the lack of food. He read somewhere that starving is a more painful death because it drags out for longer. He takes a long sip of whiskey, allowing the bitterness to pepper his tongue.

Then he notices a metal square on the wall, about the size of a TV screen. After setting his glass down on the bar, he makes his way over and presses a finger to the cold dusty surface. It's a door with a handle on the bottom, much like a garage. He pulls it up and reveals a compartment—a dumbwaiter, of course. It's been ages since he's seen one. But his attention is more drawn to what's inside.

A candelabra lies on its side, covered in blood.

Fresh blood.

He takes it into his hand, staring at the thing, trying to remember where he's seen it before. It was…it was in the last room. Yes, it was there, sitting on the side table, next to the pill bottles.

He didn't see what happened, but Crystal's screams reverberate in his ears, followed by the sickening *thunk*.

Like she was hit in the head.

Buck turns to look at the sleeping Melanie, her body curling into itself. He watches her for a long while, weighing the bloody candelabra in his hand. Finally, he sets it back in the dumbwaiter and closes the door. He slowly approaches her, his heart so heavy that it's sinking through to his intestines.

Reaching down, he roots through a dusty carboard box, removes a quilt, and throws it over Melanie. Then he turns, sinks into the reading chair, and closes his eyes.

# Melanie Brown

SOMEONE IS CHIPPING away at Melanie's skull with a dental pick—the kind archaeologists use to carefully excavate bones from the ground. Her head pounds, the aching strong enough to stir her from sleep but not enough to pry her eyes open. She's on her side, the floor beneath her warm but hard. For a minute she attempts to coerce herself back to sleep, but even the slightest movement jostles her stomach and a wave of nausea overwhelms her. Moaning, she lifts her lids inch by inch and the room comes into view.

It's hard to focus on anything other than the tacky film covering the insides of her mouth or the searing pain rippling through her temple. Melanie collects fragments of memories like picking up a trail dirty clothes on her bedroom floor. The Manor. Winnie dead. Crystal dead. Attic. Whiskey? Buck—

Buck.

She jerks her head too fast, her migraine screaming in protest, and finds the attic empty. Where is he? She sees the empty bottle of liquor sitting atop the bar.

Her first thought is dismal. Buck is dead. The Manor took him while she was passed out, and she did nothing to save him. She doesn't want to imagine how it happened, sure her creativity doesn't breach Mortimer's when it comes to a grisly demise.

A sudden creaking snaps her to attention, followed by a soft thumping from below. She realizes the attic hatch is still open, leaving her susceptible to whatever might come snooping for fresh blood. Her legs feel unsteady as she tries to run over to slam it shut, but she's too late. A figure pops up through the opening.

"Buck!" she shouts with relief, ignoring how her own volume sends sharp pricks through her head. "You're okay!"

He hoists himself up, his injured foot bare except for a clean cloth wrapped neatly around the big toe. The other is still wearing a boot, which explains the clomping. He sets down a full bucket—a thermos, a purple quilt, a few knives, several tins of sardines, and—

Melanie lifts a roll of toilet paper.

"Er, yeah." Buck blushes. "It's… Well, if ya gotta go…I wasn't too sure you'd be all that jazzed to head back downstairs for the latrine. I figured the bucket could be…ya know."

Her bladder *is* bursting. And she has no desire to traverse backward after all the trouble it took to get up here. She almost wants to laugh. In all the horror novels she's read, never once did any of the characters have to stop and use the bathroom while they were fighting off ghoulish monsters. Buck dumps out the contents and hands the bucket to her before turning away. She takes it behind the bar and when she emerges, Buck double-checks aloud before turning back around.

"I found this in the kitchen and filled it with water." He hands her the thermos. "Drink as much as you want. I had plenty straight from the faucet."

She gratefully guzzles the lukewarm water. The stale taste along her tongue is gone, but her stomach still gurgles in retaliation.

"Guess so. I found some canned food in the kitchen—only grabbed what could fit in the bucket, but we can always go get more. And there's water. So we'll last…I don't know…a few months?" He sighs. "At least this is less gruesome, right? When we run out of food, we'll go peacefully."

She's not exactly sure dying of starvation is a serene experience, but he's right. It's nothing compared to the brutality of the deaths they've witnessed tonight. They can spend the next few months wandering the Manor, living in it as Mortimer might have. It could be relatively fine, as long as Gia doesn't disturb them.

"He's got a lotta books," Buck says, like her inner musings are on display. "Might not be so bad."

A ghost of a smile—she might never fully grin again, but this feels like a start—stretches across her cracked lips. "That's very authorish of you to say."

Her hangover twists her brain stem, reminding her of its presence like an unwelcome bang on the front door.

She winces, clutching her head.

"Me too," Buck agrees, blowing air from his lips. He reaches for the thermos.

"I drank it all," Melanie says apologetically. "But I can go back downstairs. Wait here. It's my turn to help."

She retraces her steps back through the master bedroom. While she tries to keep her eyes on the floor, not wanting to see the bodies of Winnie and Crystal, a human urge beckons her gaze upward. To her surprise, the room appears completely normal, not a body nor speck of blood in sight. It's terrifyingly plain.

Melanie hurries back through the secret passageway to the kitchen, fills the thermos again, and makes her selections from the pantry as quickly as possible. She does *not* want to be alone for long. When she returns to Buck, she reveals her spoils: two foil-wrapped pastries—the kind scientists say could survive a nuclear winter.

"Excellent!" Buck drools. "I ain't one to be picky, but these look a hell of a lot tastier than sardines."

They decide to tear into one now, their stomachs gnawing. It's a miniature loaf of sponge cake with caramel-colored frosting drizzled on top. Melanie breaks off a bit of mold on the corner to make it good as new. It's a small victory, one that should be celebrated.

They sit together, Melanie on the reading chair (bedsheet still strewn over it) and Buck on the ground. His toe stub is starting to smell rancid.

"What do people do?" she asks abruptly after a comfortable bout of quiet. "When people are about to die, what are they supposed to do?"

"I guess they think about everything they did in life," Buck says. "All their best moments. Like a highlight reel, ya know?" He reaches into a cardboard box and hoists up a large crystal award in one hand. Pilsworth Literary Honor, 2013.

"I've never won anything like that," she says. It's not a self-pitying remark, just factual reporting. "Never achieved anything, really."

"I'm sure that's not true."

"That's just what you're *supposed* to say. Don't people think about their regrets when they're dying? I have a lot of those." She notices he's waiting to bite into his half of the pastry until she does. So she sinks her teeth in. Regardless of its age, sugar tastes heavenly.

Buck follows, then talks with his mouth full. "What are your regrets?"

"Petra, my sister, always told me I needed to do things for myself," she says. "I never did. I can't think of one thing."

"That's a cryin' shame. Because you seem like you deserve it."

"You think?"

"Definitely."

"Thanks, Buck."

A gust of cold air settles in the room, less like a breeze and more like lukewarm water in a chilled lake. Melanie looks up at the outer edges of the room and finds a pair of glittering white eyes blinking back at her. Gia hovers in wait, still watching.

Choosing not to inform Buck, Melanie takes a deep breath and licks frosting off her fingers. If they're going to exist in the Manor for as long as they can, Gia will have to become like a spider on the wall.

"Is it better than sugar-free pudding?" he asks.

"Oh yeah," Melanie says, ignoring the eyes boring into her. "Dog food tastes better than that."

Buck laughs so loudly that his face turns pink, and he starts coughing, beating his fist with his chest. Once she's sure he's not actually choking, starts plucking crumbs off her lap one by one.

"Especially walnut cake," she adds. "I'm not usually a huge fan of nuts in desserts, but this is the exception."

"Walnuts?" he says, and Melanie hears that his voice is suddenly raspy. "There are walnuts in there?"

Confused, she creases her brow. She lifts the plastic packaging and turns it over, squinting at a faded nutritional label. "It's...it's a walnut-maple loaf," she says. "Why? What's...what's happening? Are you okay?"

Buck's hands fly at his throat, his skin transitioning to an urgent splotchy red. He makes a sucking sound like he's attempting to draw air in from a too-thin straw.

"What should I do?" Melanie screams, bounding to her feet. "What should I do? Tell me!"

She knows enough about allergic reactions to understand how quickly bad goes to worse. Buck collapses, his fingers tearing at the buttons on his shirt.

Whirling toward Gia's eyes, still blinking through the shadows, Melanie shouts, "Help me! Help *him*! He's dying! Please!"

Buck gives a strangled cry and stops thrashing. She knows his heartbeat has stopped because a flap in the ceiling opens and a set of stairs unfolds. She pauses, her hands hovering over his body. Then she springs into action.

In a high school CPR class, an instructor told them that a person's heart can stop beating for a total of eight minutes before it results in death. But restarting his heart won't mean anything if she can't get him his EpiPen, one that he had mentioned having in his truck during dinner. His truck, parked right outside. With a surge of determination, she bolts up the stairs.

Emerging out onto the roof, she gasps as her lungs welcome cold, fresh air. Deliciously chilly rain smatters her face, and the sky is a light blue, the sun settling into its morning position. She steps out onto the widow's peak, a small square on the roof with tiny iron spikes surrounding the edge.

"Oh my God." She splutters in shock. "Oh my God."

Melanie can't believe she made it out. But now isn't the time to celebrate.

She never really considered what would happen once she got here. There doesn't appear to be a way down. Peering over the edge, she sees how tall the Manor truly is. Maybe this is another one of Mortimer's tricks.

"You could do it, if you wanted," someone behind her says.

It's not a surprise that Gia has appeared next to her, though she looks as human as she did when first greeting the guests.

"You could jump," Gia says. "But I don't think Mortimer would have wanted that. He put so much effort into this plan for you."

"I need you to get me down," Melanie orders, rainwater flying into her mouth.

Gia reaches her hand out, and Melanie flinches instinctively. "But of course! I'm at your service. You're the Manor's new owner after all."

Melanie suddenly feels cold, and then there's a jerking sensation—like a hook tugging on her navel. The world spins, and suddenly, she's standing on a spot of grass, the Manor to her left. Her knees buckle as she struggles not to collapse.

She sprints to the other side of the house, kicking up gravel as she gets to the cars. It's not hard to figure out which is Buck's: a massive red truck with tractor-sized wheels. She wrenches open the door—thankfully those small-town sensibilities made sure he didn't lock it—and yanks open the glove compartment to search. And there it is. The EpiPen. She grabs it and races back to the Manor's front door. It opens for her without delay. Remembering her and Buck's detour, Melanie sprints to the parlor room and up the secret passage to the guest suites.

Somehow, the Manor feels different now—the air easier to breathe, the walls no longer growling. In a blur, she's back upstairs in the attic, crouched next to Buck.

She stabs the EpiPen into his thigh, through his pants, and begins CPR. Her skinny arms barely make a dent as she does compressions against Buck's chest. Puffing up her cheeks, she counts in her mind: *Seven…eight…nine…ten…*

A minute passes and he doesn't stir. Her arms are burning, but she continues.

Suddenly, his eyes fly open, and he gasps for breath. He's panicked, though, and it's hard to keep him calm while the rest of the epinephrine does its job. Finally, Melanie feels him relax under her touch, and he starts breathing deeply in and out.

"Holy shit," he says to the ceiling, once he's able to speak. "How did you…?"

"I can explain later, but right now, we need to get out of here." Melanie glances around. "The doors are all open, but I can't promise they'll stay that way. The Manor might feel…cheated. Can you move?"

It takes another minute for him to stand. Melanie is on pins and needles. She was free mere moments ago—what if she gets trapped again?

"Rule number two." Buck grunts, starting toward the door. "Run fast."

While they don't move as fast as Melanie would like, she and Buck make it out to the parking lot. "You don't know how to hot-wire a car, do you? Gia has all the keys."

"'Fraid not. We'll have to go on foot."

Melanie nods, and the two run toward the woods, then duck into the shadows of the trees. Part of her wants to check over her shoulder to see if Gia is chasing after them, but that seems like a mistake. *No, you don't waste time looking back—that's a rookie move.*

Her quads ache, her body throbbing from the hangover. In the distance, past a long series of bare-bones pine trees, is a house, and she doesn't stop until she gets to its door. Buck has fallen slightly behind, but he arrives a beat later, choking on the cold night air.

It's a simple modern cabin, the kind people retreat to when they want to be off the grid. Little do they know what's going on nearby.

Melanie grabs the doorknob and twists. She's expecting resistance but finds that it's unlocked. After sweeping inside, she slams it behind them and turns the lock.

"Hello?" Buck shouts. "Anyone home? Please! We need help!"

When no one replies, Buck throws Melanie a look, and they begin scoping out the place. The cabin is one room with a tiny twin-size bed, a kitchen table, and stone fireplace. Above the hearth is a moose head, its eyes glassy. After checking to make sure the front door is properly locked, she searches for a phone. Instead, she finds an old-fashioned typewriter sitting on a small desk, a piece of paper stuck in its platen.

She steps closer. It's a letter.

Addressed to her.

Dear Melanie,

*I've written thousands of words over the course of my career, but nothing has ever given me more pleasure than what I'm about to inscribe now.*

*I hope you've enjoyed your time at the Manor, because it's yours now. While this was not originally a component of our deal, I suspect you'll be pleased.*

*I've never been a kind man, but in my final days of life, I wanted to be. To put those monsters out of their misery, their every waking step burdened with the evil acts they committed, is a thing of mercy.*

*As I discussed during our afternoon together, those monsters may have attempted to sway you to feel empathy for them. Did you grow fond of them, Melanie? Did you consider them friends? I should hope not, but to err is to be human. If this is the case, I implore you to visit beneath the floorboards for a reminder as to why we made these arrangements.*

*When we first met, you had so little to say but such a wrathful hunger to put words on the page. Now take what you've experienced and tell it to the world. This cabin—built a mere acre away from* the Manor—has been crafted for your every need: food, water, shelter, a typewriter, paper, and most importantly, inspiration. You may stay as long as you like.

There are so many monsters in the world. Not the ghouls and ghosts we authors often create, but true forms of evil masked beneath soft flesh, friendly eyes, and steady hands. I am giving you mine. Take them and turn them into something great.

My publisher is at your disposal, ready to take your call when you are ready. Upon your submission of pages, my attorneys have been instructed to transfer all my money and assets to you.

As for the Manor, do what you will with it. You cannot destroy it, though I can only assume you will try. You may, however, starve it if you wish. It's a kind of predator that sits in wait for its victims rather than goes into the night to hunt.

But, dear Melanie, some people do terrible things in life. Some people, like the ones you've met from my past, deserve to be punished. Are you going to tell me that you can't think of anyone who should be given what they are owed?

*All my best,*
*Mortimer Queen*

# Melanie Brown

FOR A MOMENT Melanie thinks this cabin must be alive, too, because it feels like it's swallowing her whole. Her foot accidentally kicks the leg of the table, jostling a stack of blank paper with Mortimer's letterhead on them. She backs away from the typewriter until the lies marring the page are too blurry to read.

They are lies, right?

*Yes!* She whirls around and marches toward the door. *This is another trap.*

Although…

A thread of hesitation pulls her to a stop. Mortimer predicted she'd be skeptical. What did he say? To *visit beneath the floorboards?* Her palms, lying by her sides, itch with grim fascination. They should leave this place, find safety, call the police. But deep within her is an unhealthy hunger for answers. If she goes now, she'll never get them.

"Find somethin'?" Buck asks from the other side of the room.

Melanie quickly tears the paper from the typewriter and turns it over. "Nothing helpful," she replies.

*Five minutes*, she tells herself, scanning the floor. *You get five minutes to look.*

Turns out she doesn't require all five because the outline of a trapdoor is clearly marked on the floor. It even has a sleek black handle, which she tugs on, opening the entryway to the basement.

"I don't think we should go down there," Buck says, coming up behind her. "What if we get trapped again? Let's get out of here while we can."

He takes a step and puts his injured foot on the trapdoor, his boot landing with a *thump*. Melanie scrutinizes him, watching his eyes dart from her to the front door.

"I want to see what's down there," she says.

He looks long and hard at her before moving aside, letting her pull up the door. Without another word, she climbs down a ladder and gazes around the darkened room. The only light coming in is from upstairs. When her fingers brush a switch, she flicks it on.

And then everything changes.

The basement is covered in gray photos, documents, and newspaper clippings, a chaotic art exhibit with six familiar subjects:

Petey, Chester, Scott, Winnie, Crystal, and Buck.

Not every shot makes sense, but when she steps back and puts them together, they tell a cohesive tale. There's a framed manuscript of *Shrieking and Shrinks* with Mortimer's name as the author, plus a sticker marked EXTRA COPY. Alongside it is a printed-out email from Petey. It reads, I got your messages and your threats. What's done is done. You have no proof of concept, and I have the copyright. So let's just call this what it is and leave well enough alone.

"What the hell…?" Buck whispers, finally joining her as he steps down from the ladder.

She continues down the wall, her gaze falling on a screenshot of a news report. An anchor is standing outside a building, her microphone brought up to her mouth as the frozen ticker underneath reads TEEN JUMPS FROM HOTEL ROOF. Melanie squints, and in the background, she can see Chester standing there with his hands in his pockets. There's another shot of him—another screen grab from an Instagram story. He's standing in the hotel lobby, towering with a snarl on his lips over a small black-haired girl. Among other newspaper clippings announcing the tragic death of Mary McKinnon, there is one that immediately catches her eye:

**SUSPECT IN TEEN SUICIDE CASE ARRESTED. POLICE SAY, 'HOMICIDE MAY BE BACK ON THE TABLE.'**

The clipping next to it is even more damning.

**KEY EVIDENCE IN TEEN SUICIDE CASE LOST; SUSPECT DISMISSED. RULING FINAL.**

Melanie gets to Scott's section of the room. A cluster of photos shows him in the middle of an alley, kicking a man curled up on the ground. A *New York Tribune* article is taped up, ripped from its magazine.

**MORTIMER QUEEN: A FALLEN KING**

Once a giant of the industry, Mortimer Queen—author of beloved classic *Monster House*, among other classics—has officially been snubbed from the *New York Times* list. His last effort, which was released in a spectacularly understated way, has sold a meager number of books, making his final bow more of a stumble. While the book itself is a finely crafted work, many bookstores claimed their shipments failed to arrive on time, if at all. The promotional tour was ill organized, the novel is not available on any online platform, and Mortimer's social media profile has gone radio silent. Either Mortimer doesn't care to showboat anymore, or his PR manager phoned it in—

Melanie moves quickly away. Scott, her fearless leader who nearly cried when she split from the group, was not only a liar but twisted, cruel.

"I...I don't think we should be down here," Buck croaks. "We should go."

Next is Winnie. A series of camera photos, their dates marked on the bottom left-hand corner, show her walking out of a town house and into the one next door. There's a flurry of text conversations between Winnie and someone called Betty, whose minuscule profile picture next to her name is the BCA News logo.

> **Winnie:** Did you do it?
>
> **Betty:** I told you I would.
>
> **Winnie:** When will the article be out?
>
> **Betty:** It's in production.
>
> **Winnie:** ????
>
> **Betty:** A week.
>
> **Winnie:** 😵 😵
>
> **Betty:** God, can't you be a little less eager to destroy a man's reputation?
>
> **Winnie:** Just text me when it prints. I'll want a lot of copies.

And clipped beside the string of texts is, of course, the BCA News article detailing Mortimer's alleged abuse. The possible murder of his ill wife.

"Melanie," Buck pleads, but she's in another world. His voice is far away now, unimportant.

She fears Crystal's betrayal will be enough to send her spiraling. If Mortimer was telling the truth this entire time, then that means…

Crystal's display contains a Google history search:

*Is arsenic traceable in an autopsy?*

*Arsenic symptoms vs. pancreatic cancer.*

*How to get weed killer out of clothes.*

*Trips to St. Croix for two.*

Melanie physically gags, unable to stomach it. A scream rises from the lowest section of her chest, but she pushes it down.

Buck's rugged features and jolly smile pierce her heart as she scans the mosaic of photos of him. There he is at Deacon's Group Publishing, shaking Mortimer's hand and giving the camera a thumbs-up. Maybe that was his first day. A gold plaque hangs on the wall with his name emblazoned at the top: RECOGNITION FOR TWO YEARS OF HARD WORK. Another photo shows him slumped over his desk, a flask dripping from his pocket. There are several versions of this image; he's wearing a different tie in each one.

A cassette tape hangs from a red string, the label reading, LISTEN TO ME. Melanie unties it from the string. A cassette player is on the ground before her. She sticks the tape inside and presses Play, then waits with bated breath.

"Wait." Buck extends an arm but appears stuck to the ground. "Don't."

For a while, there's only static. Then Buck's voice comes clearly over the speakers.

*"Actually, sir, before you…decide on anything…" he drawls.*

*"Decide?" Mortimer chuckles. "I've already made my decision."*

She lifts her chin to look present-day Buck in the eyes as the recording plays on.

"I just wanted to give you your messages. Two messages, really. A Crystal Flowers called, sir. She wants to know if she can pack a second checked bag for your trip to London this weekend. She also mentioned that she'd like it if you could book the same couple's massage as last time. Now, ain't that the girl who was in here the other night? The one half naked, bent over your desk right there?"

He goes on to blackmail Mortimer into approving the publication of his first book.

"That's…that's made up," Buck stammers, the lie plain on his lips. "It's not me. He's trying to trick you, Melanie. I didn't do anythin'… I didn't!"

She stares at him for a moment and gives a curt nod.

Right away, he responds with a watery smile, his shoulders relaxing.

"We should go," she says flatly, grabbing the ladder and starting to climb.

She pulls herself out and peers down at Buck, who's halfway up behind her. Searing, passionate indignation twists in her belly as she looks at him. It's a sensation she hasn't experienced in a very long time but one she greets like an old friend. She grabs the hatch door and slams it shut, yanking the lock in place with a loud *clang*.

"Wh-what? Melanie! Lemme out!" Buck thunders, jostling the floor. "It won't open from this side! Melanie! Melanie, no! Don't do this!"

His high-pitched begging is even worse than Crystal's was. Melanie should have known they were all bad after realizing how *horrible* Crystal was. They were all alone in the master bedroom, and the Manor saw to it that Melanie had the opportunity to strike her over the head.

Melanie felt sick about it afterward, but now her decision feels even more warranted. She righted a wrong. Crystal deserved it. They all did.

Mortimer wasn't the one rewriting the past—these *monsters* were.

Melanie spins on her heel, ready to run out of the cabin and never look back, but her toe catches on the carpet, and she goes down hard. Her head cracks onto the floor…

*And it*

        *all*

                *comes*

                        *back.*

# Melanie Brown

### *Before the Manor*

A N OBSCENE HONKING is coming from the other side of Petra's bedroom door.

Melanie clutches her laptop closer to her chest while imagining her sister tucked into the lavender comforter, a flurry of used tissues and cough drop wrappers decorating the bed.

"Are you sure I can't come in?" she asks, leaning on the door. In her hand is a bag of cold medicine, plus a can of chicken noodle soup.

"No!" Petra says weakly, though it sounds like *doh* because of her stuffy nose. "Just leave the medicine. I don't want you getting sick. What took you so long? I'm dying here."

Melanie bites her lower lip and sets the CVS bag on the ground. "I was…" She stops, thankful the door is there to shield her face. "I was just running late. Sorry."

She can't tell her sister that she was sitting in the darkest corner of a café, banging her fists on her keyboard. After twelve rejections, Melanie has come to realize her newest novel is an eighty-thousand-word pile of mush—a bowl of oatmeal she's left sitting on her kitchen counter for a record number of days.

"Don't tell me that *she* made you go back to get your eyebrows waxed," her sister growls.

Petra doesn't like to refer to their mother as…well, their mother. It's always *her* and *she*.

"Well, yeah." Melanie lifts the beanie and delicately feels the swollen pimply spot between her brows. "But that was yesterday."

"What?" Petra gasps, which leads to a bout of coughing. "You went back to the salon? But you had an allergic reaction to the wax last time!"

"It's fine."

It's not. Which is why she's wearing her beanie low: 60 percent of her face looks like it was stung by hornets. But Petra doesn't need to know that.

"Melanie, you need to stop letting her boss you around. You're not her little doll to mess with—"

More coughing. It takes her minutes to stop, and when she does, Melanie can practically hear her deflate into the pillows.

"God, I wish I could just get as far away from here as possible," Petra moans. "Far away from *her*."

"You shouldn't leave your apartment key under your doormat," Melanie can't help but add, trying to jump off the topic of Cynthia. "That's sort of the most obvious place to find it."

"This place is a shithole. Anyone who would break in would just feel bad for me."

Melanie has to agree. The apartment, which Cynthia has forbidden her to visit (oops) smells of wet algae and stale cigarettes. Petra refused to let their mother pay for housing after college, so with her small teacher's salary, this is where she landed.

"This is the worst day ever." Petra sniffles.

Melanie bites her bottom lip. "I'm sorry, P. Lucky it's just a cold, though! You'll be better in a few days."

"It's not just that!" Petra says passionately. "Mortimer Queen is at Joseph Beth Bookstore for a book signing! I've tried for weeks to get my hands on *Phobos*, and he's selling a limited number of copies today."

"*Phobos*?" Melanie wrinkles her nose.

"It's the god of terror."

She can tell Petra is rolling her eyes. "Can't you get a copy off Amazon?" Melanie asks.

"Didn't you hear me say, 'I've tried for weeks?' They're nowhere to be found. My book club was gonna read it this month, but they gave up looking for copies and moved on to a *comedy* novel. Bleh."

"Bummer." Melanie feels tired of talking to a door. "Anyway, I have to go."

"Wait, wait, wait! Could you go for me? I'll send you money—please! I'll love you forever!"

"Petra, no," she whines. "Please don't make me do that."

The *last* thing she wants to do is go to an event celebrating an author's success when she's only just accepting that it's something she'll never have.

"Melanie!" her sister begs. "It's his last book *ever*. He's done writing after this one—do you understand? He's done! Please, please?"

Melanie hesitates, bending under the will of her sister. "How crowded will it be?" She loves bookstores but hates crowds. "Will I have to talk to…? Who is the author again?"

"Mortimer Queen," Petra says quickly. "He's my *favorite* horror writer. Oh, and do something for *yourself* while you're at it! Buy a latte, read a book for fun, or ask a cute guy out."

Melanie doesn't verbally agree to do it, but then again she doesn't verbally do much of anything. And regardless, there are few things she wouldn't do for her sister. So she leaves the care package at the door and heads to Joseph Beth.

Considering how highly as Petra talks about Mortimer Queen, the line to get *Phobos* copies signed is underwhelming. When she's only a few people away from Mortimer Queen, Melanie's phone rings from her pocket, but she ignores the jaunty tune.

A round-faced woman wearing too much blush informs her, "Your cell is ringing." The woman is standing behind her in line, looking positively overjoyed to be there.

Melanie acknowledges this with a curt nod before waiting for the ringing to stop.

"Are you all right?" the woman asks, putting a hand on her khaki-clad hip.

"Me?" she squeaks and clears her throat. "Yes. I'm fine."

She turns away from the woman and promptly realizes she's up. Melanie steps forward and places the book into Mortimer's hands before he has to ask.

"Please make it out to Petra Brown," she says, hoping he'll be quick.

"Thank you for being a fan, Petra," he says with as much gusto as a tired older man can offer. He seems oddly defeated for someone at his own book signing.

"Oh, I'm not Petra," she says and instantly regrets it. Why couldn't she have pretended? Why did it matter? "This is for my sister. She loves your books."

"Is that so?" Mortimer asks, smiling softly. "Would you like a signed copy for yourself?"

"No, that's all right," she says quickly, averting her eyes. "I…I haven't read any of your work before."

She can't believe what just came out of her mouth. Her hands stretch out, wanting to snatch Petra's signed book from his hands and bolt out of the store. But Mortimer isn't angry. In fact, he seems to be intrigued.

"What's your name?" he asks.

"Melanie Brown," she answers, her throat dry.

"Melanie." Mortimer smiles. "Are you in school?" He motions to her laptop, which she's perched on her hip.

"Huh? Oh! N-no," she stumbles over her words. "I was…writing." *Stupid, stupid, stupid. Stop talking.*

"Writing?" His eyebrows arch. "You're an aspiring author?"

Melanie hadn't expected so many questions and so much eye contact. "No. I mean, I guess so?" Her voice cracks.

"You don't sound so sure." Mortimer coughs out a laugh and reaches into his pocket for a yellowed handkerchief. "Writers must have confidence."

Melanie waits for him to hand her the book back, but he's watching her like he expects a response. "I've sent my manuscript to everyone in the *Writer's Digest* index," she admits. "But all I get are rejection letters."

The admission comes out before she can stifle it. This very clearly successful author doesn't need to hear about her failures—but he doesn't look like he's faking interest; he's pursing his lips in thought.

"Not to be rude, but you're taking a long time," complains the woman behind her.

Mortimer leans to the left and holds up his forefinger. Then he turns back to her. "Melanie, right? How about you stick around after the book signing and you can show me what you've been working on."

Her tongue shrivels like she's just chugged a gallon of salt water, but Melanie nods. Finally taking the signed book from Mortimer, she steps to the side and gathers her thoughts. Did he really just say he'd read her work? The bookstore has a little café in the back, so she takes her things to a table and orders a coffee and pumpkin scone. But she lets her drink go cold and only picks at the pastry, her nerves sitting hard in her stomach.

Melanie's phone buzzes, and a text from Petra comes in.

Did you meet him???

She stares at the screen, tugging her beanie down tighter on her head.

Yes.

Another text comes in two seconds after Melanie sends her own.

AND???? Is he amazing?

She glances toward the front of the store to see a sniffling, teary woman taking a selfie with Mortimer. He gives a weak smile, then hacks into his handkerchief again. Some iteration of this interaction happens at least fifteen more times, and the line dwindles. Mortimer gives a subtle hand gesture to someone standing off to the side, and a man steps out of the wings, holding up his arms.

"All right, everyone," he announces loudly, though it's not necessary. There are only about six people now. "Thank you so much for coming out today, but the book signing is officially over. Please check Mortimer Queen's website for future tour dates."

"When are you going to get more copies of the book?" asks a lanky man wearing a T-shirt that says *Feel the Fear*.

Mortimer ignores this and tugs on his collar like he's letting steam out from beneath his clothes. He slowly gets to his feet, wincing and rubbing his knees.

Melanie holds her breath as he scans the store until his eyes finally settle on hers. He makes his way to the café, lifting a finger at the barista behind the café counter. Right as he makes contact with the chair across from her, a cup of steaming tea and a packet of honey are on the table for him.

"Thank you for waiting," he says, ripping the honey open and drizzling it in. He takes a long sip and grimaces. "Ugh. Forget this. Let's go next door and get a drink."

"Oh, I don't—" she starts to say, but Mortimer is already up and headed toward the door. The only thing she can think to do is gather up her things and follow.

All eyes are on them as they walk down the sidewalk to the bar next door. Melanie glances at the neon flickering sign hanging in the window: ROODIES—with two *o*'s. The minute she steps inside, she inhales a whiff of Red Bull and nail polish remover. There's no one else inside, save the bartender scrolling through his phone.

Mortimer struggles to hoist himself onto a barstool, and she takes a seat next to him, trying to ignore how sticky the leather is.

"What can I get you?" The bartender barely looks up from a game of Candy Crush.

"Scotch. Neat." Mortimer coughs. "And whatever she wants."

The bartender finally looks up and stares at Melanie, skepticism written all over his face. Before he can deny her, Mortimer slides a clump of bills across the bar. The man's eyes bulge, and within seconds, the money is in his pocket.

"I…I really don't…" Melanie mutters to Mortimer, her face growing warm.

"She'll have the same as me," he says for her.

A glass of honey-brown liquid is set in front of her. Mortimer finishes his in a flash and flicks another wad of bills at the bartender, who accidentally smashes a bottle of liquor as he hurries to refill his glass.

"Just throw it back," Mortimer advises, his voice gravelly. "Only hurts for a second."

Like a toy soldier, Melanie complies. Fire licks down the back of her throat, and her eyes stream.

"All right," Mortimer says, drumming his fingers on the bar. "Show me what you have."

Melanie throws open her laptop and scours her manuscript folder, where dozens of her books have been left to die. She clicks her most recent project and turns it toward Mortimer, who pats his pockets until he finds his tiny rectangular reading glasses. He narrows his eyes and stares hard at the laptop screen, and Melanie's heart floods with—

"No," Mortimer says. "Not good. What else do you have?"

She could vomit then and there. And not because of the alcohol churning in her stomach. She fumbles with the laptop, clicking open another manuscript and offering it over again.

His furry eyebrows pull together in concentration as he reads.

"This one actually sparked some interest," she says, trying to be lighthearted. "An agent told me it had potential, but it wasn't a fit."

"That's what they say when your book isn't good," Mortimer says, using a single finger to push the laptop back across the café table. "And it's not. Anything else?"

If Melanie weren't so gutted, she'd have cried. But her system is in so much shock that all she can do was pull up yet another manuscript. Surely *one* of them would—

"I'm afraid this one is no good either," Mortimer says as he finishes the first page.

She jerks to her feet, slapping the laptop closed. "I'm sorry to have wasted your time." She starts to get down from the stool.

Mortimer takes another swig of his drink and holds up a finger. "*Sit.*"

Melanie slides back onto her seat, stricken.

He presses his fingertips together and says matter-of-factly, "You can't write if you have nothing to write about. Your stories are lifeless, dull."

"Oh."

Mortimer sighs and beckons the bartender over again. This time, he requests shots. Of what, Melanie isn't sure. They're dark gold but taste medicinal.

"What if you *had* something to write about?" Mortimer pounds the shot glass onto the bar so hard, she's astounded it doesn't shatter. "I mean really write about. Something with grit, with *meat*."

"Yeah. That's a…um, that's the common reception I get from publishers." She wipes her clammy hands on her jeans. "That I don't have anything to say."

Mortimer surprises her by grumbling, "Ah, fuck publishers. They're all bad, even mine. You don't need to have something to say—you just have to be able to write. And you can!" He jabs his tongue against the inside of his cheek. "The world is overcrowded with stories. So many things to say…not enough writers to get it out all there. Some of the really good ones fall through the cracks!"

"Writers?" Melanie asks, confused. "Or stories?"

"Stories!" he says with such aplomb that a few years shed off his face.

Two more shots appear. This time, Melanie knows what to expect and is careful not to let the liquid touch her tongue, sending it straight down her throat.

*That's my last one*, she thinks, feeling woozy already. *Speak up next time. Say no.*

"Take me, for instance," Mortimer says, a hand to his chest. "I…" It's like a thought occurs to him. "I'm going to tell you something, Melanie. But I need you to keep it between us."

She bobbles her head, which only makes her sway more on the barstool. This feels weird.

He leans close. "I'm dying. Soon, I'll be gone. And there isn't enough time for me to write all the stories I want to. Important ones. Some of the most significant of my life."

"I'm so sorry. Are you…sick?" She whispers the last word like it's vulgar to say aloud.

"I am." He nods. "I've made my peace with it. Lived my life the way I wanted to. It would be a peaceful exit into the afterlife if only…if only I could get my final story out."

Melanie's mouth is sandpapery, so she asks the bartender for something to drink. He misunderstands and slides a pink cocktail glass over, an umbrella sticking out of the top. This, which she sips idly, is at least tastier than the others.

"We could help each other, you know," Mortimer continues.

She shoves the beanie off her head and itches the rash along her eyebrows. The bartender makes a face, but she feels too warm and good inside to feel insecure about it. Should she drink more often?

"How?" she slurs in a voice she doesn't recognize.

"I bet you want to travel around the world," he says, his eyes ablaze with fervor. "To get out of this town. I have the money to do it. I could close my eyes, point to a spot on a globe, and be there by tomorrow afternoon. There's a theory out there—a *theory*, mind you—that there are advanced beings out in the galaxy. That they could spin our earth like a toy. And you know what would happen? The centrifugal force would become so extreme that one side of the planet would be plunged into darkness forever. Can you imagine? Half the earth plunged into eternal blackness."

"That would be awful." Melanie slurps down the remnants of her pink drink and is disappointed when it's gone.

"No, it would be wonderful!" He chortles. "I recommend you try it, Melanie. Take the world into your own hands and add a little darkness to it."

She remembers Petra then, probably still tucked into bed, oscillating between a fever and chills. "I should go home." She meant to only think it, but the words come out. "My sister is waiting for this book. Where is it? Here it is. See? Oh my gosh—I forgot. You wrote it."

"Melanie." Mortimer grabs her hand, and the loopy cheerfulness in her cheeks deflates. "Listen to me. We can do this together. You need a story to tell? I have *six*. Help me expose them, and I'll help you experience things that will change you as a writer forever."

His voice is fading in and out as he tells her his plan, his home, his victims, which is just as well, because so is her vision. But that doesn't stop her, maybe nothing could, when she finally swivels in her seat and looks him in the eye.

"I'm in," she announces.

Then she tilts slightly to the left and careens off the stool, smashing her face into the floor.

And the world goes dark.

# Melanie Brown

### *Two years after the Manor*

MELANIE TRIES TO curl a piece of hair behind her ear and finds it's no longer there.

Several weeks have passed since she cut her head into a neat pixie, and she's still not used to being so bare. Even though Cynthia won't stop telling her how much she hates it—*You look like a prepubescent boy!*—Melanie never knew how much braver she could be without a curtain of hair to hide behind.

It's uncomfortably chilly in this room, her cold hands near purple underneath the unflattering fluorescent lighting. Petra says the temperature in office buildings temperatures is set for the metabolic rates of men, but Melanie has no time to even thinking about fighting the good fight over thermostats. The air smells of stale coffee and printer ink, a lethal combination that has her itching her nose every two minutes. She tugs at her light-gray blazer—it's snug and accentuates the curves she didn't know she had. She's not one for fashion, but the matching pleated pants and flats certainly don't hurt her confidence.

How long has she been waiting here? She gets to her feet and paces, rubbing her hands together. It would be great if Petra were here with her now to ease her nerves, but that's a selfish thought. Melanie bought her sister a ticket to Barcelona a few months ago, and Petra's been having the time of her life since. She even sent Melanie a selfie of her pressed cheek to cheek with a cute guy over a bowl of paella.

Her sister always wanted out. Now? She is out. Maybe for good. It's bittersweet.

The room's door swings open, and Becca Anne bursts forth, fluttering her hands in the air as she sings, "Are you ready to *kill it*?"

Melanie smiles—her publicist is anything but subtle in her bright pink dress and giant bug-eyed sunglasses. Becca Anne hugs her, enveloping her in an all-too-sweet cranberry perfume.

"Are you excited?" she demands. "Are you thrilled?"

"Both." Melanie grins.

Becca Anne is only a few years older than her and has not only been essential in the book's launch but has become a good friend, something Melanie's never had before. Their afternoon coffee sessions and late-night Netflix binges (Becca Anne introduced her to something called *Desperate Housewives*, and they've been flying through all the seasons) have become her favorite perk of this new career.

Well, one of her favorite perks.

"Okay, so here's the deal," Becca Anne says, shoving her sunglasses on top of her head and whipping out her phone, "the center has a cap of a thousand people, but there's a line forming outside. People are dying to get in and see you."

"That many people?" Melanie blurts. "Just to hear me read?"

"Yep." Becca Anne flashes her a thumbs-up. "Don't forget you'll also be answering questions from the audience. Oh, and there's a raffle for your new book. But I don't know how they pick... I wonder if we could..."

Melanie is only half listening now, her heart thumping loudly over Becca Anne's instructions.

"...and afterward, security will bring you to the side entrance for a quick, discrete exit," she's saying.

"Is that really necessary?" Melanie intercepts this idea. "I mean, why would I need to make a quick getaway? It's not like there are going to be hordes of people after me."

She laughs, but Becca waggles a finger in her face with a serious look.

"You don't realize who you are now, do you? You're Mortimer Queen's protégée—people have been waiting for you to reveal yourself ever since he died. This is like if Oprah announced she had a younger host taking over the show. OH, BANANA SNAKES!"

The last bit is how Becca swears—it makes Melanie snicker every time.

"I completely forgot you have an interview with *USA Today*. We're meant to meet her in convention room D. Are you ready?"

Whether Melanie is ready or not, within minutes, they're speed walking down the hallway. Even though Becca is in heels, she's much faster. Melanie practically chases her past all the convention center's back offices to room D.

There sits Farrah Carmichael, associate editor and C-list celebrity. She's tall, her blond hair in a long braid down the back of a gorgeous white pantsuit—and she's ecstatic to see Melanie.

"I had to fight tooth and nail to be the one to interview you," she gushes, offering her a seat in a silver fold-out chair. "I loved your collection of short stories. Very J. D. Salinger meets Agatha Christie. And this goes without saying, but I'm *so* excited to read your book."

Becca, who is standing off to the side, air claps so that only Melanie can see.

"That's very nice of you to say," she says, smiling. "I'm honored."

It took three days to write *Six Short Stories* in that cabin in the woods.

Initially, this collection of works didn't have an official title. She was just calling it that because that's exactly what they were. But Becca Anne *loved* the idea and ran with it. She doesn't divulge the number of copies sold (mostly because Melanie decided she doesn't care to know), and money is somewhat insignificant because of how much she now has, but it's not hard to surmise how well *Six Short Stories* has performed. Her new modest apartment, perched over her favorite hometown coffee shop, is constantly swarmed with fans.

"I guess I don't mind it that much," Melanie said during a long-distance phone call with her sister. She was peering out from her front window at the gaggle of girls clutching copies of *Six Short Stories*. "Gives more business to the coffeehouse, so that's good."

Petra said something in Spanish, and in the background, glasses clinked and laughter spilled over. "Tell me again why you can't move in a nice private New York City penthouse? Or come travel with me? I can't figure out why you want to stay at home!"

They had that conversation often, but Petra still pressed it every time they talked—which was at least twice a week.

"Because Cyn—I mean, because Mom is here," Melanie repeated, as usual.

She'd started refusing to call her *Cynthia* any longer, and the reception was more or less lukewarm. But it was undeniable that her mother had become kinder to her since her return from the cabin. Melanie, who had found a prepaid cell phone taped to the underside of the cabin desk, called home just once the entire time she was away to say she wouldn't be back for a while. It was clear her mother had thought that meant her youngest daughter was leaving forever and had been openly relieved when she came back.

"It's so weird to hear you call her 'Mom' again," Petra grumbled. "I was just getting used to 'Cynthia.' It's not like she deserves the title, anyway. Or all the money you're giving her from your book deal. Even if she's being nice to you now, that doesn't change what she's done. You know that, right? She's still a monster."

"I know." Melanie pressed her forehead against the cool glass window. "But people are just monsters we love, right?"

"You're so weird. Call me tomorrow. Love you!"

Back in the interview chair, Melanie crosses and uncrosses her legs.

"Where did you come from?" Farrah asks, shaking her head. "I mean, it's like you materialized out of thin air. Where have you been hiding?"

"I've wanted to be an author my whole life, but I just never found right the story to tell."

"I'll say," Farrah says. "Your publicist allowed me to read an excerpt of your newest book—how can such a scary story come from a sweet-looking girl like you?"

Melanie laughs—it's a fake laugh, a strategic one. She's practiced it over and over again. Genuine hilarity has become something of the past now, even with Becca or Petra, a price to pay after experiencing the Manor.

"I have a vivid imagination," she tries to smile.

More like vivid nightmares. Writing this second book was easy—she just put pen to paper about everything she saw when she lay her head on a pillow.

"And quite the mentor, I hear. Mortimer Queen took a liking to you and helped you get published in the last bit of his life. What was he like?"

Melanie considers this, careful to breathe evenly while she answers. "He was…encouraging. And misunderstood by many."

Farrah waits, obviously anticipating more to Melanie's answer. When she doesn't oblige, Farrah moves on. "Clearly. I heard he left you everything he had in his will—is that true?"

Melanie glances over at Becca, who gives a shrug and nods, telling her it's okay to answer. She has a team of six lawyers, thanks to Mortimer, who assured her that she can say practically anything and they'll protect her. But still, she likes to keep things private for the most part.

"Yes, he did," she allows.

"All his accumulated wealth, his share of a publishing company, all his book royalties, and even a house, if I'm not mistaken?"

Melanie shifts in her seat. "Yes."

"Do you intend to live in the house?" Farrah asks.

"No. No, I don't."

Recently, her mother sheepishly asked if Melanie would consider letting her visit the Manor. "We could remodel it into a country vacation home!" she suggested hopefully. "Spend some time together up there."

When Melanie vehemently refused, insisting she didn't ever want to go back there, her mother offered to go alone.

And, though she's ashamed to admit it, Melanie considered letting her. But it was a fleeting, horrible thought. She assured her mother that nothing would ever come of the place and that, if she wanted, they could look at buying a home somewhere in the Carolinas.

"Maybe you'll turn it into a museum of sorts? An ode to Mortimer Queen?" Farrah pipes up. "I'm sure people would love to—"

"No," Melanie says, louder than she meant to. "It's... The place is old. Condemned. I'm leaving it be."

"Oh." Farrah frowns for a millisecond, then plasters on a professional smile. "That's a shame. So, did Mortimer Queen read your collection before he passed?" Her tone turns sympathetic, making Melanie nauseous.

"No," she says simply. "He didn't."

"Ah, I'm sorry to hear that. It's an even greater feat, then, the fact you did it alone."

Alone. Right. Melanie suddenly feels very far away, her gaze fixating on a figure that's appeared behind Farrah's shoulder. Her mouth goes slightly slack, and her palms turn clammy.

"You okay?" Farrah asks.

"I'm sorry, who is that?" Melanie grips the arm of her chair.

It's a large man looming a few paces back, his face masked by the shadows along the edge of the room. She can see his mitt-sized hands twitching, clenching and unclenching.

Farrah turns, her hair like a whip. She purses her lips and looks back at Melanie. "Ah, who?"

"That, who is that?" She demands, standing up. Her feet refuse to carry her toward the man, but her eyes strain to see. "Who are you!?"

The man takes a step, and she sees his face is gaunt and sallow, his bloodshot eyes wide and unblinking.

Buck.

She presses her palms to the sides of her head and screams, squeezing her eyes shut and wishing him away. This should be easy, seeing what she did to him. During those days at the cabin, the typewriter was loud enough to drown out his pleading, but at night, she lay awake and listened to him beg for forgiveness. Looking at him now, she almost opens her mouth to address him with a thank-you—this wouldn't have been possible if he, along with the others, hadn't died.

Someone is pawing at her, repeating her name.

"Melanie?" Becca asks, stepping in. "Mel? You good?"

She opens her eyes and realizes she's still sitting quietly in the chair. Buck is gone, and Farrah's brows are furrowed. Regaining composure, Melanie feigns a yawn and rubs her eyes.

"Sorry, I just spaced," she says with an apologetic smile. "I didn't sleep much last night—too excited about today."

"You're totally fine!" Farrah says, too cheerful to be genuine. Melanie knows she's just relieved her interview hasn't been cut short. "Let's move on."

"Yes." Melanie sits back and stares at the empty space where Buck was. "Let's."

The rest of the interview goes off without a hitch. She realizes she's not worried about misspeaking, talking about all of them. There's no one left to be outraged. Their disappearances have all been explained, taken care of by powerful figures still under Mortimer's payroll. Winnie now lives a quiet life in Paris. Petey is in hiding. Scott had a mental breakdown and is in long-term rehab. Crystal has sworn off social media and values "privacy" now. Chester shut down his website and moved to Russia.

Before she knows it, Becca is ushering her away from the interview room and onto a stage.

Melanie stands alone in the center at a large chestnut podium. Her book sits waiting for her, the chapter she's going to read aloud bookmarked.

When she looks into the crowd, this time Melanie isn't surprised to see who is in the middle row of chairs. They're there—all of them— charred skin, bloodied skulls, torn flesh. Petey, Chester, Winnie, Scott, Crystal, and Buck stare up at her, seemingly invisible to the people around them. But Melanie isn't frightened. She cracks open the book, clears her throat, and fixes her eyes directly on them.

"It's been an honor to be welcomed into this community after my collection of short stories was published," she starts. "And I feel so blessed to bring forth my first novel. This book… It's my first. But it won't be my last."

Her gaze never leaves the six, even when the crowd applauds and Becca whistles from the wings. Mortimer was so successful because he had so many tales to tell, so many monsters to display in his books. These were *her* monsters, and thanks to the Manor, she's grown strong enough to pry their stories from their cold, dead hands. No longer will she quietly wait in the shadows for words worth saying—she'll go out and take what she wants to take and say what needs to be said.

She continues to stare them down, moving so close to the microphone that her lips press against the hard surface. This is important.

Her message to them must read loud and clear: "I'm not going anywhere."

Then, like chimney smoke carried away in the wind, the six vanish, and Melanie basks in the glow of the crowd, its members now on their feet. Melanie knows the six will be back. She can feel their eyes on her, even when they're gone. But it's okay—because this, all this…

She'd kill for this.

# Reading Group Guide

1. Qu
2. Qu
3. Qu

# A Conversation
# with the Author

**Qu**

Ans

# Acknowledgments

People say writing your first book can be tough, but no one talks about the difficulty of penning a decent acknowledgment section. I'm not one to complain, however—how lame would that be? Griping about thanking people for helping you accomplish the dream you've had since you were six? *Egad!*

First, I have to thank my agent, Courtney Paganelli, from Levine Greenberg Rostan Literary Agency, who took a chance on me—and then another chance and then another. Thanks for never giving up and poking the bear (me, I'm the bear) whenever I felt discouraged. I'm sure you're aware of this already, being the witty, beautiful, whip-smart lady you are, but this book wouldn't have happened if not for you.

To MJ Johnston and everyone at Sourcebooks and Poisoned Pen Press for not only believing in my work, but for believing in *me*. You aren't just publishers but assets to making this story come to life (teehee!).

To my writing group, who, I laugh now thinking about it, are mostly made up of lovely, sweet romance authors. Thank you for devouring my pages no matter how gruesome they were and for spitting up edits and feedback that made my book what it was. I apologize for the nightmares.

To my junior high literature and English teacher, Paula Knight. For as much of a blip as my time was in your classroom, you remain a cornerstone of my writing success through your early support. I always promised myself that if this ever happened, you would secure a spot in the acknowledgments. Thank you.

To my mom and dad. From the day I scribbled out my first story in (most likely) backward letters, you encouraged me to make this happen. You saved every looseleaf paper, every journal, and every story I ever gifted to you, and as a child, I took note. It made me feel like my words mattered enough to be cherished.

To my siblings, Davis, Amelia, and Max, for keeping our childhood creative and fun through story-writing, comic-book-making, and picture-coloring nights. And for inspiring me today with your humor, intelligence, ambition, artistry, and devotion to our family.

I do not subscribe to the phrase "last but not least," because I come from a dessert family, which is served last and is almost always unapologetically better than the meal that's eaten before. So I will simply continue my thanks by acknowledging my one and only, Corey, who is currently listening to me loudly *click-clack* this letter out on the thick keyboard he gifted to me because he knows I like the sound of a typewriter. You are the only thing that can pull my nose out of a good book, because you make my reality better than fiction. I love you.

# About the Author

Mallory Arnold is a magazine editor and writer who lives in Nashville, Tennessee, with her husband and three cats. When she's not penning a scary story, she can be found curled up with a book, running, listening to podcasts, painting, eating pickles and drinking Diet Coke (*not* together), or bopping her head to Southcourt's music. This is Mallory's debut novel, and she hopes to continue writing until the cows come home (though she wonders where the cows went in the first place).

Feel free to follow her journey on Instagram—if you dare. @malwriteswords

Printed in the USA
CPSIA information can be obtained
at www.ICGtesting.com
LVHW091927051224
797942LV00002B/2